The Aftermath
of Oliver

The Aftermath of Oliver

Hazel Hucker

WARNER BOOKS

A *Warner* Book

First published in Great Britain in 1993 by Judy Piatkus
This edition published by Warner in 1994

Copyright © Hazel Hucker 1993

The moral right of the author has been asserted.

A CIP catalogue for this book
is available from the British Library.

ISBN 0 7515 1135 8

Typeset by Phoenix Photosetting, Chatham, Kent
Printed and bound in Great Britain by
Clays Ltd, St. Ives plc

Warner Books
A Division of
Little, Brown and Company (UK) Limited
Brettenham House
Lancaster Place
London WC2 7EN

For Michael and Sally, with love.

1

'And do you think that handsome daughter of yours is still a virgin?'

The question landed in my mind with a quiet slap somehow reminiscent of the way in which the splodge of excreta from a passing bird had hit the back of my hand ten minutes earlier. I had risen from my chair in the sun then and groped my way through the shadowy house to remove the limey streaked mess at the kitchen sink, relieved as it sluiced away. Oliver's question could not be dealt with so easily, but it was similarly exasperating and unnerving. Perhaps it was the effect of dealing with so many sex cases in my career at the Bar.

'Sara's only sixteen.'

'Positively elderly by today's standards, Annabel.'

'Well, I don't know. I hope so. She isn't very mature.'

'I have frequently heard the words "my boyfriend".'

'Referring to a different individual almost every week.'

'Safety in consecutive numbers?'

'Oh God, Oliver, I don't know. Don't be so bloody. It's too hot.'

'Sorry, darling. I was just interested, mildly, in the problems of rearing a daughter in these times of co-education, sex-lessons and post-feminism.'

'Heaven knows there are plenty.' I raised myself with difficulty on the reclining chair, and stared across the flagstones to where he lay outstretched upon a similar chair. 'Do you know something I don't?'

'Good Lord, no! Sara doesn't talk to me. No, having contemplated her somewhat abandoned posture on that rug over there, I did wonder what stage her development had reached. No more than that, Annabel.'

I said reproachfully: 'Mothers, like wives, are usually the last to be told. Didn't you know?'

His grey eyes examined me. He made no reply.

I flopped back in my chair, disturbed now. Oliver's questions had brought to the surface an unease I'd been struggling to suppress. Sara hadn't talked to me recently like she used to do, comfortable gossips over the potato peeling or the drying-up. And she was such a big girl; full-breasted, broad-shouldered, darkly sullen: she looked far older than she should and she coveted the friendship of those beyond her own age. Her physical development had always been faster than her mental growth. I shifted uneasily on the taut canvas. I wished it were not so hot.

'Push your glass across and I'll pour you another drink.' Oliver reached for the glass jug on the white cast-iron table between us. Pieces of orange and lemon and mint jostled on the lip of the jug and then flopped into the glasses.

'The ice has all melted,' I grumbled, sipping.

'It's still cool,' he said soothingly. He waved the jug towards the bottom of the garden. 'Shall I pour some for Sara?'

'No, I know it's mild, but it is alcoholic and I don't intend to encourage her in that. She drinks more than enough at those parties she goes to.' (Oh, hell, why did concern always sound like condemnation?)

2

I turned to gaze across the grass to where the still body lay in the brightness, the shadows of early afternoon darkly sharp beneath it. Sara had dragged her rug to the far end of the lawn, establishing herself as far away as was possible from her mother and her mother's old friend. She lay spread-eagled upon her back, exposing the maximum permissable area of glistening skin to the late June sun. Her bikini, bought for her last year and now clearly too small, barely preserved her decency. I saw that the top was undone: the tiny piece of fabric lay limp across her breasts and slack flesh spilled from beneath it. Beside her on the rug lay the scattering of objects which she considered essential to her afternoon's enjoyment: enormous white-rimmed sun-specs, a plastic bottle of suntan lotion, several glossy teenage magazines, an old cassette-player giving out an endless selection of pop music, and, flung just out of reach on the grass, a battered copy of Jane Austen's *Emma*, one of the set texts for the next term's sixth-form English literature course. But Sara was reading nothing: her eyes were closed against the bright light and against any form of activity. She was concentrating upon browning her body to the deep colour necessary to draw her friends' admiring looks. No shadow cast by a book should interfere with the work of the sun's rays.

Why had Oliver asked that question? Suspicion stirred in my mind, thoughts nudging each other sharply. Those parties that Sara went to, did they resemble the student parties of my college days? Sometimes she stayed all night. 'It's not fair to ask Daddy to get the car out so late.' Did the boys stay too? I remembered the grousing over her own party last spring: 'Other people's parents go away for the night – they don't hang around and snoop and spoil it.' My imagination filled in what happened in the parents' absence. Sara would say little afterwards. 'Oh, it was all right, I suppose. Usual thing.' I hated to be called a snoop;

I left it to her to confide if she wished. And that youth from the Technical College Sara had liked for nearly three weeks – he had a car . . . I'd never done it in a car, the contortions involved were unappealing and there was always the fear of intruders. But the young nowadays let nothing worry them.

But Sara had been brought up carefully. We had often discussed such matters in the days when we did still talk easily. In a giddy world from which moral absolutes had vanished my headstrong Sara needed guidelines, I'd decided. I had emphasised the importance of a stable relationship, and spoken of the need to keep one's self-respect. I'd remembered with a nasty clarity what it felt like to lose it, though naturally I had not told her that. Surely Sara could not already have discarded all my teaching?

The whining electronic noises from the cassette player were unattractive. Sara's toes were twitching with the beat; clearly the sounds were giving her pleasure. I wished she would turn it down, or better still off. I wanted to shout to her, but I could never shout in front of Oliver, it was inconceivable. I considered walking across, but the effort was too much. Oliver lit two cigarettes and passed me one. I smoked little, and there are not many people I would care to have do that, but Oliver had been lighting cigarettes for me since we first met at university twenty years ago. I liked the little intimacy. Sara's tape came to an end and to my relief she did not replace it. We smoked in silence.

The sun moved imperceptibly down the sky, lengthening the shadow of the terraced house behind us until it crept over our bodies. A rose soundlessly scattered a flowerhead of petals on to the flagstones. A faint breeze came from nowhere, cooling my face. It was foolish to allow a friend's idle words to distress me. There was no

4

reason to suppose Sara promiscuous, no real reason at all. I should enjoy this leisurely afternoon, the rare opportunity to sit in the garden instead of working in it. If my husband, Richard, had been at home we'd have been weeding, but Richard, Reader in Politics at Princes, a college of London University, was having tea on the terrace of the House of Commons with some elderly alumni celebrating the splendidly vast number of years since they had graduated.

I turned my head to look at Oliver. I was glad that our long friendship made constant conversation unnecessary. When a man drove himself as ruthlessly as he did, he needed to relax. After his wife Melissa's death from cancer last year I had told him always to come when loneliness threatened or depression hovered. And he took me at my word, and often came. Sometimes he talked with Richard or argued politics, calling us: 'Pathetic pinks, unconvinced and unconvincing Socialists!'; sometimes he brought his violin and played duets with his namesake, my thirteen-year-old son Ollie, encouraging him, teaching him without apparently seeking to do so; occasionally he was just here, like today, pale, self-contained, speaking little, simply here. I thought sadly that I should not have been cross with him for asking questions about Sara; he was so rarely provocative now.

His mother had asked me to keep an eye on him after Melissa's funeral. 'Let us know if anything worries you,' she had said. 'Oh, I don't know, if he is ill, if things don't go right . . .' Her voice had faded, there had suddenly been a stillness about us and the cold rank smell of the earth thick in the air. Then Mrs Malet had said: 'He will need friends like you and Richard to help him through this. We live too far away and we are getting old now. But you are close to him. You understand him.'

It was the greatest compliment of my life. My widowed

5

mother considered all men special – more worldly and trustworthy than women – let alone men in Top Jobs like bishops or politicians or barristers: members of the Establishment were people you read about, not people you knew. She couldn't quite believe in me. And subconsciously I must have absorbed some of her awe, for I always thought of my friendship with Oliver, a wealthy Queen's Counsel and an old Etonian, as being a wonder and a privilege. I was proud to be asked to help him.

He was lying back with his eyes screwed up against the light; perhaps he was falling asleep. His hands were lightly clasped over a flat stomach – thin hands, immaculately tended. His shirt was open at the neck to reveal the blond fuzz on his chest; neither there nor on the well-shaped head were there any signs of fading or greying hairs. He was remarkably attractive for a man in the mid-forties. There was a beading of sweat on his temples: as I watched a drop moved and blended with its neighbour. I knew a maternal urge to smoothe away the annoying moisture with a forefinger and to push back the clump of hair that had fallen, boyishly untidy, over his forehead, but at the thought of touching him the urge became sexual and I suppressed it swiftly because it made me feel indecent and guilty. Recently such thoughts had kept coming into my head and I wished they wouldn't. If I allowed them to develop the whole basis of my successful marriage would be undermined, and I didn't, on a logical level, want or need anyone but Richard in that way. But it must be horrid for Oliver on his own; I wondered how he managed and then smothered that thought too. I could not do anything to help him there. My help must be of the sensible unobtrusive sort that any kindly friend could give. Perhaps he would remarry one day – in the far future, of course. The stray thought passed through my mind that on the whole it was a good thing I had slept with

Oliver once, all those years ago, because if I hadn't curiosity might have led me into the most awful tangle. As it was, I knew he was good, but I knew Richard was equally good, and some of the aphrodisiac qualities of change and curiosity were removed by that knowledge.

Sara was stirring; she stretched and rolled over, grunting irritably as she did so, flapping a hand at an intrusive bee that strayed from the nearby phloxes. The bikini-straps slid from her shoulders, the naked breasts flattened beneath her. She took a fresh cassette and poked it into the machine.

Piano chords crashed through the warm air, loud, insistent, repetitive. A hoarse male voice bawled out its message: 'Girls of fifteen, sexually knowing . . .' My pretty garden blurred through a red haze of exasperation as the air vibrated with the lascivious sounds. I leapt to my feet. 'Sara!' I pounded across the grass, clutched the machine. Which of the identical knobs would turn the ravings off? I pressed at random. The machine grunted, made whirring noises, stopped and restarted.

'Hey! What are you doing? Jesus, watch out, will you? You'll wreck it.'

'I want that filthy racket off.'

An outraged stare, as outraged as my own. 'But it's The Who! It's historic! It's nearly a collector's piece – valuable!' She wrested the machine back from me, examining it tenderly.

'I don't care who it is. It's obscene. Turn it off!'

'I'll turn it down,' she said sullenly, pushing a knob. The noise continued, minimally reduced.

'Not down. Off.' The constant repetition was wearing.

'Oh God, I can't do anything without you moaning.'

It was at the same moment that we both noticed the naked breasts, pressed against the cassette player. 'Look what you've made me do,' she snarled, turning her back

7

and struggling to do up the bikini top. 'It's you that's obscene. Oh, for Chrissakes, I'm going in.' She raked her possessions together on the rug, flung it over her shoulder and rushed off into the house.

I walked slowly back to Oliver, embarrassed by the scene. Why did Sara always appear at her worst when he was with us? I flung myself on to my chair, silently daring him to mention it. This was supposed to be a restful afternoon.

Oliver pursed his mouth and enquired in a reproving falsetto: 'My dear, whatever will the neighbours think?'

Despite exasperation, I felt my lips twitch. 'A vital point. But, if you noticed, one that I failed to make.' I had more than once amused him with reminiscences of my penurious childhood in a pebble-dashed semi in Woking. My circumstances appeared to bear for him the same charm of unreality as a journey in a foreign country. Mother's constant preoccupation with the neighbours' thoughts had particularly fascinated him.

'Darling Annabel, I could see the words hovering over your head, comic strip fashion.'

'That,' I said firmly, 'was the evening's mosquito hordes gathering. You know how they love to bite me.'

He paused for a moment's contemplation. 'A voice is coming to me out of the past,' he murmured. Then, 'I have it now,' he said triumphantly. '"It's a phase, and phases pass." Remember that one?'

'Lord, yes!' I was smiling properly now. 'When Sara threw three-year-old tantrums – and when Danny refused to eat vegetables!'

'And when Oliver insisted on taking his pillow everywhere with him.' He always gave young Ollie his full name, the only person who did so. 'Remember how filthy it used to get as he trailed it behind him, and how you worried about germs?'

I repeated the words slowly: '"It's a phase . . . and phases pass."' Deep breath. 'I must hang on to that. You are a comfort to me, Oliver.'

Of course, it was easy for him to be flippant, being childless himself, but it was curious how often a few words from him could put my problems back into perspective. He'd always had that capacity, even way back in our university days together, when he'd helped me to recover from my first disastrous love affair. No matter that the method he had used had been highly irregular, it had worked.

It's a phase . . . Much more sensible to look upon the intermittent warfare with Sara as a passing problem on a par with potty training or three-year-old tantrums, than as the imminent collapse of a once good relationship.

2

On a July evening a few days later I drove through Lincoln's Inn Fields, passed through the wrought-iron gates into New Square and round to park near the archway by Wildy's bookshop. I switched off the engine and sat and looked. The mellow square was at its best: its turf impeccably striped, its great plane trees dappled by the slanting sun, the scent of roses stronger than London's traffic fumes, birds wheeling against a fading sky. Even fourteen years of practice as a barrister in Chambers there could not dim its charm; affection warmed me, my flagging spirits revived.

I needed a break to collect my thoughts and to recover from the mental concussion caused by the harangue I'd been listening to on the radio by a fellow barrister, Martin Hanley, on the iniquities of our criminal justice system, particularly in regard to the trial of sexual matters. Then I would go into Chambers where I would cheer Tom, our clerk, with the happy outcome today of my case at Maidstone Crown Court, drink a cup of coffee and pick up my brief for next week.

It had been a long day with a worried, fussing client and a testy judge. My lorry driver client, Steve Pike, had been accused of attempted rape. The girl was a singer hitching a lift to the next gig. On a hot spring day she'd flopped in the cab beside him with her arms outflung and her thighs, according to him, spread equally wide. 'And her little skirt up to her fanny,' middle-aged Steve had told me morosely in conference. 'An' could she talk? Gigs in Liverpool, gigs in Marbella – been all over, she had. Flung off the railway station in Milan 'cause she wasn't behaving decent . . . I'm not bloody surprised! Real proud of that, she was, little show-off. Anyway, she goes on and on about her singing and her shows and all the different cities she's spent the night in and the fun she an' her boyfriends've had . . . the booze, the dancing, the laughs. More'n I get in my trade; lonely, it is, driving like I do, long-distance. At the time she was a ray of sunshine. Huh! Sunray? Deathray, more like. Then she gets to scratching up her thighs, says she's got an itch there. Mosquito bites, she says. I reckoned it was another sort of itch. I reckoned she was leading me on . . . hot for it, she was. Sorry, miss, but you know what I mean. Well, you must do in your line of work, mustn't you? An' I've gotta tell you, haven't I? So, like I'm saying, I looked for a lay-by where we could have a spot of . . . well, a spot of fun. But when we get there I've hardly put my hand on her knee before she's leaping out the cab and hollering, "Rape!".'

Steve had put his head in his hands. 'Some chance!' he'd gone on indistinctly. 'There was two other vehicles parked in that lay-by anyway. An' she'd only got to push me away and say "No!" nicely, hadn't she? I'm not that sort. I don't need to force myself on anyone. It's an insult, it is, what she says. An insult.'

I had believed him. But I'd doubted whether the judge or the jury would. In the weeks while my client had been awaiting trial the singer's song had not only reached the charts but climbed to number one. Her skirt length, on the other hand, had dropped to mid-calf. The judge was sharp with both of them, the jury openly appreciative of Salome Keane – young factory workers, middle-aged housewives and denim-jacketed college lecturers alike. But, to my surprise, its members didn't believe her. According to the usher they were a cynical lot: the young men thought she was an all-singing, all-dancing invitation to anything, a real cock-tease, the college lecturers disliked the lack of medical corroboration, and the house-wives thought her a born liar mad for publicity. 'Not guilty,' they said, to the noisy disgust of the representa-tives of Females for Freedom and Women against Rape up in the gallery.

Martin Hanley would be disgusted too. Head of Cham-bers in a flamboyantly trendy set which took on only those defence cases which proved its members' own point of view, in his broadcast he had declared British justice to be in a state of terminal decline. He had his own suggestions for reviving it, including having independent judges to investigate and prepare criminal matters for the courts rather than the police, while all police evidence would have to be corroborated by independent witnesses as a matter of law. He took a sour view of the police, Martin did. He wanted, too, stronger laws on sexual harassment, while in rape and other sexual matters he demanded that the accused's evidence in defence be corroborated by independent evidence. I wondered how. Rape is not normally a public performance, nor can knickers speak. In other words, where one woman's word is pitted against one man's, the woman's is to be preferred. A new double standard was being raised. Proud as I am of my sex, I cannot believe we are all like the young George Washington, unable to tell a lie. Certainly Salome was caught out in one. She'd denied my client's story of her exploits in Milan, and was shattered when we produced an old newspaper report of her arrest for indecent behaviour, including a photograph of her lavish toplessness. The men on the jury had relished that piece of corroboration.

In the clerk's room, Tom was congratulatory: 'I thought you were on to a hiding for nothing there, ma'am. A good win.'

'And what am I doing next week?' I asked.

'A nice little stabbing,' he said with relish, 'attempted murder. Prosecution. At Inner London. Expected to run for a couple of weeks.'

'Lovely,' I said absently. I liked Inner London Crown Court. And two weeks was just right. School holidays started then and I needed to be at home to ride herd on the younger generation, who were inclined to buck a bit and play up if a strong hand wasn't kept on the bridle. Richard would be home too, but he tended to withdraw into his study, where he was writing what he swore would be the definitive book on the history of political thought in the nineteenth and twentieth centuries. Interruption by teenage offspring not appreciated.

'And,' Tom added, 'you've another big case for next term. Probably come up in November. New solicitors: Bryant and Morley. Their Mr Hoffer saw you win in the Old Bailey recently, and gave you his seal of approval.'

'Decent of him', I said drily but cheerfully. Bryant and Morley were based in the West End and handled long firm frauds and big drugs cases, mostly privately paid. Such a new firm of solicitors was especially good news. It meant a fresh source of work, my own not Chambers', more indefinable kudos, more clearly definable money for Sara's clothes, Danny's books, Ollie's violin lessons, holidays in the sun. The third of such pieces of good news in as many weeks.

'At the rate your practice is moving we'll have you in the six-figure bracket soon, Mrs Bateman,' Tom murmured.

Tom worked on the principle that flattery would get him everywhere. What had he got up his sleeve? I shot him a sharp look but his chubby face betrayed only the satisfaction the thought of his ten per cent of that figure brought.

When I had first started at the bar Richard had spoken slightingly of my meagre earnings as, 'Your pin money.' My brief fees were minute, paid months if not years later, and reduced to half their worth by the costs of travelling and books, Chambers' dues and Tom's slice. 'Is the game worth the candle?' Richard would grumble as he went to bed alone night after night, leaving me to work on my briefs. Now my earnings after expenses equalled his. Tom's estimate was an exaggeration, but even so I knew I would soon rocket past Richard. What would be his reaction to that?

'A nasty one,' Tom said, handing me a hefty set of papers tied in pink tape. 'Here we are. Incest, this time.'

I woke from my reverie in shock. 'Tom, what is this? Of my last half dozen cases four have been sexual. Now this. A corner in sex crimes? Not my idea of a good varied practice!'

The door opened and two of my colleagues came in, both criminal practitioners, smiling with Friday night cheer, greeting me, wanting Tom's attention. One was my old friend and regular would-be seducer, Gerald Lees, the other a young woman called Paulina Grey, intense and driven, proud possessor of a Cambridge first, who had been in Chambers for less than a year and was notorious for her pickiness over the briefs she would handle.

'Oh, Annabel,' she said now, 'did you hear that wonderful talk by Martin Hanley on the radio? I thought it was inspirational. He's so clear, so succinct, so caring, and he puts everything I think and believe in into words that the most ordinary person can understand.'

15

'Really?' I said, but before I could say anything more, Gerald, a cheerful, bouncy man with an unexpectedly sharp tongue, got in first.

'He does, doesn't he?' he said sardonically. 'Such basic tenets as judging a case before you've heard the evidence on both sides – like you – never mind the cab rank rule of accepting any case that's offered because all defendants are innocent until proved guilty. We can't soil our hands with anything nasty, can we, Ms Grey? Not if we're followers of Martin.'

'Oh, stop it, Gerry,' Paulina said with spirit, 'you know it isn't like that.'

'Of course it damn' well is! How else is it that I hear you fussing over your cases almost every time I'm in the Clerk's room? And like dear Martin, you won't prosecute, will you?'

'Oddly enough,' Pauline said, 'I would thoroughly dislike to feel myself responsible for some poor chap being locked up twenty-three hours a day like a caged animal, with only some psychopath and a stinking pot for company.'

Gerald gave her a thoughtful look. 'And serial murderers and arsonists? You'd leave them free to create havoc and misery? Or do you, like Martin, simply prefer to leave the dirty work to someone insensitive like me? Leaving you free to defend precious little darlings you can call victims of society. Where do you draw your line between the victims and the vile, Ms Grey, and more importantly, how do you draw that line?'

The telephone rang. Tom picked up the receiver, holding up a finger for silence while he spoke to the solicitor on the other end of the line. 'A con at five-thirty on Wednesday for Mr Groom? Let me just check . . .'

I said softly to Gerald: 'Remember Crispin Groom's views? He wouldn't prosecute until his flat was burgled – then he couldn't wait to get at them.'

16

'Christ, yes, I do,' he said happily. 'The sods attacked that immaculate flat he and his wife had. She was in tears for days. There was ketchup all over the kitchen and they shat on her lovely chaise-longue. What would Paulina do with such precious darlings, I wonder?'

Tom put down the telephone and remarked severely that peace would be appreciated. He swivelled his chair to reach into the pigeon-holes behind his head and pushed a tape-tied bundle into Gerald's hands. 'Here you are, sir. Goodnight!'

'Okay, Tom,' Gerald said. 'Have a peaceful weekend!' He went out, winking at me as he disappeared.

Paulina stood by Tom, statuesque, her face expressing outrage. 'So condescending, so patronising. Just like most of the men in Chambers! They take a view of the Bar and British justice when they're in pupillage, and never imagine thinking for themselves. The status quo incarnate is what they believe in.'

'Yes, Miss Grey,' Tom said calmly. 'A lot of us are like that. Still, you have a particularly interesting case next week, think for yourself about that.'

Paulina sighed and shook her blonde head. 'Preaching to the unconvertible, that's what poor Martin Hanley is doing. One can see that pressure will have to come from sources other than the Bar.'

'The meddlesome media,' Tom muttered, drawing the Chambers' diary to him and settling down to work again.

Paulina ignored him, her eyes on the bulky package under my right arm to which she nodded. 'Another big case?' Paulina liked to know everyone's business; she was even said to sneak into the place at dawn to check the diary and gauge the pace of progress of her immediate rivals.

'Not your scene,' I said briefly. 'An incest.'

'Defending?' She shuddered dramatically. 'I don't

17

know how you can! Incest? Rape within the family!'

'Perhaps you think I should prosecute? A trifle illogical, aren't you?'

'Sex crimes are different,' she retorted. 'And what will your own family think of your defending that sort of horror, at their ages?' She did not wait for my reply, but flounced out.

I stared at the closed door for a moment then turned to cock an eyebrow at Tom. 'I know that smug look of yours. What have you given her?'

He avoided my eyes, his pencil posed over the diary. 'Defending the third man in the gang in a robbery with violence. They beat up an elderly spinster to make her reveal the whereabouts of the savings she never made.'

'You're quite the strategist,' I commented, and left him to his work.

Paulina's last words had stung. I could see that I would have to be a strategist, too. She had asked what my own family would think of my defending the horror of incest. I have to admit I didn't know and hated to think. I didn't bother with the cup of coffee I'd planned; I left Chambers hastily to begin the drive home to Richmond, pondering the problem. Perhaps they would understand. In fact, I rather doubted Sara would. Still, no need for her to know, of course. No need at all.

3

It was towards the end of the summer holidays that Oliver
again lay in the sun with me in the garden. He had been
lunching with friends in Hampshire and called in on his
way back to return a book Richard had lent him, a politi-
cian's newly published autobiography. Richard was out; I
suggested Oliver should stay to supper to see him and he
accepted. We relaxed in the August heat discussing politicians' passion for publication of their memoirs and certain
recent fascinating revelations of a cabinet minister's
sexual indiscretions. Sara, who had been lying reading on
a chairbed, gave us a sour look and removed herself to her
room.

When I went indoors to cook supper I found the sun
glinting sideways through the graceful fanlight of the
front door, catching gleams of light from the old copper-
framed oval mirror on the hall wall. I stopped to check my
appearance before going to the kitchen. There are not
many women who can say that middle age has improved
their looks. The improvement was purely relative, naturally. I was better looking for forty-two than I had been as a
young woman, despite the blurring jawline. At twenty,
my light brown hair was of the shade that bitchier friends
called mouse. By forty, some happy chance of nature had

deepened it, 'To the colour of the best tobacco,' said Richard. And my figure was good. I tucked my navy shirt more firmly into my designer jeans and patted myself approvingly.

I went into the dining-room to lay the table, enjoying the task: the room's admirable proportions, its moulded cornices, carefully repaired by Richard when we moved in, its marble fireplace, its swagged cream silk curtains, the softly ticking longcase clock, all combined to make a pleasure of any job performed there. On the table was a bowl filled with honeysuckle; it trailed elegantly, admiring its reflection in the shining mahogany.

We had come a long way from our origins, Richard and I. There was no trace here of my mother's 'forties Utility furniture, or my parents-in-law's mock Jacobean suites. Over the years we had furnished our early-nineteenth century house on Richmond Hill as much in character as was sensibly – and financially – possible. The result gave us enormous satisfaction.

I felt sometimes that we should put up memorial plaques to the two old ladies who had made it possible for us to realise our dreams: Mrs Percy and my Great-aunt Florence. Mrs Percy lived to the age of eighty-nine, seventy of those years in this house according to those who had known her; for the last twenty of them alone, and without doing any repairs or redecorations. Because of her neglect the house sold cheaply, at a price we could afford – just.

It was summer when we moved and university lecturers have long vacations. Richard ripped out old pipes and wires and installed new plumbing and electrical circuits with the aid of incomprehensible diagrams over which we struggled every evening. We camped out, first in one room, then another. Oliver and Melissa came, bringing hampers of picnic food and sensible suggestions which we generally adopted: their Queen Anne house in Hampstead was my idea of perfection. We scraped and painted. The children toddled in the newly scythed garden. We sweated from our efforts but we revelled in the transformation.

If we owed our house to poor old Mrs Percy, it was Great-aunt Florence who provided several of our best pieces of furniture. She died at ninety-five, in the same year as Mrs Percy, leaving all her furniture, which included some beautiful eighteenth-century pieces, to my mother. Mother, who preferred the sentimental claims of her marriage furniture, gave them to us. Our friends were stunned by our luck in inheriting such antiques.

It was too hot to enjoy cooking. In the kitchen I pushed up the bottom sash of the window and a smell of exhaust fumes came in from the road beyond, together with three wasps. I swotted the wasps with a rolled-up copy of *The Times* and shut the window, opening the door to the hall instead and letting in the sound of pop music from Sara's room. Even Salome Keane's noisy lecherous voice in 'Hot Love' was marginally preferable to wasps.

Oliver strolled in, poured us both drinks and perched himself on a stool. I put peanuts in a dish for him to nibble.

'I must get a move on,' I remarked, glancing at my watch. 'The boys should be back from their swim soon, they're bound to be ravenous.' I moved rapidly from cupboard to cupboard, collecting ingredients and dumping them on the table.

'What are you giving us?'

'Curry. Chicken curry. A good sweat will cool us off.'

'You have all the right ideas,' he observed, and crunched peanuts.

Sara appeared in the doorway, wrapped in a towel and apparently nothing else.

'Sara, what do you think you're doing? Don't wander about like that when we've a guest here.'

'It covers a lot more than my bikini does. Anyway, I don't count Oliver as a guest. He's always around.' She spoke as if he were an inanimate object. Was she being deliberately provocative or simply deliberately rude? 'He saw me naked often enough when I was little.'

'You're far from little now. What do you want?'

'I forgot to tell you. I'm going down to Lucinda's tonight.'

'What for?'

'Oh, the usual sort of thing,' she said impatiently. She picked at the peanuts and added with sarcasm, 'Don't worry, we won't be smoking pot or rolling about having orgies on the floor.' I looked at her. She moderated her tone. 'We'll be listening to her latest CDs, I suppose. Talking. You know.'

She'd been out late nearly every night this week and it didn't improve her temper. 'Be back by eleven for once, then.'

'Eleven? Eleven! Don't be ridiculous. Nobody leaves that early.'

'You're looking tired. Be sensible, Sara.'

'I'm fine. Christ, I'll be seventeen by the end of the year. I'm old enough to get married and you fuss as if I was twelve.'

'There's nothing grown-up in overtiring yourself. Eleven.' The less time she spent with Lucinda, the happier I should be. Lucinda was nearly a year older than Sara, a startling redhead with an excess of self-confidence. I disliked her manners and suspected her morals.

Sara groaned and padded off, muttering something that sounded suspiciously like: 'You'll be bloody lucky!' I pretended not to hear, chopping onions with vigorous strokes, averting my head as my eyes smarted from the

22

fumes. Life with Sara was a series of uneasy compromises, an effort to avoid an all-out confrontation – which neither of us seemed to want at present.

'You did say that Richard was at his mother's, didn't you?' Oliver asked.

I sighed. 'Yes, she demanded his attention yesterday, quite out of the blue. He drove to Bromley this morning. He'll be back in half an hour or so.'

'I'm surprised she didn't demand the attendance of the whole family.' Oliver knew Mrs Bateman of old.

'We escaped this time. She said she needed to consult him on personal affairs.'

'Does she lean heavily on him since the old boy died?'

'Who else?' His grey eyes were watching me. 'I expect she wants him to read her new will. It's been the excuse for her to call here or to demand his presence there at least once a week for the past two months.'

'Good God. I hadn't imagined she'd have so much to leave.'

'She hasn't. She has so much time to kill.'

'Always a problem in those circumstances,' he said thoughtfully.

'I suppose you think I should be sorry for her? Well, I'm not. She nagged old Mr Bateman to death.'

'I'm not criticising you, Annabel. How could I?' He tilted his head to smile at me. 'I think you're remarkably patient with the old trout.'

I grimaced back ruefully, accepting the compliment. I thought I was, too. Bertha and I had never got on, not from the very beginning. She had settled it that Richard should marry her god-daughter, Elizabeth, a home-loving girl. She mistrusted those over-educated university women: they were restless, got above themselves, never made good wives. But Richard chose me and spoiled her plans. I was rejected in advance, tolerated only for

23

Richard's sake. She clung to him, as she clung to all her four children, because only through them did her life have meaning: she wanted to bind them and to rule them and that was her understanding of love. Richard was in his late-forties; he was still her boy.

I started to cut up the chicken, stopped to take a swig of my drink and saw that Oliver was staring into far distances, his eyes unfocussed. It frightened me to see him do that. Quite suddenly he would withdraw into himself and a dreadful bleak look would tighten the skin across his face. In the first months after Melissa's death that look had been a regular occurrence; recently I had seen less of it. The contrast with his normal social self was horrible. I must try to drag him back: wherever his mind had gone, it was clearly not into pleasant places. I opened my mouth, but before I could speak the boys erupted through the front door, making us both jump.

'Hi there!' Fifteen-year-old Danny's newly acquired bass voice boomed through the house. 'Sara! Hey, Sara! We just saw that bird-brained friend of yours, Lucinda. She wants you to go round to her house earlier than she said. Sara!'

'Stop shouting, Daniel,' I groaned. 'How many times must I tell you? Sara's in her room. Either go up there or wait till she comes down.'

The two boys came into the kitchen, tossing damp towels and trunks on to the table among the onion peelings.

'I'm not running round after Sara,' Danny said cheerfully, opening the fridge door and surveying the contents. 'She can come down. Can I have this piece of cheesecake? Thanks.'

Sara came into the room on bare brown feet, dressed now in a fussily flowered crimson and blue blouse over elderly jeans. 'Somebody call me?'

'Yeah. Lucinda says she wants you to go their house half an hour early to help her get organised.'

'Did you drag me all the way downstairs just for that? You could've called up, couldn't you?'

'I asked him not to,' I said. 'I'm tired of all the noise and shouting in this house.'

'I suppose it's not good manners,' Sara said offensively, 'but dragging people out of their rooms when they're only half-dressed, that's all right.' She turned to stamp her way back upstairs, but found the stamping ineffective without any shoes on. She slammed her bedroom door instead and followed the bang with a series of thuds from within the room.

Ollie turned from the fridge with a can of Coke in his hand. 'What on earth's she doing?' He tilted the can to his mouth.

'Kick-starting her broomstick, I shouldn't wonder,' said Danny.

The comment caught Ollie's sense of humour. He choked, spluttering horribly, spraying the sticky brown liquid across my tiled floor.

Danny peered at his cheesecake. 'Thanks for coughing all over my food, brother. I'll savour that as flavour of the month.'

I shook my head, laughing myself, ordered Ollie to find a floorcloth, then changed my mind. The kitchen was stuffy enough without all these large male bodies in it. 'No, on second thoughts, don't bother. Just go. And take those wet swimming things and hang them up outside. Now! Vanish! I'll mop up myself, properly.' I found a cloth and wiped with care. 'We eat in half an hour,' I added.

'I suppose I should go and practise,' Ollie conceded. He towed his brother with him from the room, grinning at Oliver and tilting his head in a gesture that was a replica of Oliver's own.

The physical contrast between the two boys was very obvious as they jostled together in the doorway. Danny's dark and brawny bulk already made small shopkeepers twitch nervously when he galloped into their premises, while thirteen-year-old Ollie, who was slim and blond, had the sort of quiet good looks which inspire confidence. Odd that we should have produced a strikingly fair child after two so dark. Fondness stirred as I watched them go; they were no trouble despite the noise and the aggressive posturing.

'Confess, Annabel, it'll be a relief when the law term starts,' Oliver said.

I began to fry the onions. 'I'll be back to rushing from court to court, but yes, I confess I'll be glad. One can take just so much of domesticity!'

'What are you doing this term?'

'The mixture as before: a murder, a mortgage fraud, incest . . .'

'Incest? Particularly unpleasant. But he'll plead guilty, surely?'

'No. No, the solicitors tells me our client is adamant that whatever his daughter says, he never laid a finger on her. He's insisting on an early conference because he wants us to find out somehow, God knows how, why she's telling these terrible lies.'

'What's the story?' Oliver enquired.

'Simple but sad. Dad and Mum were divorced a year or so ago, with the mother keeping the two girls and the matrimonial home, the father having access and able to take them away on holiday. He took the younger girl camping with him at Easter, and, it's alleged, the first offences took place in a tent. The older girl, who's sixteen, had an illegitimate baby about four months ago. Interestingly, though, no allegations against the father from her. Karen, that's the older girl – the younger one, I'm

26

sorry to say, is called Fern – Karen only backs up her sister's story in minor aspects: that she did see her Dad emerge from Fern's room late one evening when they were staying in his flat, Mum being away nursing her sick sister, and that Fern did become prone to fits of crying that she couldn't or wouldn't explain. Karen says Fern was always her father's favourite.'

'Fern,' Oliver said ruminatively, trying the name on his tongue. 'Fern.'

'Yes, I know. It makes one think of woodland glades and still pools of water at dusk.'

'And don't forget the startled deer!'

'The jury are going to be one hundred per cent for Fern.'

'And you are going to be the beastly bullying counsel forcing the poor girl to relive her terrible experience in public, in order to try to get an evil man off his just punishment.'

'Yup.'

'As you were with Salome Keane. Does Sara still hold that against you?'

'One hundred per cent. She plays Salome's number one when she's annoyed with me.'

'I noticed. Though I would imagine she'd have enjoyed the vicarious fame of having you involved.'

'She did. But Sara's good at having her cake and eating it. Women's Rights look like becoming her latest involvement, possibly even displacing vegetarianism and Animal Liberation.' I stirred curry powder into the pan and rich smells arose. 'In a minute I must make an animal-fat free sauce for a quorn curry for Sara. No, seriously! But I won't let her lecture you on quorn's food values!' The shrill summons of the telephone splintered the air. 'Damn! Why do people always save their calls for when I'm busy? It's probably for Sara anyway, though she won't bother to answer it.' I waited, stirring, and she didn't.

27

'Would you like me to go?'

'Oliver, would you? Thanks!'

I had just time to start on the quorn before he returned, an odd expression on his face. 'Richard's mother.'

'Oh God!'

'Give me that frying pan. Keep stirring?'

'Oliver, you are good. Yes, please.'

'Well,' crackled my mother-in-law's voice, in tones struggling between affront and triumph, 'that gave me quite a shock, I must say, to hear my son's telephone answered by a strange young man.'

'There's nothing strange about Oliver Malet, Bertha. He came to return a book Richard lent him and he's staying to supper to see him.' To my annoyance, my voice sounded defensive.

'Mr Malet? I sometimes think that man might as well move in with you! I know he's lost his wife, but that was some time ago. Before I lost my dear George. You mustn't let him impose upon you, Annabel.'

'He doesn't.'

'We folk who have been bereaved have to learn to live with the absence of our loved ones. He can't expect other people always to put themselves out for him. I've had to manage on my own.'

'But then you're a competent woman,' I said smarmily. I managed a passable imitation of her own reproving style as I added: 'Of course, I've always believed that friends should put themselves out to care for one another in times of trouble. That's what friendship's for, surely?'

'Not when it comes to men friends coming to the house when your husband's out,' she shot back. 'I can hardly believe that Richard would care for that.'

'Oliver expected him to be here, but Richard gave up his day to helping you. I do hope he was able to sort out your problem for you?' She made me as self-righteous as she was, and then I disliked myself.

A moment's pause, then her voice, oddly smug. 'Yes, I think you could say we made progress. I have some very interesting news, Annabel. I'm going to come . . .' She stopped. Clearly over the line had come the sound of her door chimes. 'Someone has called. It looks like that Mrs Cross from next door. So annoying, people calling at any old time. Richard will have to tell you my news. Goodbye.' A click and the line purred softly, emptily.

I put the receiver down, pulling wild faces at it. She was up to something. I disliked the self-satisfied note in her voice. I returned to the kitchen and took over the cooking from Oliver.

'Trouble?'

'I don't know,' I said slowly, trying to work it out. 'She bitched a bit about your answering the phone, but it wasn't that.'

He remarked disarmingly: 'I can't imagine why anyone should be antagonistic to you, though clearly she is. One could hardly describe you as a tough social tennis player.'

I grinned as I remembered Oliver keeping the score, not quite sotto voce enough, during one of mother-in-law's trivial altercations with me. 'Thirty-forty!' 'Deuce!' His handsome profile had turned constantly from one to the other of us. She gained the upper hand and he looked at me reproachfully. 'Advantage striker!' She heard and was furious. She would not be mocked. Another black mark against me for having such a rude friend. Women should not have men friends; men only look for one thing in women. She watched me hopefully for signs that I was indulging in that one thing, called at the house uninvited when Richard was out. She had discovered, many years ago, a certain episode to my discredit. Leopards – and leopardesses – don't change their spots according to

Bertha. The jungle was all around us, she'd catch me in all my true spottiness one of these days. In the meantime she kept up appearances; nobody could say she hadn't done her best with me.

It was her righteousness I found most difficult to combat; it unnerved me. Richard excused her personality by saying that she'd had a struggle to bring up her family: if she had doubted herself she would have failed. She had, he maintained, performed miracles on next to no income. His father, an accounts clerk who called himself an accountant, had been an encumbrance rather than a help. I didn't see how that excused her. My mother had brought me up single-handed in similarly straitened circumstances: it hadn't turned her into a humourless old bag.

What was Bertha up to? My mind kept returning to her last, interrupted sentence. 'I'm going to come . . .' Where? When? To do what? Hurry home, Richard, and relieve my suspense.

I turned the gas jet low beneath the curry and turned to Oliver. I must distract myself. I began to tell him about the party Richard and I were planning to celebrate our twentieth wedding anniversary. We'd have a drinks party first for lots of friends, then a chosen few of our dearest would stay to an informal supper. My bridesmaid, Clare, and her husband, both old university friends, would be coming. 'And you'll come, won't you?' I asked Oliver. 'On the Saturday. We couldn't have it without you. After all, you gave me away.'

He smiled and said: 'Yes, of course,' but his eyes were bleak as a wintry beach and I realised with a lurch of my heart that I was being cruelly tactless, because his own marriage had taken place only ten weeks before ours. It was a relief to hear the sounds of a car braking outside and a door slamming sharply.

'Here's Richard,' I said, and turned to greet him.

He stood in the doorway, a massive man, his grizzled hair haloed by the evening sun. He paused, staring at Oliver, and for a horrible moment I anticipated a sharp remark. There was a tension about Richard for which I knew no reason. Then he moved heavily forward into the room. 'Oliver,' he said. 'Good to see you.'

He bent to kiss me, his invariable practice. 'My love.'

'Mmm. Hello darling. All right?'

'No, I'm afraid not. All wrong.'

'What? I knew it – your mother! What's she up to?'

Deep breath. 'She wants to come and live near us. She's put her house on the market, reckons she has a buyer already, and thinks she'll move before the winter.'

Through the stunned silence came a shriek of anguish from Ollie's violin. The wail on the E string resembled the noise I should have liked to make if Oliver had not been there. Instead, dignity held me to a relatively mild protest. 'Oh, hell, no! You can't be serious?'

Oliver, for once almost tactlessly tactful, murmured: 'I think young Oliver needs assistance,' and took himself out of the room.

'You told her not to – you dissuaded her, didn't you?'

Richard looked at me with a cool thoughtfulness, his bushy eyebrows drawn together. He said slowly and clearly: 'Her mind was made up before I got there. From most points of view it's a sensible decision. I can't stop her. She can live where she pleases.'

'It's expensive here,' I said feverishly. 'She won't get much for her money.'

'She won't want much. She'll be moving to a smaller house.'

'But she's lived in Bromley for – God, it must be nearly half a century. She'll miss her neighbours and friends. She'll find it difficult to settle here.'

'I told her that. But she hasn't so many friends and she

31

despises her neighbours. She's thinking in terms of the Richmond side of Kingston, nicely between us and Jane at Hampton. Then she won't get lonely any more.' He picked up a handful of peanuts and stood scrunching them while I fumed impotently. Then he caught sight of my expression and his own face twisted in sympathy. He put his arm round my shoulders in a hug, and said, his voice muted by peanuts: 'I'm sorry, sweetheart, I don't like it any more than you do, but we're just going to have to put up with it.'

4

Curry and vexation do not go well together. Even as Sara and I cleared the table and loaded the dishwasher I was aware that my stomach was as uneasy as my mind. The thought of Bertha's loud voice and dominating presence daily invading my peaceful house made me feel ill. She had told Richard she did not want to be a burden, did not want to interfere; she only wanted to do the sensible thing. Of course, she was devoted to her family; she had dwelt on how lovely it would be to see her grandchildren frequently without that tiresome journey across London.

I could visualise all too clearly how lovely it would be. Sara, always her favourite in our family, encouraged to defy me over homework 'A fat lot of use books will be when the baby's got colic and the dinner's burning!' Danny nagged over his noisiness and his outbursts of bad language: 'It's sad to see Richard's eldest son being allowed to develop into a lout.' As for Ollie, he would be slapped down at every opportunity. She had never shown any real affection for him. 'You spoil that boy, Annabel. In my family we believe in treating all our children equally.' She objected to our paying for him to attend a London public day school, not because Richard and I had abjured our principles in paying for such education, but because it

33

was against her principles: 'Why should one child have a privilege the others haven't had?'

Sometimes I felt guilty myself, but Ollie had worked hard to win the music scholarship that paid a fair proportion of his fees, damned hard; it was a reward, not a privilege. Besides, the music teaching at the comprehensive school was terrible and Ollie was described by his teachers as being musically gifted. He deserved better than an elderly and deaf alcoholic who switched off his deaf-aid when his classes burlesqued the songs he tried to teach them. Sara and Danny didn't mind the defeated alcoholic. To them music was a loud noise with a beat you could dance to and further than that they had no interest – which was strange, because Richard and I had. They had all been brought up in a musical atmosphere but only Ollie had responded. Bertha thought that listening to Beethoven or Bach was pure snobbishness. 'There's no tune to it,' she said.

Sara turned the dishwasher on, took a cloth and began to wipe over the working surfaces. She was often perceptive and helpful in domestic matters, though she tended to perform them in a silence that left me guessing as to whether she really wanted to assist me or thought she had to. 'I'm off now,' she announced as she finished.

'Thanks for helping. Have a good time,' I responded.

Soon after Sara left the house my old friend Angela arrived. Richard, Oliver and I were drinking coffee and gazing gloomily at the nine o'clock news – the usual stories of European Community manoeuvres and machinations, health service inadequacies and murders in Belfast. Danny let Angela in. I think he hoped it was one of his friends. 'I'll go,' he called when the bell shrilled, and she was in before any of us had moved.

She was wearing a purple jacket over an embroidered cheesecloth blouse and pink sateen trousers gathered in at the ankles, Russian-style. Her feet were bare and dirty. She gave no reason for calling and I suspected that her strong-minded daughter, Lucinda, had dismissed her from their small house to make more room for her own friends. It would not be the first time.

'You do remember Angela, don't you, Oliver?' I said, rapidly muttering something about Princes College as an aid to his memory.

I saw Oliver's eyes survey the gaunt face and flicker over the unnatural metallic red of the hair that had once shone in a copper aureole round her head.

'Goodness, yes, Angela. How are you?' He held out his hand but she ignored it, making a sign in the air instead with a nicotine-stained clawlike hand, a gesture halfway between a priest's benediction and a Red Indian peace sign. Worry beads swayed from her fingers.

Richard pushed himself out of his chair, switched off the news and poured us all drinks. Angela accepted her whisky with a pleased smile and turned to me.

'How do you like my blouse?' she demanded, indicating the limp fabric, undone almost to the waist to reveal the bony dips and bumps of her frontage.

'The embroidery is pretty,' I said with economic truth.

'Isn't it? I found it at the Oxfam shop. It must be quite old. Genuine peasant, you know.' She patted herself happily. 'Fashionable this year.'

Oliver leaned forward. I had a momentary fear that he would ask Angela how Miles was, provoking an outpouring of that sordid story from her, and not only that story, for plenty more than Miles had happened to her over the years since they last met – but no, he commented that he had met her beautiful daughter on a couple of occasions and asked how old she was. Dear, kindly Oliver. Although Angela had reappeared in my life as a near neighbour only a month or two before Melissa died,

Oliver would not have forgotten what I told him then.

'Lucinda?' Angela's face showed her pleasure. 'She's seventeen, nearly eighteen. And she really is striking, isn't she? Quite lovely. People comment on it the whole time.'

'She's at the same school as Sara, I believe.'

'Yes, the local comprehensive.' Her mouth twitched, the thin hands gestured nervously. 'Miles insisted she should go there when St Hilda's . . . after she left St Hilda's.'

'And what will she do next? University?'

'Miles wants her to, but Lucinda shouldn't be stuck in stuffy libraries pouring over books. God, how I loathed it! Miles has no right to interfere. Money or no money, he forfeited his rights long since by his behaviour. The courts are so stupid about these things.'

'But what do you think Lucinda should do?'

'She should be a photographic model, something in that world. It would be a shame to waste her beauty.' She leaned back on the Chesterfield, inviting our approbation, and crossed her bare feet at the ankles, knees swung carefully sideways together in a sad parody of her old elegance. 'But naturally Lucinda will make up her own mind. I would never try to dominate her as my father dominated me.' The worry beads raced through her fingers.

'It must be difficult, bringing up a daughter on your own,' said Oliver.

She downed the remains of her whisky and held out her glass for more. 'It's dreadful. My money problems are never-ending – a tangled web. But anything's better than living with the wrong man. I was very unlucky in my husbands, you know.' The plaintively resigned tone put them into the category of natural disasters, matters over which she could not possibly have had control.

I recalled Richard's caustic comment of a few days ago. 'If the silly woman were to quote Shakespeare she would want to re-organise his words to suit herself: "The fault, dear Brutus, lies not in ourselves, but in our stars . . ."'

We were silent. It dawned on her then that it was her turn to show interest, her turn to ask the polite questions.

'Your wife died, didn't she? I'm sorry about that. Do you have any children?'

Oliver's voice was quiet. 'No, no children. You're lucky there, you see.'

Oliver had known Melissa was incapable of having children when he married her. She'd had a hysterectomy at an incredibly early age. 'My female insides were hopeless,' she said regretfully, and poured out love on her friends' children. Richard and I disappointed her by producing our first two in the Midlands while he was lecturing there. When we returned to London I started Ollie. If ever a woman could share another's pregnancy Melissa shared mine. She questioned me upon every symptom, insisted that I stop smoking, worried about my vitamins. She held my belly in her hands to feel the child kick and tears of emotion ran down her thin brown face. 'It's wonderful,' she said. Richard suggested that the baby should be called Oliver or Melissa according to sex. Melissa was thrilled. After Ollie was born she never stopped watching me for signs of fatigue. 'Let me have him for a weekend to give you a rest,' she would plead. I let him go, but worried at first – for her, that is – but Oliver said: 'He gives her so much pleasure. He helps us both, you know.'

Angela said that children were a mixed blessing. 'The adolescent mind can be very difficult to understand. Annabel keeps so calm. Meditation helps me to cope'.

'Meditation?' Oliver queried.

She leaned forward eagerly. 'Every day I set aside a time

for meditation. It is a great help in my troubles.'

'It helps you to escape from their pressures?'

'No, no. One must be careful that in seeking The Way one is not falling into escapism. That is a wrong path. One seeks a heightened sense of awareness, an inner strength.'

'A positive approach.'

'Yes, indeed. You know, Oliver, alcohol, sex, drugs, all these can give a sensation of having reached a new understanding of the cosmic forces, but they are merely a temporary self-deception. I know, I've tried them all. I was on the wrong path until a friend showed me the value of meditation. It really has helped me.' She accepted a cigarette from Oliver and added unexpectedly: 'I can see that you are suffering, Oliver. Depression. You, too, could be helped.'

He looked startled. He made a negative gesture with his hands and smiled politely. 'I know nothing of these . . . movements.'

Angela was pleased to explain. 'Meditation helps us to live and to think fully, to allow our senses to operate in balance. It helps us to deal with sorrow. You will have heard of transcendental meditation – everybody has – but there are other ways. Zen, Tibetan and so on. You might call them the modern equivalent of prayer.'

I watched Richard, his eyes on his ill-assorted guests, his dark face impassive. Richard had no need of meditation, his senses worked in balance, he was at one with his world, the select world of the university, of academic life. He preferred London to Oxford or Cambridge; his ambition was to soar to the heights at Princes College, where we had taken our degrees, to be Professor Bateman; it looked as if he might achieve it. He had always known who he was and where he was going, and that inner certitude communicated itself to others, so that they trusted him and relied on him. He was not always an easy man; he could be abrupt and often impatient with those whose minds worked more slowly than his own, but he did not know what it was to suffer from discontent. It was that male assurance and strength, lacking in my fatherless childhood, but in Richard wonderfully allied to an acute intelligence, that had first attracted me.

The goals of position and wealth which had stimulated people like Richard and myself could not arouse Oliver, who had possessed them from birth. It was Melissa who saved him from becoming an amiable dilettante. She, too, was a barrister with a civil practice, competent and cheerfully ambitious. He found himself forced to compete with her to preserve his self-respect and discovered that he enjoyed the competition; they applauded each other's successes, commiserated over lost cases. Now that Melissa was gone Oliver was struggling with sorrow and with loneliness, but his prescription for them was very different from Angela's; I had heard it in the past when he had been concerned about me. I had been weak with the lassitude that comes with self-disgust. Work, books, food, everything that normally attracted me was repellant. 'Action is the only answer,' Oliver had told me. 'Nonstop. No brooding. Fill every moment with people and interest – it doesn't have to be noisy or energetic, but it must eliminate those moments when nasty thoughts could sidle insidiously back.' He had helped me to follow this prescription and it had worked. It was later that I found it strange he demonstrated so close an acquaintance with melancholy. Nowadays it was his intimate companion. He took on an ever heavier load of work, forcing his mind to concentrate on the problems of others, but if the old prescription helped him, it had clearly not yet made a cure. No, Oliver would not care to meditate.

The windows were open to the thin summer darkness.

From the distance came the familiar sound of a plane descending into Heathrow, and from above us, the sound of Ollie's violin, a cascade of notes in a minor scale. Small moths were flying into the room, blundering into the lights, beating their wings against the taut silk shades.

Angela's high-pitched voice was wearying in its persistence, its unceasing talk of self-awareness and mystic communication and kharma. In the right mood Angela could be very amusing, whether consciously or unconsciously. But tonight, with Oliver, the mood was wrong.

We were rescued by Sara. She prowled in through the French windows, making us all jump as she glimmered from the darkness. She eyed us without expression, remarked that the place was alive with insects and murdered a few messily beneath a table lamp.

'Good to see you back so early,' Richard said encouragingly.

She looked revolted. 'I've got a headache.'

'Too much sun, I expect.'

'And I was bored.' She turned to Angela. 'Lucinda says you're to go back now and make coffee for them.'

Angela rose in a flurry of nervous movements, gulping the remains of her whisky and stubbing out her cigarette in the glass. Oliver rose and said he must go too.

'There's a gem of a concert on Thursday week at the Barbican: Handel, Purcell and Bach. If I can get seats I'll telephone you. Agreed?' He smiled at me and kissed my cheeks. 'That was a superb curry, Annabel. Thank you. You're very good to me.' He was suddenly exhausted and there were marks like thumb prints beneath his eyes. I suspected he was sleeping badly and thought: I wish I could do more for him, but I can't take his grief away. There is so little anyone can do.

Sometimes I wondered how I could live if anything happened to Richard. Through my awareness of the

40

extent of Oliver's loss I had come to the alarming realisation that Richard, too, was mortal and vulnerable to
disease, to accidents, to a heart attack. I remembered my
father, killed in a road accident when I was a toddler. I
kissed Richard goodbye with a special fervour in the
mornings in case it should be the last time. I asked of the
fates that my own luck should hold.

Sara collapsed on to the carpet, a limp rag doll, limbs
sprawled everywhere. She leaned her head against the
sofa and closed her eyes.

'Poor love,' I said, then murmured: 'Late nights!' provocatively.

One eye regarded me balefully. 'Two of them were
baby-sitting, just flopping on Mrs Foster's sofa. The baby
didn't even wake.'

'But you weren't in bed till well after midnight.' I fetched
aspirin and a glass of water. 'Come on, idiot, take these.'

'Thanks.' She sipped, looking pathetic. 'It was awful
tonight. Too many people packed into that hot room. And
the boys were so boring.'

'Boys? Boring?'

'Yeah. All they know to talk about is school and sport.
Who cares about fucking football, anyhow! And then they
think you're so fascinated that you'll be thrilled when they
grab you and put their pimply faces all over yours.'

Not boys in general, one specific boy, I deduced;
rejected and scorned. I remembered the agonies of that
age, the yearning for someone attractive and different, the
exasperation at persistent bores. But I suspected that I'd
let them down more lightly than Sara would. I sank on to
the sofa beside her and after a moment she moved her
head to rest it against my knee. I sat very still, not allowing
my pleasure to show; gestures of affection were examined
with suspicion. The incense smell of Angela's house was
thick in her hair.

41

'I'm glad you're not like Angela,' she said.

'Oh?'

'Mmm. She's very silly sometimes. She drives Lucinda crazy.'

I said nothing, simply waited. Too close an interest in what Sara thought or did could shut her up like a slammed book. It was easy to ask the wrong questions.

'She's got a new boyfriend – at least, that's what she calls him – lover, I suppose, though I don't see how she could. Have you seen him?'

'No. They come and go.'

'You haven't missed much in this one.'

'Oh?'

'He's awful – you can't imagine. Old and slobby. Lucinda says he's the creepiest creep that ever crept round her mother. Yuck! He's got a great fat beer gut; not a barrel, a jelly-belly.' She giggled faintly. 'Lucinda says she can't imagine how they do it – think of all that quivering belly getting in the way.'

I shivered, took a deep breath, tried to keep my voice light. 'Lucinda says too much. Poor Angela, having her sex life discussed with all the neighbourhood. She can't have any privacy.'

'She doesn't want much,' Sara observed shrewdly. 'She likes to think people are talking about her and her men. She wants to be interesting. I can't think why you and she were friends at university. You're totally unalike.'

'People change. She was different then.'

'How different? What was she like?'

'Smart,' I said promptly. 'Stunningly smart. Way-out high fashion. I was terribly impressed.' Everything about her was impressive to me then: her posh-school accent, her acquaintance with people whose names were of household significance, and those clothes . . . like nothing I'd ever seen at home in Woking. I had a vision of

Angela nonchalant in the lecture hall, clad from head to foot in emerald green, the **in** colour of that particular season – slim ski-style trousers, shoes, eye-shadow, even her fingernails were green, making the other girls' eyes slide sideways, first to this strange phenomenon, then to each other, in envy or disapproval.

'She's a weirdo now.'

'Yes. And it's sad when I look back to what she was.' But the distance between the two was not so great. Angela had simply toppled over the dividing line that separates the extreme from the ludicrous.

'She never got a degree or anything, did she?'

'No. She was thrown out at the end of the second year for not working. She was glad. She'd always wanted to be a fashion designer but Daddy said it was purely an adolescent yearning. He insisted she should go to university. Why economics and politics I can't imagine, except that probably they're what he'd have liked to study himself.' Poor Angela. Daddy was a Socialist MP, one of a group of wealthy post-war idealists who lived in Hampstead and never quite made it to cabinet rank. He believed that people would better themselves if one could only open doors: he opened doors for Angela, but she never went through them.

'I wouldn't let you or Dad tell me what to do. It's my life. If I make a mess of it, that's my business.' Sara's voice had the easy scorn of her years. 'Anyway, go on. Didn't you disapprove of Angela sleeping with her boyfriends? Grandma says that in your day, same as hers, you were supposed to be good little girls.'

'Angela was.'

'Christ, you're joking? Was she really? Why the great change?'

'She didn't sleep around because it wasn't generally done then. But it's the fashion now – divorced people take

43

lovers. Angela always follows the fashion, doesn't she?'

Sara's head moved, rubbing against the calf of my leg. 'That was bitchy.' But her voice sounded amused.

'Cynical, perhaps.' I hoped she saw the point I was making.

'Can I ask you something, Mum? I mean, without you being cross?'

'I'll give it a whirl!'

'Did you sleep with Dad before you were married?'

'Yes. We lived together.'

She exhaled noisily. 'Naughty old you! Weren't you taking a risk? Wouldn't you have been in trouble with the college if you'd been found out? After all, Dad was your tutor!'

'Only in my first year. We certainly weren't sleeping together then.' Expecting someone grey-haired and benign as my tutor, I'd bristled with resentment at the forceful young rugger-type who never let up in his demands on my brain. And the following year I'd abandoned economics for law, to his disgust, though it was he who had originally suggested I should do a paper on Elements of English Law. It was in my finals year that we'd fallen in love.

'But when you were living together, he was a lecturer and you were still a student?'

'True. Yes, we'd have been in trouble if it had got out.' I couldn't tell her how nearly it had, because it would mean telling the whole story, and that I could not do. Richard's mother had discovered that we were living together, found us sharing a bath, to be exact, and pronounced herself deeply mortified that a son of hers could commit such sins. But it was on me that the full force of her venom fell. Men were weak vessels, easily tempted; women must be strong. She made no distinction between fornication and adultery: to her, they were equally wrong and she was convinced that a woman who had done the first would commit the second; she would be an unfaithful wife – bound to be. She therefore attempted, using this and certain other information she had unfortunately acquired about me, to blackmail me out of Richard's life. It didn't work because he knew all there was to know: she'd banked on his being ignorant. When it came to the crunch she wasn't prepared to wreck his career; together, we'd called her bluff.

'You were being trendy then!' Sara said.

'I suppose we were.'

'I can't imagine it now. You take yourselves so seriously.'

I grinned. 'Perhaps not as much as you think. But we're trying to bring you lot up on a firm foundation.'

'Grandma tries to bring us up too. But she's stuck in a time warp.'

'Yes.'

'But she's all right, really.' Sara sat up and scratched her leg vigorously. 'Blast those mosquitoes! Lucinda has a T-shirt with Females for Freedom all over her boobs. Well, I reckon I believe in what they say, too, but imagine what Grandma would make of it! Lucinda's got lots of stuff like that. It's mostly show-off.'

Richard's voice came from behind us. 'How you do pick folk to pieces, Sara. Can't you find anything pleasant to say, even about your friends?'

I gave him a meaningful look and a shake of the head as he crossed the room but he was impervious to such signals.

Sara scrambled to her feet and said without rancour: 'But it's much more fun to pick folk to pieces. You can't just praise them, can you?'

'Why not?'

'Only boring self-righteous people do that. It's boring to

be good – all dull and worthy. I suppose you'd like it if I was like that! Well, I'm not, so you'll bloody well have to put up with me like I am, won't you? I'm going to bed. 'Night!' She stalked off without waiting for any response.

Richard said softly: 'I want to go to bed, too!' He put out a hand to pull me up from the sofa.

I rose, grumbling affectionately at him: 'You never learn tact, do you? Specially not with bed on your mind! You interrupted an interesting discussion then, the first for ages.'

'Was I tactless? I'm sorry.' He didn't sound it. His hands undid the buttons on my shirt, his fingers played with my nipples. 'Relax, lover. You worry too much over Sara. Come on, bed! At least she's in early tonight. No need for you to lie awake, worrying.'

'I'll worry about your mother moving here instead,' I said, and pushed him away. Then I changed my mind and pulled him back again. 'But afterwards, darling, afterwards.'

5

It was an unexpectedly warm September day when the first conference was held in my incest case. Lincoln's Inn was dusty. The trees were the dark green of late summer, their leaves motionless in the windless air. The faint roar of the traffic outside the square was like the deep note of a distant organ. I sat quite still in my car for a minute after I arrived, looking at the late roses, letting my muscles relax after driving through central London, bracing myself for what I suspected might be an unpleasant hour.

As I walked into Chambers I had a mental picture of what my client would look like. John Pockett was the manager of a furniture shop: I saw him as largish, plumpish, with an ingratiating manner and a pallid face sheened with sweat. That picture had been with me for weeks, but when I had climbed the stairs to my room there were two men in their shirt-sleeves sitting waiting on the chairs outside. One was a self-confident six-footer with navy blazer over his arm, the solicitor, Howard Hoffer; the other was a slight man of medium height with floppy brown hair and light brown eyes in a tanned face. His skin was quite dry. He was wearing a Marks & Spencer shirt and trousers and an unobtrusive tie. I told myself that one could not, of course, go too much by appearances.

My room was stuffy. I flung up the sash of the window as high as it could go, displaced a pile of briefs from my desk, replaced them with the contents of my briefcase and we got straight down to work. 'Mr Pockett, I have your proof of evidence here and I'd like to start by clarifying one or two points – '

'Mrs Bateman, before you say anything more, there is one thing I want to clarify absolutely, now and for ever – that I am not guilty, that I have never touched my daughter, Fern, in any way that could possibly be construed as sexual, and that I am totally at a loss to understand how she or her mother could allege such things against me.' He looked at me from under the flopping lock of hair, blinked, took glasses from a pocket to see me better, blinked again and said: 'Now, can we go on from there?'

We could. We did. We clarified many matters: his marriage, his divorce, his relationships with his two daughters and the mounting difficulties over access, but we could cast no ray of light over the allegations of incest.

Mr Pockett did not prevaricate, on the contrary, as in that first brief outburst, he was clear, concise and firm. His marriage had been a disaster, but not an utter disaster. He and Tina had bickered endlessly, but they had not often screamed at each other – not to start with, that is. He took off his glasses and smiled sadly. 'We never cared enough for that.' She had been his girlfriend for a short while, differing only from other girlfriends in that she got pregnant. He had done the right thing, knowing even then that it was the wrong thing for them both. 'Abortion? I wouldn't have cared to murder my child. No more than my daughter Karen did. And Tina was too disorganised. She put off the unpleasant decision until it was too late.' It hadn't been all bad; there had been the two little girls. They had made it worthwhile – then.

He stopped to polish his glasses. 'Tina wasn't much of a mum – she was always one for a good time, would never stop in of an evening, so I had to. And I was the one who went to their school open days, who talked to their teachers. Yet the divorce judge gave Tina the girls while I only had access. A man alone shouldn't bring up teenage girls. I only saw them every other Sunday.'

'Why the divorce after all those years?'

'There had always been other men sniffing after Tina. I looked the other way. What the eye doesn't see . . . But then I was forced to see. They were in my bed, and he was one of the salesmen from the shop. After that we screamed at each other. Home truths. There's nothing nastier than home truths with no holds barred, Mrs Bateman. And then we divorced. I got a mortgage on a flat about ten miles away and I thought – well, I was fool enough to think she'd let me have access without too much fuss.'

'But she didn't?'

'Not for long. Within a month or two she was making difficulties.'

'Such as?' I prompted him when he seemed to have dried up.

He was swinging his glasses from one earpiece. Round and round they went; I was oddly reminded of Angela's worry beads. 'At first it was excuses not to let me have the girls. They'd been invited to a friend's house for the day, she'd say, or she'd got her awful cousins or her mother coming and they'd want to see Karen and Fern, wouldn't they? But other times she'd want to be away herself and then it was fine for me to sleep on the sofa in the lounge and look after the kids for the whole weekend. Then more recently it changed; she'd yell abuse at me when I came, real vicious stuff. Stuff to make you cringe and wish the neighbours were all deaf mutes. She didn't want me

49

coming to the house, not at all. I've got a car, a company car. I'd always picked the girls up. Mostly I'd just park the car and wait outside, to keep away from Tina. Now, if she let them come, they had to come by bus. That shortened our time together.'

'Can you date the time when the pattern changed?'

When I was first at the Bar my pupil-master had given me two useful pieces of advice: look for changes in a person's pattern of behaviour, he'd said, they're often a clue when you're trying to solve a problem. And never reject any piece of information, however small, that doesn't fit the pattern. Make a note, record these things. People have set patterns of behaviour, particular ways of living; anything out of the ordinary can be a pointer – to what, you may not know yet, but if you keep probing something will turn up.

'So when did the change come, Mr Pockett?' I prompted.

He put his glasses back on, as if they'd help his mental focus. They didn't. 'Sometime in the winter, I suppose,' he said vaguely. 'January? February? I can't remember.'

'Keep it in mind. Let me know if anything occurs to you – a particular argument between you and your wife, some difficulty with one of the girls, perhaps. Now, Mr Pockett, tell me about the two girls. How well do you get on with them – no sorry, I meant, how did you get along before all this trouble blew up?'

He gave me a suspicious look. I smiled faintly back and nodded encouragingly. 'Take Karen first. Tell me about her and her baby.'

The hands that had been loosely clenched in his lap now balled into tight fists. 'It's a little girl. She's six months old now. Lara, she's called. I've only seen her once, just after she was born. I have to keep away, it's one of the conditions of my bail. Wicked, isn't it? My own grandchild, and

50

I'm not allowed to see her.' His voice was thick with outrage; his fists pounded my desk once and were still, as if shocked at the noise they had made. He gulped.

I waited. John Pockett's hands uncoiled and he removed his spectacles. 'Sorry,' he said. The rhythmic swinging of the glasses began again. 'Karen was only fifteen when she started the baby. I couldn't believe it at first. I thought Tina was winding me up; it's the sort of thing she would do. Then I tried to find out who the father was – well, whoever he was, boy or man, he'd committed an offence, hadn't he? Karen wouldn't tell me. She clammed up and cried every time I asked. Finally it turned out she couldn't tell me. There'd been more than one in the month. Would you believe it? At fifteen!'

'Had you no idea at all that this sort of thing was going on?'

'None. Well, not really. You hear about young girls getting up to all sorts of things before they're half fledged, but you don't connect that gossip with your own daughter, do you? It sounds silly to say it, in view of the evidence, but Karen's not like that.'

'What is she like?'

'Quiet, a bit shy. Nervous sometimes.' Pause. With a half-smile he added: 'What the teachers would call a nice girl. No trouble. Oh, she had the occasional boyfriend, but the one or two I saw were quiet boys, nothing to get a dad's wind up.'

'And Fern?'

'Ah, she's different. Chalk and cheese, the two of them are. Fern's a big girl, big-built, and she's a much stronger personality. Look,' he said diffidently, fishing out his wallet from a back pocket, 'I've got a photograph of them.' He leaned forward and pushed the picture on to the desk before me.

Two girls standing by the wooden garden gate of a

51

semi-detached house; an amateur's snap with a cheap camera. Mr Pockett pointed out Fern on the left, Karen on the right. I studied it.

Fern did not resemble her name. Nothing of the quiet woodland pool about this girl. There was a resemblance . . . to Sara, I thought in some discomfort. Not a striking likeness, simply the physical type, I supposed; big, dark, sulky, looking older than her years. Karen, on the other hand, did look like Oliver's startled deer. It was her large shy eyes that did it.

'And does Fern attract the boys?'

'She's very young,' he said quickly, protectively. 'I've only ever heard of one, that was round about Christmas and a month or two afterwards. Otherwise just as friends. They do have boys who are friends at the comprehensive.'

Was the protectiveness the natural reaction of a caring father or the jealous reaction of a man caring in the wrong way? It was impossible to gauge. But the police surgeon's statement was clear on the subject of Fern's sexual experience: from the condition of the vagina and the absence of the hymen Fern was not a virgin; on the contrary, appearances were that she had been regularly penetrated.

'How do you account for the medical evidence then?'

'I can't. I just can't. It could have been one of the boys from school. It must have been. It certainly wasn't me!'

'Fern states that it was you.'

'It wasn't! It never was.'

There was a sheen of sweat on his face now, but his voice remained calmly firm.

'Is Fern a truthful girl?'

A pause. A sucking in of breath. 'Mostly. The occasional lie to avoid trouble, like most kids. Nothing major that I've ever discovered.'

Nothing major?

'Is Fern like you in character?'

A shake of the head. 'No, Karen's like me, if you like. But Fern, she's not like anyone. She's herself.'

'Easy to get on with? Difficult?'

The glasses were swinging again, agitatedly. 'We got on well when she was small. She was great – bright, quick, go-ahead. Now . . . well, it's different when they're teen-agers, isn't it? Everyone says how awful they are. Specially when there's been a divorce in the family. Fern took it all so much harder than Karen. She changed.'

So Fern was difficult. 'Yes?'

'But we got on all right. Mostly. Till the last few months. Till . . .' His head went down, his voice smothered. 'Till there was . . . this.' Silence, then his head reared up. 'I don't understand it. I can't understand it, not whichever way I look! It's – it's a nightmare, it's a nightmare that goes on, and on, and on, and I never wake up from it.'

Either he was both a consummate liar and a consummate actor or he was telling the truth. No way to tell which, as yet. Give him the opportunity to produce some ingenious explanation.

'Mr Pockett, can you think of anything, anything at all, you have done which an inexperienced girl like Fern might misinterpret as sexual? Please be absolutely open with me.'

'Nothing. Nothing at all. No need to think. I've thought and thought till I'm sick.'

'The first of these alleged offences took place in a tent in Devon when you were on holiday. Were you sharing a tent with Fern?'

'No. We had two tents. She had a two-man tent, which she usually shared with Karen. I had a one-man tent next-door. Karen didn't come because of the baby, of course.'

'Of course,' I echoed. 'Were there any caravans there, or mobile homes?'

'Mostly tents. One or two weekender caravaners. It was half-empty, being early in the year. The tents were on one side of the field, the caravans the other. Fern's tent was the last in the row.'

No real hope that the other campers could prove or disprove anything. 'Fern says that you went to her tent in the night asking to cuddle up because you were cold. Which night was that?'

His lips tightened. 'I never went to her tent on any night for any reason.'

'Then tell me the reason, some reason, any reason, why your daughter might have it in for you – enough to make such an allegation against you. You say she had been difficult recently – any nasty arguments? Or was there something she wanted that you were blocking her from having? Think hard, Mr Pockett.'

A lengthy silence, then: 'There is one thing. I don't know if it's relevant. Sometime in early February, I suppose it was. Karen was nearing her time and Tina wanted to go to her sister's wedding. A second marriage it was, but they made a ruddy big do of it, a knees-up in the evening and all. In the Midlands. So I stayed in the house. Fern was going to a disco with a friend and I said I'd take them there in the car. She was late in getting ready, as usual, and I went to her room to speed the process. There were a lot of things there I'd never seen before.'

He stopped, marshalling his thoughts.

'What things, Mr Pockett?'

'Well, there was a portable colour TV set, and a CD player. And on her chest of drawers there was some gold jewellery set out that she was choosing a piece from, to wear that night. I asked her whose they were. She darted me an angry look and said they were hers. Then she seemed to want to push me out of the bedroom. She came towards me and snapped at me to go away and she'd be

54

down soon. But I wanted to know how she'd come by them. She muttered something about presents and how her boyfriend had given her things. She'd just had a birthday at the end of January. But I knew that was all rubbish.'

'How did you know that?'

'There was no one who'd give her such expensive presents. The gold bracelet and the necklaces and the earrings were spindly, like the fashion is now, but even so they'd have cost a fair bit and so would the other things. Tina doesn't work except for the odd bit of barmaiding when the local pub has a busy night, and she's always moaning on about how what I give her wouldn't feed a cat. And Fern's boyfriend then . . . he was fifteen and had a newspaper round. So where'd she got them? I insisted. It was her Christmas money and her birthday money and her boyfriend too, she said. What, hundreds of pounds' worth? Well, there'd been the January sales, hadn't there? She wriggled and she groused and she wanted to go out 'cause Tracy'd be waiting for her, and in the end we were both shouting and swearing at each other. Was I accusing her of stealing? she yelled. And I said I wasn't, but I'd still like to know where it all came from. Ordinary shops, you stupid git, she said. Christ, where did I get such a shit of a father from? she said. So then I got very quiet and serious and told her that items had been known to walk from shops and she'd better tell me if her boyfriend said they'd fallen off the back of a lorry, or he'd bought them from a fellow in a pub, because receiving stolen goods was a very serious offence. In fact, I said, so serious that she and I ought to go to the police before she got any further involved.'

'What on earth did she say to that?'

She denied it all, as angrily and firmly as I'm denying the allegations against me. She went very red and said it was libel and I was a scumhead even to think of such things. She went all dramatic and tumbled the contents of one drawer – all her hankies and scarves and bits of make-up and tissues – on to the floor and scrabbled round in them finally to produce a receipt for the earrings. That seemed genuine enough.'

'And then what happened?'

'Nothing.' He shrugged. 'I gave up. I wasn't getting anywhere. I gave up and drove her to the disco.'

'A strange story. Did you ever discover any more? Did any further expensive items appear in her room after that?'

'I don't know. That was the last time I went to the house.' He had been slumped in his chair. Now, suddenly, he sat bolt upright. 'That was the last time I ever went to the house!'

'The change in pattern!' the solicitor and I said in unison.

'Yes, that was when things changed! But wait, it was Tina who changed, not so much Fern. She was sulky with me but she still came on the access visits, or most of them anyway. It was Tina who was screaming and shouting after that.'

'Hmm,' said Mr Hoffer, looking at me. 'Something definitely out of order there, one would think.'

'Something odd,' I agreed. 'Mr Pockett, did Tina have any new items for the house or any new clothes about that time?'

He thought, shook his head. 'Can't really tell you. Nothing new in the house that weekend, but you wouldn't catch Tina buying things for the house – she was hardly ever in it. Clothes and jewellery were her scene, but I never really saw her to tell. She kept me well away. And if she'd had any new stuff, she wouldn't have brought it out in my honour!'

We talked on for a while, but we could think of no real explanation for this story. Or, rather, we could think of several, but none of them gave Pockett a let-out.

Finally he pocketed his glasses and said: 'What I want is a private detective looking into the matter for me. I have to find out what's going on. I have to. I could pay, you know.'

'I'm afraid you'd have to,' Howard Hoffer said gloomily. 'Can't see the legal aid authorities forking out for an enquiry agent, not for the sort of flimsy lead you'd be giving them.'

'Well, like I say,' John Pockett said impatiently, 'I'll pay. Can you find me an agent, thought? I wouldn't know where to start.'

'Oh, I can put an enquiry agent on,' Hoffer agreed, 'but I doubt that sort of thing will turn up much. Futile, I'd say. But if you've the money and you're ready to risk wasting it, then there's a fellow does work for us at Bryant and Morley called Alan Greening. He's pretty good. Thorough, you know. Looks ordinary, so people trust him. Tell him the most extraordinary things, too, sometimes. Best you put some money down with us. Are you still working?'

'No,' Pockett admitted, blinking rapidly. 'Damned bastards my employers found out about the case and they've suspended me.'

'With pay?' I asked, suspecting the answer.

'No pay. They say they'll make up the back pay if I'm found not guilty, but they can't take the risk otherwise. But I do have savings. I've always been the careful sort, thank God. And I'll just have to pray your man comes up with some evidence of what the hell's going on.'

'Waste of time,' Howard Hoffer said after Pockett had left. 'Might as well plead guilty now and have done with it. We're on to a hiding for nothing. No jury could help but convict.'

Sara was waiting for me when I arrived home. As soon as I opened the door she was there, ready to unburden herself of some monstrous complaint. I knew all the symptoms: the hunched shoulders, the lowered eyebrows, the heavy breathing that indicated barely restrained ire. It was a nerve-racking prospect. I wondered who had offended her. The boys? Her father? Some unwary shop-keeper who'd sold her the wrong type of suntan oil? No, I discovered, it was me.

'Daddy says that conference you went to was in a case of incest, and you're for the defence. It's not true, is it?'

'Why shouldn't it be?'

'Incest?' she said, ire freed from restraint and fuming hotly at me. 'Are you joking? Incest? Rape of a daughter by her father? You think that's all right?'

'I think it's revolting and horrific. But this man is pleading not guilty. He has a right to challenge the evidence.'

'Challenge his own daughter? What sort of daughter would say those things against her own father – her own *father* – unless they were true?' Sara had always had a good line in rhetoric, and on these occasions she used it to the full. 'You really are getting down to the pits of the earth, Mother!'

'Just doing my job, darling.' I walked briskly into the kitchen to proceed with my second job of the day, feeding the hungry hordes.

'What sort of a job is it to defend filth like that?' she demanded, following me. 'Not the sort of job I ever want my mother doing! What you did to Salome Keane was dreadful, but this is much worse. I agree with that man in Parliament who says all rapists should be castrated. That would stop them fast enough. They wouldn't like that, would they?'

58

I opened the fridge door and peered around for meat. 'And supposing for some reason they had been wrongly accused? Plenty of jealous women bring wrongful accusations against men and have done so throughout the ages. Castration is horribly final.'

'The MP said it should only be one testicle on the first offence,' Sara retorted triumphantly, 'in case there's a mistake. Then, like you said, the second one would be the ultimate deterrent. I think that's really clever, and so do Angela and Lucinda.'

I shut the fridge door hastily. Raw steak had lost all appeal. 'Oh God, no, you haven't discussed my case with those two, have you?'

'Yes, I have, and why not? They think very seriously about these matters, both of them. They belong to Females for Freedom and I'm going to join too. Protecting our own sex I consider highly important, and so should you, Mum. They're going to send me the forms and all the leaflets and pamphlets so that I understand all the implications of the movement. It's – it's a radical and meaningful organisation set up to secure full rights under the law for all women.'

'Very worthwhile,' I said seriously. 'Very worthwhile, so long as it is done in a dignified manner – and, Sara, most importantly, so long as men's basic rights are not infringed in the process.'

Females for Freedom was a noisy group I'd met hoisting banners outside the Bailey, whose energies and emotions, in fact, ran more to recruiting fodder for the gender war than to the cerebral effort of drafting the clauses for peace.

'You should join, too, Mum.'

'Me? I'm no joiner – I haven't the time. I demonstrate for women by competing successfully with men in my career, not by holding a placard. We have to consolidate our gains now that the main battles have been won.'

'Won? You're joking. Just look at Dad.'

'He's his mother's son, my lovely. Intellectually he likes to describe himself as a supporter of the cause. But deep within his subconscious lurks the traditionalism he was brought up in. Domestic chores will never be for him. But at least he doesn't give me a hard time about working.'

'You bend over backwards to be fair – but one of these days you'll bend too far and fall flat,' Sara threatened me, 'and then he'll trample on you.'

'Maybe I shall fall flat over this case. I don't know. You say that I shouldn't be doing it. But if I were barred from representing men because of my sex you'd be horrified. Exceptions are wrong – and they make bad propaganda. True equality is what we must win.'

'Yes, well, you're not doing much about winning it, are you?' Sara snapped. 'And what's more, I'm not helping you in the kitchen tonight. The boys can do it. True equality? Huh! You don't know what it means.'

6

Our wedding anniversary began auspiciously. It was one of those days when getting up is easy; like being a small child again, seeing the world as bright and full of surprises. My body was light, the flesh taut over the bones; happiness seemed to dissolve the heaviness of middle-age. I pulled back the curtains. Dew was sparkling on the grass and the air was still. The shrubs were festooned with spiders' webs, scraps of lace sewn with pearl beads of moisture. I could hear the sounds of the terrace coming to life: the chink of milk bottles, a door shutting, a robin practising his autumn song. In the bed Richard stirred. I did not have to turn to know what he was doing; I knew his hands were searching for my body, they always did.

'Annabel? Where are you, my lovely love?'

'It will be fine,' I said with certainty. 'It's a good omen for our celebrations this evening.'

More movements. The bedclothes heaved. 'This evening? What are you talking about? There's only one true way to celebrate twenty years of you and I intend to do that now. Come back in here, woman!'

I knelt on the side of the bed, shaking my head, luxuriating in the cool air on my skin, in his warm hands grasping for me; tantalising myself as well as him. This was going to be good. The hands tugged and I tumbled across him, laughing. His bristly morning face scratched mine deliciously; his hands travelled over me. After twenty years sex hadn't palled one bit. Whoever said that familiarity breeds contempt was a fool. Familiarity breeds contentment, not contempt. Richard knew my body as if it were his own. It was his own.

It must have been some sound, a cough perhaps, to clear her morning catarrh, that reminded me of my mother-in-law's presence in the next room. I stiffened. I disliked making love when she was in the house. Disapproval radiated through the walls, her unseen presence inhibiting me. 'She'll hear,' I whispered. 'Your mother.'

'Nonsense. The walls are far too thick.'

'But I just heard her.'

'Imagination.'

'She'll come marching in to suggest that it's time we got moving.'

'That's what I thought we were going to do!' His breath puffed against my hair. 'Oh, all right. To keep you happy I'll lock the door.'

He slid from my arms and the air blew coldly across my body. He held me once more, but the carefree loving urge had dwindled. It was not perfect. I was out-of-proportion disappointed.

I grumbled as we pulled on our clothes. 'I don't know why you had to invite her to stay for the whole weekend. As if there isn't enough to do already – and Clare and Colin to stay overnight, too.'

He said with patient sympathy: 'You know she invited herself, sweetheart. But it was only sensible to agree to the suggestion when she had half-a-dozen houses to view and the party to come to tonight. The travelling would have been impossible.'

'Good.'

He bent to pull on his underpants, an undignified stage. 'You realise how it would have ended if she hadn't stayed here, don't you? With me acting as her taxi-driver for hours on end.'

'You could have said you were too busy to drive her. If it's so much trouble to get to view the houses she might even give up her idea of moving.'

'Fat chance.' He opened a drawer and selected a shirt from the pile, rumpling several as he removed it.

'You haven't said much to dissuade her.'

'There's little to be said, seeing she's definitely found a buyer for her house now.' He tucked his shirt into old grey trousers, zipped himself up and crossed the room to take me in his arms, pulling me to sit on the tumbled bed with him, cuddling me like a child. 'Darling, I don't want to squabble with you – not today, of all days! It isn't like you to get things out of proportion. I doubt we'll see much more of her when she's moved than we do now. She isn't that fascinated by all our doings.'

I laid my head against his shoulder, pressing my face into his cool clean shirt. You don't know, I thought miserably, and you don't want to know either. He turned his newly shaved face to kiss my cheek and the familiarity of his special smell struck me as earlier the familiarity of his body had. There was a particular blend of scents that was unmistakably Richard. And as certain smells mingled to create the particular one that was him, so certain attributes and interests combined to create his character, a character that appealed because it fitted mine as notches in a key fit and work the tumblers in a lock. Yet we were two distinct people, however close we became. His mind could only understand mine through speech and gestures. Although as time passed we translated more easily their fullest meanings, the gulf that could fill with misunderstandings was still there: the tumblers moved and worked smoothly, but could not fuse with the key. And this was part of the mystery, that despite all our loving communication there should be room for incomprehension.

Knuckles rapped on the door, Ollie's voice called through the wood: 'Mummy? Daddy? Are you up? Grandma says she thought you'd have wanted an early start today of all days.'

Walking from the kitchen to the drawing-room with yet another plate of food, I paused to survey the party. From where I was, half-hidden by the door, I could see our guests talking but not distinguish their words. It was a bit like watching television with the sound turned down; a curiously meaningless display, as if they were so many actors going through the motions of having fun. The party looked successful, all was movement and laughter, but in a moment of self-doubt I wondered whether the success was more apparent than real. I could not believe that either my mother or my mother-in-law could have found a soul-mate in Angela, for example, despite the animated conversation. At least she would provide them with material for gossip afterwards.

Further down the room Professor Morton-Rycroft was braying at Oliver, or rather, at a point somewhere beyond Oliver's left shoulder. It was one of the Professor's many quirks that he looked no one in the face, leaving the impression that he regarded us all as beneath his notice. With exasperating inevitability characters Richard and I had sworn to keep apart had been drawn together; Oliver's detestation of Morton-Rycroft had been a college joke. 'It was hate at first sight, darling,' he once told me, 'though I suppose I should be grateful to the man. Listening to that affected voice monologuing interminably so sickened me of his subject that I switched to law, a far better idea.' It surprised me that Richard, not an easy-going man, put up with him year after year. I saw that Oliver was not listening to the Professor; he was staring into space, his eyes empty. I took a deep breath. I would do my duty – I would rescue Oliver and pause to sympathise with the Professor over the latest government cuts in funds, a subject near to his heart.

I was forestalled by Richard, towing a senior lecturer from King's, an old friend. I should have known I could trust him to deal with such situations. The man from King's was given solace from the bottle in Richard's right hand and left to his fate while Oliver was detached for amusement elsewhere. A neat manoeuvre.

'Marriages are made in Heaven,' my mother said, blinking with sentiment, her flat chest heaving beneath well-worn blue Lurex.

'If marriages are made in Heaven,' Angela retorted, 'then all I can say is, God had some off-days when He made mine.'

Bertha Bateman planted her feet in their sensible shoes well apart on the carpet and inclined her head of iron-grey hair, freshly corrugated for the occasion. 'Marriages,' she pronounced, 'marriages are made on earth by two people working together. Working hard and unselfishly, what's more – and having the sense to forget the off-days.'

'Annabel thrives on the hard work,' Mother said, speaking of me as if I weren't there.

'She's worn well, hasn't she?' Angela's comment made me sound like a serviceable coat, good but dull. Tweed probably. Tweedy was hardly the style of her own clothes. Today the embroidered peasant blouse was replaced by one of pink satin, thrust into purple velvet trousers and surmounted by a silk patchwork tabard-like garment, clearly homemade. My mother-in-law looked her up and down, metal-rimmed glasses flashing ominously.

'You're admiring my waistcoat,' Angela smiled. 'It's delightful, isn't it? It was made by a friend of mine from the Psychic Growth Group. It's imbued with the spirit of the past, with the feelings and yearnings of those who once wore the garments from which these materials came. This piece here,' she indicated a white bit all of one inch square, 'this came from a pair of Queen Victoria's drawers.'

'Did it really? May I touch?' Mother leaned forward with reverence. 'Fancy – material that's been against Queen Victoria's skin!'

Bertha Bateman said: 'On her backside.'

I said: 'Do somebody have a taste of this savoury dip!'

'You've trained your offspring well, I see,' said Clare.

I thought of Richard's threats and my bribes and kept quiet. I watched them. Sara, disgruntled at the waste of her Saturday evening, was carrying good manners to the point of burlesque, presenting her dish of food to Professor Morton-Rycroft with eyes cast down in deference, thanking him for helping himself. She had earlier refused to touch any plate that might contain what she called: 'Dead animals contaminated by cruelty and unnatural additives!' but luckily I'd foreseen this impasse and persuaded her to take charge of crudités and dips, and she organised some deliciously original mixtures with panache and flair before boredom finally set in. I saw that I should shortly have to thank and release her, but in the meantime at least she was still being helpful.

Danny was standing by his Aunt Jane, my favourite among Richard's three sisters. In Jane, as in Richard, their mother's bluntness was tempered by understanding. Impatient with Jane's failure to notice his offering, Danny was nudging her with his elbow. Bite-sized sausage rolls slid greasily across the plate. He righted it in the nick of time, shrugged and pushed a couple into his mouth before moving on to the next group of guests. He looked endearingly like Richard; there was the same impatient rejection of polite formalities, the same self-assurance. Ollie I could only catch glimpses of, but I knew he was helping steadily, pleased by our reliance upon him, impressed by the occasion. As Sara had insisted, all three were helping equally.

'How are your two?' I asked Clare.

'Growing up and growing away,' she sighed. 'Simon's off to Cambridge shortly and Amanda's gone back to school. They're both healthy and happy and I rarely see them. They lead their own lives now.'

Clare was a link with the beginning of the twenty years Richard and I were celebrating. We had shared a flat when we were at university, enjoying night-time confidences about ambitions, love and sex – about which last Clare had always been luridly revelatory. We were sympathetic audiences to each other's worries and disasters. Our squabbles were rare, generally over borrowed clothes. Clare had married a fellow student who had become a schoolmaster and now was deputy head of a preparatory school in Sussex. It was unfortunate that Richard found Colin's particular combination of condescending pedantry and schoolboy humour quite unbearable: because of this and because of the full-time nature of Colin's calling we saw little of them; nevertheless, when Clare and I did get together we were able to drop back easily into our old intimate relationship.

'And so you're free again. What will you do now?'

She swung round on me. Her voice was harsh and strained. 'What does one do after the children leave home? Make innumerable cup cakes, dig the garden, write letters to old friends and from time to time look back to say: "Didn't we do well?" What can I do, Annabel?'

I was taken aback. I had heard Clare complain before about the boredom of life in a small village, about her lack of career or status – 'I'm not even Mrs Pritchard to the parents, I'm Mr Pritchard's wife' – but there had not been this note of despair.

'You could get a job,' I suggested.

'What as? Where?' She took a gulp from the glass of gin and tonic in her hand. 'You live in London, Annabel, I don't. Not many jobs about near us, not unless I drove to Brighton or Lewes. And not then, not for me. Who'd want a middle-aged woman with nothing to offer but a twenty years stale degree? Anything I could get I wouldn't want.'

'You could teach.' I knew she'd helped out at the school when they were short-staffed.

'Teaching bores me.' The rejection was impatient and total.

I looked anxiously into her face. There were hollows under her eyes and her cheekbones were too prominent. Heavy tan foundation lay in lines I had not seen before. Beneath, the untouched skin of her neck was sallow and dry.

'Is everything all right?' Stupid question – it clearly wasn't. 'I mean, you do look rather off-colour.'

She gave me a long look in return, partly assessing, partly defiant, a look I found difficult to decipher until she said: 'I'm recovering from an abortion, if you must know.'

I rocked backwards on my expensive party sandals. People shouldn't spit remarks like that at you in the middle of a party. What can you say in reply? I glanced round but no one was near enough to hear.

'Clare, how awful for you. But what happened? Why?'

She shrugged. 'A failure of contraception. I couldn't have it, could I?'

'Why not?'

'Christ, Annabel, it would be impossible in a hundred

68

ways. Surely you see that?' I wasn't aware that my face was expressive of disagreement, I don't think that my brain had progressed that far, but almost at once she said: 'No, you don't see it, do you? I suppose you'd have gritted your teeth and gone on and borne it – literally.'

The was a baffled pause while I thought about this one – and about the occasion when I had been ready to do just that. 'Yes, I would.' I couldn't deny my own feelings to soothe hers, though the temptation to take the easy way out was there. 'I'd worry all through the pregnancy in case there was something wrong because of my age, but I don't think I could have it aborted.'

Another pause before she said drily: 'It wasn't only because of the age factor. I had a different problem. It wasn't Colin's.'

More shocks. 'Oh, Clare! Whose was it then?'

'Peter's. Peter Marsden. You met him once when you came over. Red hair. He teaches mathematics.'

'Did Colin know? I mean, is that why . . .?'

'God, no! You know Colin. He carries his personal double standard higher than the school colours! Him having it off with the school secretary, that's all right. But if he heard so much as a whisper that I wasn't holier than thou, I'd be out in a flash. And where could I go?'

'To this man Peter?'

She shook her head vehemently; limp wisps of hair tumbled over her forehead and I glimpsed white hairs in among the brown. 'Peter's married. Got children. He's younger than me by four years. Hell, we were having an affair, not a love affair.' She grinned. 'An antidote to boredom!'

Richard appeared with a bottle; our glasses went out in silent unison. He touched my hand, poured and vanished into the throng once more.

'So what did Colin feel about the baby – about the

abortion? I take it he knew you were pregnant?'

'Oh, yes, he knew that. Funny – it was incredibly simple. He agreed whole-heartedly when I said I was too old to go through with it. He wants the headmastership when old Holtman retires next year. A screaming toddler would be a shocking handicap. It would show incompetence, wouldn't it?'

'Didn't you want it at all?' I asked curiously. 'Not in any mood?'

She drank deeply. 'Not really. Whenever I pictured the baby it had Peter's flaming red hair. How could I risk that? I couldn't see myself flaunting my bastard about the school for the masters and the boys to giggle over in corners.' She shot me a sideways glance and added: 'I'm not brave like you.'

'It's easy to be brave in theory. I've not had to face taking such a decision.'

'*Haven't you?*' Her eyes caught mine in a curiously intent gaze, then directed them down the room. The social eddyings of the groups of guests had left a gap like a tunnel. I followed Clare's eyes along it; at the far end stood Oliver, his hand resting on Ollie's shoulder, on his face an unmistakable look of tenderness for the boy. 'If you want me to believe you, Annabel, never let Oliver and Ollie stand together like that.'

Incredulity was my immediate reaction. She couldn't mean what I thought she meant; I must have misunderstood her. Then the shock came – a gasp for air, a rising nausea. A group nearby shifted and the two of them altered position, each leaning an elbow on the marble shelf over the empty fireplace, not stopping their conversation. Their stance was identical, mirroring one another: one leg braced, the other bent, the blond heads tilted to one side, the long backs straight.

'Don't be ridiculous,' I said breathlessly. 'Ollie's

70

Richard's.' I moved backwards to lean against the cool mahogany of the piano. I felt confused and horrified. I suppose I had already registered the likeness, but only in pleasure that Ollie would be a similarly good-looking man. I must have been blind. The resemblance was uncanny. How many other people had come to the same conclusion as Clare?

Her voice was low and hard with scorn. 'Come off it, Annabel. It's inescapable. Look at their colouring, their build! You surely can't expect me to believe such a likeness came by chance!'

I knew I had flushed violently with shock; it must look like the flush of guilt. I pressed my hands to my cheeks, then snatched them away. My mind, from working slowly, was working fast. I must kill this misapprehension. It seemed imperative that I should convince her, as if by so doing I could cure all other smirched minds.

I spoke indignantly, in staccato bursts. 'They're alike by chance and by choice. By chance because Ollie's long and slim and blond. But so was my father, I believe. By choice because Ollie's always admired Oliver and copied him in every way he could. And why not? He's an admirable man.' My heart was pumping hard. My voice was too vehement. I tried to calm myself, to sound convincing. 'They've been great friends since Ollie was tiny, you know that. It's hardly surprising he should have picked up some of Oliver's mannerisms and ways.'

'I can't believe you,' Clare said, but she was clearly wavering. My mind in its nervously alert state could understand hers as if she had spoken its thoughts aloud. She was thinking that I had never hidden things from her before, that her own revelations should have made it simple for me to admit the truth. Her eyes glanced at me, flickered back to them. All the same . . . could it be that I was unable to admit it, even to myself?

71

My blood became hotter and hotter, racing through my veins. My armpits prickled. Anger was welling up like sickness. 'You shouldn't judge other people by your own low standards,' I said. 'Your belief or disbelief makes no difference to the truth. And the truth is that I've never been unfaithful to Richard in all our twenty years. I've never needed to be.'

'Really?'

'Absolutely.'

'Interesting,' she muttered to herself. I received a hostile look. 'It sounds almost too good to be true. Don't tell me you've never been tempted!'

I remembered Oliver lying in the garden; I thought of two or three other men. I told her: 'Sometimes I think, "*He's* attractive . . ." when a man's near me throwing out sparks. But I don't let it lead anywhere. I'd hate to hurt Richard. And besides, if you've just had a good meal you don't want to go scrumping someone else's apples, do you?'

Clare wriggled her shoulders. She said ruefully: 'It hasn't been like that with us. At all.' She picked up her glass from the piano's glossy top, but it was empty. She put it back, took someone's half-drunk tumbler of whisky and dispatched that instead. She patted her mouth with the back of her hand. 'But I still find it unbelievable that Oliver should be here so often and nothing have happened between you. What a waste – I'd drop my knickers for him any day! He's a fascinating man and quite irresistibly sexy. And when I think what he was like in the old days . . .! Remember those leggy blondes he used to collect?'

'I remember. But that was before Melissa. He adored her. There was never anyone else once she arrived on the scene.'

'Odd how folk change.' She contemplated Oliver, deep

in earnest dialogue with Ollie. 'I'm sorry if I got you wrong, Annabel, but I thought – we both thought – it was self-evident.'

I sensed I'd won with Clare, or at least beaten her into temporary submission. I hoped her doubts wouldn't resurface when she was back at the school with Colin, living her own erratic life once more. It is easy to imagine that other people must think and act as you do – and she enjoyed a gossip. I said: 'You know, I don't think I could perform with anyone but Richard. After so many years a different body would feel totally wrong. He's left his imprint upon me. Another man wouldn't fit – like a square peg in a round hole!'

The ludicrous inaptness, not to say crudity, of the last sentence struck us both at the same moment. We doubled up in sniggers, clutching at the piano for support.

'And may I share the joke?' Bertha looming beside us acted like a douche of cold water. We spluttered, shook our heads and subsided. She flashed a smile at Clare, then turned to me. 'Annabel, Professor Morton-Rycroft and his wife are about to leave. Don't you want to join Richard in seeing them out?'

I was just saying goodbye to the last of our departing guests when Sara's friend Lucinda arrived.

'Hi!' she said, mounting the steps, all long hair and long limbs in wet-look PVC thigh boots and the skimpiest of yellow hot pants. 'Sara free yet? She said she'd got to organise your party for a while, but we could come round after.' She stopped, hands on out-thrust hips, waiting for me to move out of the way. 'We've brought some new CDs she wants to hear,' she added, and I glimpsed two boys behind her.

Oh lord. 'We haven't eaten yet, I said, 'and this is a special occasion for the family.'

Sara appeared from behind me. 'Oh Christ, count me out. I don't want food. I've been eating bits all evening. I'll be sick if I eat any more. You wouldn't want that, would you? Me puking all over!'

I opened my mouth to reproach her – and closed it again. Sara aggrieved could effectively ruin any celebration. And she had been helpful today. 'All right, treasure,' I said. 'If you're sure you're not hungry.'

Sara looked surprised but pleased. She pulled Lucinda towards the stairs and the two male figures behind her came in from the darkness. 'That's Dave and that's Tony,' Sara said.

I smiled at them as I turned away only to swing back in a double-take. Dave was wearing battered denim jeans and a torn red sweatshirt, quite normal. But Tony was wearing a dinner jacket and bow tie. As Dave slouched past his curly head jerked, puppet-like, and he muttered, 'Hi!' as if in his mind a distant memory had jerked the string of polite behaviour. Tony bowed with the grace and gravity of a bygone age and shook my hand; for a moment I almost thought he would kiss it.

'His gear comes from the Oxfam shop,' Sara told me.

'Don't take any notice of him,' Lucinda added. 'He's mad.'

'A pleasant form of madness,' I said.

'Middle-aged ladies all drool over him,' Lucinda concluded resignedly.

'Thank you, Lucinda.'

Tony retained my hand for a further second before letting it go. 'I've heard all about you,' he said. 'You're the brave lady who's daring to represent an incestuous dad.'

'A dad alleged to have committed incest,' I said warily. Sara really shouldn't discuss my cases with her friends.

'You're right to do it,' he informed me solemnly. 'Sara and Lucinda are one-sided in their views. They've taken an overdose of feminism. They reckon men have behaved badly for so long, made women suffer so much, that now women must punish them. But only the guilty must be punished.'

'Absolutely, Tony,' I said with equal seriousness.

'Sara doesn't understand that a girl could be evil enough to make a false accusation of incest against her father, but she's naive. Teenage girls can be dreadful!' He cocked an eyebrow at the outraged pair waiting for him. 'I've met some. Men aren't the only nasty animals around. Don't misunderstand me, I love girls, but I've never thought they were perfect – not since my sisters arrived on the scene!' He grinned then added: 'I don't suppose you had the misfortune to be at a mixed comprehensive, Mrs Bateman, and I've only been at one since I left Winchester after my parents split up two years ago, but I'll tell you this – it teaches you plenty about how the other half lives as well as what makes the other sex tick. I'd lived a sheltered existence before, and I didn't know it. You can see the potential trouble-makers and the tarts by the end of the third year.'

'Tarts? At thirteen or fourteen?'

'Lots of the girls have started by then. That's nothing out of the ordinary.'

'Proper little Lolitas,' Dave remarked with a happy leer.

'Do you think you can get your client off?' Tony asked me.

'The outlook is bleak, not to say black, so far,' I said. 'Perhaps the trial will shed a clear light, perhaps it'll shed none. It'll rest with the jury, God help them!'

'Don't you believe the dad then?' Dave asked, looking puzzled.

I shook my head. 'I've no reason to so far. Not on the evidence.'

'You mean you're sticking your neck out for nothing?'

'No,' Lucinda snapped. 'For a shit of a sick incestuous bastard! All right for you boys to sneer and leer, but think about this – how'd you like your fathers, your *own fathers*, coming sliming into your rooms in the night, wanting to bugger you?'

Nobody spoke. I wondered, not for the first time, whether Angela's boyfriends always kept their hands to themselves when Miss Longlegs was around. Poor girl.

'No need to get emotional,' Tony said quietly. 'We know all that and it's not what we're talking about. We're talking about a fair trial.' He turned back to me. 'I'd like to do work like yours.'

'Seriously?' I asked him.

'Yes. That or be a solicitor. I've got an uncle who's a City solicitor, but I don't know enough about the court work side to decide between the two. I tell you what, perhaps I could talk to you – '

'I thought we were going to listen to music?' Lucinda interrupted.

I said hastily: 'I'd be glad to talk to you another time, Tony, but right now I have to get dinner for nine people. Nothing elaborate, only salads and ham, but I need peace.

'You need help,' he said with admirable courtesy. 'We'll help. All of us. I'm a New Age man, I believe in the men and the girls working together. Where's your kitchen? And then you can tell me about the Bar.'

And within a few minutes he had marshalled the other three into the kitchen, despite their protests, and had them chopping peppers and tomatoes and gherkins and carving ham, while squeezed lemons for a dressing and cross-examined me upon my work at the Bar, what one had to study to get there, and how the pupillage system was managed.

'What you might call an academic obstacle race,' he remarked pensively after I'd warned him of the need for a minimum of an upper-second degree, and the competition for pupillage places in Chambers. 'I knew it would be hard, but I didn't know how hard.'

'You've got to have an amazing memory for all that law,' Dave said, pausing in his carving.

'And a sharp mind to pick out what's relevant in the evidence,' Lucinda added.

'And be mug enough to face working evenings and often half the night when you have to prepare last-minute briefs and submissions and things,' Sara shrugged.

'Hmm,' Tony said, giving a final stir to his dressing. 'But think of the high when you win a case – you know, establishing some poor soul's genuine innocence, or if you're prosecuting, getting some beastly villain put inside. Do you feel that still, Mrs Bateman?'

'Of course,' I said. 'When I'm sure we've got it right.'

Tony straightened himself and looked at me. 'What I really need now, I suppose, is to get into court and observe. Could I?'

'Why not? If you want to listen to a criminal case you can go to any Crown Court and watch the proceedings.'

His smooth confident young face twisted momentarily with a mixture of hopefulness and embarrassment. 'Well, what I suppose I'm asking . . . Could you? . . . I mean, would you mind if I came with you and watched you do one of your cases?'

I looked at him. I liked Tony and his lively mind. If he was Sara's latest boyfriend, then she'd chosen well. 'No problem. You could spend the week of your half-term with me. And you needn't sit in the public gallery. We'll call it work experience and you can sit behind me, with the solicitor.'

He sighed ecstatically. 'That would be fantastic. Thank you very much indeed, Mrs Bateman.'

And so it was arranged.

Then I thanked the four of them heartily for their help, we carried the food into the dining-room, Sara and her friends went upstairs to their pop music, while, for the first time in about nine hours, I sat myself down.

7

The last of our guests left the house by four o'clock the following afternoon, with the exception of mother-in-law, but even she was temporarily away from the house, out in the car with Richard, viewing new areas that she might consider blighting with her presence. I made a cup of tea, dragged my weary body into the drawing-room and flopped on to the Chesterfield, putting my feet up. My brain was churning like a washing machine, round and round in endless circles, dirty rags of thought appearing in the window of my mind, then flicking out of sight into the general whirl.

Did other people perceive what Clare had? Did other people believe what she had believed? It was incredible that I hadn't seen the likeness – and the danger – before. I thought of Bertha Bateman's habit of appearing on my doorstep at unexpected hours, clearly watching for something, far more suspicious than my sins of more than twenty years ago would justify. Was this the explanation? I thought of various neighbours and friends who at one time or another had commented, with smiles that now seemed meaningful, how different my youngest was from his brother and sister. I remembered Lucinda chatting to Sara in the hall, unaware that I was behind her, asking:

'And is your mother's boyfriend here today?' I'd dismissed the question as only to be expected from one of her upbringing, joked about it to Sara. But she hadn't smiled back. She couldn't think . . .? No, of course she couldn't. She knew me too well. Besides, she was too young for her mind to explore such slimy pools.

I took a sip of tea, scalding my tongue. What about Richard? He must know that Ollie was his. But how loathsome to think that so-called friends should suppose I had cuckolded him. Richard would never admit to a favourite among his children, but he was closest to Ollie. Were there those who secretly smiled when he showed his affection?

I leapt to my feet. I would not lie and brood; I must work off this angry energy. I went to the guest room, stripped the bed and began to remake it with fresh sheets. Oliver would telephone this evening to thank us for his evening's entertainment. He never forgot the formal courtesies. I would apologise to him for my stiffness. I must be quick when the telephone rings, I thought, and take it in the quiet of Richard's study. Perhaps I could even tell him why I had been curt. I played with the idea for only a second before discarding it. There would be an awkwardness between us then; I would not be able to continue to help him as I had done over this last year.

It was because he wanted to thank me for my kindness that he had come into the kitchen last night. I had been scraping dinner plates abstractedly, and when Oliver put his arm round my shoulders in a hug I shied like a startled mare and dropped a plate. It shattered on the tiles with a noise like the shot from a starting pistol.

'Don't!' I gasped, and tried to bend to pick up the pieces but his arm tightened like a vice and stopped me. His grey eyes looked into mine from far too near. I could see small amber flecks on the irises, and that the whites were

80

bloodshot. The thought that he was sleeping badly again flashed through my mind.

'I'm sorry,' he said plaintively. 'I didn't want to cause chaos and destruction, only to say thank you for yet another delicious meal.'

I wrenched myself away; shock, exasperation at the broken plate, and, yes, desire, combining to make a witches' brew of blistering emotions. The noise of the crashing plate would surely bring someone peering round the door. I was terrified of the misinterpretation that would be placed upon the friendly consoling arm; I was terrified by the agitation inside me. I wanted him to go a hundred miles away so that I could regain my peace of mind.

He crouched with me to pick up the pieces and our heads bumped, hard enough to rock us back on our heels. He said ruefully: 'Darling Annabel, I can't do anything right tonight. I wanted to say beautiful things to you in line with the occasion and instead it seems all I can do is damage!'

Damage? I did not yet know the extent of the damage he had all unwittingly caused. I rose to my feet, muttering: 'You said a lot of complimentary things when you made that speech earlier on. You don't need to say any more.' I took the broken pieces of plate from his hand and threw them, with mine, into the rubbish bin.

He stood, reached for my hands and took them in his. 'No, don't pull away, Annabel. You're upset . . . something has gone wrong, hasn't it? Not the party – that was a great success. Not between you and Richard, surely? Is it your mother-in-law?'

'You're like a bloodhound on the trail,' I said, searching my mind for an explanation that would satisfy him. 'Clare made a remark about one of the children that upset me, that's all.' Would that satisfy him? Would he demand to know what?

81

'It hit a raw spot?'

'Oh, I don't know. Perhaps I'm over-reacting. I don't want to talk about it. I just want to be alone. Rude, I know, but please, Oliver . . .'

'Dearest Annabel. You're such a good person. You deserve your peace, if that's what you truly want.'

He let go of my hands and turned away and I understood that I had hurt him, but there was nothing I could do. Twenty seconds later Sara appeared, her talk of equality in domestic chores apparently held kindly in abeyance, and began rapidly to help me sort out the remaining muddle of dirty glasses and dishes. We worked until everything was clear; the glasses tucked away in their cupboards, the gay enamel saucepans in their racks beside the onion strings.

Bang! The front door was shut by a vigorous hand. I jumped and was recalled from my trance by the guest room bed. Richard and his mother must be back. I had stood for too long; I should be downstairs, preparing yet another meal. I was thankful I would not have to be in court tomorrow morning. The judge was going to be away for the day attending a seminar on sentencing. It would give the rest of us a welcome break; only my client, found guilty late on Friday of shop-lifting gold watches, was gnawing his nails over the weekend in agitation lest the judge should have his heart hardened by the experience. I started downstairs. Only a mere six of us for supper tonight, and I had a beef casserole from the freezer and French beans and garlic bread, and the older amongst us would enjoy a good claret.

Halfway down the stairs I encountered Mother-in-law, padding up as softly as a well-fed Persian cat. 'A worthwhile trip, Annabel,' she said. 'Definitely. Richard took me to an area I hadn't previously visited.'

'Oh, yes?' I squeezed past her.

'Tomorrow I shall make enquiries and study the position with care. Wherever I move, it must be Right. But I am pleased with what I've seen.'

'Oh good,' I said, pausing for a second. The sooner she was settled, if settled here she must be, the better. 'Where?'

'I shall come and help you in just a few minutes. Then I shall tell you all about it.' She spoke as one conferring a great favour.

Richard was in the kitchen, helping himself to a chunk of Stilton. 'Ah, there you are,' he said placidly, presenting a cheek for a kiss. Since he had left the house I felt as though I had been to hell and back, but here he was, comfortably untroubled, chomping cheese and breathing the fumes over me as if the world were totally good.

I flung myself into his arms and clutched at his jacket – a dark blue Puffa, which inflated him like Michelin man, all big and comfortable. He crammed the rest of his cheese into his mouth and clutched me in return. 'Hey,' he said, blowing crumbs of Stilton across my head, 'what's the matter?'

I burrowed my face into his shoulder. 'I'm down, that's what.' When you've been married twenty years you don't need long explanations, you talk in shorthand.

'Anti-climax, I expect,' he said, retrieving a piece of cheese from my hair and popping it between his lips. 'All that work – and now the dullness of clearing up and the excitement over.'

'Mm. Perhaps.'

'More than that? You've been very subdued today.'

'I'm tired.'

'Not surprising.' He was sympathetic without gushing, his hand rubbing my back. 'You worked very hard. Everyone said what a superb party it was.'

83

I couldn't tell him what was troubling me, but just being with him helped. I leaned on him. 'I love you,' I said.

'Good,' he said. 'I love you, too.'

Footsteps sounded in the hall; we drew quickly apart as Mrs Bateman walked in.

'I must put in half an hour's work on my last chapter. Revisions – I'm not happy with my conclusions,' Richard informed us, and withdrew.

Mother-in-law drew a chair up to the kitchen table. 'Are we eating those beans tonight? We are? Then I'll top and tail them if you'll kindly pass me a knife, Annabel. Thank you. Now. This afternoon. We had a worthwhile drive.'

'Where did you go?' I turned on the oven, fetched the casserole.

'Walton-on-Thames.'

I remembered Oliver suggesting it. An excellent idea: a pleasant place and not over-near. 'Why ever didn't we think of it before?'

'I can't imagine. I liked those Tudor-style houses with beams and diamond-paned windows. They're much more interesting than the flat-faced stuff so many folk seem to like. Everyone to their own tastes, of course.'

'Your Jacobean furniture would fit well.'

'That's what I thought,' she said with satisfaction. 'And Richard says he has a morning free from lectures or seminars tomorrow, and he's going to take me house-hunting again. Isn't that kind?'

'Very,' I said, sighing as I gathered plates and cutlery together. I had been looking forward to a quiet morning in the study with him, Richard working on the Utilitarians, me on my next case, the antiques warehouse burglary. Both of us were getting behindhand on our work schedules. Which reminded me, I must contact John Pockett's solicitor, Mr Hoffer, and hear whether his enquiry agent had come up with anything useful, and whether there were any further lines of enquiry to be followed.

As if Bertha could read my mind she said: 'I wanted the opportunity to talk to you, Annabel. About this nasty man you're defending in a case of – I can hardly believe it – of incest. How can you defend people whom you know are guilty? Especially disgusting men like that!'

Misguided friends were always asking me such questions. I had my standard answer and trotted it out now, not for the first time, to Bertha Bateman.

'You can't *know* that a client is guilty unless he tells you that he is. In which case he pleads guilty and you deal with the mitigation. But if your client says he's not guilty then a barrister's job is to test the evidence on his behalf and argue his case. Remember that in this country there is a presumption of innocence, not guilt.'

'You've told me that before, Annabel. But there must be times when you know that a man is guilty, whatever he tells you?'

'How can I know? Only God can know. Now if my client actually tells me that he is guilty and asks me to think up a clever line of defence to get him off, then I must either persuade him to plead guilty, or drop the case like a hot brick. Those are our rules. And we stick to them – or if we don't we are disbarred.' I shoved the casserole into the oven and slammed the door, wishing I could shove Bertha away and slam the door on her.

'But this case is quite another thing. Girls don't go around accusing their fathers of that sort of horrible behaviour unless it's true. So how can you defend him?'

'Because the girl may be lying. Because she may be hysterical, among other hypotheses. Hysteria is not unheard of, unhappily, in adolescent girls. Do you believe in witches, Bertha?'

85

'Witches? Of course not! What have they got to do with anything?'

'Remember the witches of Salem in the seventeenth century? Arthur Miller's play?' No, of course she wouldn't. *The Crucible* would not be her idea of light bed-time entertainment. 'Hysterical and evil girls made accusations of witchcraft; all sorts of unbelievable tales. Yet they were believed, and the unfortunate accused went to a horrible death through sheer malice.'

'That was different. That was then. That couldn't happen nowadays.'

'No, not with accusations of witchcraft. But witchcraft was quite a commonly heard-of offence in those days. Nowadays sex crimes are common: rape, incest, sexual assaults of various kinds. A girl who was maliciously inclined against her father could have him cunningly put out of circulation for a while if she so wished, her lies unnoticed among the mass of similar accusations of crime similarly difficult to prove because they depend upon one person's word against another's.'

'Well,' Bertha drew in her chins, 'I don't know, I'm sure. That all sounds very clever, but I'd believe the girl. And I do know this, Annabel – no one in our family should get mixed up in such things. They're sordid and shocking and not for us. Sara feels it strongly, she's told me as much, and Richard does too. And the boys, I'm sure.'

Did they? I didn't know. I didn't know anything. I pushed the garlic bread into the oven to crisp up. Was I dealing with hysteria or cold-blooded callousness? Was the girl's accusation against her father motivated by tee-nage tantrums or sheer evil? Or was Mr Pockett the evil one, the convincing liar, the consummate actor? Yes, I must get in touch with that enquiry agent. Whatever was his name? Alan Greening, that was it. I needed to know what he'd discovered, even if he'd discovered nothing.

86

Negative answers were a form of evidence. But if only, I thought, if only something would break, one way or the other.

Danny's voice came bellowing down the stairs: 'Mum! Mum! Mother?'

I went to the door. 'Yes? Quietly, Daniel, please. What is it?'

'Can you come up for a sec? I want to show you something – well, ask you something.'

A mystery; embarrassment in his voice; something he did not want his grandmother to see, perhaps. I ran up the stairs.

'Supper's nearly ready. This won't take long, will it?'

'No. I don't suppose . . . look, my school blazer. Ollie and I had an argument, well, a bit of a fight. You know how it is! The sleeve got ripped, can you mend it? Please, dearest Mum!' He handed me his blazer with a four-inch rip at the shoulder, luckily along the seam. No, he'd not want his grandmother to see that. 'I'm sorry. Really.'

'I suppose I could do it after supper,' I conceded grumpily. I looked round his room. Chaos: mildewed games shorts, huge trainers without laces, torn advertisements for pop concerts, school books – all strewn across the carpet, tawdry in the evening sun. 'And while I'm doing it you can blitz this room tidy. Now, I don't suppose this is the only thing you have that needs mending, is it? Come on, let me have the lot while I'm at it, let me know the worst.'

'Well . . .' Danny did a mock squirm. 'There's a button off my shirt cuff, and the zip on my school trousers is pulling away – that could be catastrophic if it isn't done soon! Oh, and hell, I've been meaning to tell you for weeks and forgetting – the sleeping bag I took to camp last month has a tear in it.' He reached into a cupboard and pulled out a crumpled sleeping bag split at the top and showing its filling.

I gathered it into my arms and my mind rushed back more than twenty years. The split sleeping bag – I'd forgotten! How could I have forgotten? It was the break – the break I'd been hoping for in my incest case!

Fern was alleging that her father had forced himself on her in her tent. Her statement told of his creeping in saying he was cold, and pleading with her to let him into her sleeping bag to warm up. But it can't be done, as I well knew but had so stupidly forgotten. You can't squeeze two people into a sleeping bag, let alone get up to anything in there. In fact a girl in a sleeping bag might as well be wearing a chastity belt for all the fun she can have in it.

Danny piled his mending on top of the sleeping bag and I staggered downstairs to put it on the Chesterfield, ready for my attention later.

Twenty odd years ago in a field in the Lake District Richard had attempted to slide into my sleeping bag – and promptly got stuck. He couldn't go up and he couldn't go down . . . I began to laugh softly as I remembered it. Then the bag had split; it was an old one and tiny feathers filled the tent. We got them up our noses and in our mouths and we were spitting and cursing and half the camp woke up and started muttering, and then we saw the funny side of it and laughed and laughed out loud and all around us we could hear other people becoming infected and starting to giggle at us because we couldn't stop laughing, until the whole dark field seemed to be alive with mirth. How incredible, that comic scene, and it had quite gone from my mind – until now.

I had to tell someone of the leap forward I'd made so I went into the study to Richard. He looked up, still poised over his work, as I entered. But his reaction to my excitedly poured out story was depressing, snubbing even.

'Is the point really of such vital importance?'

'It shows that she's lying! And if she's lying in that she may well be lying in the whole story.'

'It could simply be a matter of inaccurate recollections. In a life-shaking trauma like that, one that I gather she suppressed and kept to herself at first, some inaccuracies are to be expected, surely?' A judicial voice, pouring cold water.

'Some, perhaps. But this was so detailed! *Too* detailed. Those details seemed at first to give strength to her story – matters like her father wanting to cuddle closely because he was cold – but now they seem more like carefully thought out lies.'

'And you seem to me to be giving too much weight to a trivial matter. Besides, don't psychiatrists tell us that heavily traumatised children are often found to tell stories that are basically true, despite their over-elaborate and inaccurate details?'

'I have heard that,' I admitted, 'but this child isn't that young, she's fourteen, and she doesn't look immature.'

'You don't believe the father, do you?' Richard asked me curiously.

'Up till now I just didn't know. I was neutral.' One shouldn't get involved anyway; in my job one has to stand back, otherwise it would be too easy to ignore pieces of evidence because their implications were upsetting to a pet theory. In several notorious cases recently the police had been in trouble precisely because of this. But in the Pockett case I knew they had been into the details carefully. They were not all soft-hearted suckers for sob-stories, the police; they too tried to stand back and analyse. And neurotic women screaming rape without reason were not unknown to them, thus neither was cynicism. But they had found nothing to make them cynical in this case. On the contrary: the dates of the father's abuse given by the girl were borne out by the mother's diary notes of access dates; even, once, corroborated by her school. The police surgeon's evidence, too, appeared to uphold the tale. But that ridiculous sleeping-bag story had stirred my cynicism. 'Now, Richard . . . well, I'm beginning to believe that my client might, just might, be telling the truth.'

We looked at each other. His eyebrows went up; he shrugged.

I could not believe it. I had not believed his mother. I put it to him: 'You disapprove of my doing this case, don't you? Your mother said you did, but I thought that was her imagination.'

'Approval or disapproval doesn't come into it,' he said, putting down his pen. 'How you run your working life is your affair. You must do what you think best.'

'Oh, very good, very impartial.' I was beginning to get angry. 'But I'm not impartial about your work, I back you entirely. I always have done, to the hilt. So why this sudden refusal to back me?' We'd always stood together in the past. It felt strange, unnatural almost, not to have him supporting me now.

'No refusal, that's an exaggeration. But when my mother spoke of her concern that you might become notorious for your connection with high-profile sex abuse cases, then I had to agree with her that this wasn't the best time for such involvement.'

'Not the best time? You mean, because of *your* career?'

'Jonathan Morton-Rycroft will retire in three years' time. He could retire sooner, you know that. That's why I am working all hours on my book – a successful publication would attract me considerable support as his successor, particularly with certain persons who are impressed by glossy books and media publicity . . .'

I interrupted him: 'And, don't tell me, those certain persons would be horrified if their precious professor's wife clashed in public with Females for Freedom, especially over a child abuser!'

'They would, yes, and I deplore that sort of attitude. But you can hardly expect me to welcome the prospect of bad publicity.'

I leaned my hands on his desk and faced him over it. 'Let me say this, then. Although I dislike their noisy methods, I do agree with Females for Freedom and Women against Rape that there's still a need for reform, particularly where child witnesses are concerned – the present reforms fall short of the Pigot Report's recommendations, and the shortage of closed-circuit television facilities is deplorable – but it isn't my job to instigate or implement reforms. It's my job to defend the accused, and I can't wait until the system is perfected before I do so. Do you back me in this at least?'

He leaned away from me, pushing back his chair. 'Can you doubt it? There's no need to get uptight, Annabel. I've never yet interfered in your work, and don't intend to start now. I repeat, I leave these matters entirely to your own judgment.'

I stared at him in frustration. This was not the reassurance I'd sought and my confidence in him was shaken. I might have said more, told him that Oliver would support me, but my mother-in-law's voice cut between us.

'Annabel! Annabel!' she was calling from the kitchen door. 'Are you coming? The beans were nearly boiled dry. I've had to dish them up.'

'Help! I must go. Supper, Richard. Come now, will you?'

I rushed into the hall, thanked Bertha for her help, called the others into the dining-room and went back to the kitchen to load up an elderly trolley with the food. Richard followed me, so I made him useful by thrusting the bread board into his hands.

'Richard, just out of interest and all that, but how much longer is your mother going to be here?'

'Give her a week to have a really good hunt and then I'll speak to her.'

Mother-in-law's refusal to drive to strange places unaccompanied was a menace. 'A week? No, Richard, that's too much. She must make other arrangements. It's difficult having her underfoot; she's perpetually critical of the boys and she takes up too much of your time. You say yourself you've urgent work to do on your book if it's to be finished by Christmas, and I'm going to be busy in court virtually non-stop till then. Why can't she stay with Jane at Hampton?'

'In that tiny house? It's overflowing with children and pets already. Whereas we do have the room.' He saw my protesting face and added quietly: 'You know, since Melissa died we've devoted ourselves to Oliver, given him infinite amounts of our time and our sympathy, but he isn't the only one who's had a bereavement, is he? Don't you think my mother might need help too?'

Richard could always find the right words to disarm me. I didn't care to think of myself as a hard-hearted bitch, carrying enmity to the point of ignoring mother-in-law's loss. Nor could I argue over Oliver's needs. I did not believe that their losses were in any way comparable, but I dared not start to discuss them; Clare's suspicions impeded me. I was speechless and Richard took my silence for acquiescence.

All evening I sat stiffly in front of the television with Danny's mending, watching faces and places come and go as meaninglessly as the scenery beside a motorway. 'Nice to have a little relax after all that fussation,' Bertha remarked. Sara sidled out to visit Lucinda. 'I suppose nobody's going to object if I just go to see my friend?' Danny bolted up to his room. 'Shit, I forgot to do my

92

French homework and it's going to take me ages, *and* I've got my room to sort out.' Only Ollie stayed beside me, a bag of humbugs on his lap, sucking squelchily.

All evening I had a sense of impending disaster, as if the world about me were going to collapse totally. I kept instructing myself to calm down, telling myself that in a year or two I would laugh at this ridiculous reaction to Clare's misconception, yet hour by hour the impression grew. I sat distractedly, my mind agitated, my body stiff, my needle pricking my forefinger until it was red and sore.

At eleven we went to bed. Oliver hadn't telephoned. Several other friends had. I told myself that perhaps he gave up when he couldn't get through. I was disappointed, though. I had a feeling, not even a coherent thought, just a vague feeling, that if I could talk to him my sense of dread would disappear.

It was a long time before I could sleep. The muscles of my body refused to relax. Each time I reached the edge of sleep a muscle would jump, giving me the hateful sensation of falling from a cliff, startling me to full wakefulness once more.

The dread did not diminish, rather it gathered in strength and was joined by the uncomfortable feeling that is associated with a forgotten item of importance lodged at the back of the mind. It was while I struggled to remember that I fell asleep.

8

In the morning it was worse. Beyond the curtains birds were screaming and a pale sun shone mockingly. Nightmares had plagued me all night; I was always on the edge of consciousness and visions of grief and illness kept flowing through my mind.

Oliver. My last dream was connected with Oliver. It was gone directly I woke, like the dreams of fever, but it left behind such a sense of oppression that I could barely move or breathe. My body was weighted down, as though rocks had been piled on my chest. I did not understand what was happening; I only knew that something was irretrievably wrong and that I must discover what it was.

There was no time to think over breakfast. There never is on a weekday morning. It was a temporary lull for my troubled mind, a short relief. I worked swiftly, making the correct movements, the correct responses, acting like an automaton. 'Daniel, go back upstairs and brush your hair, please.' 'Ollie darling, would you get the milk in?' 'Sara, pass to the toast to your grandmother.' At last the children were gone, the house shuddering at Daniel's whirlwind exit, late as usual. Mother-in-law plodded upstairs to make her bed, Richard stood in the hall frowning at the morning's delivery of bills and I went to draw back the study curtains.

It was then that I knew; knew in a single bolt of horror what my subconscious mind had been struggling to tell me in the night while my conscious mind rejected it. The light fell on the telephone, an inoffensive object, contemporary beige plastic, squatting on the desk. Silent.

I must have cried out because when the first pain cleared Richard was beside me, taking my elbow, holding me. 'Something's wrong. What is it?' His face came and went through clouds of misery. I leaned on the desk. 'Annabel, tell me! You've been in such a peculiar state, I've got to know.'

'Oliver,' I said. 'It's Oliver. Richard, something's happened to him. He should have telephoned last night. He always telephones. Always.'

The glare of the sun showed finger-marks and dust on the telephone as if it hadn't been touched for weeks. I couldn't bear to speak what was in my mind – as though words could affect reality. I gazed into Richard's dark face in a silent struggle to communicate.

His eyes held mine for a second, then shifted. He frowned. His hand slid to my wrist; I could feel the pulse beating crazily against his fingers. He said slowly: 'He may have found the line engaged when he tried.'

I knew he was using this explanation to reassure himself as much as me. 'No one rang after half-past nine. You thanked God, don't you remember? But Oliver rings late in the evening.' He knew our habits; he knew we never went to bed before eleven. Richard liked to play the piano, I liked to read; sometimes we listened to a concert on the radio. We appreciated an hour together after our offspring had gone upstairs. Oliver would phone and chat; it had occurred to me that the human contact was a relief before he faced his lonely bed.

Richard put his hand out tentatively to the telephone, took it back again. 'He'll think we're mad,' he said, trying a half-smile.

'Please, Richard.'

He dialled and we waited. The sound went on and on. 'Perhaps I misdialled it.' His blunt forefinger fumbled round again. At length he put the receiver down. 'He could have gone into Chambers early.'

'No, not his habit.'

'He could have taken sleeping pills'. The fear sprang into his eyes, reflecting mine. 'Oh God, Annabel. All I meant was, if he took a couple, he might be sleeping on heavily. There must be an explanation, there must be . . .'

Silence. Bertha descended the stairs with slow, heavy footsteps.

'I'll drive over. I'll have to. I can't bear you looking like this. Oh hell, it's the rush hour, it'll take me forever. Wait a minute, what's his next-door neighbour's name? The nice old boy? No, I can't think of it either.' He grasped my shoulders, holding me for a second. 'I hope to God you're wrong in your fears, Annabel. I'll telephone you.' He strode out, nearly colliding with his mother whom he removed from his path with minimal ceremony.

'Well, really, Richard!' The front door crashed. 'What on earth is he doing?'

Her solid bulk filled the doorway. What could I say? My fears must sound ludicrous to one so welded to down-to-earth commonsense. Yet I must tell her something – Richard had driven off in the car that was due to take her house-hunting in Walton-on-Thames. I explained briefly.

'Well, I don't know! I never heard of such a thing.' Bertha was vexed. 'I suppose he's forgotten that I was to go to the estate agent's this morning. What a fuss! Possibly the man was with friends last night. Perhaps he has the 'flu. Why, it could be anything.'

'Yes, I suppose it could,' I murmured, trying to take reassurance from her scorn.

'There are a hundred and one explanations for missing a telephone call. His line may be out of order. Mine was like that once. Jane was trying and trying to reach me and the silly machine was making the right noises at her end, but none at mine.'

'Let's hope that's the explanation, then.' I prayed that she was right. Oh God, oh God, please make it so! A childish scream to a deity long since denied.

The study smelt of stale wine and old books. It was hot and airless. Oliver liked to come in here; he and Richard would lean back in their chairs and drink wine and talk and lend each other books they had enjoyed. My head throbbed. Oliver, oh Oliver, are you all right? 'I must make our bed,' I said dully.

Upstairs there was even less air. I opened windows but nothing moved; the curtains hung limp. The birds were silent, the sun had gone. Sun before seven, rain before eleven. The jingle rang in my head. Perhaps a storm was brewing. Was it the time of year for storms? I couldn't think. My mind baulked as I tried to lead it away from the one subject. I told myself not to be hysterical because for once in his life Oliver had stepped out of his normal pattern. I tried to think that Clare's accusation had temporarily unbalanced me. Nothing helped.

At half-past nine Bertha called to me. I found her in the kitchen. 'I am making a sponge cake for the children's tea,' she told me, whisking eggs vigorously. 'I can't sit idly waiting all morning. I don't know where you keep your sandwich tins, but perhaps you'd kindly find them and grease them.'

I did not bother to remind her that the children ate dinner with us. I did as she asked. The cake would be eaten; she made excellent sponges.

I picked up a duster. My nice cleaner, Mary, would be here tomorrow to deal with such chores but I must keep moving. Steady movement kept the sick tension at bay. Ten o'clock. Ten-fifteen. Why didn't Richard ring? Ten-thirty. All the downstairs rooms were shiny and tidy. I would try the Hampstead number. I went into the study and as I put out my hand the shrill jangle made me jump violently. I snatched up the receiver, hardly able to hold it for the sweat on my palm.

'Richard?'

'Annabel.' The line crackled. He didn't speak. A sound like a long breath. 'Annabel. Darling, I'm sorry – '

9

The receiver fell with a sharp crack upon the desk. I knew now, but I had known for hours. Richard's strained words were the confirmation I hadn't wanted. Oliver was dead. Dead. Oliver. A voice cried out; it was my own. The sound was forced out from me as though a great hand had tightened upon my chest. I sucked in gulps of air, trying to keep control.

Mother-in-law was beside the desk, picking up the telephone, speaking to Richard. Her big body was rock steady in front of mine, pushing me out of the way. I retreated backwards. My throat closed up, choking me. I didn't want to talk; I couldn't. But she didn't have to gabble on. Oliver was dead; that was enough. The room was grey and very still. Her words came and went.

'Was he gone when you got there? Sleeping tablets, I suppose? What do you mean, you don't know? Annabel suspected. . .' Her chin drew back into the fat neck; she shifted the receiver to the other ear and I heard Richard's voice in sharp crackles. 'Did you call an ambulance? Ah, the doctor came. . .' She listened, tongue licking her lips. 'No letter? Nothing at all to show what. . . ? Extraordinary. My poor Richard. No, I'll tell her. I'll keep an eye on her, don't worry.'

I turned to the window, trying to blot out the sound of her voice. The darkening sky scowled at me. I pressed my forehead on the cold glass. Outside a daddy-long-legs clung, motionless. The first drops of rain spattered; the insect quivered and was still. My tears trickled down the pane, indistinguishable from the rain. Mustn't give way in front of *her*. I pressed the sleeve of my pullover against my eyes, turned back to the room and sat in Richard's chair, gripping its wooden arms. I understood now the Arab women who wailed and shouted of their grief, pulling at their hair and rocking their bodies. I wanted to scream my rejection of Oliver's death, to fill the void with a wave of sound that would prevent me from hearing my thoughts. But English women curb their feelings; they make no display. I sat in the chair and presently Bertha thrust a cup of tea into my hands.

I sipped and protested: 'It's sweet. I hate it sweet.'

'It's for shock. You've had a nasty shock. I used to serve it in the war, in the air raids. The doctors said hot sweet tea was best.'

I drank. The tea lay uncomfortably on my stomach. Bertha poured herself a cup and sat down to drink it, her eyes watching me over the rim.

I said with difficulty: 'Did Richard tell you what he was doing? When he'd be back?'

'He'll be a long time. Seems there's some doubt how Mr Malet went. The doctor said he couldn't tell. There's a lot to be done and no one there to deal with it.'

'No.'

I thought of the handsome empty house. There was a housekeeper, a quiet woman; she did not live in but came in the mornings from Belsize Park. She would be very upset. She had worked for Oliver and Melissa for many years.

'Richard will have to tell the family. Not a nice task, that, breaking it to his parents.'

'No.' Oh God, oh God, the Malets! Mrs Malet's nightmare had become reality. How could Oliver have done such a cruel thing to her, to all of us? A picture of Mrs Malet came into my mind, her face white with shock, her hands trembling alarmingly as she had struggled to help Oliver with the administrative details that Melissa's death had brought last year – the funeral arrangements, the newspaper announcements, the searing telephone calls to friends and relations. Tears had poured down her wrinkles. I could not imagine Bertha Bateman weeping for a childless daughter-in-law, but Mrs Malet had accepted Melissa and loved her. That was a different death from this. Melissa's had been expected, longed for even, after months of terrible sickness and pain. Even so it had hurt and aged the Malets. How would they cope with their son's rejection of life?

'I don't see why Richard should have to deal with all this unpleasantness.' Mother-in-law's distaste was clear. 'He has an over-developed conscience about such things. Soft, I call it.'

I thought: She has no idea of friendship. To her, only family counts, a limited, tight little world. Other people's problems have never concerned her. They are as unreal as serials on television, fit to be talked over, but not to be taken seriously.

'He's been friends with Oliver for so long, it wouldn't occur to him not to help. The Malets are old now and they'll have to come up from Sussex.'

'There's a brother, isn't there?'

'Yes, Peter. They weren't close. He lives in Kent somewhere.'

Bertha was saying something about the police, about an inquest, sordid matters it was better not to think about. Her voice came from a distance, a remote irritation like the planes from Heathrow.

'I suppose there'll have to be a post-mortem.'

'Oh no! No!' The protest burst from me. What did it matter how Oliver had died? How much he had taken, of what and when? If he had chosen oblivion, that should be enough. The law should not have to interfere. I had grasped the idea of Oliver's death; now, inexorably, the reality was showing its ugly face. I visualised his body lying on a marble slab, naked, defenceless, empty; his eyes being closed and his limbs straightened by hands that would be brisk and uncaring, reaching out in the next moment for a cigarette or a cup of coffee. Once, those arms had held me all night, those legs twined with mine, our bodies dovetailed together. I have never seen a body more perfectly made.

When I first began my law degree I used to watch Oliver and Richard playing squash. I would sit in a corner of the gallery at the college courts, hoping they would not notice me. I was shy of them – Oliver, my unexpected new friend, and Richard, my unexpected old tutor. The gallery was glassed in, airless and warm. The sound of the ball would come up to me, slap, slap, slap, as it ricocheted off the walls and floor, and the sounds of their grunts and their laughter would filter through the glass. At first I had expected Richard to beat Oliver, because he was the more powerful man, but it didn't happen that way. However hard Richard slammed the ball, Oliver's swift returns sent him racing after it once more. Oliver's movements were controlled and graceful; I was fascinated by his co-ordination; brought up in a house without men, sent to an all-girls school, I had known nothing of men's bodies. My pleasure in watching him was immense.

Oh Oliver, where are you? What are they doing to you?

Soon the indifferent hands would destroy that beautiful body, using a scalpel to slit him open, taking the contents of the stomach for analysis. There would be no real bleeding, but there could be no healing. When the hands had done all they had to do they would lift him into his coffin. Oliver. Mutilated. . . .

Fluid gushed into my mouth. My stomach revolted. Grey spots floated across my vision, blotting out the face of my mother-in-law. I stumbled to the door, reached the lavatory just in time. I was more sick than I could ever remember being. I could not stand, had to kneel beside the bowl. Afterwards I collapsed against the cold tiles on the wall, shuddering weakly as the churning in my stomach subsided. The churning in my brain went on and on.

'Annabel?'

'I'm all right.' I rose awkwardly to my feet, my legs cramped. I opened the door.

'You'd better lie down.' She took my arm. Something like sympathy was in the broad face. Sickness she understood, had dealt with many times in her own family. 'I've poured you a little brandy. It'll maybe settle you.'

It did. Warmth spread out from my throat and stomach. I lay for ten minutes on the Chesterfield and gradually my mind settled also. I would go to Hampstead. I wanted to be with Richard. I needed him desperately, wanted the comfort of his big living body. And perhaps I could be of use there. There was nothing to occupy me here, only tasks that were ridiculously trivial. What did today's dinner matter, or working on some case, when all of life was wrenched from its true course? I telephoned for a taxi. I could not face the drive.

Mother-in-law came out of the kitchen, a smell of hot cake clinging to her. She protested: 'But you're not well.'

'I'm not ill. It was the tea. I couldn't take it.'

Her lips tightened. 'And who is going to tell the children about Mr Malet's passing on?'

She startled me deeply. I had thought of that and then

pushed away the thought as too painful for immediate decision. They would not return from school until late-afternoon. Now my mind flooded with images of Ollie's shock and desolation. Sara and Daniel would be upset, as they had been over Melissa's death, but it would not hurt them as it would Ollie. I let the idea of telephoning his headmaster and asking him to break the news worm its way into my head and then dismissed it as contemptible. Only Richard and I could help him through this.

'I shall be back,' I told her.

I had thought I would break down in the obscurity of the taxi, but I was calm. In some strange way the violent vomiting had relieved me. I struggled to understand why Oliver had taken his life. It did not occur to me that his death could be anything but suicide, despite Richard's attempt at denial to his mother. I had felt it; I knew. But why? Why? The loss of Melissa had been terrible; grief and shock had altered him, draining him of vitality. But he had wrestled his way through the first months and I had hoped that he was emerging on the far side of grief. His life was not worthless; he had a successful career behind him and awaiting him. He was likely to have been made a High Court Judge. He was a man of wealth and position. Many people loved him; they had understood his lone-liness and worked, as we had done, to fill the empty spaces in his life with their friendship and care. His death seemed like a punishment for daring to assume that any-thing we might do could compensate for his loss. The sense of rejection was overwhelming. He was a kindly man – how could he not have pictured this? Rain sprayed across the taxi windows, great drops chasing down the dusty glass. My mind jolted on, searching for the truth.

And then it came to me that perhaps his death had not been the purposeful act that I had visualised, the act that horrified me with its disregard for our feelings, but rather

106

a seeking for oblivion in a moment of intolerable despair, when he was already worn out by months of striving to forget. Perhaps, I thought, he allowed his fingers to take too many pills from the bottle in order to blot out the pain and loneliness and futility and did not care what the result would be. It was a faint comfort. But beyond all other thoughts one thought persisted: that in the end he had rejected himself, and this was more heartbreaking than all the rest.

It rained and it went on raining. The streets of London were grey and dim beneath a coating of water and they smelt dank. The late flowers in my garden, weak-kneed from their drenchings, leaned down to the soil and mud spattered them. Bertha grumbled as she dealt with the boys' sodden macks and shoes, but I did not care how much it rained. It was right that the weather should be gloomy; sunshine would have been an insult, like the wearing of bright colours.

I felt as though I had fallen into a deep river, sinking into a blurred and icy world where I gasped for relief but where no one could reach me. A swirling current shoved me over sharp rocks that lacerated me with pain: the obituary in *The Times*, the funeral, the memorial service in The Temple church, the inquest (an open verdict). There was no time to recover from the one before the next loomed.

The worst moments came at the funeral.

It was held in the Sussex village where the senior Malets lived and where Melissa was buried. Her grave had been dug beside tombstones with other Malet names upon them and dug deep enough to hold Oliver's body when his time came. I had thought when we buried her that the links between the living and the dead were unpleasantly close in this place, but it had not occurred to me that his time could come so soon.

The sky was a wrinkled grey sheet from which oozed continuous moisture. It hung in mist under the yews, it sprinkled itself in droplets on hair and woollen coats, it squelched in the shaggy grass. The churchyard was full of people whose strained faces bore tribute to the affection he compelled. The men stood bare-headed in the drizzle; the women wore dark hats. How odd it was that men took off their hats to show respect while women put them on.

Beyond the grave Peter Malet was surreptitiously wiping lumps of mud from his shoes on to the matting that covered the fresh earth. He was next to his parents, but slightly apart from them. His face was like Oliver's yet not like: a caricature. His head was the same sculptured shape but deposits of fat were beginning to mar the jawline and the skin beneath the eyes was pouched unhealthily. The droop at the corners of the wide mouth gave him a petulant expression. He looked up at the horse-chestnut trees beyond the yews, his face abstracted as if absorbed in a calculation of his new riches; presumably most that had been Oliver's would be his. His two sons fidgeted beside him, their faces unnaturally solemn above carefully pressed grey school suits. The Awfuls, Oliver had called them, occasionally the God-Awfuls. Oliver. He was in that box. I could not believe it; I could not bear it.

The rector's nasal tenor stopped; the coffin was lowered, bumping awkwardly against the sides of the hole. Old Mrs Malet leaned closer to her husband, clasping both hands convulsively round his arm. His free hand covered hers. He stood like a stone.

The sobs came without warning, heaving their way from me like sickness. I cried as a noisy protesting child might. A movement went through the groups of mourners; faces turned towards mine and back to where the earth was falling. Richard gripped my elbow, drawing me backwards. I wanted to run from that place. I did not know what to do. I tripped against a vase of wilting dahlias. Green water filled my shoe, its icy stream as effective as a slap on the face. Silently, Richard handed me the handkerchief from his breast pocket, holding me as I rid my shoe of water. My face burned, drying the tears. Shame mingled with my grief. Grief should be private, a purely personal concern.

I wanted to separate myself from the other guests at the Malets' house. They were talking quietly in the drawing-room, stiff faces beginning to loosen now that the funeral was over. They had murmured condolences to Oliver's parents, choosing the words with care, people who would produce the right gestures on all occasions. If tears had left their eyes in the churchyard no one could have told in the damp air; they would not gulp and cry out.

Richard was drinking sherry and listening to Peter Malet, the impassive look on his face that I knew signified annoyance. It seemed Peter wanted to discuss the will; Richard was one of the executors. As I drifted past them on my way to the door I heard Peter saying: 'One would think he'd have remembered his own nephews. Well, I mean, wouldn't one? One would have thought they'd have been important to him when he had no children himself. All those bequests to dozens of folk one's hardly met – godchildren and so on – and nothing special for poor Alexander or James.'

At the end of the hall was the small sitting-room Oliver had called the garden room; I would go in there and be silent. Little had changed in the room. It gave me an odd feeling, not unpleasant. The same photograph of Oliver at university stood on the same walnut side table. The Chesterfield still faced the fire, too large for the room but comfortable; I'd had it in mind when Richard and I bought ours. The rug by the fire was the same silky Bokhara, more faded perhaps but definitely the one on which we had made love, Oliver and I. I bent to touch it and remembered vividly the softness of it against my buttocks and the warmth of the log fire on my skin. And Oliver . . . Oliver saying: 'Don't be shy, Annabel.' And later, with surprising emotion: 'Oh, darling, I've wanted to do this with you for such a very long time.'

With my first lover, Angela's cousin Roddy, what he called lovemaking resembled more two people competing for a prize – with me the invariable loser. Oliver's awareness had brought reactions that were remote imaginings before. I came for him: it was the first time. He had kissed me lightly on the nose as he left. 'What a surprising girl you are,' he said, smiling. 'Like one of those sherbet sweets – quiet and smooth to start with and then an exciting fizz!' 'I never fizzed before,' I confessed. He lit us both cigarettes and then questioned me. I can remember every word of that conversation. 'Then this is a special occasion for you,' he said, and finally: 'My opinion of that flash Harry has never been lower. How could there possibly be anything wrong with you? You're entirely delectable. Heavenly!' And his fingers had gently hooked my bra.

He had joined me in bed that night, after his parents had returned from their bridge evening and gone to their room. 'I want to hold you,' he said, clutching me tightly, his whole body shaking strangely. He said he was cold, but he felt perfectly warm.

Next morning he had a migraine and stayed in his room. When at last he did appear I was holding a trug for his mother while she dead-headed the roses. He had walked across the lawn as if he were treading on hot nails. His face was very pale. 'I'm sorry,' he said, and to this day I do not know whether he was referring to his sickness or to the events of the previous evening. Two days later there was a small parcel in my pigeonhole at college. In it was a gold brooch, a little knot of gold. 'In memory of the special occasion,' he said when I thanked him. We never spoke of that night again. It was as if it had never happened.

I understood, or thought I did. We could meet easily enough in the classless atmosphere of the university, but outside were other worlds, and Oliver's world was not mine. But I wished I could have told him how much he had done for me that weekend. My affair with Roddy had been a disaster, a silly girl's dream that turned into a nightmare of terrified pregnancy and ended in a car accident and a miscarriage. Afterwards I had despised myself and hated my body. It was paradoxical that it was through my body that Oliver's greatest help had come. He hadn't known about the baby, but he had understood that I was depressed over Roddy and tried to help by inviting me for the weekend with his parents. He had helped me – in a very different way from what he had intended. I didn't believe for a moment that he had deliberately set out to make love to me; it had just happened. I suppose that I should have had pangs of conscience, but my conscience had remained firmly quiescent. I hugged the loving warmth of the occasion to myself and felt better than I had done for several months.

I looked at the photograph in its silver frame; the striking young face was the one I had first gazed at in admiration, not the worn face that had worried me over the last year. This face was almost, but not entirely, serious. It had that not-quite-smiling look I used to see on it when he was teasing me and struggling to keep himself from laughing. I had thought he had changed remarkably little over the years and in a way that was true; the shape of the eyes, the mouth, the jawline, they had remained the same; no sagging or pouching had spoiled his features. But as I studied the photograph I realised that there had been

111

changes, more than I thought: sadness in the eyes and tiny lines around them, a tired set to the lips, a loss of vitality.

Odd, but now that I looked closely I thought I detected the shadow of the sorrow that had dimmed the older Oliver. Something in the setting of the eyes, perhaps.

10

Richard told me of Oliver's bequests to our family while we were driving back to Richmond after the funeral. Dripping hedges and skeletal trees rushed past the car windows in a grey blur as I forced my mind to grapple with the significance of his generosity. I could have wished he had acted differently. I could take no real pleasure in his bequests to us (his George I kneehold desk for Richard and for me the Sheraton sofa-table I had always admired) because of my apprehension over the legacies to the children. Already I found myself in a posture of self-defence, all the dread that Clare had awakened at the party rushing back over my body. It was the extent to which Oliver had singled out Ollie that frightened me.

When I could speak calmly I asked Richard for his opinion. To my amazement he said that he thought the will fair, although he did admit that it might cause ructions between the children, for which we should be prepared. Oliver had given him an idea of what was in his mind when he asked him to be one of the executors. Richard's opinion then and now remained the same: that Sara and Daniel must learn that life would not throw plums into their laps unless they had earned them, and the sooner they learned this lesson the better. They had been generously treated in any case. I didn't know whether to be impressed or exasperated by his attitude. He was imperturbable.

His mother, unfortunately, was not. Richard told the family of the legacies towards the end of the evening meal that day. There was no point in waiting until Bertha was absent; she was found to ferret the news out eventually.

'I never heard anything like it!' she exclaimed when Richard had finished speaking, and she buttered a cream cracker with such energy that it shattered into a dozen pieces. 'Ten thousand pounds for Ollie and only two and a half thousand each for the others. What an extraordinary thing to do! Well! I only hope young Ollie appreciates his luck.'

Ollie's body was rigid, his face very white. I could see that tears were not far from the surface; his mouth tightened with the effort of controlling himself. He glanced at his grandmother with distaste. He said nothing.

'Of course,' she continued, 'in my family we've always believed in treating every member equally. I wonder whatever could have made Mr Malet give preference to Ollie like that?' And her eyes shifted from face to face round the dinner table, inviting us to join in her speculations; it was only too clear that her mind was loitering suggestively in dark corners.

'I think it's disgusting,' Sara said angrily. 'Why should Ollie be given so much more than Danny or me? And the violin, too. What's he want two violins for? It's not fair. Just because Ollie's such a creep. . .'

Danny jerked upright in his chair. 'Shut up, you stupid cow!' he snapped, in a tone I'd never heard him use before. 'You're lucky he left you anything. You never bothered to talk to him. You didn't even like him much. And you bitch because it's only two and a half thousand! Christ, you've got a cheek!'

114

Richard had opened his mouth to blister Sara, but closed it again when Danny demonstrated that he could do it equally effectively. He pushed his chair back from the table and listened, his eyes two icy points of blue light.

'Well, what did Ollie do for him that's worth all that?' Sara asked sullenly.

'He liked him, didn't he? They were real friends. And Ollie had the guts to talk to him about Melissa – he didn't block her out as if she'd never existed, like most of us do about dead people.' Danny was going very red, whether with indignation or embarrassment I couldn't tell, but he continued determinedly: 'Look, I liked Oliver, I liked him a lot in fact, but I didn't have anything in common with him, not like Ollie with his music. I know it gave Oliver a lot of pleasure playing with Ollie because I heard him say so to Dad more than once. You didn't do anything like that for him, nor did I. Far as I'm concerned, two and a half thousand pounds is bloody generous . . . and it's two and a half thousand pounds more than I expected.'

'Precisely,' Richard said with a sharp nod.

Sara shot both of them a look of dislike. 'Well,' she muttered, retreating but trying to cover her withdrawal, 'nobody cares about the silly old fiddle, but ten thousand's an awful lot for somebody of Ollie's age – and I think it was rude of Oliver to make such a big difference. It's as if he was saying he didn't think much of Danny or me.'

'Jesus, what a load of rubbish,' Danny gasped. 'If someone thinks two and a half thousand quids worth of me, I think that's terrific. Anyhow, Ollie was his namesake.'

'So what?'

'Well, that's like being a godson. People always leave their godsons something extra in their wills, don't they?'

'A namesake can hardly be compared with a godson,' Bertha pronounced. She felt safe on religious grounds, a

115

missionary among the heathen. 'Godparents have special duties to perform. It is a quite different thing.'

Richard interrupted in a voice that grated like a shifting glacier: 'If Annabel and I had been churchgoers, no doubt Oliver would have been asked to be a godfather; as we are not the point is purely academic. I suggest we leave the whole matter. I find this discussion offensive. Oliver's bequests were Oliver's business and there is no gain to be made by arguing over them.' He rose to his feet, glaring down at his daughter. 'Sara, you will help your mother to clear the table, please.'

Sara's eyes widened in fury at this sexist command, but Bertha interrupted; she had not yet finished. She addressed herself to Ollie, her dentures bared in a smile that was totally synthetic. 'We haven't heard from Ollie yet. What do you think about your exciting windfall then, dear?'

Ollie stood so abruptly that his chair swayed danger-ously backwards. I steadied it quickly, watching him. I hated to see the look of hurt on the drawn, loved face. His chin trembled and I hoped fervently that he would not let himself down. Then the chin lifted, jutting forcefully; for the first time I saw a resemblance to Richard. 'I don't care about the money – I don't need it. I'm glad he liked me enough to give it to me, that's all. And his violin. I wish I could thank him. I wish I'd told him how much I liked him while he was alive.' The half-broken voice could not take the strain of the emotion; it cracked into falsetto and he had to stop to control it. Sara giggled faintly, unforgiva-bly, and I saw his hands close convulsively on the edge of the table. He shouted: 'No stupid money or anything else can make him come alive again! I'd give it all up if it could, but it can't. And I wish you'd all shut up and leave me alone.' His hands released the table to make an unexpec-tedly violent gesture towards us.

There was a horrified silence. I reached out to touch his shoulder but he shook me off and rushed from the room. Richard swung round to follow him, calling: 'Oliver, wait!' I watched the damp fingermarks on the mahogany gradually fade as their voices rose and fell in the hall. Eventually Richard took him into the study and the door shut. I hoped Richard could reassure him. It would be wicked if a sense of guilt were to be added to his loss.

I felt suddenly middle-aged and exhausted. Beside me Sara was collecting and stacking plates, attempting to hide discomfiture behind a righteous assumption of helpfulness. Across the table Danny was slumped in his chair, gazing at her as if he'd never seen her before.

'You bitch!' he said furiously. 'You tactless, interfering, vomit-brained bitch!'

'Really!' Bertha gasped. 'That any grandson of mine should use such language!'

Two weeks passed. Signs of autumn appeared, the days visibly shortening, the first fallen leaves freckling the grass. Looking from my bedroom window in the early mornings, I could see mist steaming from the sluggish river to hang among the trees in the park, waiting for the sun to shaft through and banish it.

I was out of the house most of the time, working. When I was in the house I was still working: organising my family, cooking the meals, and, when the clearing-up was over, analysing the day's notes on whichever case I was engaged in at that moment, studying the statements, preparing submissions or my speech for the defence, always with something to be done. Work was the best therapy for my tormented and miserable mind, it demanded total concentration, blotting out all other thoughts. And dealing with men in trouble helped to put my own troubles in perspective.

My mother-in-law was dividing her time between Richmond and Bromley, an arrangement my family did not approve of. The peaceful atmosphere I tried to maintain was evaporating from the house like the mist from the park. Bertha bridled, she sighed, she sniffed, she commented. Ollie's violin playing went straight through her head; she didn't know how we could stand it. Of course, she realised some people had favourites among their children, but she never had – it wasn't her way. She couldn't help worrying over my passion for buying books: 'Such an extravagance nowadays!' 'The children read them too,' I said defensively, 'they're helpful for their education.' 'My dear Annabel,' said Mother-in-law, 'you'll be telling me next that they can learn about Real Life from books.' Since something along those lines had been in my mind, this was unanswerable. She turned to leave the room. 'Fact,' she observed heavily, 'is stranger than fiction.'

On an evening at the beginning of October I drove from court back to Chambers to collect a couple of large cheques that Tom had told me had arrived and found the report of the enquiry agent sitting in my pigeon hole, sent on by the solicitor, Howard Hoffer. The envelope looked pleasingly fat; I pocketed it for after-dinner reading, my fingers crossed for useful revelations.

Once I would have shared the news of both cheques and report with Richard; now, uneasily tactful, I said nothing, but crept into the study to scan the report while he was watching the nine o'clock news.

The fat envelope was an indication of Alan Greening's verbosity rather than any useful discoveries, but he had clearly searched for information like a lively ferret, digging away in every possible location, and reporting in full everything he had turned up.

It appeared that on the small estate where the Pockett house stood most of the women worked full-time to help pay the mortgage; they had hardly time to cope with their own lives, let alone poke their noses into other people's troubles. Mr Greening had garnered little here. Besides, the other half of the semi-detached house had been empty and up for sale for months, while across the road the two bungalows had their bedrooms on the road side, giving their occupants little chance to watch the Pockett women's comings and goings. The elderly widow from one, after recording her shock at the decline of modern morals – 'That young lass having a baby at only fifteen and the father attacking the younger one, well, it wouldn't have happened when I was young, not on a nice street like this!' – did go on to remark that the house got a surprising number of visitors who stayed quite late. She heard car doors slam and saw headlights on her bedroom ceiling just when she was trying to doze off. She thought Mrs Pockett was a lively one, but who was she to criticise? It could be the visitors were relatives come to cheer her up – the Lord knew she'd need it.

Alan Greening, I discovered as I read on, had an endearing habit of quoting the people he interviewed verbatim, or semi-verbatim, making his report consider-ably more lively than most of the documents I had to read. I concluded that he carried one of those miniature cassette recorders in a pocket or a bag in order not to lose a word.

He got plenty of words from the owners of the local post office-store, Mr and Mrs Patel, caught at a slack moment. Both Tina Pockett and Karen cashed their child benefits here and used the store for their food shopping. Only the thriftless and the lazy did their main shop of the week at the Patels, Mrs Patel explained to Alan Greening, because supermarkets held a wider range of goods and were cheaper; what people generally popped into them for

119

were things they had forgotten or needed for unexpected guests. But the Pocketts bought lavishly and at all hours, Mrs Pockett particularly lavishly at the off-licence section at the back – canned beer, cheap wine, gin, cigarettes. The Patels did not approve, despite the extra sales: this was not how their frugal, hard-working lives were run. Of Karen there was little said; she was a fair enough mother, but what a disgrace to be one at her age! Of Fern they had plenty to say, but most of it was of the exclaiming variety, of no use to Mr Pockett's case. Mr Greening abridged it to one sentence quoted from Mrs Patel: 'I always thought she was a sulky, awkward young madam, but when you hear what her father put her through, well, you can under-stand why the poor girl was like that, can't you?'

Similar words were spoken up at Fern's school. Alan Greening had hung about the school bus lane at going-home time, posing as a caring dad, and had attempted conversation with the staff on bus duty. On the first occa-sion the middle-aged male teacher told him brusquely not to bother him, he was not interested in gossip about any of his pupils, and particularly not Fern Pockett; the matter was in the hands of the police. On the second day Green-ing chatted up Fern's own tutor, a young woman in a bright turquoise and yellow track suit who had just come from refereeing a netball game. Miss Goodwin was full of energy, indignation and information freely given. No, Fern was not a good games player – could have been, but never had the team spirit; equally, she had a good brain but only did the minimum work to keep out of trouble, and not always that. Recently, Alan Greening heard, she had done almost no homework, and her concentration in class was shocking; she seemed as if half-asleep.

Miss Goodwin had been really worked up over Fern: here was a badly traumatised girl, raped and possibly buggered by that terrible father, who needed all the help the law could give and yet our creaking old system of justice was making her wait, not just weeks but month after month, for her case to be heard. It was not surprising she showed no interest in school work, not surprising she had no team spirit. Miss Goodwin felt horribly guilty about poor Fern, she said. Because of her difficult behaviour she and other teachers had always been hard on Fern; now their hearts ached for her. As her tutor for more than two years, she felt that she herself should have recognised that something more than just the parents' divorce was upsetting her. And there had been evidence that she had ignored. Twice other children had complained that Fern had jeered at them over their sexual ignorance and told them unpleasant stories. And once during the morning tutor period she had confiscated a comic that Fern was passing to another girl. It was a violent comic, a horror comic, its pictures full of men viciously attacking other men. Fern had added in ballpoint pen what Miss Goodwin primly termed 'erect organs' to the figures of the attackers, giving the stories a surrealistic effect of quite stunning nastiness. She had taken Fern and the evidence to the deputy headmaster, and both of them had talked to the girl. Both had come to the conclusion that Fern was 'having difficulty in coming to terms with her adolescent development'; neither, Miss Goodwin mourned, had thought of looking further. Miss Goodwin had no doubt at all, Mr Greening concluded, as to the guilt of Fern's father.

On the third day of Mr Greening's efforts a bored-looking bearded man had been delighted to have a chat with someone adult while the shrieking children fought their way on to the various transports, but while he knew all about the incest case from discussions with his friend Miss Goodwin, he had to admit that he had not personally taught Fern and wouldn't know her if he saw her – until

Greening owned himself an enquiry agent and produced a photograph.

'Her? Is that Fern Pockett? Well, I know her all right! Saw her with a senior boy last spring – locked in the supreme stage of heterosexual affection in Smokers' Dip, they were, when they should have been in class!'

Greening enquired further. 'Smokers' Dip?' the bearded teacher had replied. 'It's on the far side of the playing field, between a shrubbery and the boundary fence. Somewhere to go to be undisturbed, hence its name. I usually check it out when I'm on duty. Were they shocked when I interrupted them? Hell, I didn't interrupt them. No, it might have given the lad a shock his libido would never have recovered from if I'd done that to him. I took myself off.'

The fact that the boy could also have made the girl pregnant didn't seem to occur to him. I sighed and read on.

'Don't think either of them saw me. Nope. But I know it was her all right. Seen her around a lot – she's a fairly obvious type, if you take my meaning. Not a nice kid. Lippy, you might say. Still, given that she's who you say she is, that's not surprising, is it?'

Pressed as to the date on which this episode occurred he could not be accurate. Spring? 'Well, early in the summer term. I remember it was warm so I was lightly clad – and so were they!'

Interesting, a pointer, and at first sight exciting. But in the final analysis not useful evidence. In her statement Fern had claimed to be a virgin, innocent about all sexual matters before her father's assaults. But this was after the Easter camping holiday and any competent prosecution counsel would suggest her desperate for normal affection, making mincemeat of any deductions I might try to make from the incident.

The report's final paragraphs noted that an enlarged photograph of Fern had been recognised in two shops in the local shopping centre, a jeweller's and a music shop. The jeweller's was a well-known multiple selling at the lower end of the market. The two middle-aged lady assistants had not recognised Fern, but the dapper young male trainee had. Yeah, she'd been in several times; she always came to him for help, he expected because he was younger than the others. She knew what she liked, all right, she'd bought a bracelet once, and then some earrings. Yeah, he had been surprised she could afford them: he'd seen her in school uniform, knew she was young. But lots of kids have jobs, he always had himself. The music shop was a plush gilt-painted place, selling everything from reproduction eighteenth-century harpsichords to magenta electronic guitars, from sheet music to CDs. They knew Fern in there, all right. She was a regular, had bought her CD player from them and fed it new CDs almost every week. Sometimes she had a girl friend with her. No, no hint of shop-lifting. No, she had plenty of cash. Parents who spoiled her, probably.

So Fern's anger at her father's suspicions was genuine. Her boyfriend had not been on the make, buying dubious goods in a backstreet pub or shop-lifting to impress his latest girl. All was above-board – or was it? How did she, or how had the ex-boyfriend, come to have so much free cash? Was she working on Saturdays or in the evenings? Alan Greening had picked up nothing, and she was free to spend at least some of that time revelling in her shopping. Was she stealing money from somewhere? No evidence of that. Strange, I mused, very strange . . . all that cash. But even if we found out where the money came from, would it necessarily help John Pockett? What could it prove?

And the unpleasant interest in sex – what did that show? Did it arise from her father's attacks upon her?

Where else could it have come from? Neighbours, friends and school teachers were clearly of one view only. After ten minutes or so of brain battering I gave it up and went to watch a detective story on television: that was always satisfactory – by the end of the programme one knew for certain who was the guilty person.

'Mum, when is Grandma going to go? I mean, seriously, when?'

'When she's found a house she likes.'

I knew as soon as Danny sidled into the kitchen on Saturday afternoon that something was wrong. Two unnatural pieces of behaviour together proved it – Danny never moved quietly and he seldom closed doors.

'But that could take for ever. She finds dozens of faults in every house she looks at.'

'She is fussy,' I agreed.

'Fussy? Christ, she fusses about everything, not just her new house.' Danny's normally good-humoured face was screwed up into a mask of passionate resentment. 'Whatever Ollie or I do it's wrong. I can't stand much more of her.'

I squeezed garlic heartily in the presser, wondering wearily what the problem was this time.

'She was getting at me about my clothes and my hair and everything again. You'd think she'd let me wear what I like on a Saturday, wouldn't you?' He glowered broodingly at the pastry base of the vegetable quiche that I was making for supper. 'God, I wear that dreary school uniform all week. I told her you let me express my own personality at the weekend.'

I started slicing courgettes, then stopped and focused my eyes on him. If his appearance was expressing his personality then it was an aggressive one. It was also calculated to give maximum annoyance to his grandmother. For a start, he hadn't bothered to shave. As with Richard, the beard growth was black and the scruff made his face look dirty. His hair, though not unduly long by modern standards, would have been the better for a trim. Through a hole in an elderly games vest poked a couple of the wiry chest hairs that he had been proudly cultivating recently. Below the vest came faded and shrunken jeans that gripped his thigh muscles and outlined his genitals. I was glad that my son looked uncompromisingly male, but I could understand that Bertha found his appearance offensive. Privately I thought he looked touchingly like a boisterous bull-calf preparing to challenge the leader of the herd.

'You do look a mess,' I commented in a neutral voice. 'Not the picture of how every grandma would like her grandson to look. What have you been doing?'

'Helping Dad in the garden. I don't have to dress up for that, do I?'

'No, of course not. But might I suggest that you shave and put on a respectable shirt before supper? To please me,' I added hastily.

'I might,' he conceded. He sat on the edge of the table and picked bits of bread absently from the loaf. 'And she was going on at Ollie about his music again. Pretending to be interested but really bitching at him. You know.'

I did know, only too well. Since she'd learnt of Oliver's bequests Ollie had joined me as a constant target, but being younger, he was more vulnerable.

'She keeps on telling him how lucky he is to have inherited such a valuable violin and asking him if he knows it. Then she says to think how dreadful it would be if anything happened to it. The way she goes on he'll never dare to play the thing – he'll be so jittery he'll drop it!'

I cursed her hard beneath my breath. For the last two

125

weeks Ollie had been unnaturally silent, going off to school in the mornings as if it were a relief, returning in the evenings to shut himself away in his room. 'Essay to write,' he would say if I attempted to lure him into the kitchen to talk as he used to do after school, or, 'Got a difficult piece to practise,' and his feet would steadily mount the stairs and his bedroom door close with a Keep Out click. Coping with his first grief at Oliver's death had been simple in comparison with this. Answering the frantic questions of 'Why? Why? Why?' as he sobbed against my shoulder had been easier than breaking through a wall of stoical endurance.

Richard said: 'Leave him alone. He'll come to terms with this in his own time.' Perhaps he was right, I didn't know. My own impulse was to persuade Ollie to talk it out. Thirteen is over-young to cope alone with the total loss that is death. Perhaps it was easier in the days when belief in an afterlife was generally accepted; nowadays the finality is frightening. Ollie had never been the confiding type who tells all with much heavy breathing and circumlocution, but neither had he been averse to asking for help or sympathy when he needed them. His withdrawal was frustrating to my maternal feelings, increasing my own sadness. I longed to be close to him, to comfort him, but he couldn't, or wouldn't, let me. The time when none of my children would need me seemed suddenly within touching distance.

'We did a good day's work,' Richard announced as he came into the kitchen. 'Got that long border sorted out.' The smell of chrysanthemums and fresh earth clung to his pullover. He scrubbed his hands vigorously at the sink, spraying brown water on to the tiles behind, dripping over the floor as he looked for the towel. I picked it up from where Danny had dropped it beneath the radiator and put it into his hands.

'Richard – play for Ollie tonight,' I said. 'He's been practising those Mozart sonatas. He needs an accompanist.' His eyes met mine; he nodded.

'I'm taking Mother back to Bromley after we've eaten. Then I will, if he wants me to.'

'I can't imagine how he can like that sort of music,' Danny said. 'It's dreary.'

'Nonsense,' Richard said. 'Those records you play are dreary, if you like. Fashionable, yes. Good, no. Nothing musical about them; only noise.'

'Oh God,' Danny grumbled. 'Now it's Dad getting at me. It isn't like that. It's a question of taste. You don't understand.'

Sara strolled in, wearing a tight pillar-box red jersey that emphasised her breasts and tight white trousers that exaggerated the length of her legs.

I said mildly: 'When teenagers complain that their parents don't understand them, they usually mean that they understand them only too well.' I pushed my quiche into the oven and shut the door.

'Parents never understand their children,' Sara said. 'How can they? You don't know what I'm thinking. You never have done.' She leaned against the table, arranging her body carefully, watching the effect in the glass of the china cupboard opposite.

'No need to be mind readers to understand you,' Richard said. 'It isn't the same thing, you know.'

'Christ, no. We don't have to switch you on like a radio to hear your thoughts,' Danny said. 'Your clothes shriek them, "Wowie! Get me!" Right?'

Sara blinked her annoyance. 'You think you're so bloody clever! Lucinda's got a bit of a party going tonight. I want to look reasonable, don't I?'

'That silly girl again?' Richard frowned. 'I'll admit there's one thing I don't understand – why you should

127

spend so much time with a butterfly-minded, worthless piece like Angela's offspring.'

'She's fun,' Sara said indignantly. 'She's not dead from the neck up like most folk around here. And she gets me invited to all the good parties – I'd die of boredom if it weren't for Lucinda.'

'Come to think of it,' Richard said, 'I've seen remarkably little of you recently. I thought it was agreed you would only go out on Friday or Saturday nights during termtime?'

'I babysit for Mrs Foster a couple of times a week,' Sara explained impatiently. 'I told you, Daddy. She goes to evening classes and her husband does too. Italian. The baby's too big for his carrycot so she has to have a sitter.'

Julie Foster was half-French, a lively brunette who had taught French at the comprehensive school until shortly before her son was born. Judging by the frequency of her calls upon Sara's services, she found it irksome to stay at home. Sara benefitted from her restlessness: she liked to sit, she said, the baby was gorgeous, with his mother's warm brown eyes, and the money was always welcome.

'I'm not sure I approve,' Richard said. 'What about homework?'

'I take my books with me, of course. I can do those boring essays just as well at their house.'

Not for the first time I wondered whether boring referred to the endemic dreariness of regulated school work – after all, who would claim to enjoy homework? – or whether she was genuinely not interested in what she was doing. When asked, Sara would shrug: 'It's okay, I suppose,' and change the subject.

'What if the baby cries?'

'He hardly ever does. He's terribly good.'

'I see. But last Thursday wasn't baby-sitting for Mrs Foster. That was a pop concert. What about our agreement?'

Sara leapt from the table as if a coiled spring had been released. 'Oh God,' she exclaimed, 'all you two ever think about is work. Why can't you be like Grandma? She understands me. She says a girl of my age should be having fun, not sticking her nose into books every evening. I have to get away from the gloom in this house anyway – it's like a bloody morgue!'

11

When the Monday of half-term arrived Tony appeared on our doorstep at an early hour, immaculate in a dark suit, determined that I shouldn't leave for court without him. He said he'd had his breakfast, but he kept me company with a trio of hot croissants anyway. He thought Sara should come to court too, but when she appeared she refused point blank.

'No thanks!' she said, examining a croissant and then tossing it back on the plate. 'I've been before and it's nothing like the plays you see on telly. Dull? The witnesses go over and over the same stuff for hours.'

'But you have to look for clashes of evidence,' Tony protested, 'and that's interesting. Besides, it's related to our Wednesday classes on justice and human rights.'

Sara shrugged and grinned. 'If that's what you reckon, you go for it. Me, I'm spending the day shopping in Bond Street and Sloane Street and the Kings Road with Lucinda. We're going to suss out the fashions from the top to the bottom and choose what we want for our birthdays and Christmas. And that's serious.'

'What sort of case have we got today?' Tony wanted to know as we drove off down Richmond Hill.

I liked the involvement implied by the 'we'. 'Murder,' I

replied cheerfully. 'We're doing a murder, and we'll be in Court 1 at Inner London Crown Court. We're for the defence. My client is a Turkish-Cypriot accused of killing his wife by pushing her out of a third-storey window, and there's an admission of guilt on tape – with a duty solicitor present. But he's insisting on pleading not guilty.'

'You think it's a loser?' Tony asked, sounding taken aback.

I shook my head. 'Oh, no. There are some interesting features to this case. To start with, I shall challenge the admissibility of the confession. I say *I* shall, but perhaps I should explain that normally a silk leads for the defence in a murder trial. My unfortunate leader was rushed to hospital at the end of last week and not only was there too little time for a new leader to be fully briefed in all the details, but both my client and the solicitor insisted they wanted me, not some unknown quantity, however learned. So it's an important occasion for me, taking on my first murder – and for you, Tony. You're going to play an important role – taking a full note as if you were my junior and analysing the evidence, searching for any telling details that might help our client's case. Can you do that?' I braked to allow a pushy taxi-driver to nip his vehicle in front of mine and glanced at him.

'You tell me what you want and I'll do it,' he responded, clearly delighted at the prospect of acting a real part in the courtroom drama. 'I've got plenty of pens in my pocket.'

'No hope that your racially integrated school has given you a command of Turkish, I suppose?'

He laughed. 'None. Is this chap's English bad?'

'Abysmal. Look, while we're driving along, I'll give you an outline of the story, then you'll see where our problems lie. The client, one Mr Hamad, lived with his wife in Peckham, in a dismal Victorian tenement block. It's scheduled for demolition any day now, and not before time. They lived in a flat on the third floor; most of the flats around them were either boarded up or occupied by squatters. Litter everywhere, kids aimlessly kicking empty beer cans, a stench of urine in the stairwells, drunks . . . you get the scene?'

Tony wrinkled his nose. 'Loud and strong.'

'Yes. Mr Hamad's forty years old, and admits he's a heavy drinker; his wife was about thirty-six and an alcoholic. They were housed in that building because they were difficult tenants, fighting and screaming when they were drunk, and she, in particular, abusive of the neighbours. In conference at Brixton Prison, Mr Hamad told us – that is, myself, my learned leader, and the solicitor – through an interpreter, that on the evening of her death they had been drinking together in their flat. When the drink ran out she insisted they must go to the off-licence for more, but he was demanding a meal and there was nothing edible in the flat. They had a row over this and she hurled a couple of saucepan lids at him. He decided to go to the shops for a couple of take-aways and she staggered after him with booze in mind, but he shoved her back and locked her in the flat, using the Chubb lock. That second lock had been put on their front door by the council because of the thieving squatters, and he had the only key.

'He says he locked her in because he didn't want her yelling abuse at him all the way to the shops and back. When he returned with the kebabs it was dusk, an April dusk. The outside door was still locked, but inside his wife had vanished. Eventually he saw that the bottom half of the sash window in the bedroom was open. He leaned out but could see no one. He mooched vaguely around the flats and the courtyard, searching for her, then abandoned the problem in favour of his take-away. The police found him half an hour later asleep in his chair, the unsavoury remnants still in his lap.' I paused while I swung the car out of the steadily silting-up inner lane and over to the outer lane of the Hammersmith fly-over.

'But what happened?' Tony demanded. 'Where was she?'

'Well, oddly enough, no one saw Mrs Hamad fall, whether pushed or not. But at some point during Mr Hamad's absence a man walking across the rear courtyard saw a woman lying bruised and semi-conscious on the concrete, reeking of drink and groaning. He dialled 999 for an ambulance. At the hospital she was briefly examined in a crowded casualty ward by an exhausted and over-burdened young doctor. He had her placed in a quiet room to sober up before she was treated. When he had a free moment to check her condition he found her dead.'

'Ah! Poor doctor. A nasty shock for him!'

'Beastly. The police were informed and came to find Mr Hamad. He identified his wife and told them in his broken English how she had been locked in. They made enquiries of the residents of the flats and the squatters, heard from them of the Hamads' fiery relationship, and about the shoutings and clatter they'd heard earlier that evening, and they came to the conclusion, particularly the Detective Sergeant, that Hamad had thrown her out of the window in the course of the row and then rushed out to try to provide an alibi.'

We were almost at the great glittering palace of Harrods. I turned right into Beauchamp Place and along Pont Street towards Eaton Square, with Tony questioning me all the way.

'Could this drunken woman have overbalanced and fallen out of the window by accident? I mean, was the sill low?'

'No, not that low. Very unlikely.'

'Then if the sill was high, wouldn't it have been hard for

her husband to have pushed her out – a struggling, raving drunk?'

'She was undernourished, the post-mortem report said.'

He strummed his fingers on the car dashboard, his sleek dark head tilted to one side. 'Then could she have climbed out? Were there drainpipes she could have tried to shin down?'

Defence counsel had gone on a recce, viewing the scene of the alleged crime. I shuddered as I remembered the rear of the tenement, its broken windows, its rusted iron pipes snaking their way erratically across and down the crumbling and slimy brickwork. 'Not to my mind. Not unless she was a skilled mountaineer or a member of the SAS. There were pipes near, but none immediately below the window. No.'

The sun was shining on Eaton Square, shining from a soft blue heaven and illuminating the last tawny leaves on its trees and the handsome façades of its terraces, chocolate box in their charm. Did the square's inhabitants get drunk and fight? Did they suffer and die as the inhabitants of Nunhead Buildings did, behind those great façades? It didn't seem possible. *'Busie old foole, unruly sunne . . .'* shining on all impartially.

Tony was eyeing the houses, too, but with different thoughts in mind. 'Three storeys up – quite a smash. What else did the post-mortem say?'

'It said that her back was broken and that the backs of her heels were badly bruised and damaged, and the conclusion drawn was that the broken back was a fracture caused by a fall of some forty to fifty feet.'

'Mmm. And the police had arrested Mr Hamad.'

'He was interviewed at the police station by Detective Inspector Spode and Detective Sergeant Finch. The interviews were taped. There was a duty solicitor present. No one bothered to discover if Mr Hamad could read or write English, which he couldn't. All he could manage was his signature, which he scrawled to accept the solicitor. Then on they pressed with the interviews. Mr Hamad apparently agreed with a lot of what was said, and as time went on it appeared, by his saying "yes" to various questions, that he was making an admission. In the small hours he was charged with murder, and next day the magistrates remanded him in custody to Brixton.'

'But you said his English was abysmal. Did he have an interpreter?'

'No interpreter.'

'No wonder you're challenging the admissibility of the confession!'

'Precisely. Though in fairness to the police, Mr Hamad does at first appear much more at home in English than he actually is. He spreads his hands and nods and shrugs knowingly – and then he says "Yes", when he should have said "No", or vice versa, and you realise he hasn't a clue, not a clue, as to what's been said.'

'That's terrifying.'

I nodded. 'Too true. And there's more to it yet. We realised the full extent of the problem when we had a conference with him in Brixton. My then leader and I were questioning him from a transcript of the tapes that we'd insisted on having in full. We started off in English, but soon had to switch to using the Turkish woman interpreter we'd obtained, and still we were getting distinctly odd replies. Suddenly the interpreter asked if she might speak to us outside the interview room. She was very agitated. She said that Mr Hamad had no understanding of many of the words in his confession in Turkish, let alone English. He was a peasant of low intelligence, nervous of anyone in authority, anxious to please the police, whom he feared, and she was concerned that he might have signed his name to a confession without any real idea of its contents. In his answers to the questions we'd put through her, one thing only was clear – he absolutely denied pushing his wife through the window.'

A pause. I braked at the end of Birdcage Walk to allow a snarl-up of morning traffic to resolve itself, and then we inched our way towards Westminster Bridge.

Tony said tentatively: 'He could have faked stupidity.'

'Doubtful,' I pointed out, 'because he fairly dropped himself in it, didn't he? Anyway, we investigated. I recommended that an educational psychologist should assess him with the interpreter present, and that's what was done. In essence the report agreed with the interpreter – that Mr Hamad has problems in understanding.'

'Hold on,' Tony exclaimed. 'What about the solicitor? What's his view? He must have been present right through the interviews.'

'The duty solicitor was, but he seems to have been a passive sort of fellow. When I listened to the tapes I heard him intervene once, just once, to remark that his client might not have understood something. Soon after Mr Hamad got to Brixton Prison he asked to change solicitors: my instructing solicitor, Mr Goldstone, is a very different sort, far more on the ball.'

'He'd need to be,' Tony grunted.

Once over Westminster Bridge, I drove speedily round the back of Waterloo Station, weaving round taxis each containing one solemn commuter clutching his briefcase, and on down to the bleak urban muddle that was Newington Causeway, home of Inner London Crown Court. Parked, I leapt from the car, grabbed my briefcase and red bag containing my robes and wig tin, and told Tony to follow me. Time was moving on.

By the robing-room door I ran into David Plunkett; just avoided cannoning off his hefty stomach, in fact. He was a large, ginger-haired, genial man who was also a highly competent senior treasury counsel. I liked him; he was straight up and down, metaphorically if not physically.

'Hah!' he said to me now. 'Annabel! Are we against one another in Hamad?'

'Good morning, David. Yes, it would seem we are.'

'Is there anything you want to tell me before we start?'

'Yes. I'm objecting to the admission of the interviews. Do you intend to open without them?'

'No,' he said. 'No, I can't. We'll have to deal with it as soon as the jury is sworn. You know, I had a horrid feeling you might say that, Annabel. How bothersome of you, and on a Monday morning, too.'

I laughed, and introduced Tony to him as a Chambers mini-pupil, then I robed, to Tony's admiration – 'Wigs give such gravitas to a person!' – took him downstairs to Court 1, met the solicitor and the educational psychologist, Mrs Croft, and introduced Tony to them, and then Mr Goldstone, Tony and I went down to the cells to have a few comforting words with Mr Hamad.

I found my client shaking with nerves. He was a swarthy, cadaverous individual, with a drooping moustache and drooping bloodhound eyes, whose looks were not the sort guaranteed to instil confidence into the onlooker at any time; today he was at a new low. Normally a prisoner's wife would bring him a clean shirt for the start of his trial, but Mr Hamad's wife lay broken in her coffin and nor had he any family in this country. So he was wearing the clothes he had been arrested in, dirty and crumpled from more than thirty-six unpleasant hours non-stop wear as well as six months' bundled up in a prison cupboard. There were sweat marks in the armpits of his cheap jacket, old salty rings as well as new dark stains where fright had started up further secretions. He looked terrible and smelt worse.

When he saw us he burst into incomprehensible speech, a pelting muddle of Turkish and pidgin English. Mr Goldstone and I nodded and made meaningless soothing noises, struggling to calm him. The awful thing was that I couldn't tell him all would be well, because it might well not be.

I introduced Tony, who shook Mr Hamad's hand, clasping it for a moment in both his hands, an international gesture of goodwill that made Mr Hamad blink and take a deep breath before speaking again, this time more clearly.

'Mizz Bateman, I say you – I come England, I have friend say come, much money. Now my friend he dead. I have wife; she dead. One man, one man friend I have in kebab shop. Now I in prison, much prison, and today – bad day. More prison come, I not know. And now I have no friend. But I do nothing, *nothing!*'

I said slowly, seriously: 'You have friends, Mr Hamad. Mr Goldstone and I are working very hard for you.'

Simon Goldstone, a dark-faced, dour, seen-it-all man in his forties, nodded and said firmly: 'Yes, Mr Hamad, yes, that is so.' He added to me, 'We spoke just now of you, and I can confirm he's happy for you to do this case on your own.'

As we went up to the court I asked Tony whether he'd jumped to the conclusion that Mr Hamad was innocent. He looked surprised, then said: 'Oh, the handshake! No, no conclusions. It was just . . . well, his surroundings were so awful and he looked so nervy and pathetic that I wanted to make him feel better, calm him down. Poor bastard. Nobody should have to face a judge and jury in his state. And you're soft-hearted, Mrs Bateman, you told him you and the solicitor were his friends!'

The defendant duly arraigned and the jury sworn in, my opponent, David Plunkett, stood up and said to the judge: 'There is a matter of law to be discussed with your lordship.'

139

The jury left the court, David said that the admissibility of the confession was being challenged, and a trial within a trial was held before the judge alone.

His Honour Judge Morton was approaching seventy – a tight-lipped, heavy-jawed man who wore thick gold-rimmed spectacles that gave his eyes a stony, fixed gleam. This dire appearance was at least partially deceptive for while he was undoubtedly tough, I hadn't so far found him other than fair and courteous, if abrupt. He inclined his massive head to listen to the tapes, twitched thick eyebrows together as the interviewing officers maintained that the defendant had made his admissions voluntarily, blinked at the translation of Mr Hamad's tearful evidence on the nightmare of the night of his wife's death, chewed on his lower lip as the educational psychologist informed us that Mr Hamad was a man in the lowest range of normal intelligence, with a poor grasp of English, intervened to be assured that he was not actually subnormal, listened to my submissions, and then gave his ruling.

During questioning of the defendant, he said, there had been no breach of the code laid down by the Police and Criminal Evidence Act, 1984. The defendant was not an intelligent man, but he was not subnormal. He appeared to understand what was said; there had been a competent solicitor present to protect his interests. Consequently the jury should hear the interview tapes.

I silently swore while behind me Tony muttered furiously. The jury shuffled back in, young, middle-aged and elderly, white, brown and black, seven women and five men. As they sat down Tony tapped my shoulder.

'That ruling would be appealable, wouldn't it?'

'Oh, yes,' I said flatly. 'Insufficient weight given to the language problem.'

For a moment irritation flared in me, then a bout of coughing and hawking from my client thrust his unsavoury appearance once more into my vision and I gave Simon Goldstone strict instructions as to how he should address the prison officer and Mr Hamad on the necessity for cleanliness and a fresh shirt. His present guise of human refuse would only incline the jury to dismiss any story of his as unfit for human consumption. God knows, his linguistic inadequacies were enough to contend with, without additional handicaps.

The jury sat down. The first witness, a Rastafarian tenant of Nunhead Buildings, was called to give his evidence of finding Mrs Hamad virtually insensible, battered and stinking of alcohol on the concrete of the courtyard 'After work – when it was coming dark, like', and we got down to work.

Tony enlivened the drive back to Richmond with his comments on the inability of the witnesses to remember the exact time at which Mrs Hamad had been found: 'Not much hope for an alibi so far, not with this dozy bunch!' and his disapproval of the ambulancemen's approach to the comatose woman: 'Even if they do get cynical about damaged drunks, surely they could still look out for internal injuries?'

As we drove up the hill he asked if he could come in when we reached my house so that he could speak to Sara. He wanted to invite her to some film the critics had raved about, tomorrow evening or the day after: 'If that's all right with you, Mrs Bateman.'

'Of course,' I said, unlocking the front door. 'It's half-term.'

But Sara was not at home.

'She must still be with Lucinda,' I said. 'Wait if you like.'

Tony did like. He accepted my offer of a cup of coffee, sat at the kitchen table and discussed circumstantial evidence and the implications to be drawn from the demeanour of the witnesses with lively interest. Scenting coffee and conversation, Danny joined us. He was not repelled by Tony's regaling him with today's witnesses' descriptions of the dying Mrs Hamad's groans and black eyes, but when I started to prepare dinner and suggested that he might lay the dining table, a look of horror came over his face and he claimed an urgent appointment in the loo.

Tony finished his coffee, radiating waves of disapproval. 'Don't your family all help you?' he asked. 'Automatically?'

'Sara does, mostly,' I said. 'The boys don't seem to have grown to it yet.'

'My stepmother would be disgusted if I didn't,' Tony said. 'Or my father, come to that. She's a doctor, a GP. She has evening surgery and urgent visits to do before dinner, so Dad and I cook. Sharing chores is right. Seems to me you're put upon.'

With that he thanked me gravely for an interesting day, assured me he'd be with me early tomorrow, and departed. 'I'll have to telephone Sara later,' he said.

If the ambulancemen had been defensive in giving their evidence, the twenty-six year-old casualty officer, Dr Cartwright, was aggressive. Yes, he snapped in reply to David Plunkett's questions, he remembered that Friday night in April last only too well. It had been an exceptionally busy night, and he'd been exhausted before he began work by weeks of inadequate sleep. In addition one of the three nurses on duty with him had gone off sick halfway through the evening and there'd been no replacement. He considered it disgraceful.

Yes, he had examined Mrs Hamad. She was definitely under the influence of alcohol. He had known by the smell of her breath. He would call it overpowering. There were contusions on her face and body, but they were not life-threatening. No, she had been unable to speak, though she moaned faintly. He had looked for injuries to the head and found none. No friend or neighbour was with her; he could only deduce by what he saw.

To me he said, 'No, he had not suspected a broken back. He had no reason to do so. He had patients urgently requiring his attention, therefore he had decided to put her in a quiet room to sober up. Twenty minutes later, no more, he had gone to check her condition and found her dead. He added that he did not believe anything the hospital could have done would have saved her life.

The jury were sympathetic to Dr Cartwright's evidence; breaths were sucked in, heads were shaken in disapproval of National Health Service limitations. The pathologist's evidence, and, in particular, the photographs they were shown of Mrs Hamad's injuries, riveted them.

Dr Barrington was in his fifties, a grey bespectacled man with a high-domed head and a long nose. In reply to prosecution questions he told the court that the cause of death was a broken back, brought about, in his opinion, by a fall of some forty to fifty feet. Extensive damage to the heels of the deceased supported this conclusion, as would the compression bruises on the torso and on the face. In laymen's terms, the force of a fall from a great height would cause waves of jarring to a body, resulting in lines of marks.

We looked at a photograph of Mrs Hamad, lying dead and naked on a slab. The compression bruises of which the pathologist spoke were visible as rings, almost like tiger stripes, across her body, and similar marks crossed her cheeks. Under the mortuary lights the body looked putty-coloured and bony, with a poor, pitted skin. A pathetic relict.

We were told that Mrs Hamad had nearly four times the legal drink-driving limit of alcohol in her body at the time of death.

I rose to put my questions.

143

'Dr Barrington, did you notice any bruising other than the compression marks on the body?'

'No.'

'Were what looks like bad black eyes caused by the jarring of the fall?'

'Yes, that is how it appears.'

'There were no indications that any person had battered her, that day or previously?'

'None that I could see.'

'No scratches even?'

'None.'

I glanced at the jury. They stared back, impassive. I sighed.

I scrutinised the photographs, leafing through them. There was something that had puzzled me, something odd I'd noted earlier . . . There it was!

'If you'd look at the photograph of Mrs Hamad on the slab, Dr Barrington . . . yes, that's the one. There appear to be dark marks on the palms of the hands. Do you see what I mean? Are those bruises?'

The pathologist took off his spectacles and short-sightedly lifted the photograph close to his long nose. He said: 'Ah, yes. I have no bruises in my medical notes. I remember it as black paint – very old heavily leaded paint, like oven blacking, which was stuck to her hands.'

In a flash of illumination I saw the scrawny figure tottering drunkenly on the windowsill, grabbing for the decaying pipe barely within reach, saw the sticklike fingers slipping helplessly on its greasy surface, saw her plummet to the concrete below.

While the jury peered at the photograph I swung round to the solicitor behind me and in a rapid mutter asked him to get hold of someone, some clerk, some enquiry agent, to go at once to Nunhead Buildings and obtain a sample of the paint on that drainpipe.

Tony's eyes lit up. 'Oh, wowie, yes!' he muttered.

By lunchtime the next day I was able to tell David Plunkett that we had obtained a specimen of the paint and it tallied with the pathologist's description. He raised his eyebrows, shrugged his shoulders and grinned. He would accept that Mrs Hamad must have held on to that pipe if it produced that particular mark. 'I shan't challenge it,' he said.

The taped interviews having been played to the jury the previous afternoon, and the police officers' evidence dealt with that morning, the prosecution case had closed at lunch-time. Now I put my client into the witness box.

My efforts to get Mr Hamad cleaned up had resulted in some improvement; at least he had shaved properly and his clothes were not visibly dirty. In giving his evidence he was nervous and mumbled at first, but the court interpreter patiently ensured he understood the questions and relayed his answers.

No, he had not thrown his wife from the window. He would never do such a thing; he was not a man of violence. Perhaps she had climbed from the window? He would never have imagined she would. He would not have locked her in if he had thought that. Yes, when she was drunk she thought she could do anything.

No, he said of his apparent confession. No, he had not understood what the police were asking. It had been a nightmare for him, that evening, that night. His wife had not been an easy woman, but suddenly she was dead, and she was all he had in England. He had needed to weep for her, but all the time there had been questions, questions, questions.

Under cross-examination he maintained that he had said, 'Yes, yes, yes! because the police demanded it, because his mind was muddled with shock, because all he wanted was peace.

145

His bloodhound eyes were damp with tears. The jury stirred in their seats, embarrassed by his emotion. The judge's face was carved in granite.

On the way home Tony told me he'd definitely decided to become a barrister. 'It's something real,' he said, looking pleased with himself. 'You're where the action takes place, influencing people. Making sure that justice is done.'

It was good that he was enthusiastic; young people need enthusiasm to carry them over all those academic hurdles they have to face. And I wished my own young could each have so clear a vision of their future lives. But I didn't want Tony to view a career at the Bar through some rose-coloured glow.

'That's great. But please, no sentimentality. Life at the criminal Bar is not a crusade against injustice and police mistakes or malice – far from it. Oh, they exist all right, but they're rare. On the whole the system works as fairly as any system can.'

He shifted in his seat. 'But you take your cases seriously.'

'Always. But many of my clients deserve to be behind bars. They're hardened professional criminals. They go for a trial like they might go in for the pools – hoping for the unexpected win.'

'You sound cynical, Mrs Bateman!'

'Not cynical. Realistic. My job is to ensure they haven't been framed for a crime they've not committed and try for a reasonably short sentence.'

'Mmm. Prison's never a positive option, is it?'

'Let's put it like this. There are basically two categories of offender – those who have a problem, and those who are a problem. The first are often inadequate people, poorly educated, often unemployed, in debt. There may be a difficult wife, or too many children, or chronic illness.

146

Under pressure they commit petty offences. They can be helped. The probation service does a great deal here. But for those who are a problem, who see crime as a way of life, who enjoy the kick of excitement a burglary gives, or to whom violence is nothing, then prison is a necessity, however unpleasant.'

'Those who have a problem and those who are a problem,' Tony mused. 'Mr Hamad's one of the first group, isn't he? I like that analysis. It makes sense. It's clever. Perhaps I ought to read some criminology.'

When we reached my house I asked him if he wanted to come in and see Sara. It might improve her temper, so sour of recent weeks.

'No, thanks,' he said. 'We were out last night. I mustn't be tempted again.'

'Cinema good?'

'Yes, terrific. But right now I feel inspired to work!'

On Thursday morning I called the educational psychologist on behalf of my client. Mrs Croft was a tall middle-aged woman with a brisk no-nonsense manner. She informed the court that she had submitted the defendant, through an interpreter, to various standard tests. The results had shown him to be a man of barely normal intelligence. His command of English she dismissed as: 'No greater than your average two year old's!' He had a vocabulary of around a hundred basic words and he understood a number of others in context.

Yes, he liked to please people by pretending to comprehend more than he did. Yes, it would be a matter of pride with him.

His vocabulary in Turkish was also poor. He understood only half the number of words that would be used by an intelligent educated person.

In reply to questions from the prosecution she agreed that, yes, he could lead a normal life. But it would be a struggle for him, particularly in this country. Yet he had succeeded over a period of nearly two years? Yes, so she understood.

My last two witnesses were the man from the take-away food shop who had sold Mr Hamad his kebabs, and the enquiry agent.

The first could say little of any real assistance to my client. Yes, he had definitely seen Mr Hamad that evening, but as to the time, between seven and eight o'clock, say. Pressed, he thought probably about half-past seven. No, he could not be definite. No, he seemed perfectly normal.

The enquiry agent was far more specific with his evidence. He presented a cloth black with the crumbling paint and soot of ages and told us on oath that it had come from the drainpipe that passed at an angle to the side of the bedroom window.

The pathologist, re-called, confirmed that the black substance on the cloth was similar to that which he had found on the dead woman's hands.

My speech for the defence ended the day, to Tony's delight.

'The jury will go away with your words ringing in their ears,' he told me as we drove along the Cromwell Road. 'And there'll be all night for them to sink in. I don't see how they could possibly convict. You made it very clear that his so-called confession was rubbish, and any fool could see how she must have tried in her drunken state to scramble down the pipe and gone crashing to her death. If he'd thrown her from the window, how'd she get that black on her hands?'

His Honour Judge Morton summed up next morning, straight down the line, presenting the facts clearly and concisely, ending with the words: 'The essence of this case, members of the jury, is, surely, whether the defendant's confession is true, or whether he signified agreement to the case put to him by the officers without any real understanding. You will convict if the confession is true, you will acquit if you feel if it is not true, or may not be true. But, before you can convict, you must be sure that it is true. Now, members of the jury, retire and consider your verdict.'

One hour . . .

'What's taking them so long?' Tony wanted to know.

Two hours . . .

'They should know their minds by now, for God's sake!'

Three hours . . .

Tony paced the floor. 'This is silly,' he said disgustedly. 'What a collection of . . .' Rude word, for which he apologised. 'It's the pressure,' he explained.

Four hours . . . Tony was beyond speech. I felt wrung out.

Four hours and twenty-two minutes. The jury returned.

'You have reached a verdict?'

'We have.'

'And that is . . .?'

'Not guilty.'

'And that is the verdict of you all?'

'It is.'

Tony gave me a fright by hissing: 'Sensational!' in my ear; Simon Goldstone shook my hand and congratulated me on an unexpected win; Mr Hamad, lost at first as to what to do with himself, thanked me in even worse English than normal: 'Most thank you, very much good! Very thank you, Mizz Bateman. Now I home go Cyprus. England no more bad come.'

David Plunkett was congratulating me on pulling the carpet from under his feet when the usher plucked at my gown. 'The judge would be glad to see you in his room, if

149

you would be so good. On a matter that has nothing to do with this case.'

I excused myself and followed him, puzzled as to what he could want of me.

Judge Morton rose as I entered and smiled. 'You handled that case with skill. No more than I would have expected from you, but still, I thought I should say it was excellently done.'

Praise from Judge Morton was rare and to be prized. I thanked him.

'Now, would you be going back to Chambers tonight? Or soon? I borrowed some books from your Head of Chambers and for obvious reasons I'd rather not post them.' He indicated a Harrods bag bulging with hefty tomes. 'Perhaps you could return them to him? I'd be most grateful.'

'I expect to call in there early next week. Would that be suitable?'

'Certainly.'

He passed me the heavy bag and I turned to go.

'A moment. Have you applied to be an assistant recorder yet?'

'I've applied, but I've not heard of any decision.'

'Right,' he said, jerking his heavy head in approval. 'I shall give you my full backing. You may be assured of that.'

As Judge Morton was a senior judge whose opinion would be sought, this was especially good news.

I thanked him and went to drive Tony back to Richmond, warmed by his words.

As I was dropping him off outside his house, Tony turned to me. 'If you hadn't thought of everything, and asked all those questions, and tested every possibility,' he said, 'then the right answer would never have emerged. And that poor innocent fool would've been locked up for

150

years. Hell, that's horrifying, isn't it? A lazy barrister who thought his client probably guilty anyway could easily let a case like that go by default. I've learned a lot from you this week, and I can't tell you how grateful I am. Sara's lucky to have a mother like you.'

I blinked, pleased but embarrassed. 'Well, thanks for the praise. But you've been helpful, too. You took a good note, and, more than that, you discussed the case in endless detail with me in the car, and that made me focus on the points that mattered. I wish you the very best of luck in your career. If you need any further advice or help, you can always come to me.'

I drove on, relieved that it was the weekend. Dear God, I was tired, tired to my bones. It had been a tough week, and I'd been up late the previous night, making notes on my speech for the defence. Richard had grumbled his way off to bed without me. I'd have to work late on Sunday, too, on the final preparations for the mortgage fraud I was starting on Monday. Right now I must do the weekend shopping, thankful as always that Richmond's food shops stayed open late on a Friday night. But in between, some-time, somehow, I would find a time to unwind with my family.

12

'Lust is evil!' A small woman in a battered black velvet hat emerged abruptly from the doors of Reading Crown Court. 'Beware of the lures and wiles of the devil in your body!' she trumpeted, while homebound solicitors, jurymen and court clerks turned to stare and grin uneasily. 'Moderate your eating to ease your body from Satan's snares!'

The car park, once a military parade ground, had heard many orders bellowed over the long years of its existence, but never any quite like these. The woman's eyes travelled towards me; she called something I could not catch. I unlocked my car and slid hastily inside. Perhaps she had been listening to the sexual abuse case in Court 3. Perhaps she was part of it. An usher made a hurried way towards her.

'Moderate your married love to be close to your child,' the voice intoned.

Strange. As if love could be divided into slices, like cake. And nothing would persuade me to moderate my love for Richard; it was the solid centre of my life. or had the woman used the word lust? Lust? I wouldn't want to moderate our sexual relationship, or to denigrate it by calling it lust. In twenty years our love-making had not lost its magic . . . or had it?

The air smelled coldly dank. I turned on the car engine, shivering. We'd made love rarely these last weeks. After Oliver's death it had seemed indecent to enjoy each other's bodies, to revel in that most vividly alive of all sensations. Since then we had both been low in spirits. Frequently there had been Mother-in-law lurking in the next room. I realised that I had been using the subterfuges of the reluctant partner – tiredness, work to keep me up till the small hours, a headache – to put Richard off. He had accepted my rebuffs without question, turning silently away. I had been grateful for his forbearance; now, thinking about the implications, I was uneasy.

The little woman was being whisked away round a corner. I sent her a silent message of thanks. The effect of her words had been the opposite of her intentions, but she had alerted me to a real danger.

Tonight, I told myself, tonight we'll make love. I wanted Richard to hold me with passion, to blot out the misery and the worry, to reassure me with all kinds of familiar declarations. I drove home in a haze of sensual thoughts, planning all the delicious things we might do and say to each other. And afterwards, I thought dreamily, afterwards, when we talk together without barriers as we always do, I'll confide my anxieties about Sara and her increasingly wayward behaviour, and about Ollie and his withdrawal, and pave the way to a proper discussion of their problems.

With teenage children in the house it becomes impossible to make love when you will; they are always about, alert eyes noticing everything. I wanted my offspring to have a broad education, but not that broad. Sex had acquired its fixed hours, as meals do. Halfway through the evening I had a bath, a deep, scented, bubbly one; it seemed as good a way of passing the time as any. I lay in a voluptuous stupor, watching the foam eddy when I stirred my fingers and toes, listening to the distant sounds of Richard playing a Haydn sonata, the C major. It had a cheerful, almost flippant opening, that one, I liked it.

I was galvanised into emerging by a finger that leaned long and vehemently on the front door bell. I cursed whoever it was and cursed more furiously when Danny rapped to tell me it was Angela. I sensed trouble, for which she would demand maximum attention, but my head was filled with Richard and our loving linked bodies. How could I push out Richard for Angela? 'Say I'm in the bath.'

'I told her. She says she'll wait.' Danny lowered his voice, not very successfully: 'She's in an awful jittery state. Lucinda's been arrested.'

'Dear God! Whatever for?'

'She didn't say. Shall I tell her you're coming?'

'Yes, yes. I'll be down shortly.'

What had Lucinda been up to? Demonstrating with Females for Freedom – with brickbats? Joy-riding in some poor fool's stolen car? Drunk and disorderly? Whatever it was, I prayed Sara was not involved. Had Angela come for a sympathetic ear, for counsel's advice, or to warn me? Sara was out, baby-sitting again. I pulled on a dressing-gown; Angela might depart more rapidly if a state of undress hinted at an early night. A wasted hope – Angela was in no state to notice anything, still less to draw inferences.

'They actually dragged us both off to the police station! Would you believe it? For something as trivial as cannabis and a trifle of cocaine!'

'Yes, I can.' Richard twisted round on the piano stool. 'The police don't regard possession of any prohibited drug as trivial. It's their job to eliminate it.'

'Oh, but that stuff's not dangerous, not like heroin or

155

crack. I mean, really, Richard, they behaved as if they'd found corpses littering the place!' Her fingers writhed together as she poured out her indignation over the accusations the police had made against her as well as Lucinda and told of the horrors of having one's house searched. 'Like burglars – the sense of total desecration. I shall never be able to meditate in my bedroom again. Never! The police dog lifted its leg against the doorpost, ugh, and they turned out all our drawers, no please or thank you – all my most intimate things. You should see the mess!'

I cut through the lamentations: 'To what extent is Sara involved in this?'

Angela stopped in mid-flow, peering through a frizzled mat of faded red hair, clearly surprised. 'Sara's not involved, not that I know of. That's not her scene, is it? I mean, she's bound to have tried pot at parties once or twice. But, hell, everyone does that.' She accepted a whisky from Richard and took a couple of gulps, saying, as if it excused everything: 'It was Dave, she was keeping it for him. The police have raided his house once already. We never thought they'd go for Lucinda.'

What sympathy I'd had for Angela was evaporating rapidly. So hard, coping alone with that erratic young woman, I'd thought, something like this was bound to happen. But as it became evident that Angela knew what was going on, or, at least, had a fair idea, so my feelings of commiseration dwindled. Why hadn't she stopped this nonsense? Did she consider a criminal conviction of no importance? Wasn't she worried by possible connections with drug-pushers? She appeared to have no normal protective maternal reactions. But then Angela never did have. She believed in Fate, from which there could be no protection. If she were fated to have a difficult daughter then she could only lament that fact with sympathetic friends: poor Angela, feeding on sympathy as others feed on success. Now she was hinting that we might lend her the money if the magistrates imposed a fine. Richard pointed out, not ungently, that Miles was Lucinda's father; he would have to be told; he should pay.

'Oh God,' she wailed, 'but he'll lecture us for hours, you can't imagine!'

We banned Sara from Lucinda's house for the present. She was furious: events had happened in her absence; it was ridiculous that we did not know the finer details and would not let her rush off to Lucinda to find them out.

'But I can't not talk to her – she's my friend.'

'A bad friend,' we said.

When Sara was upset she swung erratically between the offensive and the defensive. 'Christ, you're so silly – you get everything out of proportion. You'd think she'd beaten an old lady to death, the way you're going on,' she said, unconsciously echoing Angela as she raged about the kitchen, kicking chair legs. 'OK, Dave's a fool to touch coke,' she said, sitting down to argue her case, 'but pot does no harm, for God's sake. I don't like it much – all right, yes, I did try it once – once, I said – but for those who do, well, it's no worse than having a cigarette or a drink.'

We spent half an hour not resolving that argument, mainly because none of us knew enough about it and each kept accusing the others of ignorance. We were interrupted by Danny: 'Hell, if it really does lower the sperm count I don't think I'll bother!' and by Ollie, drooping white-faced in the doorway. 'Please could you keep your voices down? I'm trying to go to sleep.' I apologised to Ollie, accompanied him upstairs, gave him a kiss, which he permitted but did not return, and went back down to suggest that bed would be a good idea. It was midnight.

My thoughts of a night of love long since discarded, I wanted only cool sheets and oblivion.

Sara slouched to the door, her dark brows lowered in a scowl. 'Anyway, I shall see Lucinda at school,' she said defiantly.

'You won't, you know,' Danny pointed out. 'She goes in front of the magistrates tomorrow. And I bet you she'll be suspended from school. Mr Hamerton's had enough of her cheek already – he'll leap at the chance.'

'She won't care. It's what she wants. She's bored with fucking school. She's virtually eighteen – she'll leave home and do her own thing. God, I wish I could!'

My family had long had the habit of drifting into the kitchen while I prepared a meal; during termtime it was the best time to catch me for a gossip or a heart-to-heart. It was a wet evening at the beginning of November, a couple of days after the cannabis argument. I had driven home from Reading and was now putting the finishing touches to a quorn and mushroom pie for Sara and a turkey and mushroom pie for the rest of us, while Danny leaned against the fridge crunching raw carrots and Sara cut pastry leaves with the air of one conferring high favours.

'There you are,' she said, putting down the knife. 'Now you can show off your smart cookery. Don't know why you bother, though. It's only going to be eaten.'

'Impress Grandma,' Danny muttered. 'Show the old bag that she can cook as well as defend incestuous fathers.'

Sara tugged a bottle of varnish from a pocket in her jeans and uncapped it. 'I don't know why you're always going on about Grandma,' she said. 'She's all right. And she's right about Mum being wrong in what she's doing, too.' She laid a preliminary layer of red across her nails.

'Mum's not . . . No! Must you do that in here?' Danny protested. 'It's unhygienic and it stinks.'

She shrugged her indifference, painting carefully.

'What are you doing it for, anyway? You aren't supposed to be going anywhere tonight, only baby-sitting.'

Sara gave him a distinctly unfriendly look. 'So what? I can look nice for baby-sitting, can't I? Besides, I'm going to a party with Tony on Friday night.'

'He'll get a big thrill from your bloody red talons,' Danny jeered. 'God, they look revolting.'

'Couldn't be worse than those bloody red blobs on your face. You'd make any girl puke.'

Danny grunted his annoyance. A large hand rose to finger three pimples on his chin. 'I can't help those. Christ, Sara, do you practise to be a bitch, or does it come naturally?'

'Oh, sod off, you whingeing wimp . . .'

'Stop it, both of you,' I snapped. 'And cut out the foul language.'

Yet another exchange of unpleasantries. The unceasing friction of the last weeks worried me; I saw enmity growing between Sara and the boys and wished I knew how to end it.

The front door opened and five seconds later Bertha surged into the kitchen, a tidal wave of wet black cloth, bulging shopping bags and dripping umbrella. 'Such nasty weather,' she told me disapprovingly, as if I'd specially laid on the downpour for her inconvenience.

Richard emerged from the study to help her out of the wet coat. 'Put it on a hanger, dear,' she instructed him and passed him the umbrella. 'Put it up. I don't want it drying all creased.' She lowered her wide backside on to a chair. 'Now, you'll want to hear my news!'

'What's that?' Richard enquired, dutifully carrying coat

and umbrella into the hall. She waited for his return.

'I think I've found a house to suit me! In Walton-on-Thames!'

We could hardly believe our ears. She was taken aback by our jubilation, counselling caution. 'It needs a lot of doing – and you never can tell about the electrics or the drains.' She shook her head significantly.

'Come on, Grandma,' Sara encouraged, blowing on her finger nails. 'It can't be that bad or you wouldn't fancy it.'

'It does have its points,' she admitted. 'Tudor-style, built between the wars – now that was a good time. It's in a good position, too, the church at the end of the road, shops and buses near – and the price is about right. But I'll say no more till I've read the surveyor's report.'

She was ever wary of admitting to enthusiasm. She needed to be in a position to say: 'I told you so!' if anything should go wrong.

Before we sat down to eat Richard suggested opening a bottle of wine: 'To do justice to Annabel's cooking and to celebrate Mother's new house.'

His mother sniffed; from her point of view perhaps he might have chosen his priorities more carefully. At the table she stared as he selected glasses and poured Château Mouton Baronne Philippe. 'Surely you aren't going to waste good wine on those two young pups of yours, Richard?'

'Oh no!' Danny flashed, amazement in his voice. 'We're going to lap up the puddles outside!'

Ollie exploded. It was the first time in weeks that I'd heard his choking giggle. The more he tried to suppress it beneath his grandmother's glare, the more it burst out again. The rest of us joined in helplessly.

Bertha made a great play of spreading her napkin on her lap. Finally she stretched her lips into the semblance of a smile. 'Very witty.'

Richard put his hand on Danny's shoulder. 'You know, Dan, sarcasm is meant to be a subtle art. Yours has all the subtlety of a flying hammer!'

Sara fidgeted, prodding patterns in the tablecloth with her knife. 'I saw Lucinda today,' she announced. We looked at her. 'I couldn't avoid her,' she said defensively. 'I couldn't turn round and run off, could I?'

'Agreed,' Richard said, accepting his plateful of turkey pie. 'So?'

'She's definitely leaving school . . .'

'Expelled as a druggie,' Danny muttered.

'God, what rubbish! Luce doesn't use drugs. She was suspended . . .'

'While they discussed it.'

'Well, they haven't done anything. So you're wrong. Her father telephoned Angela and said she was to be removed and she was.' Sara closed her mouth firmly over a piece of pie.

'The governors must have been pleased,' Richard said. 'No need for them to take an embarrassing decision.'

She swallowed. 'Lucinda was amazed. Her father'd gone on and on about her having a proper education – just like you do – and then suddenly he gave in. He paid her fine, too. But he's done even more than that – you'll never guess what! He came to see her yesterday and he's going to set her up in business!'

We all raised our heads. Richard said: 'Good God!' And Danny: 'He must be bloody mad!' Sara looked satisfied by these reactions. 'What sort of business?' I asked.

'A boutique. Way-out fashions. You know. Just a small one, but her father says she can do as she likes with it, except he's to check her accounts every month. She's terrifically pleased.'

I had a momentary vision of Lucinda's window display – skimpy dresses cut asymmetrically, gold thigh-length

161

sweaters, purple leather trousers – and wondered whether her shop would be in this area, and if so who would buy such items.

'The girl sounds thoroughly spoilt to me,' said Bertha. 'I hope she realises how lucky she is to have a father who is rich and generous enough to do such a thing.'

'Some people do have all the luck,' Sara agreed enviously.

'To work in a shop?' I said. 'Fussy women, stuffy changing rooms and tired feet? You'd hate it.'

'I don't know,' she said doubtfully. 'If it was my own I wouldn't mind. But anyway, to have an opportunity like that – to leave school and do what you want. God, I wish it were me.'

'You don't really want to leave,' Richard stated. 'You just have these periods of restlessness. Everybody does at your age.'

'Most girls wouldn't want to waste their time with books,' Bertha observed helpfully. 'Jane was the only one of mine who did. Very strange. The other two couldn't wait to get away from school. Sara's just like her Aunty Valerie.'

Richard ignored her. 'What's wrong with school, Sara?'

She shrugged. 'It's such a drag. Take English Literature. The reading's okay, but Miss Cole makes us dissect every dreary bit of every book till I want to throw it at her. According to her virtually everything has social significance, and if there's something that can't be socially significant, then it's meaningful detail.' She took a mouthful of her wine, swallowed, and added resentfully: 'And she's got hairy legs, too.'

'It all sounds most trying,' Richard sympathised, his lips twitching. 'But you know, if you hack through the jargon and the clichés, she's largely right. To create believable characters the details must be perfect – otherwise they're cardboard cutouts, not three-dimensional individuals.'

'Oh God, three-dimensional. Don't mention three-dimensional people to me!' Sara managed to make the words sound like particularly filthy expletives.

'Why not?'

'They're always on about that – Mr Hammerton and the other teachers – character training, all that stuff. Do you realise I'm going to be a three-dimensional person when I leave?' She rolled her eyes upward until only the whites showed, fluttering the lids rapidly.

'And what is a three-dimensional person?' I asked.

'God knows, but that's why we have to go to assemblies and be caring and out-going!' She almost spat the last words, so great was her disdain.

'Tell them about the caring classes,' Danny said.

'Yes, please do,' Richard encouraged her.

'Well, they're on a Wednesday afternoon. It used to be the games afternoon, but most of us don't want to be jolly hockey sticks any more. The boys used to have Cadet Corps, too, for those who wanted, but now that war and violence are out that's gone, so we have Caring instead.

'And what does that involve?'

'Oh, there's a lot of options you can do, a different one each term: Caring for Endangered Species, Caring for the Environment and the Atmosphere, Caring for the Whale, Caring and Human Rights – that's about justice and equality, all that. I'm doing that this term. Trouble is, there's no textbooks – no money for them anyway. So what we get taught depends on who teaches it, and most of them are useless. Ms Cropper – she's our teacher – belongs to Females for Freedom like Lucinda and me, and she's into a Charter for Women. We reckon she's good, but most of the boys reckon she goes over the top. Oh, and there's Caring and Drama – psychiatric drama – where

163

they act out zany neurotic things. That idiot Dave does that, it's ultra-trendy.'

'I never heard anything so ridiculous,' my mother-in-law said and for once I was in agreement with her.

Sara was well into her stride now. 'And we still have these awful moral education lessons where we discuss sex and abortion and drugs and things like should we have prisons.'

'It's to make you think,' Richard said dourly.

'It makes me cringe. This week we had to get into groups, two boys with two girls, to discuss when we think it's right to go to bed together. You can't imagine! It's fine talking about these things with friends when you're in the mood – but not from cold with Dave trying to be all hard and being plain crude and that fat Samantha nearly in tears . . .'

'It's absolutely disgusting,' said Bertha, outraged, spraying crumbs of pastry from her mouth. 'Richard, you must speak to the headmaster about it. I won't have my grandchildren subjected to such pernicious nonsense.'

'I doubt I can do much,' he said. 'It appears to be the modern way of dealing with such issues. Personal viewpoints, not immutable laws.'

Her face settled into lines of sour disapproval. 'Then I shall write myself. Someone must act. The children will grow up with no moral guidelines at all.'

'Views on morals have changed and are still changing, particularly with the advent of AIDS,' Richard pointed out wearily. 'These classes are at least an attempt to show different perceptions, to try to counter old prejudices – or even new ones, with any luck.'

'Look, this is all very interesting,' Sara interrupted, scattering angry looks about the table, 'but we were talking about me leaving school.'

There was a brief pause. Richard said: 'I hoped we'd got

past that one. All right, Sara, leaving school to do what?'

Surprisingly, she seemed disconcerted by this question. 'Well, I don't know. Something interesting. I wouldn't mind working with small children – they're okay. Or in a shop.'

'Where? What as? Leading to what?' Richard passed his empty plate to me. 'Pudding, darling? Sara, I suggest you find out just what interesting jobs are available with your few qualifications before you rush to leave.'

'I knew you'd say I had to stay.'

'I have not, as you would know if you listened. When you have a positive suggestion we'll consider it. Till then, keep going. Believe me, being unemployed would be considerably more boring.'

I collected plates and carried them to the kitchen where lemon creams were waiting in the fridge. When I came back Mother-in-law was again making her opinions known.

'If she was my daughter I'd have her out of that place straight away. She'll get no benefit from the rubbish they're filling her head with. All that complicated mathematics and chemistry she did last year – what for?'

'To keep her options open should she want to go on to higher education,' Richard said tersely.

'But she doesn't,' his mother stated. 'Now, I don't want to interfere, Richard . . .'

'Then stop doing so,' he replied.

Bertha sat up more straight-backed than ever, breathing deeply in an obvious I-am-controlling-my-injured-feelings way. Pastry crumbs rose and fell on her bosom like scum on the river at high tide. She sniffed loudly and sniffed again.

Ollie looked at her with distaste. 'Do you mind, Grandma?' he said. 'Your sniffing gets up my nose!'

Danny's delighted snorts at this infelicitous remark

stopped suddenly as Bertha stood, red in the face, to vent upon Ollie the fury she did not dare to vent upon Richard. 'What a nasty insolent boy you are! How dare you speak to me like that? You've been brought up to have no consideration, no respect for others who know better than you . . .'

We were stunned by the vehemence of her outburst.

Richard attempted to intervene. 'Mother . . .'

'He has far too high an opinion of himself. He's been ridiculously spoilt. That Mr Malet, leaving him all that money – what for, I'd like to know?' Sticky foam appeared on her lips and her big bulk shook as she shouted her rage.

Ollie's eyes were huge with shock. 'I didn't mean . . .'

She pushed her face at him across the table. 'At times,' she hissed as Ollie shrank back, 'at times I can't believe you could be any grandchild of mine!'

13

She had gone too far. She saw it from our horrified faces. She stopped, licked her lips and sat down, passing a hand over her face to settle the mask. The dour transformation was as frightening as the anger. For the remainder of the meal she sat stony-faced and silent. Afterwards she cleared the table, her fat hands moving efficiently among my china, her voice creaking out how good my cooking was these days, thanking me for looking after her so well during the trying time of her house-hunting, using compliments like fresh-air spray to sweeten the atmosphere.

Despite her efforts the warning was clear. Mother-in-law knew what she knew. Oliver's will had made certainty of the suspicions she'd shared with Clare. Although she could not speak them directly – she was too cautious to do that without proof – yet, like the witches in *Macbeth*, she too could be an imperfect speaker, dropping poisonous hints, stirring up trouble, her eyes flickering like snakes' tongues over our faces to gauge the reaction. Thank God Richard drove her back to Bromley that night. I could not have stuck her for another day – not another hour.

Ten days later, as I drove through Richmond on a Friday

evening to pick up Ollie from a violin lesson, my mind was moving uneasily through the events of the last months and particularly of that evening. I could not tell whether the rest of the family understood her insinuations or whether they dismissed such words as merely an outbreak of ugly-tempered spite. They were silent in the evenings now, shut into bedrooms or study; even Danny's flow of schoolboy wit seemed to have dried up. My mind filled with visions of more nastiness to come, dividing the family one from another. Bertha was returning tonight: the surveyor's report on the new house had been satisfactory; an offer had been made and accepted. Now she needed to measure for carpets and curtains, to judge where her furniture would best fit, to plan redecorations. She would sleep with us tonight, leaving tomorrow evening.

The car slid on the greasy road, its back-end swinging dangerously close to a parked Jaguar. I had been speeding up, not concentrating, tired from the day in court, tense with my thoughts. Beneath the car wheels a sludge of wet and crushed autumn leaves made driving a precarious business. I slowed, forcing myself to relax my grip on the steering wheel.

It was a cold evening, damp and still. The lights were on in the streets, each one wearing its halo of drizzle. The windscreen wipers were working inefficiently, thrashing protestingly over the glass: like my brain, I thought, unable to clear away the problem.

The most important thing was to talk to Ollie. I had no idea how I was to approach the subject, only that the impossible had to be achieved: discovering whether his grandmother's nastiness had penetrated his mind without arousing his suspicions if it had not. For days I had tried to find an opportunity but I could never quite manage it. I wondered whether he was being evasive or whether I was being unusually slow. When I went to his room he muttered about schoolwork, bit at the end of his pen and glanced at his watch. This was not the atmosphere I needed; I left him to his mathematics.

The river was a dark emptiness beneath the bridge; the thickening rain hid any reflections. I shivered. This was an evening for staying indoors before blazing fires, enjoying a serial on television while we balanced plates of hot and spicy food on our laps. But we did not watch programmes together now.

I saw Ollie and his teacher before I'd parked in the cul-de-sac in Twickenham. They were framed in the centre of the pre-war bay window, the overhead light glaring down on their passionately bowing arms. Mr Zorab was barely Ollie's height, with the kind of swept-back long hair that film directors appear to associate with musical talent. Today he was wearing a banana yellow polo-neck pullover and lime green trousers, a restrained outfit by his standards. Normally his tastes ran to boldly checked trousers like American golfers' and shirts printed with dancing girls. Ollie had viewed him with amazement and suspicion on the occasion of his first lesson, but before a month was out he was able to assure me: 'He's super so long as you don't let yourself look at him.'

I flicked on the interior light to check my watch. Five minutes early: five minutes peace. The rain was drumming on the car roof, a soothing sound now that the car was still. I groped in my bag for one of my rare cigarettes and longed to stay there indefinitely, away from Ollie's silences and Sara's irritability and Mother-in-law's prowling presence.

Through the window I watched the water-distorted figures of Mr Zorab and Ollie, absorbed in their work, comic and improbable, puppets on a gaudy stage. Now they ceased playing: Mr Zorab was speaking, gesticulating, prodding at the music on the stand with his bow; now he was lifting the bow to play a passage, pausing, watching Ollie take up his bow to echo his movements; now they were playing together in solemn concentration, ending with a long slow stroke of the bow to its fullest length. A halt, then Mr Zorab flung his arms wide in appreciation. The tip of his bow hit the windowpane and even with the car windows wound up I could hear the glass tinkling on to the paving below. A jagged star appeared in the pane. The two bright figures started; Ollie's hand flashed to his mouth. Then they both doubled up in laughter I could not hear.

I opened the car door a crack to chuck out my cigarette end, thinking how Oliver would enjoy the absurd details of the scene – and then the rain spat at me and I jerked the door to, trembling with shock and wretchedness. Oliver is dead, you fool. Dead, totally gone. You'll never share this or anything else with him. Oh God, how I wished my brain would stop this betrayal. Don't snivel, I shouted silently at myself. You want to talk to Ollie – you'll never succeed if you embarrass him with tears.

Compounding my distress there was guilt. My thoughts had leapt to Oliver, but Richard was my husband and I loved him. How had this happened? The answer came swiftly and unpleasantly: because Oliver and I had always had the habit of swapping comic anecdotes, and because Richard and I were communicating less and less. A snapped: 'Richard, for God's sake, dinner's been ready these ten minutes!' or 'Richard, ask Sara to turn her music down, can't you – why does it always have to be me?' was the pattern now. The worries that were building up in my mind like winter stormclouds could not be shared with him. My desolation over Oliver had to be suppressed. For the first time in twenty years I was alone with my emotions and my fears. Sometimes I was convinced Richard must know what was in his mother's head, other times I wondered how he could be so blind. I considered bringing the whole thing out in the open, then shrank from possible results. I suppose I was longing for him to take over, to slap his bitch of a mother down, vehemently to reassure me. I resented his blindness. I listened to my voice reproaching him.

We'd always had a calm relationship, Richard and I. We had never felt the need that other lovers seem to have for those emotional bickerings that lead to intense sexual reconciliations. To me, the subjects of such squabbles carried the seeds of deeper, less easily reconcilable disagreements. In any case, I have never cared for disputes. Intellectual arguments, yes, any time; Richard and I had plenty of those, but they never descended to the level of personalities. I could not understand couples like Clare and Colin whose married lives were a series of lively battles interspersed with moments of passion – until now. Now I seemed to be occupying another woman's body, cursing him over trifles, wanting to test his affection, pushing at him for a reaction, any reaction. But Richard looked at me and disappeared into the study. And our lovemaking was minimal.

The front door opened, light spilled out and Ollie's silhouette appeared.

'Good lesson?' I asked as he wriggled his violin case and himself awkwardly into the car.

'Mmm. Fine. Ouch, this rain! Did you see . . . ?'

'The window smash? Yes, I did!'

'Isn't Mr Zorab hilarious? He's always doing crazy things like that. He doesn't care a bit.'

He was cheerful, amused by the incident. This was a good time to talk, relaxed in the impersonal shadows, tucked in away from the rain. The car drew away from the curb, the headlights stabbing the darkness. I cleared my throat.

'I'm starved,' Ollie said. 'What are we eating tonight?'

It was his favourite. 'Hungarian goulash and jacket potatoes. They'll be ready when we get in.'

He sighed contentedly, leaning back in his seat. I hated to destroy this mood, but I had to speak. 'Grandma's coming for the night,' I began cautiously.

'Oh no!'

'Had you forgotten?'

'Nobody told me.'

'Oh.' That was likely enough. With everyone in separate rooms so much of the time it was impossible to remember to whom I'd told what. 'Sorry.'

'Why've we got her again?' he asked querulously. 'I thought we'd got rid of her.'

'Things to do with her new house.'

'I loathe her coming. She hates me.'

A simple statement, but it knocked the breath from my body. I sucked it back again to protest stupidly: 'Oh, darling, you can't say that about your grandma.'

'Why not? It's the truth. And I hate *her*.' He didn't say it viciously but with an icy calm that frightened me.

'Why?'

The word hung in the air. A long moment passed. The windscreen wipers moaned their reluctant way across the weeping window. I gripped the wheel and peered at the treacherous surface ahead.

'Why?'

'I just do,' he muttered finally and relapsed into childish inarticulacy. 'She's horrible, is all.'

'You mean the things she said last time she was here? She lost her temper. People say things they don't mean when they're tired and cross. I expect she was ashamed afterwards.' A feeble attempt to neutralise the burning acid of her words.

'Not just that,' he said with cold scorn.

172

'What then?'

Silence. I sensed rather than saw his shoulders shrug. We were both staring rigidly ahead at the sodden streets.

I asked with difficulty: 'Does she . . . get at you . . . about Oliver's bequests?'

No answer.

'Tell me, Ollie. I can't help unless you say what. . . .'

He burst out furiously: 'She gets at me about everything, everything! You know she does.' His voice shook. 'Oh, why did you have to start this? I was feeling good for once. Now you've spoilt it. Leave me alone, can't you? Why can't everybody leave me alone?'

And that was my answer.

Sara was in a filthy mood, banging drawers, banging doors, swearing to herself as she changed to go out, swearing at anyone foolish enough to cross her path. 'Why did we have to eat so late? Bloody stupid. Just because Ollie had some fucking music lesson or something. Dan, for Chrissakes get out of that bathroom! Nobody cares about my convenience . . . nobody gives a damn if I'm late . . .'

I hunted wearily for my cigarettes in the sitting room, wishing she'd shut up and go to the silly party.

'Such language!' Bertha tutted over her coffee. 'Poor girl. No organisation.'

Richard yelled up the stairs. 'Sara, stop that noise!'

A long and unintelligible moan came back down.

'If you were so pressed for time, why not have changed before dinner? If you'll stop shrieking and swearing I'll give you a lift – will that help?'

Evidently it would. Sounds of hasty preparation continued but the decibel level dropped.

Richard appeared round the door. 'Is there petrol in your car, Annabel?'

'Drat, no, I forgot to fill up.'

'My tank's empty, too. Blast! And the garage is in the wrong direction. I'll pop round while Sara finishes ladling muck on to her face.' He vanished.

I was too strung up to sit still. I wandered round the room, smoking and fiddling with the ornaments. Many were presents from Oliver and Melissa; memories rushed back that did not fit the present atmosphere.

Sara exploded through the door, her black hair on end like a Zulu warrior, her crimson blouse open almost to the waist to reveal well-developed breasts bulging from their bra. 'Look!' she shrieked, gesturing at herself. 'Look, the bloody button's come off my blouse now, would you believe it?'

'I'll do it,' Bertha and I said in chorus. I added: 'It won't take a minute to sew on.'

An anguished wail: 'But I can't find the button and it has to match!'

A mental search of my button box revealed no red buttons. 'I'd better lend you a brooch then, Sara. Calm down.'

'What brooch?'

'My little gold knot. Take care of it though, won't you?' It was Oliver's present of many years ago. I rarely wore it now.

'Yeah, sure,' she said impatiently. 'Where . . .?'

'My dressing-table. Top left-hand drawer. In a navy jeweller's box.'

She rushed out. The house shook as she pounded upstairs.

'She should be trained to tighten buttons before they go,' my mother-in-law observed.

'Of course.'

She lifted the half-knitted sleeve of the pullover she was making for Sara. 'You shouldn't have to run around after a girl of nearly seventeen,' she said, as the needles began their stabbing run through a purl row. 'I never did.'

'No.'

A muffled curse from overhead. What catastrophe now?

'I always believed in having a mending evening every week with my girls.'

It was extraordinary how people of her type thought one would be fascinated by these domestic details. Annoyance rose to scorn but I said nothing. I poured myself a cup of coffee. It was tepid and bitter. I put it down and turned to see Sara in the doorway.

Her face somehow managed to be at once bemused and outraged. In one hand she clutched the blue box, in the other a tiny card. Both hands were stiffly outstretched as if she didn't know what to do with them.

A second before she spoke realisation came. God, I hadn't seen that card for more than twenty years; I'd forgotten its very existence. My heart pounded thunderously in my shaking body. 'Sara . . .' I reached for the card. If I had any sensible thought at all it was to hide this scene from my mother-in-law, to push Sara back through that door.

'You bitch!' she breathed. 'You fucking bitch!' She retreated a step as if I were contaminated.

'Sarah, it's not what you think . . .'

'You bitch! Oliver! All your talk about sticking to one man . . . All you say – just a load of shit! I dropped the box and when I picked it up, this . . . this was under the cottonwool!' She shook the card in my face as if she would strike me with it.

I gabbled: 'It's not true. It's old . . .'

Bertha's hand appeared from nowhere to pounce hawklike on its prey, the card and she moved away with surprising speed. Her voice boomed as if she intended the

175

whole neighbourhood to hear: perhaps she did. '"To Annabel, In memory of one happy day – and night. With my love, Oliver." Well!'

She wanted to pronounce with due solemnity upon the appalling revelation, but her lips were stretched in a rictus of triumph; she could hardly speak for pleasure. 'I always knew there was something wrong going on! My poor son. My poor Richard!'

Everything that was happening was both unreal and terrifying – like watching a horror film in an empty cinema. I spoke but no one listened. 'That was *before* Richard. When I was at university.' My voice was shaking more than my body; it sounded pathetically thin, a cat's mewing.

'Doing it in this house, I'll be bound!' my mother-in-law said. 'Always asking that Mr Malet round . . . using his wife's death as an excuse for indulging in your filthy behaviour . . . Making a fool of my son behind his back!'

'No. I didn't!'

She shook the card. 'You liar! Here's proof!'

Hot anger suddenly steamed its way through me, nauseating in its intensity. Her gleeful relish for the proof she thought she'd finally acquired was repellent. Couldn't she see how her mouthings denigrated Richard? Did she really imagine him so poor a lover that I had constantly to run to someone else for my satisfaction, so second-rate a man that I could take pleasure in deceiving him?

I managed to keep my voice low, conscious of the boys somewhere in the house. 'You may think badly of me, you foul-minded old woman, but, my God, you don't think much of your son either, do you? I've never been unfaithful to Richard. Never! That,' I indicated the card impatiently, 'that happened years and years ago.'

'Yes,' she hissed, interrupting me, 'I can believe that! About the time you started young Ollie perhaps?'

176

'No! Ollie's Richard's. Take a blood test if you like. I don't care. He's Richard's.'

'Then why is he the spitting image of Mr Malet? I never saw a boy more like his father!'

'Pure coincidence,' I said tersely.

'And his name? And his violin playing? And that money he was left?' she jeered. 'More coincidence?' Her broad face was brutally exultant, flushing purple with excitement.

The rain beat against the windows. Somewhere a door banged shut.

I turned to look at Sara. She was standing stiffly, her arms wrapped round her body, her eyes still and glaring, her bloodless lips drawn tight. I listened to her silence. I said: 'Sara! You don't believe this nonsense, do you?'

Her head jerked. She could not speak. Such naked hatred between her mother and grandmother was clearly more than she knew how to handle. She was not used to such emotional scenes; thinking herself adult she was a baby here.

'Of course she believes it,' spat Bertha. 'And that's the wickedest thing of all – to make the child suffer. That money and the violin he left to Ollie – what do you think she thought? What would anyone think?'

The knowledge of what she was doing to Sara burned into me. 'I'd hoped she'd think the truth – she's my daughter, she should know me better than this. You've built a great tissue of lies in your mind because you've always been jealous of me – you couldn't allow your evil mind to see anything *but* evil. God, can't either of you understand? Oliver cared for Ollie because they were so alike – and because he had no son of his own. Ollie filled a need in him.' Tears of fury were hot on my face. I hurled words at her like stones and they fell uselessly as leaves. 'Ollie was not Oliver's child!'

177

'What the hell is going on in here?' Richard bulked in the doorway, his dark face formidable in its anger, his huge fists clenched as if he would lash out at all of us.

No one spoke. We gazed at him in horror; our heavy breathing filled the room. A hundred half-formed sentences flashed through my brain, only to be discarded. Richard broke the silence, biting off each word as though the taste were foul in his mouth.

'Ollie could never have been Oliver's. Oliver was sterile. Ollie is mine.'

Another appalled silence. Time hung suspended while the words fought their way into our incredulous minds.

Finally his mother stuttered: 'I don't believe you.'

'Oliver had a bad attack of mumps when he was seventeen. Tests were taken. He was sterile.'

I gripped a chairback for support, the muscles in my legs trembling and jerking.

Bertha's eyes darted about the room as if seeking help from the furniture. 'He told you that as a cover-up.'

Richard said grimly: 'He told me years ago – before Annabel and I were even engaged. He would hardly tell me such a thing of himself unless it were true.'

The heavy colour had retreated from Bertha's face, the broken veins stood out in stark relief on her cheeks. 'Nevertheless,' she shoved Oliver's card at him in a last desperate effort, 'I'm sorry, Richard, but you were being deceived. I don't like having to do such a thing, but now you've heard . . . Well, look at that then!'

I made myself speak quickly. 'The gold brooch. I'm sorry, the card fell out – I didn't know it was still there. Sara found it.'

He glanced at her, a white statue in a corner, one hand still clutching the box. Comprehension flashed across his face. 'Really, Annabel! Of all the idiotic things . . .' He turned upon his mother. 'And was that the reason for this fishwives' brawl?'

'Well, I . . . you . . .' She gulped for air. 'Do you mean to tell me you knew?'

'Naturally.'

It was at this point that Sara began to cry, soft choking sobs, her face turned towards the wall.

I said: 'Oh, Sara,' weakly and started towards her. I think I wanted to tell her that I did not blame her, I blamed myself, but before I could speak she rushed from the room.

'No,' Richard snapped when I made to follow her. 'No, leave her. We'll talk to her later.' It was as if an engine inside him that had been silent had suddenly started up; he was vibrating with anger and with energy. 'I must know the extent of the damage that's been done. The boys – do they know about . . . all this?'

My mind was exhausted, my thoughts diffused. I dragged them together. 'Yes . . . No. I don't know about Danny. Ollie does, I'm certain. She's been hinting things ever since Oliver died. Richard – he was dreading her coming tonight, he said she hated him.'

'Oh my God! I must talk to him at once . . .'

'No, Richard. Wait! Not like this. Together, when we're calmer.'

He stopped by the door. 'You're right. You're quite right.' He swung round on his mother, the words coming in a snarl. 'For a woman who calls herself a Christian you have shown an incredible lack of charity. You've never stopped trying to cause trouble for Annabel. You hated having a daughter-in-law who could successfully combine both working and raising a family, and you tried to undermine her in both. When she did prosecution work you didn't know how a woman could stoop to dealing with such matters; when she was for the defence she was perverse and sick in fighting for such people. And look what your venom nearly succeeded in doing to the family, to your own grandchildren, tonight! For years I remembered the struggle you had to bring us up; I put up with you because I thought I owed you some loyalty. From now on I owe you none. Pack your bags and get out of my house – now!'

The big face stared in stupefaction. 'But my new house . . . It's raining outside . . .' Her hand went out towards his arm, placatingly. 'If I was wrong I'm prepared to apologise . . .'

'Neither of us is prepared to accept your apology. I don't want to know you. You gave no thought to my feelings in this, let alone Annabel's or the children's. If you aren't packed and gone in ten minutes, I'll throw your blasted belongings out of the window and you after them. I mean it. Now go!'

14

I allowed myself to cry that night, tears dripping luxuriously down my cheeks to soak the pillows and Richard's bare shoulder. I cried for the hurt that had been done to Ollie and was now being healed. I cried in relief that the weeks of strain were over. Most of all I cried for Oliver.

But that was later, much later, after an eternity of questions and recriminations and reassurances.

We found Ollie sitting on his bed, waiting. As we went in he looked up in fright and quickly away again. The raised voices had penetrated to his room; he knew that his grandmother had left in rancour. His hands were clenched on his knees, the skin over the knuckles taut and white. Richard sat down on one side of him, I sat on the other. As Richard spoke I saw the strain gradually leave him, while shock, understanding and relief replaced each other in quick succession over his face. At the end he leaned his head against Richard's thick ribbed pullover. 'Oliver was special,' he said gruffly, 'but I didn't want to think he was my father.'

I got up quickly to pull his curtains against the black wet night and stood for a moment, holding the material in my hands. Rows of soldiers marched across the cloth, stiffly old-fashioned in their red uniforms. Ollie had had those curtains since he was born. It was time he chose something more adult; they weren't right for him now. The pattern blurred and I blinked hard. Behind me Ollie was talkative with relief.

'I even had a nightmare that you would get divorced. Lots of my friends' parents have.'

'Not us,' Richard said.

I wanted to explain the difference between impotency and sterility, but Ollie interrupted. 'I know all that,' he said. 'I heard it on a TV programme. Then in a lower voice he said: 'All those horrid things happened to Oliver, but he still went on being nice . . .' As we left him to talk to Sara he said abruptly. 'I want to be called Oliver, please. Ollie sounds silly at my age. I was going to ask before, but I couldn't . . .'

In fact we spoke to Danny next – or, rather, Danny spoke to us, wanting to know what the hell was going on. No sounds of argument had penetrated the insistent beat of his pop music, but he had left his homework – 'Just for a quick slash, as you might say, and Christ, first there's Sara rushing past all red-faced and boo-hooing and slamming her door in my face, and then when I come out of the bathroom it's Grandma roaring up the stairs like a tank in action, guns blazing. "Out of my way, boy!" Wow, her face! What was that about?'

We moved him backwards into his room, switched off the noisy voices and told him briefly. He was not particularly shocked or surprised by any of our revelations, though he did have a few comments of his own to make. 'I always knew Grandma and Sara were a couple of idiots. I told Ollie not to get worked up.'

'You knew what was going on?' Richard asked breathlessly. 'Why on earth didn't you come to me?'

'How could I?' Danny retorted, reasonably enough. 'Anyway, no one ever said anything you could properly pin down – a suggestion here, a snide remark there – Grandma would only have acted monumentally hurt and said I was imagining things.' He looked thoughtfully at his father and added: 'I'm surprised you didn't pick it up yourself.'

Richard glanced at me and away again: that remark had already been made. 'I knew she was being difficult, Danny, particularly with your mother and Ollie, but I put the bad temper down to trauma of house-moving. It never even occurred to me that she could seriously think . . .'

'No,' Danny said kindly, 'because you were the one person who knew it was impossible. I can see that.'

We found Sara standing in the middle of her room, glaring. We laboured to convey understanding and sympathy – 'That card must have been a great shock. It was natural you jumped to the conclusions you did . . .' – but she was as suspicious as an animal that has been trapped and fears to be trapped again.

'I wasn't to know, was I?' she demanded aggrievedly.

Richard said quietly: 'No, it must have been difficult for you, caught between your mother and your grandmother.' He waited.

'And Oliver was always around the house,' she muttered.

Richard looked at her.

'And all the money he left to Ollie – it just wasn't fair!' she burst out.

To feel myself disliking, even despising, my own daughter was a horrible sensation. I tried to subdue it. I said slowly: 'Neither was it fair that Ollie was made to feel guilty and miserable over it – and worse.'

Her face was heavy with resentment: 'Of course, it's all got to be *my* fault . . .'

Richard's deep voice cut off her whining. 'Nobody's interested in whose fault it was, Sara. We're all to blame to

183

some extent. What we have to do now is to put this right. We have to talk things over – like we used to do. Grandma's gone and she won't be coming back.'

He laboured in vain. Sara's closed face looked past him. 'Grandma was the only person who understood how I felt.'

I made a fresh pot of coffee after we left Sara and we discussed how difficult it was to help someone who didn't want to be helped. 'Determined to be martyred,' Richard grumbled.

It must have been midnight when we went up to bed, and God knows at what hour we finally slept. Now that we had started talking we could not stop; it was as if we had to spill out in the one night all the stored communications of the last weeks. We stopped for lovemaking, but that was simply another form of communication; after weeks of near abstinence every gesture and every contact spoke with special significance.

Finally we spoke of Oliver. 'Why didn't he ever tell me?' I mourned.

'He never spoke of it. Just Melissa knew and his immediate family. He only let it out to me because of a row over you.'

'Over me?' I was incredulous.

'Because you'd spent that weekend with him,' Richard said. His hand left mine to reach for the glass of whisky he'd brought up to bed with him. 'Jealousy,' he muttered, swallowing, 'jealousy is a repulsive emotion, and quite illogical. I was horrified to find it in me. I told myself repeatedly that there was nothing between you and me at the time it happened, that I was lecturing in America all that year, that it had only happened once and nothing came of it. None of it helped. I was furious at myself and furious with Oliver.'

I watched him sip whisky. 'It doesn't sound like you.'

He nodded and grimaced. 'It was after a game of squash. Oliver had beaten me as usual, which didn't help. We had a shower. We were both naked – quite ludicrous. We were talking about our plans for the weekend. Oliver said he was taking his new girlfriend – Melissa, though I didn't know it then – to the races at Sandown Park. I remembered you'd spoken of a successful afternoon's racing before you both drove down to Sussex . . .'

Beneath the bedclothes his fingers gripped my thigh with bruising strength. 'I couldn't bear to hear him, to my mind, equate you with those easy-come, easy-go blondes of his. I looked at him towelling his body and all the jealousy I'd struggled to suppress rushed over me in a monstrous wave of fury. I said: "You took Annabel once, didn't you?" He looked surprised and nodded and then the wave broke in a flood of abuse. I spoke of rich men's spoilt sons who thought they could have and discard any girl they fancied, of good looks masking mean natures – God, Annabel, I called him every foul name I could think of and I was exasperated when I'd run out. He stood quite silent, the towel dangling from one hand, looking shattered. It wasn't until I snarled that of course if he'd made you pregnant he'd have been bound to have taken the easy way out that he lost control too, and told me.'

'Oh God!'

'Yes. I couldn't believe it at first. And then I didn't know what to say. I stuttered something, Lord knows what – anyway, he wasn't listening. He said flatly: 'Hell, Richard, money, looks, position, what do any of them matter when you can't pass them on, when every time you shoot all you can produce is rotten dead stuff? It's all meaningless.'

'Oh, Richard!' I had a horrifying glimpse of Oliver's pain and saw the extent of the courage that had made it possible for him to go on, never whining for sympathy, filling the breaches in his life with activities and with friends, always more sensitive to other's feelings than his own.

'He said he'd not deliberately set out to make love to you, that it had simply been a mutual flash of passion and if anyone was hurt it was him. He had been growing dangerously fond of you and it wouldn't do. I said I didn't see that. Not every woman has to have children – or was it a matter of class? I suppose the evil residue of my jealousy was still at work. I was sickened as soon as I'd said it. He didn't seem annoyed; I think he understood. He turned away and started to pull on his clothes. He said in that curiously flat voice that class didn't matter, but making any marriage work was not easy. All right in the early years when you were madly in love and ready to forgive anything – but it was in middle age that the real problems came, when the gilt was rubbed off, the tarnish beginning to show through. "Imagine a childless woman then," he said, "hearing her friends exulting in their children's successes at school or university, knowing this is something she can never have. Anticipating an empty old age . . . Beginning, not intending it, to resent her sterile husband, perhaps to despise him . . ."'

'Oh, don't' I said. 'Don't!' I buried my face in the grizzled fuzz on Richard's chest and the big rib-cage moved steadily up and down as if he were rocking me. The tears poured. The silence was oppressive. Not a car moved on the roads outside; acres of sleeping bodies surrounded us. My body craved to join them but my over-active mind denied it that relief.

I rolled over to find the tissues. 'I'm sorry,' I said.

'It's all right.'

'I understand so much more now.'

'I know.'

'Melissa . . .'

'She was his great piece of good luck.'

186

'Yes. Because they both had the same problem there didn't have to be any barriers or feelings of inadequacy.'

The bed was suddenly hot, the proximity of our bodies stifling. I pushed the bedclothes into a heap between us. Barriers, feelings of inadequacy, they were not gone yet from between Richard and me. We lay motionless, our eyes on the shadowy ceiling. I heard his breathing, heavy and rough.

'Why didn't you talk to me?' he asked.

Our thoughts had been moving in the same direction. 'I suppose I was afraid.' The words hung in the air, threatening us. I spoke with care, to wipe out their menace. 'I hated even to think of such things being spoken of between us. We've always been so . . . content together. Loving. I couldn't bear that slimy nastiness. I just wanted your mother to go so we could have our old peace again.'

'You should have spoken. We always shared everything. We were proud of it.'

He was making me feel guilty and I resented that. I had been trying to preserve something that was precious. In middle age it becomes clear how fragile your world is – relationships, love, the very structure of society. In youth you take what is around you to be constant – though you may wish to change it. But it appears monolithic. As maturity comes you watch relationships fail, love die, society change: you realise your own vulnerability. It is natural then to tread with care. Surely he could understand that? Besides, he was guilty himself.

'You said nothing. You were cold and distant, shutting yourself into the study and working endlessly.'

'The tension in the house, the tension in you – it was getting me down.'

'That was your mother.'

He moved his head on the pillow as if denying it. His eyes found mine. 'After Oliver died I hardly knew you.

187

You changed. Annabel, we used to talk, we'd chatter together for hours. But you went silent – ' He stopped short, his head rolled away.

I stared at the heavily carved profile. Unpleasant pictures of the past weeks presented themselves for review. The more I looked the more I disliked what I saw. My euphoria of an hour or two earlier appeared out of place. Bertha had missed her mark over young Oliver, but not all her darts had gone astray. Or would Richard have suffered even without her encouragement? By his own confession he had been jealous before over Oliver. I was frightened now, and angry – with Richard and with myself. We had let ourselves down badly, and over Oliver of all people, who had been a generous friend equally to us both.

I said slowly: 'I never had a brother. I don't remember my father. There were no males in my life until I went to university. I could never be at ease with men like Sara can. Perhaps Oliver meant more to me than he should have done, but it was because of that – he was the first person of the opposite sex to whom I was able to talk properly, normally. And God, Richard, we'd been friends for such a long time – was it surprising that I was upset? You were yourself.'

'Yes,' he said. 'Yes, I know.' He was past arguing, past discussion. He looked exhausted. His whisky glass was empty. He put it down.

'It's over now,' I said. 'We must put it behind us.'

'Yes.'

'Oliver's death, your mother's trouble-stirring . . . it's finished. We ought to go out more, cheer ourselves up.'

In the past Oliver had contributed a great deal to our social life. He would telephone often. 'I have tickets for Covent Garden,' he would say, or, 'There's a new play I think we ought to see . . .' And we had reciprocated. Without him we hadn't bothered.

'We will go out more,' Richard promised. A note of amusement came into his voice. 'And there's always the Morton-Rycrofts' dinner party!'

Every autumn the Professor and his wife invited us; every year the food and the conversation seemed to become heavier. 'Now that really does cheer me up!' I observed.

'Mmm. I thought it might.' We smiled ruefully at each other. 'I only hope her party-going will cheer Sara up,' he added. 'She's becoming too bloody-minded to live with – tense, rude, lazy. I don't know what she's going to do with her life, her boyfriends are her only interest that I know of, though God knows why they bother.'

'She may be better now your mother's gone. A lot of the trouble was her.'

'I trust you're right. Any improvement would be welcome.' He turned on to his side, away from me. 'Let's talk about the silly girl some other time. All I want now is sleep.'

15

I wished I could handle Sara with the careless confidence I had with the boys. Perhaps because she was a girl, perhaps because she was my firstborn, she tugged at my heartstrings in quite a different way. The boys were straightforward; even their mischief was simple – thoughtlessness mostly, noisiness, swearing, the leaving undone of things that should have been done such as homework, or kicking dirty socks under their beds instead of putting them in the washbasket. One spoke to them briskly, they looked put out for ten minutes, then all was forgotten. But Sara took criticism as a personal insult, disapproval as a sign of enmity. Even as a child her reaction had been similar – a bitter hurt and a sobbing rush to her room, from which she had to be coaxed hours later. Richard would say: 'Leave her, she'll come out when she's hungry'. But I never could. I worried. I was sure she was as furious with herself as with us, and that she craved the reassurance of our affection. Now that she was larger the reaction was larger also; it appalled me that she seemed incapable of seeing any viewpoint other than her own, and that resentment had set in as a permanent condition. But, as when she was little, it was wrong to accept withdrawal; I had to intervene. I tried, God knows I tried to talk to her, but in the event it was Sara who intervened in my life.

It happened on her seventeenth birthday, an event which we celebrated with drinks, a birthday dinner and the usual pile of presents. I'd hardly arrived home and rolled up my sleeves for the cooking before the telephone rang. It was Tom, calling from Chambers to ask me if I knew I had a prison conference the following evening: 'In that Heathrow drug-smuggling case you've got for next term. I noticed the brief lying on your desk, and it's a big one. You didn't know? I'm sorry, Mrs Bateman. Young Wayne was supposed to tell you a couple of days ago but he went off sick. Unreliable little beast. I'll comb his hair for him when he gets back. Anyway, six o'clock tomorrow.'

That meant driving to Chambers and back after dinner so that I could read the brief and analyse it tonight – not an easy task after a hard day followed by birthday celebrations, still less so in the cold small hours of the morning, to which it would inevitably stretch.

When the family assembled in the drawing-room for drinks I stipulated one drink only for me, just to toast Sara. Richard raised his eyebrows; I explained my need for a clear head.

He pushed a glass of wine into my hand. 'Oh, really, Annabel, this is too bad, spoiling Sara's evening. You drive all over the countryside every day, you work half the evening more often than not – can't your work be better organised?' He turned wearily from me to fill Sara's glass.

'It isn't Mum's fault that man forgot to tell her,' Oliver said pacifically.

'Not much fun for her,' Sara agreed. But then she saw a further problem and swung round to me, her glass dripping on to the carpet. 'Wait, you're bound to be late back tomorrow. Which prison are you going to?'

'Belmarsh – the new high-security prison. I'll have to ask the judge at Reading to rise early so I can get there.'

'But Belmarsh is miles away, over by Woolwich or something. So who cooks dinner? Me, I suppose you think? But I can't, I've got an essay to do on why Jane Austen thought no one but herself would much like her *Emma*, and it'll take me hours.'

'Do it tonight,' Danny suggested.

'On my birthday?' Sara was outraged. 'You must be joking! No, it's *you* who should be doing the cooking – but, of course, the men in this family don't cook, do they? They think it's demeaning.'

'Squaw's work,' Danny muttered provocatively.

Sara exploded. 'Right, that's it! Stupid sexist bastard! Oh, yeah, kid me it's just a wind-up – but you don't fool me. It's basic. Mum, if things don't change right now, I'm going on strike.'

Judging from the fluency of the diatribe which followed this announcement, she must have been practising it for days, weeks even. Her teacher, Ms Cropper held, and so did Females for Freedom, that attitudes and values were developed within the family, a . . . a microcosm of society, and if people got their values straight at an early age, the battle for equality was already half won. But in this family sexism was rife. Mother thought she'd won a great battle because she worked full-time as a barrister, but in the house she was still a skivvy. 'And me too!' said Sara. Yes, all right, Mary came in to do the cleaning and the ironing, but who did the shopping and the cooking, the mending and the washing-up? 'Mother,' said Sara, 'and me. What's the order every night? "Sara, help your mother!" Why the hell isn't it, "Boys, help your father!"? We've got to change the gender roles here!'

'God, listen to the jargon!' Danny muttered.

Sara ignored him. She tossed back more of the wine that

was lubricating her speech so well and continued: 'Men should have a hands-on attitude in the house. No good expecting miracles like Dad starting to cook at his age or washing his clothes either, I suppose. But I think it's sick the way he walks in at night and expects to find his meal waiting, and walks off after he's eaten without so much as taking his own plates out to the kitchen.'

Richard looked at me. I shook my head.

Sara interpreted accurately. 'Oh no, Mother hasn't complained. But she's tired and she looks pale and I reckon she's trying to do too much. I took a call from her Chambers the other day, from her clerk, Tom, and before he let me call her he was telling me her practice is really taking off now and she's one of the big earners in Chambers and we ought to be proud of her. He said he hoped we were looking after her. So when we were talking in class about division of labour and responsibilities in the house, I thought of Mum.' She turned to me passionately. 'It isn't right that Daddy and the boys leave it all to you when you're working so hard.'

'I've never considered myself hard done by,' I said placatingly, my eye on Richard. 'It's all just a matter of organisation, coping.'

Sara could not be calmed with disingenuous words. 'For Chrissakes, why should you have to cope? You're still living in Victorian times!' She gave me a despairing look and added: 'Men are so useless and selfish and women like you never encourage them to anything better. You martyr yourself in the cause of admiration – "Doesn't Annabel cope wonderfully?" But don't kid yourself this lot cares. They reckon you're the all-time sucker, like any man would.'

Danny plunged in recklessly: 'Maybe Mum is a sucker for punishment, but you're a blood-sucker – a greedy parasite taking all you can get and giving nothing. You're kept at school, everything paid for – look at those expensive clothes you've just been given. What do you give in return? You don't even do your homework! Who the hell are you to criticise Dad?'

'I'm not asking to be kept at school – no way. And Mother pays half of everything – probably more if the truth were known. So she should get a damn' sight more out of it than she does.' Her voice seesawed up and down the scales, veering between angry cadences. 'And don't tell me Dad does the garden or Dad changes the lightbulbs or Dad pays the bills, because it's a load of cock! Mum does twenty times that, day in, day out, and as with everything else I'm expected to follow in her footsteps. Well, I shan't, and I won't stand by and watch you self-righteous lot get away with your laziness, either. Ms Cropper says modern couples negotiate contracts on their marriage rights – I want a family contract on how we live together.'

I winced, her shots at my menfolk were hitting their target – but I cringed in anticipation of the painful rebounds. I was uncertain whether this was my punishment for putting Sara in the wrong, or a form of amends because she had been in the wrong. Perhaps it was both.

Richard's voice was glacial: 'If your mother is dissatisfied with the level of help she receives, she's more than capable of voicing it . . .'

I cut across him. 'I certainly am, and since Sarah's mentioned it I shall do so. But let's keep this to a quiet discussion, not turn it into a family feud.' I turned to Sarah. 'I've said before, there are two types of women's rights supporters: those who prove the capabilities of women by their achievements, who are quietly doing an excellent job – the gradualist approach, one might say – and those whose views are of the aggressive "Down with Men!" variety, who only impede the others. Make sure you belong to the right variety, please, if you're going to join the cause.' As she opened her mouth I held up my hand. 'And before you say anything more I'd like to say thank you for championing me, even if I don't deserve it. Yes, I am tired, yes, our menfolk are an idle bunch around the house, and yes, I should like more help. I've had one complicated case following another this term, and more to come.'

'Including your filthy incest case,' Richard said.

'Including that,' I agreed smoothly. 'And because I've hardly had a day out of court in weeks, I'm going to have to work at forthcoming cases at night and at weekends. It's all piling up, I'll admit it.'

'Perhaps you've taken on too much,' Richard jibed.

'Perhaps – and perhaps you have, too. It may seem overwhelming that we both have the chance of the big break at the same time, but we must each try to help the other, mustn't we?'

Silence, broken by young Oliver who said: 'I don't mind doing some cooking. That'll be good fun. But I'd have to be taught.'

I smiled my gratitude. 'Well, I don't think I could manage cookery lessons just at the moment, but come Christmas I'll teach you and Danny to grill sausages and chops and make good curries.'

'Unreal!' Oliver said cheerfully.

'And now?' Sara demanded.

'Now? I think the boys should be taking on more chores – for example, if Sara and I are to get the meal, the boys should clear up after and load the dishwasher.' That would both be fair and keep the boys and Sara apart. 'After dinner my time is to be my own.'

'And what's Dad to do?' Sara was a terrier, worrying away at us all.

My mind went blank at the thought of Richard and

household chores, but Oliver intervened helpfully once more: 'Dad can take Mum's car to the car wash and check it over regularly. That's a man's job.'

Sara raised ironic eyebrows.

'I will do that if it's necessary,' Richard said. But his voice was still glacial as he asked: 'Might our meal at last be ready?'

'More than ready,' I replied, and led the way to the dining-room. Sara followed behind me, muttering of unfinished business.

The telephone call from the school came early one evening. I was putting in half-an-hour's work on the incest case in my corner of the study, reading through the papers, trying yet again to make sense of it. We had been given a fixed date for R v Pockett, the twenty-second of November. I believed John Pockett and felt despairing; time was rushing up on me like a runaway train and I saw no escape route. The great climax would come at the Old Bailey – but the anti-climax would be the defence. It was not simply my credibility with the client and the court that would be lost but my credibility with my family, with Sara and with Richard. I read Fern's statement through for the twentieth time. I wasn't pleased when the sound of the telephone broke my concentration.

'Mrs Bateman? We haven't met yet,' the voice said, 'but I'm Mr Rudkin, Sara's sixth form tutor. I'm sure you'll have heard all about me?'

'Er . . . mmm,' I said. I hadn't.

'At this school, Mrs Bateman, we believe in a continuing dialogue with our parents; we believe in involving them in the whole process of their children's education, but especially when difficulties develop. Given a problem situation . . .'

'What problem?'

'Yes, well. We thought you and your husband might like to come over to the school to talk with us. A heart-to-heart, you know.'

'Yes, but why?' I insisted. 'Is Sara falling behind in her work?'

Hesitation. Clearly, being direct was not one of Mr Rudkin's beliefs. 'We could say that Sara is having difficulties, both in the work situation and in the social situation. We did wonder whether there were troubles at home . . .?' The rising inflexions delicately implied who might be to blame. I did not reply. He continued hastily: 'Of course, we do understand that her absences have not made her studies easy for her.'

'Her what?'

'Her poor health, Mrs Bateman.'

Sara was as tough as old beef. She'd not had one day's sickness this term.

I probed, 'She hasn't missed very much, surely?'

'Oh, yes.' His voice reproached me with lack of caring. 'If you add the days up they amount to nearly three weeks altogether.'

'I hadn't realised,' I said bleakly, and fell silent while he spoke at length of our need to co-operate in assuring that Sara achieved her full potential. My cover-up was automatic: it wouldn't help Sara to be suspended from school as Lucinda had been.

The rest of the conversation with Mr Rudkin was no improvement upon the first part. After he had rung off I tried to continue my work, but Sara's sullen face intruded between me and young Fern Pockett. It was time I cooked dinner anyway.

I wanted to discuss Sara's truancies with Richard and then for us to talk with her in unison, but he was late in coming home and Sara was going out. Richard was often late these days. He had a spate of committee meetings –

'The shortage of funds makes planning a nightmare!'; various politicians were giving evening talks to the students' union, 'My presence does help reduce the numbers of flying lavatory rolls,' and there was also mention of an American spinster of thirty, who, he said, kept requesting his help with thesis problems. Oliver used to tease Richard about being over-conscientious where work was concerned; I wished he were here to do that now.

When the meal was over and Richard still had not arrived I put his food in the oven to keep warm and beckoned Sara into the study: 'Just for a quiet word.' Like Mr Rudkin, I wanted a heart-to-heart talk, not an eyeball-to-eyeball confrontation.

I had neither. Sara responded impassively to my questions and comments, her shoulders hunched, her eyes fixed on her scuffed shoes, apparently only anxious to finish the disagreeable business quickly and escape to her baby-sitting at Mrs Foster's.

Yeah, all right, so she had bunked off lessons.

Yeah, she had forged the occasional absence note. It was easy, everyone did it.

No, she didn't hate school that much – she'd just been pissed off. Things were better now, she hadn't missed any this week. Just her bloody luck to be found out after she'd stopped doing it.

She'd mostly spent the days with Lucinda, going round factories and warehouses, helping to get the new shop organised.

Yeah, okay, she'd been told to keep away from Lucinda but we should've forgotten all that by now. People shouldn't bear grudges.

No, she thought she might as well hack on at school. Getting some dead-end job would be worse, or being on the dole. She knew that.

Yeah, all right, she'd have to slave at it. Could she go

now? Mrs Foster would go on at her if she was late.

I let her go and went to check on Richard's slowly drying dinner. Danny was in the kitchen, loading the dishwasher in the desultory, haphazard way that boys have; he flung information about Sara's latest boyfriend over his shoulder at me as he worked. Tony had ditched her after she'd left him standing in the rain the night of the big bust-up – she had refused to apologise because, she said, it wasn't bloody well her fault he got wet. This new boy was French, come over to England with his parents for a year; a tall dark boy with a moustache that the Head wanted him to shave off, only he wouldn't. Danny reckoned Thierry was a good laugh. He'd joined Sara's English Literature class recently – livened it up no end according to her.

It was long past ten before Richard arrived home. I had been working and waiting uneasily, and to hear him at last in the hall was at once an annoyance and a relief. I went to learn what catastrophe had delayed him. 'That stupid man, Morton-Rycroft!' he said. 'A meeting that should've taken an hour took nearer three. He sat there in his double-breasted pinstripes repeating himself like a stuck record. Intolerable!'

His meal was ruined, charcoal chips rather than chops. I offered to cook him an omelette, but he said he'd eaten; he'd been to the pub with Alan House and one or two others. I was vexed. He might have telephoned. Telephoned? Richard was aggressively defensive: I'd known he had a meeting. Indeed I had, but I'd expected him around eight, it was now nearly ten-thirty; I had been worried over him. I told him so.

He sat down heavily on my desk. His face suddenly relaxed from hostility to tiredness. He gave me an apologetic half-smile. 'My love, I did mean to telephone you. At least twice I nearly did. But you know how it goes

– the damned machine's engaged, or someone makes a provocative remark and it drops from your mind.'

No, I didn't know, I always came straight home. The resentment Sara's birthday words had aroused stirred in me.

'I'm sorry,' he said. He pulled me towards him for a kiss. His breath smelt of onions, and his tongue had a lingering taste of cheap meat. So I'd slipped from his mind, had I? My lamb cutlets Soubise rejected in favour of greasy beefburgers; the company of his wife and family less appealing than the male cheerfulness of the pub. I freed my mouth from his, but even as I did so a vision of Sara's brooding face across the supper table replaced the image of Richard forgetful in the lounge bar. Sara's scowl would sour the sweetest of foods. Given the chance wouldn't I have opted for the beer and conversation, the company of lively colleagues? He slipped off my desk then glanced at the papers which I'd been working on since dinner – my current mortgage fraud at Reading. I'd been at it all evening, he supposed. Better when you're out than when you're in, I responded, but he grunted that I did it all the time. His mood was unstable as quicksand; unease shifted in the air between us like fog.

He asked about the children, a meaningless question, a mere marital twitch. I shrugged, said that the boys had done their homework and were now watching television, added that Danny'd had a problem with his chemistry and I couldn't help him; perhaps Richard could have done. We both heard the implied reprimand and his eyebrows rose.

'And Sara?'

'Out baby-sitting,' I said. Should I tell him of her truancies? Sara had assured me that she wouldn't miss school again. Over-reaction by a testy Richard could provoke a confrontation which would help nobody.

'I haven't had a conversation with her in days,' he remarked.

'No, I know. Since that row with your mother she hasn't really got together with any of us. It's worrying.'

'Sara has only herself to blame if she is isolated within the family. Leave her alone, she'll come round soon enough.'

'But we can't allow the situation to go on indefinitely,' I protested. 'Sara is discontented both at home and at school. Trouble could be looming.'

'What trouble? Don't build a few pinpricks into an outsize headache, Annabel. Sara must grapple with her own problems and sort them out herself, not blame the nearest bystanders. Leave her to get on with it.' He gave me a condescending smile; he refused to take my worries seriously.

In the next room the television was suddenly silenced. The boys stuck their heads round the door. 'We're off to bed. Night!' Casual, cheerful, they pounded up the stairs.

Richard stood to stretch; large indifferent male, rejecting the concerns of his womenfolk, rejecting the demands of family, paltry matters beside his pressures. His big body and head, lit at an odd angle by the desk lamp, showed their strong planes geometrically defined, all blunt angles and brutal shapes, like an early Picasso. The effect was hard and male. Normally my body would have responded, immediately greedy, the undercurrent of antagonism between us only heightening his desirability, but these were not normal times, this detached superior male was not the one I lusted after. Grumpily I gathered up my papers and thrust them into my briefcase, thrusting away as I did so the thought of sex, shutting it out with the same snap as I shut the briefcase.

'Lock up, will you?' I said to Richard, and we went up to bed in silence.

Sara caught me by my car next morning, to ask, elaborately casual: 'You haven't told Dad about me bunking off, have you?'

'No.'

'I thought you couldn't have. No heavy lecture!'

I looked at her. She gave me an unexpected grin of complicity. She was looking unusually attractive, her hair well brushed, her shirt tucked into her skirt instead of dangling outside it in a crumpled mess – radiating, I could almost have said, a sensual self-satisfaction.

'Your father came in late, tired,' I said, watching her. 'He didn't need your idiocies on top of all his work pressures.'

'Yeah, I know. But you won't tell, will you?'

'Not unless you give me good reason.' A warning.

'Oh Christ, I won't do it again. Not worth the hassle. Anyway, you've been decent. Thanks.'

'I must go,' I said, and put the key in the ignition.

'Look,' she said, stopping me. 'Mum, it's claustrophobic being shut in with books all evening. If I did my homework first, couldn't I go out sometimes in the week? Be nice. Persuade Dad. I'd work like a beaver, truly, dearest Mum.' She was wide-eyed and pleading, unnaturally sweet.

I shook my head. 'An impossible task. Go out to do what? Hang around with boys? No way!'

'So that's it.' She grinned triumphantly. 'You're not just bothered over my work, you're fussed about my sex life. Well, that's my business – I can look after myself. Hell, I'm seventeen. I'm old enough, aren't I?'

'Prove it,' I said, switching on the engine. 'Stick your head down in the evenings, show us some good marks, then we might believe you to be genuinely mature enough to be able to spare more time for boyfriends and discos. Until then, slave! And believe me,' I added, gunning the engine energetically and raising my voice above it, 'it will be worth it. You like to think you're a feminist, don't you? One of those fighting for women to get a better deal? Well, fight for yourself to get somewhere in this world then, not to be second-rate, not to let your biology turn you into yet another down-trodden, underpaid and under-privileged member of our sex. You're bright. You can do it. Bye, Sara!' And I shot off towards the M4, on my daily trek to Reading.

I called in at Chambers as regularly as I could to collect my mail and any cheques; to pick up my briefs and to learn the latest news. I had chosen a nasty evening to do it this time, cold, wet, and with a biting wind. I blew in from the snarling, blustering November outside to find Chambers snug and warm, a cheerful group of my colleagues giving tongue in the clerks' room and a fresh brew of coffee in the making. Gerald Lees asked how I was getting on in that complicated fraud of mine and seemed in high good spirits. I sidestepped the hand that was patting my bottom, asked what he'd been doing and congratulated him on his success. Another of the men thrust a mug of coffee at me that for once was truly hot and not poisonously strong, and Paulina Grey, whose client had been unexpectedly found not guilty, expatiated happily on her successful cross-examination. It was all very cosy and pleasant until Tom wanted my attention.

'Got a bit of news I'm afraid you won't be very happy to hear, Mrs Bateman,' he said, looking up from the diary.

'Oh Lord, Tom,' I said, 'I came in here to be cheerful. Can't you forget it?'

'Sorry, ma'am. Would if I could, but . . . It's that incest, Pockett.'

'Monday week,' I said. Then, struck by a thought, I demanded: 'He's not going to plead guilty, is he?'

'No, it's not that. It's the judge. He collapsed in court yesterday. Heart attack. Not a bad one, but he won't be available for six weeks or more and there's nobody free to do it. So it's had to be put back.'

'Till when? Don't tell me – they couldn't give you a new date!'

'Sorry, ma'am. In the New Year, they say. They're very busy.'

I used a four-letter word culled from my children's vocabularies.

'Incest?' Paulina said. 'That isn't the one you were briefed in in the summer, is it?'

'It is,' I replied grimly.

'But that's disgraceful! Keeping children waiting month after month with this sort of thing hanging over their heads!'

'I'm deeply concerned, but we're in the hands of the listing office.'

'That poor traumatised girl – already her vision of parenthood and the family will be distorted. Now justice lets her down,' Paulina said, pinkening with outrage. 'Something should be done about these delays. We should do something!'

'Agreed – but who and how?'

'It must be given serious thought. That child must be going through hell.' Her eyes accused me. 'You're still representing the father, then?'

'I am.'

'Your own stance shocks and appals me, Annabel,' she said heatedly. 'In appearing for men like that you are betraying women, conniving at those who abuse us and use us as sex objects. The very thought of it makes me shudder.'

If Paulina could be grandiloquent, so could I. 'Betraying women? In refusing to act for any person, male or female, who needed representation before the law, I should be betraying humanity!'

'You might be right to say that if there weren't anyone else available to represent him,' she retorted, 'but there are dozens of male barristers who could do the case. Women should stand solid against this sort of thing. I think you should consider your position in this very carefully, Annabel.'

'How? What should she do?' Gerald scoffed. 'Assume the man must be guilty just to placate the feminists? Hardly the impartial attitude of the judicial mind, Paulina!'

A bang interrupted us and we swung round to find its source: Tom had dropped a large brief on to the floor and was looking reproachful. He told us briskly that he wanted to speak to Miss Grey, and that while he didn't wish to spoil our conversation, he did have work to complete. The men took the hint and drifted away, exchanging teasing comments about Paulina's sexism while she struggled to pretend deafness and attend to Tom.

I turned to my pigeon-hole and extracted a mass of paperwork. There were three big cheques there, too, all dating from work I'd done in the summer, all sexual matters, one of them the Salome Keane case. They totalled more than fourteen thousand pounds. Some of it would go into the joint account that Richard and I ran, but this was far more than we needed for everyday living. The excess? Spend some, save some. My tired mind revived as I contemplated the prospect: we could have an Easter holiday abroad, replace the elderly drawing-room carpet, give young Oliver those new bedroom curtains he deserved. Richard would be pleased at the money that underlined my success – or would he?

My pleasure vanished abruptly. Money derived from a different type of case, a different type of fame, he might accept, demonstrating himself as generous, tolerant and wise while lauding my successes to colleagues and friends. But, I thought unhappily, success that brought notoriety, and, horrors, that stemmed from what his colleagues would denounce as a politically incorrect stance, I could not see him swallowing. One of the recent meetings that had kept him late at college had been an urgent update of the university's position on racism and sexism – at his insistence. Richard was college co-ordinator in these matters. Better to pay some of that money into a building society account, hiding my success from him as I had hidden Sara's failure, than to have him openly denounce me.

16

Fog, freezing November fog, and I was almost the only person to arrive at Reading Crown Court on time, thanks to the television weatherman who had garnished his late night chart with blobs of cottonwool and warned of the perils facing the motorist with lugubrious relish. Set off early, he'd said, and I had. Besides, I needed to ensure that my witnesses were available and that the prosecuting solicitors had all the papers ready that we'd need today in court. Prosecuting seven defendants, all separately represented, on eight counts of mortgage fraud took considerable organisation. I hoped the fog would not prevent the jury and all the other people engaged in the matter from turning up.

We hung about. Ten forty-five, and the court clerk told me that the last juryman had just panted in but that my final prosecution witness had not appeared, a man whose evidence I definitely needed. At eleven the judge called us into court; the witness's car had been involved in a multiple pile-up on the M25; he was unhurt but stuck there. An adjournment was agreed to the next day, Friday, and we all trooped out again.

A free day – and what should I do with it? A hundred and one interesting possibilities sprang to mind, but household shopping was what I plumped for first, freeing me for once from the dreariness of late-night shopping at the end of a tiring week. I drove to the supermarket in Richmond, and that was where I met Mrs Foster.

I was pushing an overladen shopping trolley, and she was pushing a well-laden pram with her infant asleep inside, and we emerged together, shuddering at the cold. We exchanged polite greetings, falling into step, friendly acquaintances rather than friends.

'How are you?'

'Cold!'

'Such a nasty morning.'

'Your little son looks snug enough.'

Fog hung in yellow balls round the street lights, cars crawled past.

'He is a nice boy, that one who's going out with Sara now,' Julie Foster said.

I searched for the name. 'Thierry?'

'Yes, that's it. He is fun, don't you think?'

'I haven't met him.' Tony was one of the rare boyfriends I had met.

'Oh? Oh. He came with Sara to babysit on Monday. Most attractive, very . . . alive – you know?'

I did, with great clarity. So he was why Sara enjoyed babysitting. My original vision of her head bent over her books in a silent room, the baby asleep upstairs, was replaced with a new vision – that of Sara rolling on a sofa with a lively, fun young Frenchman. No puzzle now the air of sensual satisfaction. She was invariably late returning from the Fosters'. She said they liked to go out for a drink after their classes, to make full use of her. Clearly someone else was making full use of her too.

'He comes from my region of France, the Jura, near Switzerland. It's beautiful there, in the mountains.' She sighed wistfully. 'We talked of it. All snowy now, of course, not this dreadful wet fog. We ski.'

Yesterday Richard and I had gone to bed before Sara returned. I had no memory of hearing her come in. Had she been disporting herself with this boy Thierry again?

I said politely: 'I do hope she wasn't late arriving last night?'

'Last night?' The deep brown eyes blinked enquiringly.

'To babysit for you.'

'Not last night. Mondays.'

'Mondays and Wednesdays,' I said, but already my lungs were taking in large gulps of the icy air.

'No, no. My class is only on Mondays. Occasionally Sara has come at the weekends. Perhaps she goes to someone else . . .?'

'No,' I said weakly. 'No, I am a fool.'

Embarrassed, she directed her gaze towards her sleeping son, patting his blankets straight. I knew that she had realised.

We reached the car park entrance and parted in mutual relief. By the car I stood to catch my breath – dear God, the unbothered cheek of Sara! For a moment I was admiring, I smothered a laugh; I'd never have had the imagination to behave like her. But now I'd have to tell Richard.

When I arrived home I found a pile of mail on the mat. I dumped my carrier bags and flicked through it. All the envelopes were typewritten, mostly manilla; bills presumably. I took them to the study and dumped them on Richard's desk. Then, a telephone being conveniently to hand, I dialled Princes College. Better not to let Richard step unprepared into unpleasantness at home; better we should decide which of us was to take the lead in talking to Sara about her deceptions, and how we were to deal with

211

them; better infinitely I should confess my own small deception over her truancies first.

The shrill-voiced girl on the college switchboard said that Dr Bateman was not answering his phone, he must be giving a lecture. No, I retorted, not according to his timetable. Reluctantly, she offered to try other rooms: 'But it'll take time,' she warned. 'Then I suppose I'll just have to hang on,' I said pleasantly, gritting my teeth.

It took her several minutes of muttered expletives to track him down, and when she got the right extension Richard was sharp.

'Must even my working hours be invaded by Sara's stupidities? I'm trying to work with Erica Fennimore on the lectures for next term – and we're behind schedule.' I rang off, after a frustratingly brief conversation, wondering who this Erica woman was. I thought I knew all the members of the department, several of whom had once been my own lecturers. Eventually I concluded she must be the new lecturer in Political Science, the one Richard had told me had an American accent and big boobs. I wondered guiltily if he had in fact spoken of her in more detail and I had not been concentrating or had simply forgotten.

And thinking of forgotten matters reminded me that I should make a further telephone call – to Howard Hoffer of Bryant and Morley, to discover whether Alan Greening, the enquiry agent, had come up with any useful material as a result of his renewed efforts in the Pockett case. The answer was no, and he'd left a message with my husband to that effect two days ago, Mr Hoffer said reproachfully. Another brief and unhelpful conversation. I put the receiver down, damning Richard.

When the boys arrived home in the afternoon I asked casually whether either of them knew anything about an American woman called Fennimore lecturing at Princes.

No, they said. No, they'd not heard Dad mention her.

But then Danny's face suddenly brightened. 'There was a woman with an American accent rang up for him about a week ago. Funny, it was, she called me "Richard darling!" But when I said I was Danny she rang off . . . "Richard darling, thank goodness I got *you!*" You and Dad were out at dinner with the Hammonds in Kingston.' Grinning, unbothered, he trailed off to put his football gear to be washed.

Richard darling, indeed! And had she really put the emphasis on the you, the way Danny had said it? You – and no one else? For a moment questions jostled around in my brain like swarming black ants, pricking me with a myriad of painful stings: Richard always discussed new entrants to the department with me, why not this one? Were all his late evenings work evenings? Some were very late – why? Richard darling – darling? Ouch! But then commonsense came to my rescue, and the swarming ants fell back. Darling was an often bandied word. Oliver had called me darling without Richard reacting . . . I blushed for my evil thoughts. I berated myself in shame that anything so perfidious and unlikely should ever have come into my mind.

We had agreed on the telephone that Richard should deal with Sara, since I, he said, had jeopardised my position by covering up her truancies. He arrived home at six and dealt with her swiftly and tersely. She was not to go out on any evening for the rest of the month. She was to concentrate on catching up on her school work. We would ask her tutor for a run-down on where her worst weaknesses lay. Her boyfriend? She would see him at school and on Sundays. Very well, she could babysit for the Fosters on Mondays, since it would be wrong to let them down, but that was all. As December was barely two weeks away, this was, said Richard, given the circumstances, a mild punishment. The situation would be reviewed then. In the meantime he hoped Sara realised how deeply disappointed we were in her, how shocked by all the deceit.

I waited in trepidation for defensive counter-attacks from Sara, for cries of: 'You don't understand!' and 'You're so fucking unfair!', for outbreaks of violent hostility on either side, but they didn't happen. For a brief moment I hoped for real communication between us, for words that would give some explanation of her hostility and rebellion. I hoped in vain. Sara was white and silent, staring back at Richard. Antagonism in her looks, but not in her mouth. 'You may go,' Richard said.

An electrical sideways glance at me, charged with accusations of betrayal, and she left the study. Moments later the door of her bedroom banged shut.

Richard looked at me and shrugged. His heavy face was leaden with vexation; his nostrils were taut; there were shadows beneath his eyes that made him look older. I wanted to put my arms round him and comfort him, and be comforted in return. In bringing up our children I had always dealt with day-to-day matters, while tending to defer to Richard over major decisions: perhaps this deference dated back to our original tutor and student relationship. I needed him to be reassuring about Sara, to discuss ways in which we might act together to guide and help her. But Richard turned away, his broad shoulders rounded with tiredness. He sat down at his desk and began to open his mail. I left him to it.

Seconds later he followed me to the drawing-room where I was pouring myself a drink. 'This letter isn't for me,' he said, pushing an envelope into my hands. 'It looks important, too. There's a coat of arms on it in red and it says "Lord Chancellor". What the devil's that about?'

I opened and read it. 'Briefly,' I said, smiling my deep

214

pleasure, 'it appears I'm going to be made an assistant recorder. That means sitting as a part-time judge for at least twenty days a year.'

'Oh.' Richard looked disconcerted. 'Were you expecting this?'

'Yes, eventually. It's come earlier than I expected.'

'And the implications?'

'It . . . Well,' I said happily, 'it means I've made the first firm step to judicial preferment. If that's the road I wish to follow – I've many years to go yet.'

'And silk?' He hesitated then added: 'Oliver spoke of your becoming a Queen's Counsel, not long before he died. When would you hope for that?'

'I'm considering applying next year or the year after. Tom advises me that I should. But who can tell how these things will go?'

'Why didn't you tell me?' he asked plaintively. 'I had no idea how fast your career was going, that any of this was imminent . . .' His voice died away, then came back strongly. 'Congratulations are clearly in order, then. Congratulations, Annabel, I'm very pleased for you! Delighted in fact! My wife on the Bench – we must celebrate. Let me look for some wine. I'll call the children. No, it must be champagne, of course!' Having, like Jane Austen's Mr Ferrars, worked himself up to a pitch of enthusiastic generosity, he put his arms round me and gave me a hearty kiss.

If Sara was surprised to be offered champagne not many minutes after she had been thoroughly censured and gated, she took it cheerfully enough, giving me a hug and congratulations quite as warm as the boys'. 'It's nice to have something good happen for once,' she said.

'Perhaps one day we shall be complimenting you,' I suggested as I drank. 'Think hard about your future, darling – create a dream and make it come true. Then we'll

215

order a crate of champagne!'

'But when the day comes it'll be your dreams and ambitions – and they'll never come true for me because I'm not made that way,' Sara stated. 'You won't believe it, but it's true.'

'Nonsense,' Richard said, overhearing. 'Carlyle considered genius the transcendent capacity of taking trouble first of all, and since you take no trouble, Sara, your particular genius has no hope of shining. And, now, for Heaven's sake, let's leave that topic. It's a sad one, and this is an evening to rejoice.'

'Sara?' I murmured on Saturday night, opening her door a fraction when my knock was unanswered. 'Sara?' I said, more loudly. The room was dark; she couldn't be asleep yet, surely? I switched on the light. Sara's bed was empty.

I stood staring, my heart unexpectedly pounding, the glass of water in one hand, the aspirin in the other. The silence rustled faintly.

'I'm going to bed,' she had announced soon after supper. 'If I must stay in I might as well sleep. Besides, I've got a headache.'

Remembering, fifteen minutes later, that there were no aspirins left in the medicine cupboard, and that Sara had seemed off-colour at times recently, I had scrabbled through my shoulder bag, found a couple of pills in foil, and taken them upstairs for her. But Sara was not here.

Perhaps she was in the bathroom? No, the room was dark. Perhaps she was with the boys? They'd invited a couple of friends in. She could be in Danny's room with them, stretched out on the carpet, drinking Coke or low-alcohol lager, listening to music. I hoped, hopelessly. I opened Danny's door; he'd put blue and red lightbulbs under the shades and the faces that looked up were weirdly coloured: all were male.

'Sara? Have you seen her? She's not in her room . . .'

Oliver and Danny's magenta faces stiffened; eyes met and were averted. Blue hands fiddled with beer can pulls. 'Thought she was going to bed early.' 'Haven't seen her since supper.' Understanding had leapt into their eyes; understanding and embarrassment for me. 'There are peanuts and crisps and ham for sandwiches in the kitchen,' I said, retreating. 'Take what you want.'

Richard was out, attending some formal academic function; he wouldn't be back till past midnight. Strange how men were always elsewhere when catastrophe struck – I'd agreed that point years back with female friends – men had an interior radar that gave early warning signals, ensuring engagements that took them out of the danger zone.

Perhaps Sara had slipped off to the local pubs with her friends? That, she had defensively informed us when we demanded to know, was how most of her wicked Wednesday evenings had been spent.

'Pub crawling?' Richard had looked revolted. 'Yeah, why not? We play pool or we play the fruit machines – you know – and we talk. Can't afford to drink much. The boys in my classes go most evenings. Who cares?' 'I care,' Richard had said grimly. 'They are under age and so are you. The occasional glass at home is one thing, but I disapprove of your being in pubs at nights among hardened boozers.'

'You disapprove of anything that's not study. Whatever I want to do is wrong,' she had muttered.

Perhaps she was at a party? Or a Females for Freedom meeting. Or snuggled with her boyfriend in the darkness of a cinema. Or in his room. Was this the first time she had sneaked out? How could we control a girl who regarded our punishments with such contempt?

I groaned and went to pour myself a hefty whisky. The

door bell rang; my hand shook, wasting several pricy shots-worth. I almost ran to the door, but it was only Angela.

'Oh, it's you!' I said weakly.

She was unperturbed by the lack of welcome. 'Only me,' she agreed, stepping past me uninvited. 'Why? Did you hope for a lover?'

'Why yes,' I said. 'In fact several. For my usual Saturday night orgy.' My heartbeat had settled back to normal.

Angela snorted and removed her outermost garment, a hooded brown affair which closely resembled a monk's discarded habit. Beneath it she was dressed for the weather in descending tiers of unrelated items, hung about with beads and a trailing scarf of the type that strangled Isadora Duncan. On her head was jammed a black felt Greta Garbo hat, and on her feet were tarnished gold boots. She dumped four bulging shopping bags on the hall floor and flexed her fingers anxiously. 'Late shopping to do,' she explained. 'Christ, carrying this lot up the hill, I'm surprised my shoulders aren't dislocated!'

Judging by the richly alcoholic scent of her breath Angela had already stopped off for sustenance on her journey and now was visiting me for more of the same. I was more glad to see her than not: any distraction was an improvement on my own company. I poured her a whisky and topped up my own, and we sat at either end of the sofa, drinking it neat, and staring into the fire.

I wanted to discover whether Angela had known anything of Sara's truancies. It quickly became clear that this was unlikely. The shop was entirely Lucinda's affair, Angela told me plaintively: she was not allowed near Fulham. 'And me so knowledgable about fashion,' she mourned.

'Children can be very ungrateful,' I sighed.

'Still, I'm throwing a party when the shop opens,' she

218

confided and gave extensive details of the affair, including the vegetarian foods involved. 'Macrobiotic,' she explained vaguely. 'We are what we eat, Annabel,' she added. 'You must change your eating habits. You look low. It's these chemically contaminated foods. Vegetables are sprayed with poisons, animals filled with antibiotics. The flesh of unhappy animals cannot benefit you. My new lover has opened my eyes to terrible things.'

While I contemplated the repellent picture she had conjured up, she tossed back the remainder of her whisky, held out her glass for a refill and, glancing about herself, said with a reminiscent smile: 'You know, Annabel, your drawing-room often reminds me of my mother's – all gracious and polished and arranged just so.'

I took her glass, staring at her in dismay. The Lebournes' drawing-room had appeared constantly ready to be photographed for glossy magazines, while the furniture seemed to bear invisible labels saying: 'Rare' and 'Unique'. I had not cared for the house at all. I had much preferred Oliver's, which, while of the same period (early eighteenth-century), was warm and welcoming, its furniture looking as though it had lived there for generations, polished and kicked and used and loved. As was ours. No, the resemblance to the Lebournes' was surface only.

'You're like Mummy in other ways,' Angela continued, pink with warmth and whisky and oblivious to my discomfort. 'She was mad about perpetual study and examinations and things. She didn't believe in God, she believed in education instead, like Daddy did. It was to be the saviour of us all.' She belched and nodded, pleased with her analysis. 'Very like you.'

The room was suddenly cold. Was this a more accurate shot? Had Richard and I replaced the worship of the Three-in-One with the worship of A-levels, the Three-at-one-Time? Was bowing down to examinations our sure way to Heaven on earth? I believe in one comprehensive school education? Perhaps that was why Sara rebelled, unable to be a True Believer? Poor Sara the atheist, compelled to swallow great gulps of a creed she couldn't stomach, threatened with the hell-fire of eternal unemployment unless she complied. Whisky and worry and strange wild thoughts swirled through my brain.

Angela didn't leave until after the boys' friends had departed, well after eleven. I hoped she would make it back home safely; she was considerably the worse for wear. I watched her totter along the pavement and wondered whether Sara was lurking behind a car or a hedge waiting for a chance to slip in unseen. The pubs were all shut now.

On an impulse I crept up to Sara's room. Perhaps it was untrue, her absence a crazy nightmare I'd dreamed up; I would find her sleeping peacefully.

The empty bed mocked me.

But from round the walls eyes surveyed me aggressively, eyes belonging to the determined hand-linked Amazons on her strident puce and lime green Females for Freedom posters, eyes that accused me of lack of female solidarity, of lack of understanding of a daughter who, like me, had women's problems when faced with determining the pattern of her life. Was I being as strident as those Amazons when I insisted that she must deny her biology, worship the Three-at-one-Time, make academic success the stick with which to beat those men who still denied women's capacities for advancement? But Sara liked young males, and Sara, as Oliver had seen and tried to tell me last summer, was a sensual young woman. There were other ways of living than the intellectual, the academic life; there were other ways of proving women's worth than through examination success.

The doorbell shrilled. I shot downstairs.

'Me again,' Angela said, tripping over her feet into the hall, scraping more gold from her boots. 'I knew there was something I'd forgotten, something urgent. Annabel, I must have a pee!'

My pent-up breath gushed out. 'Help yourself, do!' I invited.

'I did think,' Angela said, making for the loo, 'I did think of squatting between two cars – but then I decided not.' She left the door half open, sounds of Niagara Falls emerged.

'What stopped you?'

Indignantly: 'The street lights were all staring at me!'

My lips twitched; perhaps animism was due to be her next fad.

The lavatory flushed and Angela reappeared. 'Christ, that's better. Funny,' she remarked conversationally, 'how strict the laws are about people urinating in public places when every gatepost is soggy with dogs' pee.'

'But of course. The English always put their animals' needs first.'

Angela nodded solemnly, struck. 'Of course. Why didn't I think of that?' About to leave again, she frowned: 'No Richard tonight? Where's he? Not out on the razzle, not the faithful Richard?'

'Academic dinner.'

'Uh. So you stay home alone. Faithful Annabel. I wouldn't. Mind you,' she added with an air of great fairness, 'he's 'straordinarily good about your high-powered career, you have to give him that. Can you imagine Miles? No competition in the home, he said. Male chauvinist bastard!' She headed off into the darkness once more.

One o'clock. Half-past one. Two o'clock. Half-past two. Damn Sara. Damn Richard, too.

221

I tried to imagine what each was doing and my imagination frightened me with pictures of fatal accidents, mangled machinery and gore everywhere. I paced the room.

Twenty to three. Familiar sounds of a familiar car. The front door opened and Richard's large and reassuringly whole body was there. He was humming and there was a slight smile on his lips.

'Richard! At last! Where the hell have you been?'

He was startled. 'Good Lord! You still up? You shouldn't have waited.' He gave me an awkward look, almost embarrassed. 'It was a most unexpectedly good evening, it was difficult to tear myself away . . .'

'Never mind that. Richard, Sara's disappeared!'

'Disappeared? Sara? What on earth . . .?'

'She said she was going to bed early, then she vanished. Richard, she's still not back and I'm frightened!' I swiftly told him what little there was to tell and demanded what should be done? Ring the police? What could they do? Ring round her friends? Embarrassing and probably pointless. 'But I can't go on sitting here, imagining things. I'll go mad.'

Richard was grimly angry. He used a few pungent phrases to describe his daughter, then said he would tour the streets in his car, to find her if she was walking home. I had a feeling that the French boy lived somewhere towards Kingston. He said he'd head that way.

It was a bare ten minutes before the car screeched to a halt and Richard's deep voice resounding through the quiet night outside made it clear Sara was found. She staggered at a rush into the house, nearly falling as she came, propelled by a violent shove from Richard.

'I found her strolling back along the main road from Ham, cool as you please,' he said harshly.

Sara stood with her back against the hall table. She

222

pushed at hair that had fallen across her face, looked at me and looked away.

I was too exhausted for anger. 'Sara, how could you? How could you?' was all I could say.

'I didn't think you'd ever know,' she mumbled, almost inaudible.

'So that makes it all right?' Richard asked in a half shout.

She looked up then. 'You're so strict,' she said, almost as if it were she who was accusing us. 'What did you expect?'

'Obedience,' I returned, stunned. 'Or a rational discussion.'

'I did try to talk to you . . . in the morning, by your car. You didn't want to know.'

That was true, she had . . . and I hadn't.

'You realise, don't you,' Richard asked, 'that your mother was worrying for hours, not knowing where you were or what might have happened to you?'

'But I was all right.' She sounded surprised that I should bother. 'Why shouldn't I be?'

'Vanishing until nearly three?' I said. 'And where had you gone?'

A shrug. 'My boyfriend's party.' She hesitated, then added uncomfortably, her eyes on mine: 'I didn't do it to spite you, sneaking out. I did it to save you from another row. I never promised you anything – but I promised Thierry weeks ago I'd help him. I couldn't let him down.'

'But you could let us down!' Richard's voice was rough with disgust. 'What a hypocrite!'

'No,' I said, thinking about it. 'Sara's own logic. Not a hypocrite, just thoughtless.'

But my words stung more than her father's had. She flew at me. 'Thoughtless? You can't say that! I'm always thinking about you. I do one hundred percent more for you than either of the boys – or Dad. And where was he

223

when you needed him? Out on the tiles! But you don't have a go at him for worrying you when he stays out late, he can be as thoughtless as he pleases! God, Mum, you say you're for us, for women who want real equality, but you're not, it's all a sham. Sod your gradualist approach – you worship at the male shrine like your friends do, however much you all grumble. And that's hypocrisy!'

'Sara, that's enough! Calm down!'

'At least,' she spat at me, 'at least Grandma is all of one piece, even if she is wrong. But you, Mum, you get up in court and defend men even when they've attacked women. Your sort doesn't see itself as losing, but you are – you're getting a . . . a hybrid deal with the worst of either sex. Do you think Dad'll be happy for you to be a QC or a judge and earn more than him? Don't kid yourself! He'll hate it! So whatever you achieve you lose out. Hell, no one'll catch me competing for those sorts of booby prizes. I don't want your endless battleground of a life . . .'

'Be quiet!' Richard shouted. He moved forward abruptly, looking as if he intended to shake or hit Sara and for a terrified moment I expected to see her flying across the hall. It would have been out of character; he'd never laid a hand on her. But Sara thought as I did. Faced with his looming powerful body and clenched fists she shrank backwards across the table, caught the vase upon it with her elbow and sent it crashing to the floor where it shattered.

I fell on my knees beside the shards. My pent-up emotions finally burst forth. 'My vase! You've broken it, you stupid careless bitch! You spoil everything about you. You don't care about me, you don't care about anything – hurting, smashing, destroying!' I snatched up the fragments with shaking hands.

'I'm sorry,' she said. 'Christ, I'm sorry! It was an accident.'

I scrambled back to my feet clumsily, feeling a shard cut my finger, but hardly noticing. 'It was Oliver's last present to us. Totally irreplaceable. Oh, go away, Sara! Go to bed. I can't stand to look at you any more.'

She turned and fled.

Richard bent to examine the pieces in my hand. They looked pathetic, the delicate pattern broken in pieces, the soft colours smeared with my blood. I put the cut finger in my mouth and sucked.

'No hope of mending it?'

'It can never be mended.'

17

'When I'm working I'll buy you another vase,' Sara said to me next morning as we were preparing breakfast, her voice subdued. 'I will, I really will, I promise.'

'You won't be able to afford it,' I said, slapping bacon into a spitting pan and hastily turning down the heat.

'I'll save. I know it was valuable, but I'll manage it somehow.' She gave me a pleading look. 'I couldn't rise to famille rose but I could still buy you a handsome porcelain vase. I want to. I loved that vase too, you know. It was beautiful.'

I looked at her in surprise. 'What do you know about porcelain?'

'Not much.' Her voice came muffled from the cupboard whence she was pulling cups and saucers. 'When I was helping Lucinda . . . well, there's an antique shop next door to her shop that's full of beautiful things – sofa-tables and Davenports and lowboys, small pieces, you know – and the lady who runs it sells quite a bit of porcelain, too. I went in there to look and she saw I liked her lovely plates and vases and told me a bit about them, about hard and soft paste and the influence of the Chinese and all that. It was interesting. When I was doing a library lesson at school I looked it up.'

227

Anything rather than English or French Literature or history. 'Learn anything?'

'A bit. The school library's generally pretty useless, but it did have one book with some great illustrations. So if I looked carefully and took advice, I could maybe find you something good when I've got the money.'

I didn't refuse; there were matters between us that needed salving. Maybe this was a way of doing it. I thanked her for the generous impulse.

The following morning, a Monday, I was in Lewes Crown Court. But not for long. The mortgage fraud I had been prosecuting in Reading had taken fifteen working days before the jury found the defendants guilty on all eight counts; it took barely fifteen minutes for the judge in Lewes to hear the outline of the case from the prosecution and to call for pre-sentence reports on my building society robber client, not once the man had changed his plea to guilty.

Loss of fees on the one hand, but on the other a week available for drafting indictments and giving advice on evidence: a much-needed catch-up week. I drove out of Lewes into the Sussex countryside and saw that it was glowing with that clear winter sunlight which reveals the details of every dip and hollow of the land, and sparkles from every ditch and puddle. I hummed to Beethoven's Choral Fastasia on Radio 3 and my spirits lifted.

I had turned the car towards London but in a short while I saw a signpost to the village where Oliver lay buried. It drew me. I could put flowers on the grave he shared with Melissa, sit on a bench in the wintry sunshine and commune with his spirit. I missed him still quite shockingly; missed his kindliness, his generosity, his perspicacity, the gentle teasing that put our problems into perspective. I remembered that summer's day when all our present turmoil seemed to have begun, Sara's moodiness and Oliver's reminder to me, 'It's a phase and phases pass . . .' I wished passionately that he were here now. We needed him.

I nearly turned the corner to the village, but then commonsense told me that I had no flowers and there were no shops near. And to think of him in the cold, cold ground hurt. Better to come in the spring with Richard, and combine it, perhaps, with lunch with Clare and Colin nearby. Clare! I would drop in on her for a coffee. The prep school was not much out of my way and I was in just the mood for her acerbity, her astringent humour. At the next crossroads I turned west, heading for their cottage hard by the school.

Clare was delighted to see me. 'Just the person I needed,' she exclaimed, leading the way into her untidy sitting-room. 'And not just for coffee – too late for that, anyhow, we'll have a drink. You'll stay for lunch and a good gossip, won't you? Save me from the torments of a severe attack of boredom?'

'I'd love to stay,' I said, abandoning any thoughts of an afternoon wrestling with the complexities of the Heathrow drug-smuggling, 'but a sandwich will do me. It's what I have normally.'

'Nonsense,' she said, a gleam in her eye. 'We'll eat tonight's steaks. Colin'll get cod from the deep freeze. Serve him right!'

'Do I hear a touch of rancour?' I asked, clearing a pile of exercise books to sit on her sofa. 'How are things with you both?'

'Comical,' she answered unexpectedly. She disappeared to get drinks, reappeared grinning. 'I see you've parked your car just in view of the main buildings. The very thing!'

'Suspicion and jealousy?'

'Very sharp!' she approved. 'I suspect some interfering

229

bastard let slip about me and Peter Marsden – months out of date, of course – because Colin's constantly on the prowl, no doubt hoping to catch me in flagrante. Twice he thought he had, twice he fell flat on his face. Huh! I never stooped to that level with him.'

'How did he fall flat?'

She laughed and put her drink down, leaning forward in her chair. 'On the first occasion he saw a white Peugeot parked outside. Peter has a white Peugeot, so what does clever clogs do? He comes rushing back, sees the door of the sitting-room shut, flings it open all dramatically, opens his mouth to denounce us . . . and the vicar's wife looks up and says: "Colin! How very nice to see you!"'

I chuckled at the ludicrous picture she had conjured up. 'And the second?'

'A yellow Porsche, parked close to our hedge. We're truly rural here, parking in the lane is rare. Colin must have thought I'd gone way up-market. He abandons his little boys, hurtles back to confront me – and I hadn't even noticed the damned vehicle. Ten minutes of argument of the "I'll tear him limb from limb – where's he hiding?" variety, and we go outside and fifty yards away there's a smart young woman lugging a large petrol can and looking very red.' She finished with glee: 'Not nearly so red as Colin, though!'

We roared together over that one.

Sobering up, she said: 'And how are you and yours, Annabel?'

I shrugged. 'So so, thanks.'

'That's a change for the worse. Usually you're all fine, great, and full of the hundred and one interesting things you've been up to. What's the trouble?'

'Nothing really. Just . . . Richard's overworking and Sara's being adolescent awful.'

'Sounds dreary. How adolescent awful?'

230

I hesitated. Clare let everything hang out, self-deprecating, ironic, she was uncaring; but it was not easy to reciprocate, to let her know that my bed of roses contained thorns. And her Amanda was the plump and placid sort. I said off-handedly: 'Oh, sulks, arguments, declarations that school is boring, that she wants to leave, that she'll never pass her examinations. She used to do so well, yet now we find she's even skipped some days. I've tried endlessly to talk to her . . . but I get nowhere.'

'And Richard?'

'They're hardly on speaking terms. And he says he can't be bothered with her complaints.'

My mind flicked back to the previous day when he had said: 'We've lost Sara, you know.'

I would never have said that, never have believed it, even though it was the feeling I'd been pushing away in the sleepless dark hours. I had not dared ask whether he'd meant in terms of behaviour, of academic work or as a friend, but I had replied with vehemence: 'We've not lost yet. Things could be much worse: she could be on drugs, or expelled from school, or . . . or on probation for shoplifting. All these things have happened to children we know. Even if we don't much care for her the way she is these days, she's our child and we love her.'

Richard had turned his head from contemplation of the frosty garden to stare stonily at me. 'If she weren't my child I wouldn't give her the time of day.' He had rejected my suggestion that we try talking things over with her again as: 'A waste of time.'

His defeatist attitude distressed me. He had been going through the motions of stern fatherhood, but beneath the act he was withdrawing; it was as though our situation was hardly real to him. Throughout my childhood as a lonely only child I had yearned for a real family of my own; I had abandoned my career for several years to concentrate upon my children, and they had been my repayment. They, and Richard, were the cherished centre of my life. Now I saw them threatened, our warmth and closeness ebbing away.

Clare was saying: 'Don't tell me that the good, the faithful, the ever-perfect Richard won't help!'

For once I didn't defend him against her mockery. I said sourly: 'His mind is on his work, as always. And on writing his book on political philosophies in his spare time. And he has meetings every other night.'

'Oh Christ, Annabel, meetings? The first symptom of the infidelity syndrome – take it from one who knows.'

I knew that the jibes came from her awareness that, once again, she had revealed the limitations of her own marriage, but that did not make them any easier to take.

She said quickly: 'Sorry, that was uncalled for. I'm a bitch, take no notice. I'm sure your love life is as superb as ever.'

The unintentional arrow struck home harder than the others. Superb? We were disagreeing over Sara, Richard was immersed in fascism, and after a tough day in court I hardly found that Sara's sullenness and Richard's dourness held any aphrodisiac qualities: bed, nowadays, was only for sleep.

I said: 'Even the best marriage has its ups and downs, you know. Like the economy. No endless perfect understanding. No Nirvana.'

'Don't say that!' Clare protested. 'We have to believe in the perfect marriage, the couple who entirely understand one another. My dear, don't you know you're our lodestar? If it weren't for couples like you and Richard to show us how, the institution of marriage would fade away entirely. Your faithfulness isn't depressing, rather it's consoling. It's still there in the universe, it's still real, others of us may achieve it!'

She spoke ironically, yet I could see that she meant it. It gave me a jolt to think that others might consider us image-makers. Once I might have relished it, now I felt constricted: image makers can't confess to frailties. The conversation turned back to Sara and we talked about the difficulties of the adolescent years, but in a cheerful grumble, comparing our own with our children's, asking each other why, when given freedoms that our generation never had, they still had to fight us. Over our steaks (rare and delicious) we concluded that it was the nature of the beast, and over coffee we confided our worries over our children's sex lives, terminating with a prose hymn to contraception. I talked in carefully general terms, Clare didn't.

'Do you know the level of teenage pregnancies and abortions today?' she asked me dramatically. 'A hundred and twenty thousand pregnancies a year – and fifty thousand odd of those were aborted last year. What a trade! What a world! And what wilful carelessness. My young beast Simon thought his girlfriend was pregnant last summer. For a whole three weeks he agonised and I cringed – and I had to keep it from Colin and his holier-than-thou attitude, or there'd have been blows struck between them. God, I was so angry with him. The "didn't-think-it-could-happen-to-me" syndrome. Annabel, if you do nothing else, hammer iron rules about protection into your children's heads. The irony of it is that contraception has never been so good, and unwanted pregnancies never so many!'

I left after tea. It had been a lively and stimulating afternoon, though darkened by an unease, almost a fore-boding, in my mind whenever the talk switched to my family.

I turned the car northwards to London and the M25. I switched on Radio 3 and listened to the second half of a choral evensong live from a church in Hampshire. Very gentle and peaceful it was, too, and I enjoyed it, but when the service came to an end, the next programme was announced with enthusiasm as the first radio performance of a new symphony by a composer whose name I didn't know. It opened with a series of wails on a solo violin and then silence for several beats followed by thud, shriek, grunt, bang and more wails. It would, I considered, make a suitably gruesome background to a film of violence and tragedy, but for enjoyable listening it rated nil. I switched to Radio 4 – and the all too well-known voice of Martin Hanley, which ended my period of relaxation with a jolt by reminding me of another lurking worry: the delay in the Pockett hearing.

Martin was delivering a talk on his usual topic – the iniquities of our criminal justice system. He was speaking of delays in getting matters to court. These, he said, could depend on various factors such as the hiatus in fraud and similar cases caused by the requirement to investigate further potential defendants, conspirators who had not been known about when the committal proceedings took place. This was a classic cause. Or there were difficulties when witnesses might no longer be within the jurisdiction, sunning themselves in Spain or Florida just when they were needed for interview. He had to concede that the normal long delays in the London Crown Courts had recently disappeared for reasons that were hard to explain – and despite the continual rise in crime committed. However, despite crime solving, arrests and charge rates having dropped in general, there were still shocking delays in frauds and even certain sexual cases being tried owing to the lack of suitable judges.

He was a good speaker, was Martin, easy on the ear. That he had not always done his homework carefully, or that he slurred over certain points that might have been advanced against his arguments, would not be apparent to the average listener who generally found him wonderful – as Paulina Grey did. He spoke of the horrors suffered by men and women who were held on remand, undergoing the rigours of prison before ever they had been found guilty, separated from their families, often unable to receive visits from their loved ones because they were in too distant a place. But even for those on bail, he continued, the length of time waiting for their case to come up was traumatic; it hung like a dark cloud over their lives, damping their pleasure in their everyday enjoyments, in many cases destroying their working lives, and all too frequently blasting their relationships. And witnesses – nobody mentioned their sufferings, but they could be severe, particularly in children who had been sexually abused.

The M25 loomed; I fought with a line of nose-to-tail lorries on the M23 to insert myself into its nearside lane, and then I had to tackle the horrors of actually getting on to the M25 which was too full of fast traffic for the experience to be other than harrowing. I ignored Martin for several minutes while these manoeuvres sent my heartbeat and my blood pressure soaring. When I could concentrate upon him again I heard him say:

'And there is another case waiting – a case of incest . . .'

Another case like mine?

'The unfortunate child in this case, a girl of only fourteen, reported the abuse she says she suffered as long ago as last May . . .'

No! Oh, my God, the Pockett case. Damn!

'And since that time she has been anticipating the horror and indignity of giving evidence in court, detailed evidence to strangers, on sexual matters of which most children of her age are happily ignorant – and afterwards having to face the rigours of cross-examination. Month after month she has had to worry, a child already affected by the most unpleasant form of abuse a father can inflict – and still there is no hearing date. How can we inflict such evils upon these poor children . . .?'

No prizes for guessing who gave Martin his information on this particular case – how delighted he must have been with the snippet. I could gladly have throttled Paulina Grey. No mention, I noticed, of the original mid-November date, or the unfortunate judge who was the cause of the hiatus. He was right, the delays were shocking, but oh, dear God, I could have wished he'd mentioned any other case but that. Juries could be easily prejudiced. And Richard's reaction to the adverse publicity this might produce about me would place an even greater strain on us than already existed from my rapidly rising career and the dissent caused by Sara. As the matter concerned a child and her father, the name of the accused could not be revealed for fear of identification of the alleged victim, that was some consolation – that and the hope that the broadcast might produce an early date for the hearing. I must tell Tom to ring the Bailey again.

18

On Saturday evening Richard and I drove to the inherited Belgravia flat of the Morton-Rycrofts, Richard complaining loudly all the way. The evening's entertainment, he groaned, would have all the excitement of an overdose of Ovaltine.

It made a change from his complaint all week: that even before it got to court my incest case was collecting publicity and revulsion. In a week rather lacking in news, the journalists had pounced upon Martin Hanley's broadcast and publicised the Pockett case nationwide. '. . . Though for legal reasons, we are prohibited from revealing names . . .' they had no inhibitions about discussing incest or rape in steamy details, or of publishing the agonies of those willing to reveal their suffering. One tabloid carried the headline: 'Young Girl's Torture by Sex-Crazed Father', another had the pictures and stories of five women who had been 'Used and Abused by Grandfather'. They also had no hesitation in reviling the legal profession for its cruel handling of the victims in such cases. *The Times* had a short article on today's high incidence of incest and a leader discussing the sad, but, the editor concluded, essential, need for abused girls and women, including the victims of marital rape, to give evidence in person and to be cross-examined. Various women's groups, including Females For Freedom, disagreed, their representatives proclaiming on television their conviction that this was an ordeal that should never be forced upon the frightened victims. Their statements should be sufficient.

Richard could only thank God, frequently and loudly, that none of the journalists had so far managed to trace me. Had they done so his position within Princes College as an upholder of women's rights would have been blown to smithereens. He could well have been forced to barricade himself in his room to shield himself from the women's denunciations of us both. I told him he was over the top – this was England, not the wilder reaches of California – but he told me, No, the college feminist groups were strident, especially so among those he taught – not surprising that those who studied political science should wish to be politically correct. I could only pray that the subject would not come up at the dinner table tonight.

The Morton-Rycrofts looked the same as always; the professor immaculate in expensive tailoring, his wife in a pearl grey silk blouse escaping rapidly from the confines of a black velvet skirt. I'd been acquainted with that skirt for many years; it hadn't expanded as its owner had, but clung to every bulge. Mrs Morton-Rycroft was a homely, dumpy woman. 'I'm a homebird,' she liked to say. There were no children, which was a pity; she was a kindly soul and would have made an excellent mother. But I found it impossible to imagine Professor Morton-Rycroft performing an act so earthy and self-revelatory as making love.

The Morton-Rycroft guests hadn't changed much over the years, either. The same senior members of the department were there; each, perhaps, having a touch less hair and a touch more paunch than last year, their wives showing a greater generosity with the tint bottle and the blusher, but basically unaltered.

It was the mixture as before – with one new ingredient. I noticed her the moment we entered the big room, standing in front of the fire, monopolising its heat and the attention of several of the men. She was a tall dark woman of about thirty, wearing a shrill yellow dress of some slithery material that looked in imminent danger of sliding off her preposterous breasts, breasts quite out of proportion to her slim frame. The men around her were clearly enjoying themselves.

'Erica Fennimore,' Richard said. 'My wife, Annabel.'

A smile flashed on and off like a neon sign while brown eyes assessed me. 'Pleased to know you, Annabel.' She looked from me to Richard and back again with frank curiosity. 'My,' she said, 'you're much younger than I expected – I thought Richard said he'd a daughter of seventeen?'

'We do have,' I said, for once not warming to the implied compliment. What had she expected? What had Richard led her to expect? Grey hair and wrinkles and clothes like ill-fitting loose-covers? I was suddenly glad I had put on my favourite dark rose dress and taken trouble with my face and hair.

'I didn't expect to find you here tonight, Erica,' Richard remarked.

'I was invited at the last minute.' She put a hand on his arm, leaning forward confidingly, her remarkable cleavage heaving gently beneath his eyes. 'I believe I was asked to even the numbers – with Paul!' She chuckled.

Richard laughed. I managed a smile to show that the humour of the situation was not lost on me. Paul, though not of the type to come out, was generally known to have lived for many years in great felicity with a bearded flautist.

Erica turned to me with a muted version of the confiding air, her hand still lying on Richard's sleeve. 'You know, you have a lovely husband, Annabel, just lovely. He's been so helpful to me, you wouldn't believe. He's given up hours of his precious time too – as if his own research and writing were of no account. His assistance with my thesis has been invaluable.'

'I wouldn't have expected otherwise,' I said, looking at Richard. 'He has always been conscientious, no matter who was involved.'

'Of course, I've told him he mustn't bother with me any more, he has his book on political thought to complete – but naturally you'll know all about that?'

'Naturally. Richard and I always discuss our work in depth.'

'You work? What do you do?'

'I'm a barrister.'

'Really? Are you?' She seemed genuinely surprised. She looked at Richard, whose face was at its most impassive. 'You didn't tell me you had such a clever wife . . .'

She was interrupted by Hyacinth House, who greeted me effusively, as she always did. Her husband, Alan, had joined the staff at Princes College the year after Richard. They had three daughters, all as nice and plain and sensible as Hyacinth herself. She was convinced that our having children of roughly similar ages created a great bond; she loved to compare their progress and interests in minute detail.

'Lovely to see you, Annabel dear. How are you?' Hyacinth planted her sturdy body between Erica and me in a way that was frankly rude.

'I'm very well, thank you, Hyacinth. Er . . . have you met Erica?'

She glanced over her shoulder. 'Oh, I didn't see you. It's Mrs . . . er, no, Miss Ferdinand, isn't it? Or do you call yourself Ms? So many divorced women do nowadays.'

240

'I've never been married,' Erica began, her eyes glinting.

'No, really? How sad for you. But perhaps it's not too late yet. Now, if you'll excuse me, Annabel's an old friend.' She drew me aside, hissing: 'Dreadful woman!'

I was surprised at Hyacinth, she was the last person I'd expect to find bristling like a bitch at the sight of a rival. But she even looked different tonight. Make-up, that was it; I'd never seen her made up before. She'd even matched the eye shadow to a smart new dress, but the result was not a success. Hyacinth wore the fashionable enormous spectacles in front of her myopic eyes. So thick were the lenses that they reminded me of the neo-Georgian bottle glass in estate house windows. They were reflecting the turquoise eye-shadow in rings round the edges, giving her a surrealistic panda-like look. 'Now tell me,' she said, 'how's the family?'

'Growing up,' I responded cautiously.

'Oh, I know! They do, don't they? So quickly too, nowadays. Sara, let's see, she must be sixteen . . .'

'Seventeen.'

'There you are – how time does fly! In the sixth form now. Will it be Oxford or Cambridge – or will she be like my dear Faith and fancy London and living at home? Perhaps she'll go with her daddy to Princes!'

I sipped my drink. 'I doubt whether Sara will go to university.'

'Not go to university?' The spectacles radiated blue shock waves. 'But, my dear Annabel, surely our sort of people send all their children to university!'

'She's doing A-levels, naturally,' I said. 'She's keeping her options open.' The defensive words echoed unpleasantly in my head. Naturally? My God, I was barely one degree less competitive than Hyacinth. Were Richard and I the stereotype ambitious parents of whom she was the caricature?

241

Hyacinth tutted. 'I knew the comprehensive school was a mistake.'

I was glad when the wife of a junior lecturer, squeezing past us, was seized upon by Hyacinth, who enquired in gracious manner after Alice's health and family.

'All's well? That's lovely. My word, your youngest will soon be ready for school, won't he? Such a relief when that stage comes.'

'I shall miss him,' Alice said, and her tiny simian face looked sad. Alice Edge reminded me strongly of a little monkey I used once to talk to in a pet shop window; the same engagingly snub features, the same wide-eyed reproachful look.

'But you'll be able to return to work,' Hyacinth said bracingly. 'Think of the intellectual stimulus, the new freedom. What was it you did before you were married?'

'Nothing. I married virtually straight from school.' Wry amusement. 'Oh, I did work in a flower shop for a few months.'

Disconcerted, Hyacinth blinked, but rallied fast. 'Then now's your chance. My word, the opportunities you have! Why, you could take a computer course, do teacher training, Open University courses if you wanted – they're all available for the more mature student.'

Dark eyes considered her. Alice said nothing.

Possibly conscious of tactlessness, Hyacinth continued kindly: 'But I expect you've already sorted your ideas out and made specific plans.'

'No.'

'Oh, but you must, my dear! So many mothers become depressed and lonely when their little ones trot off. We mustn't have that happening. What are your hobbies?'

'I wouldn't say I had any.' Alice took a hefty gulp of her drink.

Hyacinth was horrified. 'But I should be so dull without

my part-time lecturing, my work as a magistrate, my upholstery classes and my cookery. Whatever do you do with your free time?'

A long slow breath. 'I sit and pick my nose.'

I dared not look at Hyacinth's expression. I lowered my face to my glass, choking back the giggle that rose unwanted like a sneeze.

There was an interval while Hyacinth stuttered: 'Well, really . . . I don't see . . .' and then she discovered another friend she simply had to speak to and dashed away.

Alice's little monkey face was screwed up; impossible to tell with what emotion.

Gratuitous insults are not invariably entertaining, whatever certain comedians think. I said: 'You hurt her feelings.'

'So? Interfering cow! She's another woman like my mother, with her automatic assumption that every female will demonstrate solidarity with her sisters by having a career. A mere job is scorned by these ranters, raising a family is nothing. They won't let you alone.' Her eyes burned with feeling. 'I don't need achievements to justify my existence. I'm bringing up four children, I potter in my house and garden, I'm happy. Isn't that enough?'

'If it's right for you.' It would not be for me, but who was I to judge her needs? I tried to soothe her: 'But Hyacinth was only doing her best to be helpful.'

I was not successful.

'Doing her best? Women who concentrate on that sort of best are a menace. They perceive you as made in their image, and it's what would be their best they consider, never yours. Parents are the worst – they talk of the sacrifices they have to make, but it's their children who are the sacrificial victims. They plan for them, think for them, tie them up with endless guilt if they attempt to break

243

away from their pre-arranged fates, and finally kill in them the ability to think or choose for themselves.'

Was it the residue of the guilt she spoke of that made Alice so vehement? There was no doubt that she retained the ability to think for herself – unlike Hyacinth's daughters, who never queried her undeviatingly high standards but, like blinkered horses, headed straight for the objectives she set. It was peculiar how emotive and unsettling I found every conversation these days. Angela would say that my aura was all wrong.

God, bringing up children was impossible. Everything I believed in was under attack. Morals, every type of education, even ambition, it seemed. Should a parent be permissive or directive? Were my efforts mother-love or smother-love? How did anyone find a middle ground when the middle ground was a stinking marsh of shifting ideas and theories?

Thank God Mrs Morton-Rycroft was ushering us into dinner. I was not so pleased when she referred to her seating plan and I realised I had the honour of being placed at my host's right hand. Was that a compliment to Richard, the professor's probable successor, or did I rate above the other wives for my own achievements? His wife confided: 'Morty does like to have an intelligent woman next to him.' I cast a mock despairing look towards Richard, but failed to make contact. He was pushing in Miss Erica Fennimore's chair.

We had hardly started upon the chilly hors d'oeuvres before Professor Morton-Rycroft turned to me. 'I'm so glad you could come tonight, Annabel, especially after that interesting talk by Martin Hanley earlier this week. I wanted to ask your opinion, to make sure I have the facts straight – from a practitioner. Tell me, is Hanley right in his criticisms of Bench and Bar in these unconscionable delays in the courts?

I finished chewing my mouthful, swallowed and said: 'Martin has a tendency to exaggerate and to dramatise but, yes, in his level of work there are still delays because of a shortage of high court judges (and the Lord Chancellor says he will put this right) but what he briefly mentioned, but I don't think he has understood, is the really dramatic fall in routine work arriving at the Crown Courts. Some say that the Crown Prosecution Service has run out of funds, others say the police are demoralized and are not charging offenders, but what the public will say when they find out what's happening in the middle of a crime wave I hate to think!'

'Perhaps it will stop so many unfortunate men being shoved into prison?' David Burke, a junior lecturer, remarked provocatively.

'It would appear so,' I replied, not responding to this familiar gambit.

Hycinth was not so prudent. 'On my Bench we strive to try every possible alternative before we make a custodial sentence,' she informed the table at large. 'Correct me if I am wrong, Annabel, but as far as I remember the figures, the number of jury courts available has gone up by something like five hundred per cent since the fifties, whilst the numbers in prison have merely doubled. And that despite taking various matters such as practising homosexuality and abortion off the statute books.'

'Then what,' asked David, 'is wrong with our society that we have so many serious crimes to contend with?'

'Not just our society,' Hyacinth said swiftly, 'but the whole of the western world. To my mind the problem is entirely owing to the crumbling of our moral code. In Japan now there are tremendous pressures from parents, from schools, from community leaders, from every part of society, for their youth to put their energies into achieving status through education and work. This ethic of work and achievement together with strong social pressure against crime makes it far less attractive. And they don't have our permissive view of morality to start with.'

'And speaking of morality,' the professor said quickly, not willing to relinquish his steering of the conversation, 'Hanley mentioned a case of incest in his broadcast. An unfortunate young girl whose case had been held up for many months. It made me most indignant to hear of it. Surely such matters should be specially listed for an early hearing?'

'I happen to know something of this case,' I said cautiously. 'It was set down for an earlier date, but the judge who was to hear it had a heart attack and the Old Bailey, being as always heavily booked, could not fit it in immediately. Unfortunate, but not so reprehensible from the court's point of view as it might seem.'

'You seem to have inside information, Annabel,' Alan House said. 'You've done several sex cases recently – this couldn't be your case as well, could it?'

All eyes were upon me. I nodded.

'You're for the prosecution, I take it?'

'No, the defence.'

'Well,' drawled Erica, 'all I can say is, you must be vurry brave. In the town where I come from in the States the sisterhood would lynch you.' She rolled her eyes in mock horror and snapped at the food on her fork. The men laughed.

Hyacinth said: 'I'm glad we're more civilised here.'

Mrs Morton-Rycroft asked curiously: 'Do you think you'll get the father off?'

'Surely not?' Alice Edge said, shocked.

'I don't know. One can never tell. There are one or two straws of evidence on his side.' But it would take a bonfire of straws to destroy the evidence of the Pockett women.

A battery of eyes stared at me. Most were reproachful.

I felt as though it was I who was going on trial, charged with offences against women. To plead not guilty on the grounds that I was only doing my job was useless: if I failed to get John Pockett off I would be guilty on all counts – bully of the innocent victim, betrayer of my sex, guilty, too, of incompetence, of bias . . . God knows what the media and Females for Freedom might not charge me with.

'What do you think of your wife taking on this sort of case?' Erica asked Richard.

He fingered his wine glass. 'Annabel runs her own working life. The matter is entirely in her hands. She is a barrister who acts according to the cab rank principle, taking the cases that are offered to her.' His voice was studiedly neutral.

'You British are so easy-going,' said Erica.

'We're easy-going because we don't know where we're going,' said Alan House. 'Today's student generation believes in no sexual moral rights or wrongs, no absolutes, only competing arguments. Not surprising when so many of the absolutes were swept away in their parents' day –abortion and homosexuality which, as Hyacinth said, were once crimes, soon became acceptable – like divorce, pornography, and pre-marital sex and promiscuity, all flung into the flux. No wonder young people find it impossible to abide by fixed rules. The irony of it is that most of the big changes came during Labour's time in office – the first of the great privatisations, the priva-tisation of morality!'

Hyacinth agreed with her husband. 'All-out sexual free-dom has only injured women and contributed nothing to the growth of their status in the workplace,' she said. 'I give my girls proper guidelines.'

I silently betted that she told them nice girls don't.

It was Professor Morton-Rycroft who rounded off the

discussion. 'I had an interesting conversation with the Director not many months ago on one of Annabel's cases,' he said, 'that pop-singer, what was her name? Ah, Salome Keane, thank you, Alan. The Director and I are both admirers of Annabel; she's the sort who will triumph in what I believe are known as the gender wars. Someone who believes equally in both sexes' rights, who stands up for clients of either sex without fear or favour. A credit to her alma mater.' He lifted his glass to me.

I thanked Morty for his kind words and thought gleefully that if the Director felt my stance was the correct one then Richard had no need to worry over my sex cases in relation to his career.

I told him so in the car going home, but he didn't seem to think the point one of particular importance. 'You might remember that I have never asked you to abandon them,' he pointed out.

'True.' I yawned. We slowed for traffic lights. 'Your Miss Fennimore seems a lively person.' She had kept the bottom end of the long table in shouts of laughter, while I'd had to listen to the professor giving a monologue on the shifting political situation between Russia and the other members of the old Soviet Union.

Richard jerked the car into bottom gear and moved on. 'Erica has a remarkable wit. She was particularly amusing tonight.'

'I did notice that she was very . . . um, outgoing. It must be great for you, doing so much work with her. I'm only surprised you didn't tell me more about her, especially when you were giving her so much help.'

'Nothing to tell. I've given her assistance, but no more than I would to anyone else with similar difficulties.'

'Really?' I said gaily. 'Darling Richard, you mustn't be so modest. Judging by her praise, you've been quite special. It's good to hear one's husband so appreciated.'

'Erica has a trans-Atlantic warmth of manner that could be misinterpreted by someone who didn't know her.'

'Is that what it is?' I paused to suppress a belch; the Morton-Rycroft overdone pork was sitting heavily on my stomach. 'Perhaps Hyacinth House misunderstands her. What do you think? There certainly was an atmosphere. Or have there been, shall we say, certain passages between her and Alan that Hyacinth's discovered? Do tell!'

'I have no idea, Annabel. College gossip has never interested me, as you know.'

Richard stamped on the accelerator to overtake a crawling taxi. His driving was less smooth than usual; he must have drunk more than he should. The roads were surprisingly full of traffic for one o'clock in the morning, and this road held too many red lights. By the time we braked to a sharp stop outside the terrace I was feeling distinctly queasy.

I performed the undignified wriggle that extricated me from the car and on to the high pavement, and glanced up at the house for the pleasure its classical symmetry and restrained dignity never failed to give me. But tonight it looked odd. For a moment I was puzzled, then I realised that lights were on that should be off, glaring past undrawn curtains into the dark road.

'I'll park the car at the back,' Richard said.

'No wait, don't,' I said urgently. 'Look at those windows, something may be wrong. Come in with me, will you?'

He unlocked the front door onto silence and dazzle. We blinked.

'Careless waste of electricity,' Richard grumbled.

I sniffed. The house smelt bad, a nasty sweetish smell. I went to switch off the drawing-room lights and then I saw it, down the hall by the lavatory door, a splash of vomit across the carpet and up the skirting board.

'Somebody's been sick,' I said. I stepped over the mess to the open lavatory door. There were nasty yellowish marks on the carpet and up the tiles behind the bowl. My already unhappy insides lurched. My children . . . Gastric 'flu? Food poisoning? Were they unconscious? Oh God, let them be all right.

Richard called sharply: 'Annabel, here's Sara. In the drawing-room.'

She was lying on the Chesterfield, her head back over the arm, dank clumps of hair clinging to her forehead. Her mouth was open, every breath coming noisily. I spoke her name, softly at first and then loudly. There was no response. I put my hand on her shoulder and shook it, horribly conscious of the inert heaviness of the flesh beneath the dressing-gown. Frightened, I let go and straightened up; as I did so her hand fell from the sofa and thumped on the floor.

My legs shook. 'Richard? Richard, we must get a doctor. Whatever's happened?'

'She's drunk, you idiot. Passed out. Can't you see? Can't you smell it?'

That smell – of course. Not just the smell of vomit but a stench of spirits. Richard leaned forward to take a bottle from behind the bend of Sarah's knees; a high-shouldered bottle, empty of the gin it had once held. He dumped it in the waste-paper basket. I stood, more bemused than vexed, staring at the pallid face. We had left Sara sitting quietly in her room; this state was incomprehensible.

'I don't understand it,' I said. 'Why? Why?'

'I'll fetch Daniel,' Richard said. He stuck his head through the doorway and bellowed, 'Daniel!' with a ferocity that reverberated through the house. 'Daniel, come down here this instant!'

Danny descended the stairs, slowly, warily, scratching his chest and hitching at his pyjama bottoms. 'What the hell's the matter, Dad? It's the middle of the night.'

'Come on, come on! Don't play-act.' He gestured. 'In here! Now, your sister's dead drunk and we want to know why.'

Danny shuffled in.

'I don't know.' His face was a study in resentment. 'So she got drunk. Why ask me? Not my business.'

'Did you try to stop her?'

'Try to stop her? Christ, Dad, you try to stop Sara doing anything she wants to do! Hopeless.'

Richard nodded in reluctant acknowledgement. 'True. Sorry.'

Danny edged away, pushing at his tousled hair with a restless hand. 'Can I go back to bed, please? I'm cold.'

Sara groaned, stirred faintly and returned to her stupor. I pulled the rumpled dressing-gown over the goose-pimpled legs – and then I knew. The dressing-gown over the naked body, the damp hair, the gin bottle, her off-colour days recently. They added up to one conclusion.

'She's pregnant! That's what it is. She's pregnant!'

They both stared at me, Richard with his mouth open, Danny with a fair imitation of Richard's impassive look.

'Of all the stupid fools! She tried the gin and hot bath treatment. Right, Danny?'

He looked down at his bare feet on the carpet. He twitched one shoulder and wriggled his big toes and said nothing.

He's afraid, I thought, torn between us. He must have promised Sara not to say anything. But we have to know, so that we can help her. I felt curiously calm and accepting.

I put my hand on his pyjama-ed forearm. He was so much larger than me that it was difficult to remember how young he was. 'I'm sorry, darling,' I said softly. 'This is unfair on you. But you must come clean with us, for Sara's

sake. She'll need our help. She could have killed herself –
do you know that? She's been very stupid and reckless. I
only hope she hasn't taken any pills. Has she?'

He shook his head. His eyes were scared. 'I don't know.
I honestly don't.'

Richard sat down suddenly on the sofa by Sara's feet.
'Then she is pregnant?'

'Yeah,' Danny said. 'So she reckons.'

19

'I've taken three separate tests,' Sara mumbled from the Chesterfield. 'They were all positive. I kept thinking that it couldn't be true, but it was.'

I nodded, trying to keep calm and to remember that once I had been in her situation. It was late next morning and we were shut in the drawing-room, Richard and Sara and I.

'Angela gave me those pills that bring on your period,' she said in a bleak voice, 'so I thought if I combined them with the gin . . . but it didn't work.' Her hands moved nervously over her tear-stained face, clearing away the strands of hair that clung to it.

'Oh Sara, Sara . . .' I was sickened by Angela's stupidity, shocked by what Sara had attempted, and furious with the young man whose carelessness had put her in this condition. 'Is it Thierry's?'

'Dunno,' she said. 'There were three of them it could have been.'

'Three? In one month?'

'That's not many. I was going out with Tony first, and then with Thierry – and I went to a party with Dave in between. My friends get around a lot more than that. I'm just a little bit promiscuous, I suppose.' After all, she said,

253

you don't learn to read just to read one book over and over again, do you? You explore. So if you went out with a boy you let him have it – if the opportunity arose and you fancied him, that is. 'Everybody does,' said Sara.

I groaned. 'Everybody does, everybody does! Does that automatically make it right? Don't you have any moral code? No, what am I talking about? It's all DIY nowadays – make your own morality included. But, God, Sara, look at the mess you've landed yourself in.'

Richard stirred in his chair. 'Never mind the lecture,' he said. 'It's too late for that. We have to decide what's to be done. An abortion is the logical answer, I suppose.'

'Abortion? Could Sara cold-bloodedly have her child exterminated? Damn it, she's a vegetarian, she says she's horrified at the thought of killing animals for food – how could she have her baby killed for convenience' sake?'

'She's already tried to kill it,' Richard retorted.

'I didn't think of it like that,' Sara said, her skin the greyish-white of uncut pastry. 'You don't know, Daddy. I didn't properly believe in a real baby – I just wanted my period to come and everything to be normal again.'

'Well, Sara, you're on the horns of a dilemma,' I said, taking her hand. 'You can rid your body of our grandchild as if it were an infestation like the threadworms of childhood, or you can bring it up fatherless, as I was. And that's hard, and not just for you. Having only one parent is like missing an arm or a leg. Handicapped, that's how I felt. D'you know that?'

Sara shook her head and her tears spattered dark spots on her jeans.

'I say an abortion's the answer,' Richard repeated heavily. 'What sort of life would Sara have, lumbered with a baby at her age? And what about the embarrassment and inconvenience to us? We're neither of us at the stage of our careers where we want babies crying in the night.'

254

I turned to him. 'Richard, don't pressurise her. We must help Sara to consider the alternatives in the clearest possible light, but she must make up her own mind.' As Alice Edge would put it, Sara should decide what was for her best, not ours. That was the principle we should follow. I swung back to Sara, grappling for calm and the right tone of voice. 'Darling, it's up to you. You've heard what we each think. The fairest thing I can say is that whatever you decide will receive our backing – and no more recriminations.' I glanced at Richard and he nodded. 'Well?'

Her forehead was damp with perspiration. 'I don't know.' She swallowed. 'Honestly, I don't know. I don't want to get rid of it, not my own baby. I like babies. But I'm not ready for it now. It shouldn't have happened.' She pushed herself unsteadily to her feet.

Richard said quietly: 'But it has happened and you must decide.'

'I don't want to,' she wailed. Her hand rose to her mouth. 'Oh Christ,' she muttered, 'I do feel sick.' She looked to me helplessly, claiming my sympathy.

It came in a flood as I remembered my own pregnancy nausea. 'Poor love! My poor Sara! It's beastly, isn't it? Come on, let's get you to the loo.' I propelled her towards the door.

She leaned on me in tearful gratitude. 'Oh Mum, I'm sorry, really I am.'

'I know,' I said. 'I know.'

We got there just in time. I held her head while she emptied her stomach and afterwards I sat her in a chair, and washed her sweaty face with a cool flannel and brushed her hair. We were two women together and Richard was the outsider.

Tuesday evening. Even above the pulsating clamour of the pop music I could hear the boys talking, the broken voice and the half-broken voice, both full of indignation.

'I wish Sara'd make up her stupid mind. I'm cheesed off with all the talking and the puking and the crying.'

'Me too,' came Oliver's voice. 'I think it's awful.'

I stood on the upstairs landing, eavesdropping unashamedly.

'Dad's right. She should have an abortion, get shot of it. Sara couldn't bring up a hamster, let alone a baby. Mum must be mad. And what about the rest of us? How could I bring friends home with some smelly babe in the house bawling its head off and Sara yelling blue murder at it?'

'Hell, Danny, that's a pretty selfish way to look at it.'

'Turn the bass up a bit, will you? No, it's not. It's the same for you, too. Be honest. And Dad. After all, how would it look for him with his colleagues and his friends? Sara at her age, I mean. And it's unnecessary, isn't it? Forgetting to take the pill – Christ!'

'Yeh, I suppose it is. But whichever she decides can't be right, can it? Poor Sara.'

'It isn't up to her. She's not eighteen yet. Dad should tell her. But she listens too much to Mum.'

I had a free day at the end of the week, a day ear-marked for dealing with my personal administration, for wrestling with VAT, accounts and paperwork, but I pushed them aside in favour of Sara. I would take her for a walk in Richmond Park and have a heart-to-heart talk. She had been at home the last two days, too queasy to cope with school, crouched in a chair, freezing into a pallid waxwork when Richard and I tried to approach her, her brows moulded into a scowl. Perhaps the two of us together had been too much. One alone in the sunshine might melt her reserve, discover her real thoughts.

We walked in silence through the Richmond Gate at the top of Star and Garter Hill, and the sun lay luminous over the park, gilding tree trunks and grass tussocks, laying long wintry shadows behind them. As we approached a grove of trees several squirrels leapt from the ground beneath to whisk themselves up the trunks, chasing one another across branches, leaping perilously from one tree to another.

'Lucky animals,' Sara said suddenly. 'They don't have to worry about examinations or abortions.'

I responded as robustly as I could: 'Neither do you, if you don't choose to. For Heaven's sake, you dope, tell me what you want for your future. And do you truly want a baby in it?'

'But how can I tell what I want?' she asked me. 'You and Dad, your lives are geared to the professional and the intellectual. The boys and I don't know anyone outside your worlds, no one speaks of jobs outside them. How can I decide if I don't know what the options are?'

'We could send you to one of those career-planning institutions,' I suggested. 'They discuss your good subjects and your weaknesses, your interests and your hobbies, and feed them to a computer, and that then produces job suggestions specially geared to you.'

Sara retreated. 'But what does it matter now? If I'm having a baby I can't do anything, can I? And I'll have to leave school. Thank God!'

A thought so astounding occurred to me that I was momentarily stupified, then taken aback that anything so foolish and unthinkable should have entered my mind . . . and yet . . . I had to ask Sara.

'That wasn't why . . . this happened, was it?'

She did not shriek with affront. She stared into the distance. 'No. Well, I wasn't trying to get pregnant deliberately, if that's what you mean. But, well, I just didn't care . . . I was so pissed off with everything that I didn't always bother to take the pill. So it happened anyway.'

257

I felt sick. So that was how this horrendous mess had come about. Sara and I, whom I had once thought alike, could not have been more poles apart. At university I'd got pregnant by a man I thought I loved, despite stringent precautions, and my world had been blown apart. I thought of confessing my own past to Sara, then thought again. My whole-hearted wish to take my degree, some-how, anyhow, despite the child, and the story of the miscarriage that released me, were a thousand light years from her situation. I sighed and was silent.

Across the slope beyond us deer were streaming in follow-my-leader fashion, flickering in and out of the sun as they moved beneath the trees.

Sara said everyone wanted her to play follow-my-leader, too. And Ms Cropper had scared her with all her talk of the need for women to be more conscientious, more determined, more tough than men in order to achieve as much. What Sara had first heard as a clarion call to the fight she now saw as the sad trumpeting of a lost cause, certainly where she was concerned.

'I can't follow you,' she said, giving me a sideways glance. 'You and Dad, you've put your ambitions on the wrong person.'

'But you've not been working.'

'No, I know . . . Well, that's why. I don't know what my ambitions are, but they aren't yours. I've watched you, Mum, and I've seen you working evenings, working weekends, and having us three to bring up, and all the shopping and the cooking on top of it all – it's appalling. I don't want a life that's all work and no fun, just to compete with men.'

'But your generation will have it easier than mine, dar-ling. The old anti-women bastions have crumbled, men are doing far more in the house – '

'Not in our family! But whatever changes, I shan't. I'm

different from you – take that aboard, Mum, please!'

I laughed. 'Oh, I have Sara, I have. But having eliminated a professional career, what about the baby? Don't think you need to have it to escape from school!'

Silence for a while. We turned to walk back, the warm sun on our faces. Then as we left the park she said: 'I'm not like Lucinda and her sort. They hate the thought of marriage, of being trapped by men and children. But I'd like to have a house of my own with lovely old furniture like ours, and have a family. That's a dream I've always had. That's why . . .' She swallowed. Her voice anguished, she brought out: 'That's why I don't know what to do about this pregnancy. It's not wrong for the future . . . but it's all wrong now. If I were going to go all-out for a career then I'd have to be tough and hard and say, "No way, I've got to get rid of it." It'd be clear cut. Only it's not. It's all a horrible fog. Oh Christ, Mum, you do see, don't you?'

I did. And I saw that while our talk had brought a startling amount to light it had not solved our dilemma.

I flung back the kitchen curtains. A grey morning, as though nature had pressed a dimmer-switch in the sky. Drops of water hung motionless from the iron railings before our house. A steady gurgle came from the drains. The world was bleak and horrible.

Richard's heavy feet thumped on the stairs. I put bacon in the pan for his breakfast. He sat down, slapping *The Times*, still folded, on to the kitchen table. 'We can't go on like this,' he said.

'No.' The bacon began to frizzle.

'Sara must make up her mind. If she decides on an abortion it must be done now. Time's running out.'

'I know.' Loathsome words, more loathsome with every repetition.

Sara did not have morning sickness, she had evening

sickness, rendering dinnertime hideous. In the mornings, feeling relatively strong, she spoke of keeping the child, demanding endless reassurances that Richard would not hate her baby or force her to leave. In the evenings, dizzy and nauseated, she moaned that she couldn't face it. 'I'm too young to be tied down! Jesus, it's so unfair, I haven't started to live yet!' But in either mood any attempt to obtain a positive decision led to shrieks of: 'Why can't you stop leaning on me? I don't know! I don't know! Why won't it just go away?'

I broke two eggs into the pan and watched the whites flutter. Richard's eyes were on my back; I could feel them. I turned up the heat.

'If Sara can't make up her own mind, Annabel, we must make it up for her. Candidly, I think she's too young for the decision, for the responsibility. She needs someone else to decide.'

'No. That we must never do. How can we teach our boys to take responsibility for their actions if they see us encouraging Sara to evade hers? If she decides to apply her principles over animal rights to her baby's right to live, then we'll have to help her. Her hesitation does show that she cares.'

'But you're ignoring a lifetime of secondary problems to follow, not least for the child itself. Right in theory, wrong in practice, Annabel.'

'Not wrong in practice – just damned inconvenient and embarrassing. Be honest.' The forgotten bacon spat viciously and I whipped round to save it.

Behind me Richard said: 'All right. But have you told Sara of the baby you lost? Shown her you're human, too, not a blasted plaster saint?'

I grappled with the smoking frying pan, wincing. 'No. Not relevant.'

'Really?'

'No. People make that mistake all the time, saying: "Oh, I do understand, I had the same problem myself." But it never is the same.'

'No. It isn't, is it? You got rid of yours.'

'Not intentionally, Richard, you know that.'

'Of course I do. God, Annabel, you're not normally this obtuse. But think how different your life would have been without that accident – stuck in Woking with your mother and your bawling brat . . . No degree, no career, no fun. And no me – if that means anything to you, that is!'

'You know it does!' I put his overcooked breakfast in front of him, wincing from the picture he had conjured up.

'Think, then! His face altered suddenly, the blue eyes looked at me appealingly. 'Annabel, my love, this is dreadful. I hate to be quarrelling with you.' His hand reached for mine, pressing it hard.

I pressed his in return, but let it go. 'Eat your breakfast, Richard, do, or we'll both be late.'

He pushed the food about his plate with a bemused look, finally shoving it away, one egg uneaten. It was a fertile egg, I saw by the brownish mark. Inside Sara there was a fertile egg, gently growing. It could not be so simply abandoned, scraped away into a bin.

Richard jerked out: 'All this trouble was because of that foolish business with my mother over Oliver. It drove Sara out of the house. She was convinced of our condemnation of her and hadn't the maturity or the self-confidence to deal with the situation, so she rushed off with these young men. They approved of her. They wanted her.' Broodingly he added: 'I should have done more to reassure her.'

'You tried, I tried. The response was nil.'

'Nor was she happy at school. I didn't listen when she told me.'

'Neither of us did. We thought she was merely going

261

through a silly phase, encouraged by your mother. We didn't see how deep it went.'

He took no notice. 'I assumed that any child of mine must be academically minded. How stupid!'

He was heaping blame on himself, cursing himself for his inadequacies as a father. Compassion moved in me. The horrors of recent months had torn the pattern of his life to shreds, pounding him with the death of his friend, confronting him, one upon another, with a virago of a mother, a truanting and lying daughter, a career-obsessed wife, and an unwanted grandchild.

Softening, I put a hand on his shoulder. I yearned for the old uncomplicated warmth between us, for the days when we would have turned to each other for comfort through the hurt and the trouble, giving mutual support, standing together against the world.

'Darling, we can't discuss anything now. We're running late. Thank God I've only an eleven o'clock conference this morning. But come home early. We'll have the fire in the study . . .' I stopped. He was shaking his head, a dull colour creeping into his cheeks.

'Oh God,' he said, 'I can't. Not tonight. I forgot to tell you – I have a meeting. Sorry.'

I snatched away my hand as if he'd become red hot. 'Richard, not again? You can't. Damn your meeting!'

'I can't. It's important.'

I exploded into fury. 'Isn't Sara? Aren't I? Miss it!'

'I can't,' he said with finality. 'I'm chairing it. Look, Annabel, I'll try to speed it up. When I do get back – '

'Sara will be throwing up. And we'll get nowhere.'

My sister-in-law, Jane, arrived on our doorstep as I got back from court the next day, demanding strong drink to revive her after Christmas shopping in Richmond. She stared in amazement as Sara, sprawled in grubby jeans

262

and sweater at the kitchen table, peered at her through a tangle of hair. 'Good Lord,' she said. 'You look green and grim. What's the matter?'

I repeated the lie I'd used to the school to explain her absences. 'Sara's recovering from gastric 'flu.'

Jane was sympathetic. 'Poor Sara. Leaves you feeling chewed up and spat out, doesn't it?' Her blue eyes, so like Richard's, examined her niece thoughtfully. 'Tell you what, come and have lunch with me tomorrow and help me decide on a pattern for the patchwork quilt I'm making.'

To my surprise, Sara looked gratified. She pushed the hair back from her face. 'I wouldn't mind,' she said.

The worrying thought occurred to me that she might confide in Jane. I sighed. It wouldn't matter. Not in the long run. Someone from outside this house might help Sara to make up her mind. Jane was sensible: she would neither shriek with horror nor pour syrupy commiseration over her. It was up to Sara, I decided.

I returned home next day to trip over the boys' trainers on the hall mat. I'd just sworn, picked them up and dumped them on the stairs for the boys to take to their rooms when Sara crashed in through the front door behind me, making me jump. She was sobbing, her face ravaged.

Terror clutched me. 'What is it? What's happened?'

'Grandma!' she managed between gasps.

'She was there?' Dear God, I'd never thought of that. 'You didn't tell her? Not about the baby?'

'She was being really nice to me. I thought she'd understand.'

'Not this, Sara. Never!'

I wanted to comfort her, but she pushed me away. 'Don't!' She rubbed her hands across her swollen, wet face and took a shuddering breath. 'She said dreadful things.

"Like mother, like daughter," she kept saying. She said I was just another slut like you – that you got pregnant when you were my age, but you got rid of it. I said you couldn't have, she'd got it wrong again, like she had with Ollie. She was horrible – she shouted . . . It wasn't true, was it?'

I heard my voice saying the words; no time to arrange them carefully. 'Well, not quite as she told you, but yes, I did lose a baby.'

She looked stunned. 'I don't believe I'm hearing this . . . I just don't believe it!'

I said quickly: 'But I knew who the father of my baby was. I thought we were going to be married. And whatever your grandmother may have said, I lost it because of a car accident.'

She took no notice. 'It's unbelievable. You watched me going through all this misery . . . You never told me . . .'

'Perhaps I should have, but I didn't think so. My experience bore no relationship to yours and I wanted you to make your decisions entirely from your own needs and wishes.'

She turned away. 'Well, I'm going to get rid of my . . . foetus,' she said, her voice stony. 'I don't care what you think, not now. You can go to hell!' She made for the stairs, to escape to her room.

'Sara . . .'

'I won't have it! I hate it! I hate you, too. You're a hypocrite and you're fucking up my mind. You made me feel guilty by throwing back my principles at me about animals and killing, but you go and make money out of defending rapists and fathers who've committed incest, and you think you're doing right. What if their victims get pregnant? Is abortion wrong then? Lucinda says a foetus isn't a baby and I reckon that's how I see it. No, that's it! I'm going to the doctor first thing tomorrow!'

264

She started up the stairs, caught her foot in one of Danny's vast trainers, twisted, jerked and fell backwards at my feet, the base of her spine hitting the floor with a jarring crunch. The breath whooshed from her lungs.

'Sara! Oh God, Sara, are you all right?'

I stooped over her. For a second her eyes looked into mine, then they closed.

20

Her miscarriage took place without complications, dealt with competently at home by our local doctor. I was her nurse through its intimate horrors, when Sara seemed only half-conscious of what was happening, frightened and in pain; she needed me then. When she began to recover the time for anger and recriminations was gone. She lay silent and listless, mauve shadows round her eyes and her skin like tissue paper. And despite the shouting, despite the determination she'd expressed to be rid of it, Sara wept for her baby.

She accepted my comfort and a box of Kleenex, blew her nose and wiped her eyes, and muttered embarrassedly that she was a fool. 'I still want it both ways. I still want my freedom and my baby. I didn't know I could be so silly. But it's all so sad.'

'Yes,' I said.

'Don't despise me.'

'How could I?' I asked. 'It's how I felt.'

'Did you?' Sara said. 'Illogical, aren't we?'

'Not really. Just faced with impossible choices.'

'Yeah, you can say that again.' She shifted her head on her pillows. 'I'm sorry,' she brought out with difficulty, 'I'm sorry I shouted at you. It wasn't your fault.'

We talked. Not all at once, but gradually, over the next few days, and calmly. It was as if the fall that had knocked the breath from Sara's body and rid her of the child had somehow knocked the sullen anger from her, ridding her of tension and resentment.

It was on the fourth day that Sara's teacher, Ms Cropper, came. I'd rung the school to tell Mr Rudkin that Sara had fallen downstairs and injured herself at the base of the spine. The coccyx, I explained. True, if not the whole truth. I told him that she would not return before Christmas; in fact, I confessed, taking a deep breath, it had been decided that Sara would not be returning to school at all.

It was to discuss this decision that Ms Cropper called one evening. She thought it wrong. Sara was a bright girl. True, she had not been working well this term and, true, she had missed important work, but the staff were in agreement that Sara, whatever her own assessment of her abilities, was more than capable of making up the lost ground and still doing well in her A levels. Could Ms Cropper have a word with her?

I had imagined Ms Cropper as a forceful butch female with cropped hair and leathery skin, but the reality on my doorstep was a small brisk woman in her late-thirties, with a cloud of prematurely white hair framing an intelligent and attractively made-up face; someone, moreover, disarmingly concerned for my daughter's future. She had, she explained, been worried all term over Sara's mood swings and her bouts of antagonistic behaviour; she suspected adolescent emotional problems to be at the roots of these and wondered whether a talk might be of help.

'Sara and I seem to get on all right,' she said modestly, 'and she always enjoyed our class discussions. I'd like to have a try, if I may?'

I wasn't sure what might be gained but I took her up to Sara's bedroom, produced coffee and biscuits, and left them to it. It was well over an hour before Ms Cropper emerged, and then she was shaking her head. 'No go,' she said sadly as we bid each other goodbye. 'A failure. I'm very sorry.'

But Sara rejected the suggestion that the visit had been a failure. She'd had a terrific talk with Ms Cropper, whom she now called Maggie.

'I told her everything,' she said and looked at me with anxiety. 'I don't know why, it just came out. Maggie's . . . well, she's one of those people who can get things out of you. She doesn't judge you, I suppose that's why. But she can make you judge yourself.'

'Over what?' I asked, chucking a mess of clothes from a chair to her desk and sitting down. 'What horrors did telling everything include?'

Sara eased herself over in the bed, wincing. 'Ah! Well, I told her about my baby and losing it, but not just that. We talked about you and Dad . . . and the trouble in the family . . . the way things went sour after Oliver died. You don't mind, do you? She won't gossip, she's not that sort.'

'I don't mind,' I said. I did mind, but it wasn't an earth-shaking shock, I could bear it.

She then told me the details of her discussion with Ms Cropper, and as she spoke the troubles in my life and my marriage stood out in stark relief.

It had been dreadful, she said, that time after Oliver's death, the time of her grandmother's suspicions. It had been like living in a house you had thought was strong, only to find that every beam you touched was rotten, the walls running with slime. A nightmare. She'd believed in Richard and me and our one love for ever more. Our marriage had struck her as quaint and old-fashioned,

269

quite unreal by today's standards, and not anything she would ever want – she'd feel stifled by it – but it had been great to grow up with, warm and safe. She had never had to come home to parents screaming at each other, or walking out. You didn't put such security into words when you were young, you just accepted it, but after Oliver's death it had vanished. The strong edifice of our marriage had looked no more than a crumbling façade, a sham. It had been terrifying. Sometimes she had believed what her grandmother was insinuating, other times she had not. But all the time there had been pressure.

Then the whole business had blown up, the truth had come out, and everything should have been good once more. Paradise regained. But Richard and I were not the same; we'd gone cool. That real friendship we'd had, she didn't see it any more, Sara said.

There was cold fear in my guts, a terror that she was right. Richard was too frequently out; both of us were too involved in work to have time for each other; an icy patch separated us in bed.

Sara said sadly that our lives were changing, but Richard and I stayed static. Maggie Cropper told her students that in a partnership or out of it, a woman must have a worth of her own that was respected and appreciated, a basis for real friendship between the sexes. And men must make an input other than the purely financial, not demanding the sort of support from women that demeaned them, by leaving them all the dull chores of living and forcing them into the little woman role.

I agreed with that, but Sara was scornful.

Yeah, sure, but in this household I still took on far more of those chores than Richard did. So I didn't live up to my beliefs – I played the little woman. She and Maggie had discussed the sort of stifled sexist war that her father waged and how I let him get away with it. And she had told Maggie how she hated my lack of integrity over women's rights. Bad enough to have a mother who at home was subservient to the worn-out ideas of the patriarchal society; infinitely worse to have her fight for those filthy men who abused women. And then there had been my views on abortion, where had they put me?

Maggie Cropper's response had amazed her. She had not denounced my views; on the contrary, having questioned Sara closely she had said she saw in them a quality that made sense of the whole – goodness.

'Goodness?' I said, startled.

'Yeah.' Sara looked embarrassed but pleased.

Not a concept much discussed nowadays. But Sara had described a good person, Maggie said, a caring mother and wife, someone who had striven to help her bereaved friend Oliver despite the demands of a busy life, who had upheld the sanctity of life of an unborn child against her own convenience, someone who would defend men accused of sexual crimes because she refused to believe them guilty at the first outcry. And while Maggie would not herself want to go to the aid of the enemy while the battle was still raging, in another light my stand there could be seen as that of a brave and selfless person.

'It was strange,' Sara said, 'seeing it all through someone else's eyes. She made me feel much better! I still disagree with you about a lot of things, so does she . . . but she made me see that, well, you weren't being a hypocrite. No one wants to see their mother as two-faced.'

Maggie Cropper's views on formal contracts concerning chores and child rearing had been unexpected too. Easy for her, she said, to encourage her female students to tackle these post-feminist dilemmas head on at the start of a relationship, but it would be a recipe for disaster for someone like me to destroy the web of concessions of a traditional kind that had held my marriage together. Sara

271

should be wary of interference: women who refused to be as selfless as her mother was were divorced, like Ms Cropper herself. She warned that to be at once a caring mother, a passionate lover, and a successful professional woman, required Superwoman. The more I heard of Ms Cropper, the more I warmed to her. I told Sara so.

Sara laced her fingers behind her head and lay back on her pillows, smiling. 'She told me I was a bloody fool to leave school. She tried every argument on me that you and Dad used, but I told her I'd heard them all before. She said there was no hope with short-sighted idiots like me, but just to remember that I could always study through the Open University, and if I wanted any help ever I must ring her.'

'That was kind.'

'She is kind. She's really nice. A good person – like you!'

It had been Maggie Cropper's support of Females for Freedom and their ideas that had led to many of the battles between Sara and me, but I forgave her. She had called me good; she had rehabilitated me in my daughter's eyes. I was elated.

It was agreed that Sara should look for a job in the New Year, when she had fully recovered. In the meantime she sorted out her ragbag of a wardrobe – 'I've got to look smart for interviews!' – and helped me. Our cleaner, Mary, had succumbed to a bout of influenza, leaving me in a frantic top-spin of court cases, cleaning and pre-Christmas shopping and cooking. Sara took over dusting and polishing the furniture.

'But won't that hurt your spine?' I protested when she offered.

'No. A different bit gets bent.'

'If you're sure.'

'No problem. And I like polishing the mahogany. It's all silky and lovely when it's old.'

When I went into Chambers towards the weekend Tom told me that we had a date for the Pockett case, the seventh of January. 'Thank God!' I said. The destructive, critical devil that had inhabited Sara for the past months had been exorcised, but Richard's resentment would not be dissipated until the Pockett case was over.

Females for Freedom had discovered my address. Paulina again? Sara denied responsibility. Letters arrived varying from the violently resentful: 'In defending these men you are betraying every member of your own sex.' 'Only a totally callous person would put broken and violated women through the degradation of cross-examination. How can you sink so low as to take the filthy Judas money of the abusers?' to the deeply reproachful: 'We feel sure that on full consideration of your position you will at once reject the case. No caring woman could do otherwise.'

Sara harried me, Richard looked down his nose; both declared I deserved all I got. It was while I was concealing one at breakfast that I noticed the date on the envelope. If that was yesterday's date then today's must be . . . the anniversary of the day Richard and I got engaged. Our anniversary, and neither of us had remembered. But Richard always remembered – our wedding anniversary, our engagement day, St Valentine's Day . . . for more than twenty years each had been marked by a bottle of my favourite scent, a flower in a pot, a box of chocolates. And I had responded with a candlelit dinner and all his favourite dishes. These tokens of affection give a fillip to love far out of proportion to the effort involved. Richard had already left for the college. If I hadn't realised the date perhaps he hadn't either. He'd be grieved when he did remember. Telephone him at lunchtime, I told myself, suggest a meal out tonight, somewhere romantic . . . Italian . . . Hungarian. He'd be pleased to have my loving attention.

'This evening? Annabel, I told you, I've a late meeting; we grab a bite in the refectory first.'

It came back to me with a shock. He had mentioned it last night, but I'd been so tired that my sole reaction was relief at one less to cook for. I didn't even know which committee. Damn, damn, damn. 'But darling, it won't go on all evening. We could still meet for a drink. What about The Pagan's Head?' The Pagan's Head had sentimental significance. It was where many of the lecturers liked to drink, where we had first met as friends.

'Annabel, no. I can't be tied. We have a long agenda and we'll slog on till all the business is completed, God knows when.'

It had a smell of finance. I said reproachfully, 'I hardly see you these days. I'm sure devotion to work is highly praiseworthy, but recently you've taken it to extremes. Why, this year, are you so overburdened?'

'You know perfectly well why.'

'No, I don't. Tell me.'

'Really, Annabel. Quite apart from our financial shackles and the endless arguing and bargaining they put us to, you know that since the thrombosis in his right eye Morty's been talking of retiring this summer. My record must be impeccable, administratively as well as academically.'

'You never told me this.'

'Of course I did. I remember our discussing all the implications.'

My busy life led to minor lapses, but this was not minor. For Professor Morton-Rycroft to retire next year would be unexpectedly early and Richard coveted the professorship. My hands were icy. I said: 'I don't know who you discussed this with, but it wasn't me.'

Silence. Then Richard's voice, nervously impatient, as if trying to convince himself as much as me. 'Of course I told you. Morty's retirement isn't something to discuss end-lessly when it's far from definite, but I know we've spoken of it.'

'Not of thrombosis. Not of its being next summer.'

'I'm not going to argue. The point is, this year could prove vital to my future. Morty's hints have put some of us on our toes . . .' I had an irreverent vision of senior members of the department balancing on their toes, circling Morty in an ingratiating gavotte, bowing and scraping as they went. 'The pressure's on and my book's still unfinished – the publishers have set the end of January now as the delivery date and I must meet it. This is the last pre-Christmas meeting. Be patient, Annabel, please.'

No sooner had I put the telephone down than the urge began to pick it up again. Too much was left unexplained. And our anniversary had not been mentioned. Should I drive over to pick him up anyway? Until now it would not have occurred to me to question his pleasure at finding me waiting outside the college; now I discovered myself anticipating rejection. I could not decide what to do.

On letting myself into the house that evening I stood in the hall still cursing my indecision and found I was staring into the oval copper mirror. A middle-aged woman stared back in annoyance, her pallid skin taut over bones that were too prominent, her resentful dark eyes blurred and heaving like the sea before a storm. As I watched, her expression changed from annoyance to shock and a hand rose to touch the furrows that ran from nose to mouth. This was a person – and a character – I was ashamed to recognise. Poor Richard. I wouldn't care to take me out.

'Got a spot?' Sara's face appeared in the glass behind my shoulder.

That was one problem I had not got. 'No, that belongs to your age-group, thank God. But I was thinking how dilapidated I look.'

275

She contemplated my image. 'You do, too,' she remarked with horrid candour. 'You could do with a face mask.'

'I haven't had one for months.'

'I've got one,' she offered. 'It's terrific. Are you going out?'

I thought so. 'For a drink with your father. Our engagement anniversary. I'd better wash my hair, too.'

We cooked a quick chicken risotto for ourselves and the boys, I took off the gloomy black suit my work demanded and then Sara insisted on tackling my appearance. It was while my hair was still dripping coldly down my neck and the facemask stiffening that Hyacinth House telephoned to invite Richard and me to dinner in January. Hyacinth was Cordon Bleu and her dinners a gastronomic dream. I accepted with alacrity and she seemed pleased.

On impulse I enquired whether Alan was to be at the committee meeting tonight and, if so, when was she expecting him home, because, I explained awkwardly, I'd had the idea of picking up Richard at the college for an anniversary drink.

'Well,' she said vaguely, 'he did speak of being back for that French film on Channel 2, but Annabel, my dear, you weren't thinking of going to Princes, were you? You won't find Richard there. They're meeting in that Fennimore woman's flat. Oh yes, ever since the central heating went odd some weeks ago. She lives the nearest. Fancy Richard not telling you!'

I said: 'Mmm!' through my ever-stiffer face and thought how embarrassing it was to have one's ignorance exposed. Hyacinth rang off soon afterwards. Perhaps she was embarrassed also.

But now I was determined. I would meet Richard, I would take him to The Pagan's Head, and there we would sit in a corner and hold hands and talk; talk until the constraint and the resentments were banished from between us and we were back to our old close relationship.

Maggie Cropper and Sara had illuminated our troubles. Of the three roles demanded of me – wife and lover, mother, and career woman – I had barely managed two. Superwoman beyond me, the little woman had struggled, the lover had vanished. And Richard had withdrawn, alienated and resentful.

The deterioration had happened barely months after the triumphant celebration of twenty years of happiness together. Oliver, I thought, Oliver was at that anniversary. If he had been here he would have picked up the signs of trouble, as he had done with Sara: tactful warnings would have been dropped, suggestions made. We would have gone to plays and concerts with him, relaxed and been cheerful. There was a paradox here: alive, the world would have thought him a threat to our marriage, yet it was since his death that it had crumbled. How Oliver would have hated to see us now. But it was not too late, we could change.

As Sara gave my hair a smart blow-dry, it occurred to me that Mary, my capable cleaner, might like extra hours of work now that her two children were entering the expensive teenage stage. She could move into a house-keeperly role, taking over much of the shopping and cooking. Heaven knew we could afford it. I told Sara of my idea: she was reluctant to abandon her determination that Richard and the boys should do more, but on balance – 'They're a grudging lot, and it would be nice for you not to have to nag!'

In working on my appearance Sara was animated in a way I hadn't seen in weeks. She had recreated a younger and prettier me. 'You could pass for thirty,' she said proudly, then spoiled it by adding, 'at a distance.'

Still, I'd have passed for fifty before. I thanked her, amused and touched, but she stopped me.

'There's still one problem,' she said. 'You used to smell lovely, now you smell neutral. Why no scent?'

I grimaced. 'I've run out. Richard mostly buys it for me, but he hasn't remembered recently.'

Sara gathered up creams and lotions she had used on my face. 'Mum?' Her head was bent. 'Things aren't like they used to be in the old days with Oliver and Melissa. Nobody talks now, everyone's stiff. I reckon it's because of me. I ought to get out. I could go to Lucinda's. She rang up when you were in court today. She says the shop's fine, but she's lonely in her flat, no one to talk to, try her ideas out on . . . Wouldn't it be better if I left?'

'Sara, darling, don't be silly! You're not eighteen, you're too young to fly the nest – and you know we want you here.' The terrible part of it was that a vision of the house without Sara's difficult personality inhabiting it had passed through my mind and appealed immensely – no arguments with Richard, no scorn poured over me over Women's Lib, no fights with the boys – then vanished beneath a wave of guilt. How could I? My own daughter . . . after we'd been so much closer these last few days, after she'd been so sweet this evening? 'We're your family,' I finished firmly, 'and we love you.'

'Yeah,' she said with unexpected humour, 'you have to, don't you? It's the done thing. You're stuck, lumbered. But you don't have to like me.'

Erica Fennimore's flat was in one of those fringe areas still undergoing gentrification; a piebald area of handsome Regency and Victorian terraces abutting on to sad grey streets little better than slums. In Ms Fennimore's street the improvement was being tackled piecemeal and her flat was in one of the designer-restored houses. The contrast

278

of its glaring ice-cream white frontage with its crumbling neighbours was objectionably blatant.

The house showed lights at first floor level and in the basement. Since I could not imagine the colourful Erica burying herself below ground it was simple to deduce that hers was the first floor flat. Besides, there was something about those loosely woven curtains – semi-sheers, I think they are called – that shouted of America.

It was unpleasant sitting waiting there in the dark. Rough-looking men strolled past, eyeing me, keeping me in a state of jumpy unrest. The car quickly became chilly, then dankly cold. Ten minutes passed, fifteen, twenty. What the hell was I doing here? Still, having waited this long . . .

At last there was movement. The front door opened and sent a shaft of yellow light over the pavement. Three muffled figures emerged, talking, and turned briskly away down the street. Dear old Alan House might just make his French film. I wished Richard would hurry. I stamped my feet on the car floor, a tattoo of impatience and cold. Two more people came out, turning up coat collars, calling good-nights as they parted. Richard must come next.

I listened to Beethoven, strong and loud in the stillness. I flicked on the interior light to look at my watch; time had jumped on ridiculously. I looked up at the flat and it was then that I knew with the suddenness of glass shattering, and the knowledge ripped into me, slashing and hurting, blood flowing. The previously dark window over the front door now showed a discreet glow. The other windows were black.

21

The drive home was a nightmare; a terrifying sensation that all the cars in London were stampeding across my path, horns blaring and headlights blazing. Huge tremors of shock were passing through me, leaving me bleak with misery and cold and almost incapable of driving. The gears screamed and the car leapt and jerked as if it, too, were in pain. I was caught in a jumble of noise and gaudy lights, lights that beat their colours against my eyeballs and illuminated in garish flashes all the evidence I did not want to see. I had never felt so desolate.

I stumbled into the house like someone ill or drunk. I made straight for the bathroom and took several aspirin, I don't know how many. It seemed the logical thing to do, as though aspirin could kill that sort of pain. I could hear sounds of a play on television, and thanked God Sara and the boys were occupied, it gave me time to pull myself together. I stood in the bathroom waiting for the tremors to die out of me, the taste of the aspirin sharp and dry on the back of my throat.

'Mum?' I found Sara waiting at the bottom of the stairs. 'Isn't Dad with you?' she asked.

My voice replied with remarkable calm: 'No, I must

have missed him. Since he's not back here, he'll have gone for a drink with the others.'

Sara puckered her forehead, her eyes warm with sympathy. 'What a shame. You looked so pretty.'

My throat tightened and my eyes stung. Sympathy was dangerous; I must not give way in front of Sara. 'I have a headache,' I said. 'The drive home was dreadful. I shall sit quietly in the study.'

Sara gave me a long look before she turned away. 'All right, Mum,' she said. 'I'll tell the boys to leave you alone.'

I sat in Richard's chair, waiting, dreading his return, knowing that eventually he must come and I must confront him with my discovery. The painful minutes dragged by, each one a black night long and feverish with hideous thoughts and images. Now that I could see nothing but Richard in that woman's bed, I thought I must have been wilfully blind before. I stared at the handsome grain of Oliver's old walnut desk and fought for control; the betrayal must have been going on for weeks – months even. The pain of this was so intense that I found myself hating Richard, clenching my fists until the nails bit into the flesh of my palms, hunting for every possible fault and omission from the past that would fuel that hatred. I remembered his lack of understanding of my problems in those difficult weeks after Oliver's death. I remembered his negative reactions to my work. I remembered the lonely evenings of Sara's pregnancy. Richard should have been at home, if not holding Sara's head, at least, metaphorically, holding my hand. But he had returned late, smelling of whisky – her whisky? That he had drunk in her flat, after an evening in her bed?

It was midnight before he returned. I had put music on to calm myself: Mozart's Requiem. Was it a requiem for our marriage? As I heard Richard's key in the front door the voices of the choir mourned repeatedly: *Kyrie eleison*,

Christe eleison. Lord have mercy upon us, Christ have mercy upon us . . .

He went into the drawing-room and the clinking sounds of glass and decanter emerged. I stood stiffly and forced my unco-ordinated legs to walk me through.

'You'd better pour me one,' I said to his back.

He started, gave me a cautious glance over his shoulder and sloshed whisky into a second glass. The bitter thought flashed through my head that once he would have demanded a kiss. He pushed the glass into my hand, and the touch of his fingers, which once would have given me a thrill of pleasure, now revolted me: he was polluted.

'Annabel, I'm sorry I'm late,' he said, staring into his glass. 'We went on longer than I thought . . . we went for a drink . . . then the traffic was bad . . .'

Dies irae, dies illa. The day of wrath, that dreadful day . . . the words swelled ominously from the next room. My chest swelled with them. 'You don't need to tell lies, Richard. I know where you've been. I know what you've been doing. With *her* – '

His head jerked up. He seemed stupified. Silence for several seconds before he said: 'How – how did you know?'

At least he had the grace not to deny it. Somehow controlling my voice I told him of our anniversary, of the urgent need I'd felt to be near him and to talk things over. 'So I sat outside that house waiting for you, and everybody came but you – oh, so sorry, figure of speech, dear me – you did come, didn't you? *In her!*' I heard myself speaking in a very cold high voice, the voice of one who sits on an icy peak in judgment.

He looked appalled. 'Oh God, Annabel, I'm sorry. I never meant you to know . . .'

'Naturally not. I'm sure you're very sorry I know.'

'It was nothing, you must believe that. It wasn't important.'

'It wasn't important?' My voice rose. I never raised my

voice, least of all above Mozart's sacred music, but Richard's profane announcement was goading me to venom. 'Wrecking our marriage? Destroying twenty years of trust? *Unimportant?*'

'You know I don't mean it like that. Please, keep calm.'

The music was calm, strong but calm. I must be the same. 'How long has this been going on?'

'Not long. A few weeks. Just a few times, that's all. I never meant it to happen, I swear to you. It would have stopped at Christmas, anyway . . .'

'Why did it start at all?'

He hesitated. 'Does analysing these things ever really help?'

'I think I have a right to know.'

'Very well, then I'll tell you. Truth, absolute truth.' He swallowed his whisky and poured himself another. 'Look – I didn't initiate this . . . this thing with Erica. It just happened. Annabel, these last months you've rejected me time and time again. And I don't just mean sexually . . . I needed to be able to talk the tension away at the end of a long day, but here there was more tension. And Sara, a pain-in-the-neck manipulative little beast, pushing us apart. Drinking at The Pagan's Head after work was a relief; there were several of us who went there, Alan House for one until Hyacinth became upset. Erica was always there, ready to listen or to talk. She made us laugh. I needed to laugh. We talked easily together. She understood my problems . . .'

'Unlike me?'

'Please.'

'Go on.'

'I stayed in her flat to talk after a meeting . . . and it happened.'

'Pathetic! Pathetic story. Pathetic person. Pathetic excuses.'

'No excuses. I know there aren't any. You wanted an explanation.'

'That explains the first . . . fuck! But you went on – *and in* – time and again. Cold-bloodedly leaving me to take all the strain here while you made whoopee with that tramp! Where's your explanation of that?'

'All right, I'll give you it.' His voice hardened. 'You were so fascinated by fraudsters and incestuous fathers you forgot I existed. On your scale of importance my needs were so low they flew out of the window. First came whichever criminal you were dealing with at the moment, then Sara and her female solidarity. The rest of us, nowhere.'

'On the contrary,' I blazed. 'It was you who pushed your family out of mind. For months you've had little time for any of us. When did we last go out for a meal together, or do anything together? You ignored your mother's trouble-making, you've resented my work and my success – oh yes, that's very clear – and where was your support over the dreadful period when Sara was pregnant? You used pressure of work to keep out of the house – meetings, endless meetings, you said. Oh, yes! With her!'

'What do you expect?' he demanded, reddening. 'You'd barely time to speak to me. And you didn't want me here when Sara was pregnant – you didn't want to know my views.'

'Untrue! You were vexed because for once I wouldn't automatically take your line. Throughout our marriage I've subordinated myself to you, borne your children, run this house, given *you* the opportunity to shine. But when *I* began to shine you hated it. That's why you went rushing off to someone who would gaze admiringly into your eyes, and tell you what a wonderful person you were. Not so wonderful now, are you? Just another adulterer, taking something not your own. No better than a thief!'

I stopped, stunned, to swallow whisky. It was unbelievable that this could be happening to us: the shouting, the insults, the discord. Our life together had been dulcet, harmonious, the admiration of our friends. Tears stood in my eyes and the words of Mozart's Requiem mocked me with melancholy: *Lacrimosa dies illa*. Why had I turned to Mozart? How could he understand my tears, a philanderer himself?

Richard was looking like a goaded bull. 'All right, all right, I was in the wrong and I admit it. And I'm sorry. It was something that never should have happened. But you weren't perfection! I didn't want a bastard grandchild, I never asked for a wife who defended rape and incest. How do you think I like members of my department – and students too – haranguing me about my wife's peculiar principles? Or feminists denouncing me for something I don't agree with anyway? Since Morty's dinner party I've been attacked endlessly. People are sickened by your stance on sexual matters – and so am I. Sickened by your sanctimonious attitude. Try drumming up a defence for my case – I'm sure your brilliance could come up with plenty of mitigating evidence if you'd put your mind to it!'

'Oh, I've tried,' I returned savagely. 'But the more I look for mitigation, the more crimes I find. Crimes of selfishness, of hard ambition and petty jealousy, of lack of caring within your family. With today's discovery you've committed about every crime in the matrimonial book.'

'Thank you! Now I really know what you think of me. Discount the luxury you've lived in for the past twenty years, discount the help and support I gave you in starting your career. That doesn't enter into the equation, does it? Hell! Given the low opinion you've clearly been holding of me I'm surprised you allowed me through the door tonight.'

My resentment was stronger than self-preservation. 'So am I! Very surprised. Our marriage was based on mutual trust and respect. You've smashed both! Don't you understand that? You've shattered everything.'

'Perhaps you'd like me to go?'

'Perhaps you should!'

More goads. For once I had shed my inhibitions and let my fury rip. We were standing on either side of the mantelpiece and shouting without any thought for who might hear when Danny rushed in, looking flushed and upset.

'Stop it,' he pleaded. 'Please stop it! You've got to come upstairs – it's Sara, she's throwing all her stuff into a suitcase. She heard you shouting her name. She says the trouble between you is her fault and she's clearing out. She's in a hell of a state.'

We stood in a paralysis of shock. Danny's face twisted with impatience. 'Please – '

Footsteps sounded, stumbling down the stairs. I made for the door but Richard forestalled me. 'I'll handle this.' His big body blocked the doorway. 'What's all this nonsense, Sara?' he demanded.

The footsteps continued, accompanied by a bumping sound. I heard her reply in a low tense voice. More gently Richard said: 'You're wrong, you know. Not your fault. Not this time.'

I managed to push past him into the hall and discovered Sara standing at bay on the bottom stair, her coat slung askew round her shoulders, a suitcase in one hand, her bulging games bag hanging from the other. There was a certain dignity about her determination.

'I'm going and you can't stop me,' she insisted. 'You'll be better off without me. I've been nothing but trouble for ages and I don't belong here.'

'Of course you do,' Richard said. 'Where else?'

'No. You don't any of you think like I do about life. If I

stay I'll only go on upsetting you. I know I shall.'

'But Sara . . .' The suitcase looked so sad, with trailing bits of undies escaping from the lid. I wanted to reach her but the words would not come. It was impossible to know what to say.

'Everyone's miserable here. It's horrid now.'

'She's right,' Danny observed dispassionately. 'It's bloody awful.'

'But you can't simply walk out, darling. You've no money, nowhere to go.'

'Yes, I have! I'm not that stupid. I'm going to Lucinda's. She'd like me to share her flat, she said so!' She stepped from the last stair and heaved her suitcase towards the door, her shoulders hunched with determination.

'Richard, stop her, please!' Only a sense of our total rejection could have driven her to take this step. I was ashamed to remember my half-hearted reassurances of a few hours ago. 'Darling, you can't leave home like this.'

The look of determination on the dark young face was unexpectedly adult. 'I can and I will.'

Richard spoke abruptly: 'Then I'll drive you.'

Her eyes searched his face to see if his offer was genuine.

'Come on,' he said. 'What are you waiting for? Go to the car.'

Sara turned, ran back to give me a hard hug and a kiss. 'I'll come back and see you, I promise. And I'll telephone tomorrow. Make it up with Dad – you must!' She picked up her case and was gone.

Richard said over his shoulder to me: 'There's nothing left for either of us here. And I'll tell you this – you'd better win that man Pockett's incest case for him. It's the only thing left to redeem you now. Otherwise you stand condemned as the hypocrite of the century – the woman who champions men who commit the grossest evils in society but can't forgive one small sin in her husband.'

He left the house and the door slammed behind him with finality. Silence. The boys looked at me and the house held its breath. Not a creak, not a note of music. Mozart had finished his Requiem.

I did not wait up. I staggered to bed and slept like someone stunned. Whisky and aspirin on top of shock laid me out. I woke at seven and found myself alone in the bed. No hotel would have taken Richard that late; presumably he had taken himself off in fury to that woman's flat. Or perhaps he hadn't. Sara might know. He might, just might, have said something to her last night. Sara, who wanted to put things right.

The bleating of the telephone startled me. As if she had read my mind Sara was on the other end of the line. 'Oh Mum, are you all right?'

Yes, curiously, I was. If all right meant not being in hysterics or suicidal, that is. 'I'm fine,' I said. And how was Sara?

A sigh of relief came from the other end in response to my calm voice. 'I'm fine, too. Lucinda was amazed to see me in the middle of the night, but she was seriously pleased I'd come. It's a bit cramped here, but she reckons we can manage. Mum, about Dad . . .'

Sara had tried to talk to him on the way to Fulham, but Richard had preferred to drive in silence. Just once he had spoken. 'He was furious you'd accused him of not caring for his family. He said he'd worked all his life to give us the best. I asked what the hell that had to do with it? An unemployed father could care more. He'd never once talked to me properly about my baby. He said – unbelievable! – it was a mother's job. I lost my cool and told him he'd opted out from us all to have an affair, and he'd got to face up to what a shit he'd been.'

'Oh God. And what did he say to that?'

'He snarled at me to shut up. He revved the car up and shot the red traffic lights at Barnes Common at about eighty miles an hour. I was petrified. I shut up.'

'And what happened when you got to Lucinda's?'

'He lugged my suitcase and stuff out of the car and threw them on the step and I just knew he didn't intend to go home so I refused to let him leave – I blocked the car door actually – until he promised he wouldn't go to that woman's flat. He would have gone, too, in sheer temper at being thrown out of his own home!'

'He didn't have to leave,' I said tiredly. 'He goaded me into saying he should.'

'I know. I told him he was being stupid about it. No one could forgive what he'd done straight off – you needed to give him hell, and he should have shut up and taken it. But he's like all men. When he does stoop to give an apology, it must be accepted at once.'

'So where did he sleep?'

'He said he'd sleep in his room at Princes. In an armchair, I suppose. Oh, he did say he intended to go to Richmond this afternoon. He muttered about packing, but I don't know if he means it or if it's only a threat. He's all big drama.'

I knew then that I would not be in the house; I had not the heart for it. It was not just anger I had felt last night, but dislike. In all our marriage I had never been out of love with him before, but now the glow had vanished. Time to grapple with the unprecedented situation was what I needed. I would go and shop for Christmas presents and take tea at Fortnum & Mason's, cherishing myself. If Richard had changed overnight to a conciliatory mood and wanted to talk, then he could await my return. If not, better I should be out.

'Now, Sara darling, what about Lucinda? And what

about money? Lucinda can't support you.'

'That's all right. One thing Dad was decent about was that. He gave me a cheque for five hundred pounds and told me to go carefully with it. I reckon he's dead pleased to see the back of me, but I don't mind, it's what I want. The money will see me through till weeks after Christmas. And Lucinda says she'll only charge me for food and telephone bills to start with if I'll help in the shop when she needs it, particularly Saturdays.'

'That's kind. And what about a job?'

'I'll find something. Don't worry, Mum, I've got it all sussed out. Lucinda and I talked for hours last night. She's got it all together now.'

'How's she doing? Really?'

'Fine. She's barely covering costs, but that's more than she hoped for at the start, so she's happy, and it's getting better every week . . .'

By the time Sara rang off I was considerably relieved in my mind about her. She would be all right. Provided, that is, that the pair of them did not indulge in any more of the foolish frolics of the autumn. But I thought not. From all accounts Lucinda had grown up too.

Richard did not wait to see me in the afternoon. When Ollie and I returned home from Christmas shopping in the dark December evening he had gone and his typescript, his notes and his books with him; some clothing had disappeared from his wardrobe, but not a lot. Daniel reported that he had been put out not to find me at home, waiting for him. He had packed in a moody silence that Daniel had not liked to break. Had he left any address? No, he hadn't. But hold on, he would be in touch with Sara. He'd spoken of being concerned for her, living with Lucinda, and the pair of them so young; he intended keeping an eye on her.

Daniel had put two and two together about Erica Fennimore. Besides, we had hardly bothered to keep our voices down last night, had we? Both boys were surprised at their father, but after the first shock and indignation showed a certain male solidarity with him. Better to forgive and forget was their view. On the whole, and unlike Sara, they preferred not to speak of it: emotions and feelings were topics to be avoided. Quite simply they wanted him back home, our marriage preserved. A crack had appeared in the fabric, but cracks could be filled, painted over; the structure need not fall.

They did not blame me for his absence, however. Nor did they condone what he had done, Daniel even commenting briefly: 'You never had that sort of open marriage. It stinks!' And Oliver: 'I don't see why he had to go after someone else when you've always been nice to him. My friend Piers' mother shouts at his father – you don't.' Both demonstrated their sympathy and their affection by helping me with chores and reminding me that I was going to teach them to cook in the holidays. I wouldn't forget, would I?

The weekend passed extraordinarily quietly. I parcelled up presents on Sunday morning and then took the boys out for lunch. We ate hefty steaks in front of a log fire in a country pub in deepest Surrey, talking and joking as if the cataclysm of Friday had never happened. The angry misery of that evening had vanished with the night. Now I felt calm and detached. There was another emotion lurking that took me some time to identify. It was relief.

I didn't want Richard lying coldly beside me at night, resenting the importance my work held for me. I didn't want a husband who awarded his own work a higher priority than family problems. I didn't want to be viewed as the little woman. I wanted my lover back, my friend, the Richard who'd vanished with Oliver. I didn't want another woman's lover. Until the whole tangled mess of intolerance and jealousy and prejudice was sorted out, in Richard's mind and mine, it was better to be apart. It could even be that the marriage knot itself should be untied.

I went to visit Lucinda's shop on my way home from court on Tuesday. I had expected flamboyance, and I found it, but the flamboyance was colourful, not crude. The window display enticed me with tops and trousers and skimpy skirts that shouted of a fun life, a life without responsibilities; a life I suddenly envied fiercely.

The shop door was flung open. Sara shot out, grabbed my arm and dragged me inside, startling a customer preening herself in a burnt orange top and pants before a long mirror. 'Hey, Mum, this is great!' she said. 'I didn't know you were coming. What do you think of the shop?'

'Great!' I responded promptly. 'Tremendous fun. It's got real verve.'

'It has, hasn't it?' She turned to the customer to say: 'It fits you exactly. And it does look lovely on, doesn't it?'

The customer, a long skinny girl in her early-twenties, agreed: 'It does. You were right. Yes, I'll take it.' She beamed at us and disappeared into the changing room.

'Well done,' I murmured.

'I've sold lots already,' Sara informed me. 'Of course, it is Christmas, but Lucinda's no end pleased. She's at home, doing the VAT. Wow, that VAT, it's unbelievable!'

It startled me to hear Sara refer to the flat as home, but the break had to come. She deftly wrapped her customer's purchase for her, saw her out of the shop and then gave me a guided tour of every garment in it. 'Look at this – and this – aren't they gorgeous? I'm straining at the leash not to spend Dad's five hundred!' I understood that, and I fell for a pair of smartly cut oatmeal-coloured wool trousers: they would be good to relax in at Christmas, and just the thing to exchange for my funereal black working suits in

293

the evenings. Richard had always liked the sight of my neat butt in trousers . . . I grimaced in the little changing room. I was programmed to that damned husband of mine!

'And,' Sara said triumphantly as she put the trousers into a raspberry and white bag gaily emblazoned "Lucinda", 'Mrs Anstee-Smith, the lady who has the antiques shop next door – well, I popped in to say hello, and she says if I'm interested she could do with someone to help her in the shop for a few hours a week. She says she'll teach me, but she reckons I know a lot about the furniture side already. I guess I just absorbed it from living in our house and listening to you and Dad.'

'Well, that's all right.' I cocked an eyebrow at her. 'So you won't be bored or broke for some time yet?'

'No way! Don't worry about me, I'm fine.'

I was so relieved and pleased that I gave her a hug, which she accepted and returned with unusual warmth. Sara normally retreated from demonstrations of affection like a snail drawing in its horns.

Before I left she told me that Richard had telephoned, but only to check up on her. She was shocked that he had not got in touch with me. No, he had told her nothing of his feelings or his plans. 'But if I do get anything out of him, I'll tell you at once. He's a sod not to have let us know where he is – supposing one of us were ill or hurt?'

My last case of the term finished at the end of that week, and I was immediately flung into last-minute Christmas planning, a fearsomely complicated task in the present situation, and with less than a fortnight to go. My mother was due, as always, to join us for the week, but how to explain Richard's absence if he didn't turn up I did not know. Mother would be devastated if I told her of his affair; she was proud of her son-in-law as well as fond of him. And my sister-in-law Jane and her family normally

294

joined us for Boxing Day – and hovering behind them was the spectre of Bertha.

Sara was determined Richard should come home. Like most of her contemporaries she was always full of some new belief, some campaign on behalf of, or against, an objective pursued to the point of a cult: vegetarianism and feminism were cases in point. Now her campaign became the continuance of our marriage. Richard called in to see her from time to time and all that either of them said was reported back, virtually verbatim, in particular her scoldings when he evaded the topic of his return. I suspected that it was a tremendous release for her own sense of guilt to have Richard to attack. It appeared that he was using a lecturer friend's flat while he was in Scotland for the vacation. Sara was given his telephone number but couldn't discover the address. 'It's probably the pits of the earth with him alone in it. Imagine the unwashed socks and pants! And he wouldn't know how to wield a hoover.'

Two further things she discovered: he was spending ninety per cent of his waking hours writing, and Erica Fennimore had flown to America for the vacation only two days after my discovery. 'Dad says you overestimated her importance: there was never any question of a permanent relationship; she was a tough career woman who enjoyed sex with men she fancied as and when the opportunity came. He didn't see how that belittled you – a sweeping passion's one thing, but he risked everything for a bit of hokey-pokey in a corner. I told him!'

At breakfast-time on Christmas Eve my mother rang up in tears. 'I went to bed early last night with a double aspirin, hoping my headache was tiredness from Christmas excitement, but it wasn't. Darling, I've got 'flu and my temperature's way up. There's no way I can come for Christmas. Oh, it's so disappointing!'

I had rushed to seize the telephone, thinking it might be

295

Richard, and my own mixture of disappointment and relief that I did not have to tell Mother of our troubles left me trembling. It did more, it demonstrated to me that I wanted him back, that I did still care for him, that I was prepared to be magnanimous. But I was given no opportunity.

A card, coldly signed Richard and wishing me a Happy Christmas and a Joyous New Year in bleak print arrived on the hall mat in the course of the afternoon. I caught no glimpse of him. The boys' and Sara's presents had been bought and wrapped by me as always, and, as always, I signed their cards from us both. I had not invited Jane and her family to the Boxing Day celebrations, pleading exhaustion on our joint behalfs, so one way and another, the boys and Sara and I passed a subdued and dull Christmas. Richard telephoned when I was dishing-up on Christmas Day and it was Danny who answered the call; Richard spoke briefly to all his children to wish them a happy Christmas, but he did not ask for me, nor did he say what he was doing. The boys were hurt that he had neither appeared nor sent them anything specifically from him. Sara, tactful for once, said he was engrossed in his writing; to get it done and off to the publishers had become an obsession with him. 'I think he's missing you, Mum,' she said, anxiously trying to cheer me. 'He must do, mustn't he? But beating his breast and saying mea culpa will take a hell of a lot of bracing up to.'

All I could conclude was that if he hadn't braced up to it by Christmas Day then he never would. When my family had gone to bed that evening I turned the lights down low and sat on alone by the fire in the drawing-room, agonising over everything that had happened and everything that might happen. The might happen was worse than the past. Would Richard ever come back? I needed to talk to him, but in his present mood I was afraid of his reactions. I wondered whether his infidelity was a symptom of the disease that had attacked us in the past months, or the disease itself. Had Erica been a brief infection, or were his feelings for me dead?

The silence in the sleeping house was unending, breathless and implacable, reminding me it would not be many years now before the boys left, emphasising the loneliness of the future. For the first time the size of the house was dismaying rather than gratifying. If we separated, if we divorced, then almost certainly I would be awarded the matrimonial home, while Richard bought some smart flat convenient for Princes College. But our cherished furniture, the paintings we had collected, our books? All to be fought over and divided. And the silky Bokhara rug that Oliver had given us as a wedding present, that was an endless reminder of him and all he had meant to us – who would take that? I caressed the rug with my eyes; it was beautiful, the colours rich and glowing, mainly deep crimson, the pattern austere. Without that rug the room would have been dull; indeed, without it the room as it existed would not have been. For the rug had made its own demands: it would not tolerate the plain lines or gingery colouring of modern woods, it required mahogany with a patina to compare with its own lustre, while any fabrics in the room had to agree with its pattern and its colours. It was exacting in its requirements. Sometimes it had taken us months to track down a particular material that would blend as it should, but the results had repaid the effort. Was all that we had achieved to be wasted and destroyed along with our marriage? A structure and a pattern we had thought sound and possessed of its own beauty to be so swiftly devoured by the worms of jealousy and bitterness?

At least, I told myself, the boys would stay with me: undomesticated Richard would not want to cope. Or would he? A housekeeper would not be beyond his finances. Or another woman . . . that other woman . . . could still be a facet of his life despite his denials, my mind whispered. Would I be left totally alone, my sons considered a man's responsibility and living elsewhere, slowly growing away from me?

On New Year's Day four parcels dropped through the letter box. They were from Richard. The boys had aftershave (young Oliver's first) and Sara and I received bottles of expensive scent. She preened herself, and not only for her lovely smell. 'I made Dad do it,' she said to me privately later in the day, when she turned up for supper. 'I explained that secondhand love via a card signed by Mum was not what his family expected from him, not if he really cared. I was careful,' she hastened to add,' 'I didn't say we were cross, just hurt and puzzled. But I didn't expect all this!' And she sniffed her wrist for the twentieth time.

'So when do we expect to see him?' I asked sadly.

'I don't know,' she admitted. 'He's all edgy . . . You know, he's very strange about your incest case – as if you were deliberately defying him and all his beliefs with it. I've got a kind of feeling he looks on it as a special test for you both, something that one way or another will settle things. A watershed . . . is that the word?'

I didn't know. I waited. There was a week to go to its start.

Twice in that week the telephone rang late in the evening. Each time I was certain it must be Richard at last. But it was not. It was Gerald Lees – Gerald, who had taken advantage of Richard's absence from the Chambers' Christmas drinks party and my weakened spirits to kiss me behind a door, and now wanted urgently to speak to me.

298

22

I had a brief conference with John Pockett before the trial began. We went into the public café on the third floor of the Old Bailey, and Howard Hoffer insisted on buying coffee and buns all round: 'Got to keep our strength up!' he commented with uncalled for cheerfulness.

I asked my client hopelessly whether he'd thought of anything to assist his case, and he stirred his coffee round and round with his spoon and replied helplessly that he hadn't. I told him I'd been to the exhibits room to check the capacity of the sleeping bag, and it was obvious that two grown bodies would never fit into it. In fact, given its short zip, it would take some squirming to get one in. Howard remarked in rallying tones that Mrs Bateman should be able to have a bit of fun with that.

John Pockett gave him a sick stare, pushed away his untouched bun, and burst out: 'If it was anyone else who'd done this to me, I could get some satisfaction out of discrediting her. I'd show her up for a stinking liar, I'd sue her for everything she's got. But I can't because this is my own daughter whom I've loved and cared for all her life – my own daughter who's putting me through the tortures of the damned. And I have no way of showing that what

she says isn't true – precisely because she is my daughter.'
He lapsed into silence again.

When his angry breathing had steadied I warned him
that I would have to press his daughter hard in cross-
examination, both his daughters. Was he prepared for
that? His lips tightened. Yes, he supposed he was: he did
understand the necessity.

I did not tell him about the woman from Females for
Freedom who had accosted me on my way in, threatening
to report me to the Bar Council and demand I be disbarred
if I put that poor girl through any further agonies. Any
half-decent barrister, she told me, her eyes glaring, would
have refused to take the case, and would be protesting
against the cross-examination in open court of such unfortunate victims. I had been dignified, contenting myself
only with nodding that I had heard her.

Court 9, one of the modern courts, was packed and
claustrophobic. Smart wood panelling and wall to wall
carpeting it did have, but it lacked windows and the air
conditioning was blasting out Sahara-level heat. Journalists squeezed in, the public gallery on my left was
packed. The woman from Females for Freedom was muttering to a bunch of badged and agitated young women
filling one side; near a crowd of notebook-clutching
students on the other I glimpsed Sara. Two rows behind
her was her ex-boyfriend Tony, catching my eye, giving
me a confident smile.

Silence fell as the judge entered and addressed the
journalists, stressing that no names might be published
which could identify the alleged young victim, including
that of the accused, and stayed total as Piers Thompson
opened the prosecution case. His audience had learned
only the outline from the media, now they were hearing
the sordid details; they gave him open-mouthed attention. I had been prosecuted before by Piers, he was no

mean opponent. A tall thin man of my own age, with a dessicated face and a dry manner, he could cut through verbiage with the sharpness of a guillotine and let the blood flow. My heart sank as I listened to his bleak account of the sufferings of the innocent schoolgirl, Fern Pockett, sufferings her own father had inflicted. Fern's father sat motionless, only the draining of the last colour from his face showing his emotions.

The courtroom stirred with sympathy as Fern came to take the oath and settled again as she began to give evidence. I studied her: if John Pockett was telling the truth, this girl was a monstrous liar. She did not have that appearance. She looked gauche, wary, resentful even, but not a criminal. But then so many criminals look like normal, guileless citizens. In Fern it was the soft downy skin of her cheeks, smooth as a baby's bottom, that gave the impression of innocence; she did not look old enough to be perverse or corrupt. And she was dressed in navy, the colour of respectability, the colour of a good little schoolgirl. Not that she was little; she wasn't, she was a big girl and well-endowed by nature. I sensed a smouldering sensuality not completely obliterated by the childish mack that hung open from her shoulders, or the skirt with its below-the-knee hemline. She was about to have her fifteenth birthday, she looked seventeen.

Piers Thompson took her steadily through her evidence. At first she responded reluctantly, sulkily, as if suspicious of the authority implied by wig and gown, but Piers had handled tense witnesses before. He asked her reassuring questions about family and school matters and soon the hunched shoulders relaxed, the answers came more readily: this man was not here to catch her out. He took her through her parents' divorce and on to the camping holiday and the events that had taken place in her tent. And now the silence was broken by waves of sympathetic reactions from the gallery, its occupants shifting in their seats, muttering their disgust, sucking in breath indignantly. The sympathy and comprehension together stimulated Fern to histrionic heights and she gave her audience a tale which was wholly deserving of that sympathy, the gasps and the murmurs an applause to which she reacted with still more intimate details of her torment. Twice Judge Ottley frowned at the gallery, twice the security officer there shushed the occupants, but the sounds were never obtrusive enough to bring a verbal rebuke.

I looked at the jury. If the facial expressions of the men were anything to go by, they were besotted with sympathy for the girl and her story. The women, all middle-aged to elderly married women, were more difficult to assess; I prayed they were the hard-bitten mothers of difficult teenaged girls. There were six of them.

It was in an electric atmosphere that I rose to cross-examine Fern in mid-afternoon. I began gently with a question or two about the siting of the two tents – Yes, they were so close together that the guy-ropes crossed – and the coldness of the night on which the first incident was said to have taken place – No, not a frost, but beastly shivery cold – and, as with Piers Thompson, slowly the big body relaxed, the clenched fists opened.

'Now, Fern,' I said, 'you told the court that your father got inside your sleeping bag with you. Are you really telling the truth about that?'

She reacted as I hoped she would with an emphatic affirmative.

'Right inside?'

'Yes.'

'You didn't get out of it when he joined you?'

'No. He got in with me. He said he was cold and he wanted a cuddle, didn't he?'

302

'So you tell us. Can you describe your sleeping bag to the court, please?'

'It's that blue one over there.' She pointed to the exhibit.

I asked the usher to hold it up for the jury to see. 'A single person bag, you will note. Now, Fern, would you please get into it? Out here, in front of the jury. Standing up will do.'

Her face contorted. She appealed to the judge. 'Do I have to?'

A growl came from the gallery: the sleeping bag would hold bad memories for the child. I heard a security officer's bass voice demanding quiet, but the noise grew, people rose in their seats, voices shouted: 'Bully!' 'Let the girl alone!' 'Shame!'

Judge Ottley was a stern but fair man.

'Yes,' he said to Fern, 'I'm afraid you must. Do as counsel asks you.' Then he turned his attention to the clamorous public. 'This is a court of law,' he said icily. 'If silence is not maintained, I shall order the gallery to be cleared.'

Fern shed her mack, approached the bag reluctantly and stepped into it. The usher assisted her to pull it up beneath her arms, and zipped it.

'Yes, that's fine,' I said.

Fern stood there, her arms by her sides, holding the sleeping bag in place. She looked younger like that, and rather pathetic.

I said quickly: 'Please show the jury just how much spare room there is at the top. Pull the bag forward – yes, that's right. Now, Fern, look at your father' (she didn't) 'and tell us how a man of his size could squeeze himself in there with you?' Silence. 'He couldn't possibly, could he?' The space was minute, impossible, four inches at most.

'Well, he did!' She was very red in the face and not just from the warmth of the sleeping bag.

'You're quite certain? There is hardly room there for a tiny child, let alone a grown man. Tell me this, how did he do it?'

'Well, he did, I tell you. He did!' She looked round desperately and blurted out, 'I was less well developed then!'

A grin ran around the well of the court. Two jury members laughed aloud. My point was made; no need to press the matter further.

'Thank you, Fern. You may get out of the sleeping bag now and return to the witness box.'

I took her through the other sexual attacks of which we'd had evidence, at home and in her father's flat, questioning her closely. It had become clear during Piers Thompson's examination in chief that Fern Pockett, aged only fourteen, was remarkably knowledgeable and articulate about sexual behaviour. Now, her face sullen and hostile, she flung details at me that no child of her age should know: details about sexual positions and sexual foreplay, about fellatio and cunnilingus. I embarrassed myself about the matters I was forced to go into; I did not embarrass Fern Pockett. Her father, she said, had insisted: 'He said Mum wasn't looking after him like she should any more, and a proper daughter would take care of him and make him feel good. Yes, he did. He went on about how it would make him ill, doing without sex, so I mustn't let him down. And then he made me take him in my mouth.' This, and a lot more, she had never mentioned before, not in her statement nor in her replies to prosecuting counsel, and she was unable to explain the discrepancy.

'Mysteriouser and mysteriouser,' Howard Hoffer muttered from behind me. It was at this point that my feeling that John Pockett might be innocent turned to conviction. The burden on me suddenly increased. I put it to her point

304

by point that she was lying, that she was inventing every detail. No, no and no, she would retract nothing, she was unshakeable.

I changed my line of attack. Was her father a suspicious man?

Her eyes flickered. 'I dunno what you mean.'

'Well, was he suspicious of your boyfriend, for example, the boyfriend you had early last year?'

She thought about that one. 'Yeah, he might have been.'

'So suspicious that he accused your boyfriend to you of stealing to buy you presents, threatened to report him to the police?'

'Yeah. Yes, he did that.'

'What were the presents that your father found so suspicious?'

She shrugged. 'Just some stuff I had for Christmas and my birthday. Nothing much.'

'Nothing much? What exactly?'

'A portable TV and a CD player and some jewellery.'

'Gold jewellery? And hundreds of pounds worth of items in all?' The jury was fascinated. I took her through the items, enquired which her boyfriend had bought, where she had obtained the money for the rest, and the exact cost of each. Fern was resentful; she stonewalled. Glenn had bought her a necklace. And a bracelet. The other stuff? She could save her pocket money, couldn't she? And there was the money her mum and her aunty had given her for Christmas and her birthday. And Dad, come to that. And there'd been the January sales, hadn't there? The cost? What, a year ago? No one could remember that far back. She hadn't a clue. No, she was certain her boyfriend had stolen nothing.

'Were you angry with your father for accusing your boyfriend?'

'Wouldn't you be?'

'Lippy', the bearded teacher had said. 'I'm asking you, Fern.'

'Yes, I was.'

'In fact, Fern, I put it to you that you were so angry that you invented these terrible accusations against your father to punish him for interfering in your life. Isn't that so?'

'No!'

'Because you bitterly resented his parental control now that he had left the house and left you all?'

'No!'

'You were sleeping with your boyfriend, weren't you, Fern?'

'No. No, I wasn't.'

'You were frightened that your father would find out about that – '

'No!'

' – and then you'd be in real trouble, not just with your father but your boyfriend with the law.'

'No! It was my father who was doing it to me! It was all him!'

I couldn't move her. I asked her about her delay in reporting the alleged abuse – why had she said nothing to anyone for so long? She said she had been embarrassed, she had hoped each time that it would be the last, hadn't wanted to upset her mother, cause a scandal.

I sat down. I knew I had given the jury cause to think. But was it enough? I looked at John Pockett, at his helpless ashen face. I prayed it was. I doubted it.

Piers Thompson rose to counter what gains I had made. 'Fern, it is now nine months since you say your father first abused you, a long time for the details to remain clear in your mind. Think back to that first night in the tent. You say you were definitely inside your sleeping bag at the

306

start of the incident. Take your time and think hard – try to remember – you said your father tugged your nightdress up. Were you inside the sleeping bag at that point?'

She snatched at the let-out. 'No. No, I couldn't have been. He must have pulled the sleeping bag down while he was cuddling me. Yes, I remember him wriggling about. That's right, he pulled it off me!'

'You're sure?'

'Yes. I remember it now!' She flashed me an exultant look.

But I suspected her earlier refusal to budge from her original story would weigh more with the jury.

The next morning the first witness for the prosecution was Mrs Pockett – Tina. One look at her was enough to tell me that she and her quiet husband could never have been compatible. She was short and dumpy, her body bulging everywhere unpleasing to the aesthetic eye. Her dyed yellow hair was piled on top of her head, her eyes hard under eyebrows plucked to a curious nakedness, her blusher uneasy on sallow and furrowed cheeks. She was not yet forty; she looked old and used.

She gave evidence as to the deterioration in the conduct of her daughter, and her increasing state of unhappiness following each access day with her father, days on which he had had opportunities to be alone with her. She confirmed the dates that Fern had given in her statement as verified in her diary of last year. She had to be stopped on several occasions from pouring out poison against her ex-husband, something she was vehement in her desire to do. The faces of the jurymen and women showed their distaste for her spite; they would not trust a word she said.

In cross-examination I concentrated on Fern's sexual experience. Did Mrs Pockett know of any men other than her father who could have had access to her, to abuse her? No! Were there older boyfriends with whom she might

307

have slept? No. Her daughter's evidence had shown her to have wide sexual knowledge, far wider than the half a dozen alleged occasions of abuse by her father would have been likely to give her. Could Mrs Pockett explain this? Mrs Pockett knew nothing and could explain nothing except by reiterating her accusations against her husband.

The police surgeon's evidence was read. We did not challenge it – how could we? There was no evidence of any injury to Fern, nothing untoward, except that the condition of her vagina was that of a sexually experienced woman, and that her own evidence had strikingly confirmed.

Fern's sister Karen was the next witness to be called. If Fern had been tense, Karen was petrified. Here was Oliver's startled deer – in terror of being devoured by the hounds baying after her father. If I had not known her to be seventeen, I should have judged her younger than her sister. Only in the downy skin did she resemble Fern. She was slight and skinny and did not look like a mother.

Piers Thompson's approach was as quiet and fatherly as that austere bachelor could produce. He coaxed mumbled evidence from her that her sister Fern had been upset for several weeks after her camping holiday with her father, that this was unusual in Fern, a normally tough and self-confident character, and particularly unusual in that she had tried to avoid seeing her father, whose favourite she had always been. She'd seemed scared to be with him. Finally there had been tantrums and tears and the shocking story had come pouring out. Yes, she had seen her father go into Fern's room on more than one occasion. No, he'd never touched her, Karen. She was a poor witness, an obviously reluctant witness, but what little Piers had been able to garner from her muttered words had supported her sister's and her mother's accusations. Piers sat down.

She tried to leave the witness box and was stopped: Mrs

Bateman had some questions for her. She turned upon me a face of sick revulsion. Here was something more than mere timorousness in face of the panoply of court, I thought. She was in fear, real fear, of saying something she shouldn't – but what? There was nastiness lurking, shrouded in a fog of lies. My brain struggled . . . Someone threatening her? With what? I must gentle her as I would a nervous animal, somehow overcome her dread.

'It isn't very nice giving evidence, I know, Karen,' I said quietly, my voice sympathetic. 'But you mustn't be afraid. Just tell the truth, as you have sworn to do, and everything will come out right in the end.'

The large deer's eyes, which had been fixed on my face, fell. She looked, if anything, more troubled than before.

I enquired whether she had actually seen her father make any gestures or advances towards Fern that were more than fatherly affection. No, she had not. Not ever? Not ever. Had her father entered her bedroom or Fern's from time to time to talk with them when they were younger? Yes, he had. Often. No, she had not thought it odd that he still went into Fern's room – not at the time. Yes, he took an interest in what she and Fern were doing. A kind father? Her eyes flickered to John Pockett and away again. She gulped. Yes.

I continued: 'Now, I want to ask you some questions about certain items that your sister Fern had as presents for Christmas and her birthday last year, gold earrings, a necklace and a bracelet – I'm sure you'll remember them – and there was a CD player and a television as well. Was it her boyfriend who gave her those presents, Karen?'

A look at Fern this time. She moved her head. 'What boyfriend?'

'The one she had at that time. The boyfriend your father threatened to report to the police. The one he'd been told gave her the jewellery.'

Her face strained, she mumbled: 'I dunno, do I?'

'You lived with her, you must know where those expensive things came from, Karen. Fern had no money, no more than you. Did her boyfriend give them to her?'

Silence. She was frightened, resentful, torn – hating the lies?

Very softly: 'The truth, Karen, did they come from her boyfriend?'

The judge leaned forward. 'You must answer the question.'

Silence. Her eyes swung towards Fern again. Her lips tightened. Then: 'She had a lot of boyfriends, didn't she?' There was something strange in her tone, something quite new in her expression.

My brain was clearing like fog lifting in sunlight. I asked: 'You mean they all gave her presents? Or was it money they gave her?'

A pause, then she blurted: 'Yeah, they gave her money.' She was very white. Her look at me was one of mingled resentment and triumph.

I'd struck oil. Dear God, I'd struck oil! 'Go on,' I said gently, 'tell us about it, will you, Karen? She was being paid for having sex, wasn't she?'

A gasp of shock from the public gallery was followed by a total absence of sound.

'Yes,' Karen burst out. 'Yes, she was!' The oil gushed, black and viscous, spattering filth. 'Her and my mum, too. You can make a bomb like that. It made everything easy.' She stopped to struggle with tears.

'Take your time,' I said. 'It's all right.'

She gulped, went on: 'Dad never gave us enough money. There were bailiffs coming . . . and then they went away. We all had nice food and things . . . and my baby got a pram, really smart . . . And then my dad got nosy. He wanted to know where Fern's stuff came from, he kept asking questions, he wouldn't leave off. He went on at her when they were on holiday even. Mum said he'd got to be stopped. She said if anyone found out the Social 'ud be round like a flash and Fern'd get put in care. She's only fourteen, isn't she? And my baby, my baby . . . they'd take away my baby – ' Her voice stopped on a wail, choking with sobs.

Judge Ottley leaned forward. 'It's all right, just take it steadily. Would you like to sit down? Usher, bring Karen a glass of water, will you?'

The usher darted out and a wave of hissings and mutterings swelled from all over the court. In the gallery the Females for Freedom woman had her mouth open and sagging to her chest. Sara was staring at me with incredulity. From behind her Tony gave me a thumbs up sign.

I turned to look at my client and wished I hadn't. John Pockett looked sick, sick to the heart, and as I watched he covered his face with his hands in a gesture of despair. For him, the truth had come out and it was as unpalatable as any prison sentence.

Karen was sipping her water. As always, and strange as it seems, it had a calming effect. She did not look at her sister, who was beside a social worker, nor did Fern look at her. Fern was sitting rigidly upright, staring ahead of herself, her face unreadable; only a sheen of sweat on the pallor of her skin betrayed the emotions imprisoned inside her skull.

Since Tina Pockett was a witness, Fern was not accompanied by her mother in court, as would normally have been the case. In addition I had asked for Tina to be excluded from the court once her evidence was over, to ensure that Karen's evidence was freely given. The prosecutor, sensing that there was more to the case than met the eye, had agreed. Without that agreement, I had no doubt, Karen would never have confessed the truth. Tina

311

Pockett was an evil woman – and I mean evil in the old-fashioned sense of the word.

My heart was pounding with the excitement of my sudden success. I poured myself a glass of water from the carafe before me and sipped. The members of the jury talked earnestly among themselves. A trio of journalists darted out in search of telephones. The courtroom was becoming noisy, groups in the gallery arguing and gesticulating. A middle-aged woman shouted something clearly offensive down into the court, but her words were lost in the general hubbub. In a second a security officer was standing over her; she snarled something at him and subsided. The clerk of the court called for silence.

Karen pushed her glass back into the usher's hands and stood up again. I asked whose had been the idea to accuse her father of incest. It was her mum's, she said in a small voice. There had been no other way they could think of to remove him from their lives, to ensure their safety. 'I never liked it, see? But there was my baby . . .' It had all started slowly. Her mum had brought men home from the pub at intervals ever since her dad left home, but when money problems had become desperate she had cajoled them into giving her 'presents'. More men were invited back, parties were thrown. Many of these men fancied Fern – and she had relished their presents. 'She reckoned she was having a real fun time.'

I let Karen go and the judge gave leave for Fern to be recalled to the witness box. She turned her head from me. She would look at no one.

'Fern,' I said quietly, 'do you admit that the expensive items your father discovered in your room were paid for with money given to you in return for sexual favours?'

Silence. In the gallery someone spluttered a cough and swiftly suppressed it. Fern looked ahead.

'Fern, were you paid for sexual favours?' My voice was sharp now.

She hitched one shoulder in a shrug. 'She said it, didn't she?'

'Answer the question, please.'

'Yeah, I could've been.'

'Answer counsel yes or no!' came Judge Ottley's deep voice.

She spat it out. 'All right then, yes.'

'Those items in your room were bought with that money?'

'Yes.'

'And the accusation of incest against your father was totally untrue?'

Silence.

'Was it untrue, Fern?'

Among the jury someone was muttering to his neighbours. Fern stood rooted, wordless. Finally her head jerked in something approximating affirmation. The foreman of the jury stood to address the judge.

'My lord, the jury feels it has heard enough to reach a verdict.'

'You are all of that mind?'

'Yes.'

The judge asked if they would confirm that they intended to find the defendant not guilty: 'Yes or no?'

The foreman said: 'Yes, my lord.'

The judge then asked the jury to retire. Piers Thompson said he was calling no further evidence. Judge Ottley asked me if I wished him to take the case from the jury, I said I did, and Thompson said he could not oppose it. The jury was recalled and the foreman was formally asked, on the Judge's direction, did they find the defendant not guilty? The foreman said they did, and that it was the verdict of them all.

313

*

When I left the court John Pockett was still sitting slumped and desolate. He said with an effort: 'Mrs Bateman, I have you to thank that I am not now heading for prison. I am truly grateful for all your hard work.' His voice tailed away. What else could the poor man say? He had been relieved of one form of suffering only to have another quite as harrowing inflicted upon him. I ached inside for him. We shook hands in silence.

In the corridor outside Mrs Pockett was being hustled away by police officers, her mouth polluting the air with a stream of invective. Fern and Karen were being shepherded by the social worker in the opposite direction.

Howard Hoffer remarked that it quite defeated him how any man could have fancied that dreadful old bag. 'The daughter, yes, but that. . . ?'

The usher, overhearing, said cheerfully: 'A man was found guilty of indecency with a dolphin not so long ago. No accounting for tastes.'

Howard chortled; I snorted. He congratulated me, wringing my hand with painful enthusiasm: 'I was sure we were on to a loser, but you turned the tables on those women entirely. An incredible case, the case of the decade! There's no limit to human evil, is there?' His mind had thought the same thoughts as mine. He shook his head cheerfully and left.

I followed, looking for Sara. Presumably she would like a lift back to Lucinda's flat. I wanted urgently to tell Richard my stand had been justified, to let him know that I was not the unprincipled woman the politically correct believed me, but I was scared of appearing to crow, willing him to make the first move, wondering how soon it might come.

A scurrying of footsteps and Sara arrived by my side, pink with excitement. 'I'm sorry,' she gasped, 'I couldn't get to you before. I had to telephone, didn't I? Those

314

newspapermen are brutes! I had to fight, and I mean fight, with them to grab a phone. You'll be in all the papers tomorrow, anyway. And nobody will be able to say you were wrong this time! Isn't it ace? Heavens, Mother, you were good. I wouldn't have believed it if I hadn't heard it with my own ears . . . What terrible females those were! Real harpies! And they betrayed all women by making up wicked stories against that poor man like that, didn't they? Destroying our credibility.' She grimaced and for a moment her face was sad, then she took my arm and began to drag me off towards the outside world.

'What's the hurry?' I asked. 'And do you want a lift back to Fulham?'

'Yes, yes, yes,' she said impatiently. 'I mean, no, I'm coming back to Richmond with you. Oh, Mother, don't you want to know? I rang Dad!'

'Oh!'

'Yes! I told him about your incredible win and about that awful girl and her mother really being like prostitutes, and he couldn't believe me at first. I had to tell him three times before he took it in. I told him how you'd been right all along, and how stupid you made those Females for Freedom women look.' Her once total allegiance to their beliefs was cast aside; for the moment the fact that her mother had triumphed and been vindicated was enough. As we stepped outside into the icy air she took my arm. She said: 'Dad will be waiting for you when you get home.' Happily she added, 'I think he's ready to crawl.'

'I've never wanted him to do that,' I said.

23

'You've got to have a celebration, a proper celebration,'
Sara told me as the car trailed homeward along the dark
and fume-filled evening streets. 'And that's why I'm
coming back with you. If I'm not there to oversee it I know
what'll happen. You'll do some perfectly ordinary meal
and pass the occasion off as nothing. You're to have champagne and fillet steaks at the very least.'

'Oh? Am I?' I responded meekly.

'Yes! And you needn't worry about my cramping your
style with Father, because the boys will be underfoot
anyway. In fact, my being there could make things easier –
what if I cook the meal and get Danny and Ollie to help
me? Then you and Dad can get the show back on the road
in peace.'

'No,' I said quickly. 'No. I don't want to talk to Richard
too soon. Let's just settle down together first, feel our way
a bit.'

In the last weeks I'd veered wildly between angry relief
at being rid of Richard and misery at missing him; now
today, abruptly, I knew what I wanted. But I'd need time
to judge Richard's attitude.

'Okay,' Sara said amenably. Her hand reached out to
touch my wrist. 'I'll do anything you like, Mum. So long as

things are put right. I couldn't bear it if you didn't get back together again.'

I suddenly liked her enormously, something it had been difficult to do in these last months. An elderly friend once told me that when children were young there was unsullied love between them and their parents, but in the awful adolescent years every belief and every rule was tested, testing the love, too. Then, she had said, is when you have to hang in and hang on. If you survive those war years you have a friend for life in each of your children. Sara, I knew now, would be such a friend. We sat in a queue on Putney Bridge, behind a stinking, grunting London bus, and smiled at each other.

Then, as the traffic moved on and we turned right to run near the river, Sara lowered her head and spoke in a muffled voice. 'I want to tell you something,' she said. 'Only . . . promise not to tell anybody, ever? Oh, it's all right, it isn't about me. It's about Lucinda. Promise, though!'

'I promise. But is it all right for you to tell me?'

'Yes. She said I could. Sort of to put you right . . . Put the balance right. Only you mustn't ever, ever, tell Angela.'

Something seemed to crawl between my shoulders. 'Go on.'

'She told me last night. We were talking about sex, and men, and – well, what she thought about you defending Mr Pockett. And then she said her father, Miles – her own father – had a go at her. He wanted her to, like, do it with him. She didn't, of course, not Lucinda! She fought him off. He tried twice when she was staying in his flat. He was a bit drunk, she said. He touched her – you know. She hit him and pushed him out of her room and locked the door.'

'He always was a bit much, was Miles. But this . . . I

318

wouldn't have believed this . . . not even of Miles! God, how rotten for Lucinda!'

'He apologised afterwards. She said he cried. But Mum, that's how she came to leave school. That's how she got the boutique!'

I turned my head to stare at her and narrowly missed crashing the car into a taxi that had stopped abruptly in front of us to pick up a fare.

'You mean – she blackmailed him?'

'Yes. With Angela. With his friends. With the police.'

'Well! Don't ask me to comment on the morality of that, not ever! What could anyone say? Some form of amends. And it does seem to have been a success so far . . . But even so! To make Lucinda so manipulative!'

'But today shifts the balance again. It just might show her.'

In Richmond we stopped in Friars Stile Road to visit the Real Meat butcher, the old-fashioned greengrocer who sold proper mushrooms with gills, not the little plastic bullets to which Sara and I had a deep aversion, and then Oddbins. Then we went home.

As we walked into the hall Richard came out of the drawing-room. His presence smote me: so big, so looming, so important. Behind him were Danny and Oliver. They hovered, staring.

I put down the shopping and waited, unsure.

Richard came up to me, held me by the upper arms, and kissed me firmly on the mouth.

'Wonderful' he said. 'Congratulations, Annabel. You've had a win that will silence your critics forever. A tremendous success. You were right and I was wrong, and I apologise. I'm truly sorry that I doubted you.'

His Victorian display of manly generosity of spirit almost unnerved me; without intending it, I giggled. But after all, I thought, as the boys moved in to hug and applaud me noi-

319

sily, how else was the poor man to play the scene, in public like this?

Danny and Oliver prevented him from saying more. He stood back, silently watching me, as they demanded answers to their questions.

'How did you know about that girl, Fern? What put you on to a warped scene like that?'

'Wasn't the whole thing sick? I never heard of anything so sick! What will happen to those girls now? Will the mother get put in prison?'

'Hold it, hold it!' I said. The noise and the excitement were becoming too much. My heart was pounding uncomfortably and my knees were shaking. Reaction from all the strain, reaction to Richard, reaction to all the love and resentment still warring inside me. I wanted to sit down and be silent. But that was impossible. 'Know, Danny? I didn't know anything – I simply had to probe and test and wait for something to emerge, as barristers always do. And on this occasion it did. The girls? Karen came out with the truth, nothing nasty will happen to her. As for Fern, I don't know. She's very young. She could be prosecuted, but I doubt it. She'll probably be taken into care. There'll be a lot of decisions to be taken; much will depend on her attitude.'

'But that awful mother will be for it?' Oliver asked.

'Oh, yes.'

'Good!' he said energetically and added: 'It's terrific to know you were right, Mum.' And then he went bright red. I saw to what an extent his love for me had been tested.

'Females for Freedom ought to be for it, too,' Danny said. 'They were hounding an innocent man. People who go over the top like that against men are dangerous. They build resentment that boomerangs back against them and then blame us again. They should be disbanded.'

320

I shook my head. 'A lot of their complaints are genuine. Most of the reforms they call for are needed. But for men and women to be treated differently before the law could only harm the concept of equality. Of course victims should be handled with care, especially if they're young and vulnerable, but not to the point where those accused are hampered in proving their innocence. Today's verdict has given Females for Freedom a salutory reminder that men can be victims, too.'

'As a man,' Richard said dryly, 'I cannot imagine how I came to overlook that point!'

A grunt of amusement came from us. We didn't point out the obvious.

Richard swung round to the hall table behind him and picked up a handsomely wrapped parcel lying on it. He pushed it towards me.

'For you, Annabel. It comes from Sara and from me, with our apologies and our love.' He added thickly: 'We thought you deserved a tangible gesture . . . some recompense. Oh hell, you know . . . for what we've each put you through in recent months.'

'Be careful,' Sara said in a muted screech. 'It's fragile!'

I unwrapped the parcel carefully to discover a porcelain vase decorated with figures in landscapes on a rich blue ground. An unusual and beautiful thing. I put it on the table where Oliver Malet's vase had once stood.

'It's superb,' I said, breathless. 'Well . . . I'm just . . . Thank you! Both of you.'

'You do really like it?' She gave me a pleading glance.

'Of course – how could I not?' I hugged her.

Sara sighed her relief. 'It came into Mrs Anstee-Smith's shop last week and I've been yearning over it ever since. It's not the same as Oliver's vase, but it's the best I've seen. I wanted to buy it for you straight away, but it was too much. Then when you won in court and I rang Dad I suddenly thought, well, we could afford it together. He bought it on his way home.' She touched it with gentle fingers. 'It'll fill the gap, won't it?'

Ollie said abruptly: 'I want Mum to tell me something . . . Mum, I want to know if Oliver would have thought you right to take on that case?'

'Yes, he would. In fact, he did. We discussed it shortly after I was briefed. He was sympathetic over the flak he knew I'd get. It never occurred to him to criticise. It never would have done.'

'He should have been here to tell us,' young Oliver said. 'Things might have been different then.'

'Yes,' Richard said, his voice very quiet. 'He should.'

Sara cleared away the wrapping paper, told us that while the boys had been greeting me she'd put the champagne in the freezer for a rapid chill, reckoned it should be about ready to drink, and suggested that we celebrate. Danny remarked hopefully that with the way she'd been handling the bottles there might be an explosion shortly. Richard said he had put two bottles in the fridge when he got home. He looked reproachful. Danny said happily that with that lot we could all get drunk. Everybody went into the kitchen and toasted my success and leaned against the cupboards to talk. After a while Sara organised the boys to peel and chop vegetables and Richard to lay the table, while she made special creamed parsnips and matchstick chips and a Madeira sauce for the fillet steaks, with an omelette for herself. When the meal was ready we moved into the dining-room and for a minute there was formality and an awkward silence.

Richard broke it by saying that he had good news for us: he had finished his book, it was with the publishers; he'd given a copy of the manuscript to a respected colleague to read and preliminary reactions were good. We toasted that with relief and I prayed silently that the book would be a success, reviewed in all those papers and journals where it should be reviewed, his name linked with those great names he wanted it to be linked with: Michael Oakeshott and Karl Popper and Professor Morton-Rycroft's predecessor, Ernest Erskine. He needed that success. And I needed it for him. I needed to revere him as I always had, to admire the confident achieving male. I wanted him, too, sufficiently secure to be able to hold me in esteem, not to feel threatened by my achievements or my battles.

Sara laid down her knife and fork and leaned forward to say that she'd had a success too. Not to be compared with ours, but she was rather hugging herself with glee. So spit it out, Danny encouraged her. Well, she said, she had used the remains of the money Richard had given her to bid for a small Regency chest of drawers at a sale, removed the filthy varnish some vandal had administered to it – 'The drawer-fronts were so gungy you couldn't see their pretty stringing' – re-polished it, replaced the broken handles and sold it at almost one hundred per cent profit. Yeah! And, wait for it, Mrs Anstee-Smith had agreed she could regularly trade in a small way on her own account. Now she was working on a commode. It was, said Sara, holding her champagne glass up to the light and squinting at it, amazing how much she had learned just by growing up in our house – Mrs Anstee-Smith said she was a real find. Sara intended to go to classes in furniture restoration, and possibly art history as well. She was going to two auctions next week, and she'd been prowling round galleries and the V and A. It was all fascinating. She wouldn't mind running an antiques shop herself one of these days. We lifted our glasses to her achievement and her ambition and she grinned happily.

I had been watching her as she talked. She was wearing tight woollen leggings and a knitted top in striking pimento shades I would never have dared to touch, but which radiated a sense of health and vitality. The dark mane of her hair had been expertly thinned and cut in layers to frame her face, while the cosmetics she was using were carefully blended, no longer shrieking their presence. I saw emerging the handsome woman Oliver had foretold.

When the meal was over, Sara and the boys removed themselves, 'To watch the News,' Sara told Richard and me unconvincingly. We were left with the debris of the meal and each other. Coffee was brought by Danny and the dining-room door shut behind him with youthful pointedness.

'Do we feel ourselves under pressure?' I asked Richard with a wry smile.

'No,' he said seriously. 'Not from them. But there's presence from my own feelings.'

He left the chair at the head of the table and came to sit beside me. He took my hand. Something inside me leapt.

'I want us to get back together,' he said.

'Yes.'

'Very much. I love you. I want our marriage to go on.'

'I think . . .' Deep breath. 'I think I do, too. Both. But there's a lot to work out between us first.'

'Yes. I'm sorry, Annabel. I've been so stupid. But must we rake up the past? What can that do except hurt us both?'

'There are things that have to be said.' I took my hand from his. 'You doubted my judgment.'

'I was wrong. I was very wrong. My understanding was at fault.'

'But there's more to it than your being seduced by political correctness. Richard, you wanted me to be wrong, and you wanted it demonstrated to the world that I was wrong.'

'No, that's not true.'

'Isn't it? Then why didn't you wish me luck?'

'Wish you luck?'

'A card would have done.'

He was silent, staring at me.

I said: 'You see? For more than twenty years we were friends. We shared everything. Then we became rivals and resentments entered the equation.'

'But you won your case and I came at once to congratulate you. No resentment. I rushed home to tell you how proud I am of you.' He stood to pour the last of the champagne into my glass and brandished the empty bottle. 'We celebrated with this!'

'Yes.' I drank and put my glass down. 'But that doesn't mend our marriage. That's gone, broken.'

'I don't know what you're talking about.' He looked stunned now; stunned and puzzled and hurt.

'Certain factors make a successful marriage, don't they? Friendship, sex, shared parenthood. Over the last months they've all vanished.'

'Oh God, Annabel, what a horrible thought. I admit things were bad – I was bad, wasn't I?' He grimaced. 'But there were twenty good years. Never forget that. We can start again.'

'I hope so. Eventually . . .'

'Eventually?'

'Relationships aren't created overnight. They take time. And I want a new relationship.' My throat was tight, the words didn't come easily and when they came they sounded trite. As soon as I had spoken I realised it. I searched for better words, but Richard was not looking to mock me.

He reached down to pull me to my feet and hold me closely against him. The familiar smell and the feel and the warmth of him flooded back, stirring emotions I needed quiescent. His breath stirred my hair as he spoke. 'Sara said you thought of Mary doing some of the shopping and cooking for us. It wouldn't be the same as yours but I'm in favour of anything that takes the drudgery out of your life.' A moment's pause. 'Damn it, that sounds patronising, and I don't mean it to . . . I've had a month, a horrible month, to learn just how many tedious tasks you've always done for me.'

'Yes?'

In setting the scene for our reconciliation Sara had lit candles on the dining table. Their flickering light made muddled shadows of our joined figures.

Richard dropped a cautious kiss on to my head. 'I want to come home. I'd hate to stay away any longer. I've missed you.' Very softly he added: 'I've missed you in bed, too. There's no one like you.'

The message heartened me, but I shook my head. 'No, Richard. Give me time, give me space. If I let you back in now, then I'm frightened that our marriage will soon fall back into its bad old ways.' I moved away from him, to be free to say what I needed to say. 'I refuse to play the little woman to your old-fashioned male any more.'

He smile at me lopsidedly. 'I'll see it's not like that,' he promised. 'Truly,' He added provocatively: 'You'd be frustrated without me.'

I had an answer to that. Abstinence was a matter of choice, not thrust upon me. Gerald Lees had renewed his attacks upon my virtue, having somehow realised that all was not well in my marriage. His telephone calls had contained invitations to dinner, and more, cheering me in my misery. I told Richard that I was under siege. I did not add that I had found fidelity not simply a matter of moral and intellectual choice, but a habit of such long-standing that it had become unbreakable. Instead I added casually, smiling: 'He's fancied me for years.'

Richard was shocked. 'But you don't . . . you won't
. . .? No, I know you won't. At least, I think so! But where
do I stand? Oh, hell! You're being very difficult, darling.
What do you want of me?'

I looked at him. He sat down and absently cut himself a
piece of Stilton from the cheese-board that still lay on the
table. He ate it looking back at me; crumbs fell on to his
trousers.

He said: 'I see that mine were major faults. But think
about this – I had to watch you looking at Oliver Malet.
And it did occur to me, after that dreadful row with my
mother, that there must be others who believed I was a
cuckold.'

I thought. I said carefully: 'If you believed such a thing,
it must have hurt.'

'Yes.'

'As Erica hurt me.'

'Yes.'

A pause. With the judicious air of one redressing a
balance he said: 'Perhaps you're right. There are matters
that are sour to the taste.'

I nodded.

'My precious bruised love.'

In the drawing-room the News was switched off. The
boys ran noisily upstairs. Sara followed, shouting about a
CD she wanted. 'It's wild and it's wicked and I know you
thieving pair have got it hidden somewhere!'

I said: 'You asked me what I want of you? To be honest I
need a break from marriage and from you. Freedom to be
myself, Annabel; time to stand alone as an individual, not
endlessly as Mrs Bateman the wife, Mrs Bateman the
mother, Mrs Bateman of counsel. More importantly, I
think you need to be alone, to cope without the props I've
always given you.'

'But to build again . . . that's got to mean our being

327

together. Hasn't it?' He held out his hands to me, palms upward, pleading.

I paused, unexpectedly struggling with the demons of temptation, torn between my own needs and the desire to capitulate, to embrace and be embraced, so easy, so much more comfortable. And I did not want us to risk losing the proud role of image-makers . . . But no, I could not risk the real health of our marriage. I needed to be certain of Richard, certain so that I was sure.

Slowly, I said: 'No. Not yet, Richard. You're having to undergo a conversion, a complete reassessment of yourself, your beliefs. Saul on the road to Damascus – you say you've seen the light, but how can I trust you?'

He stood and snuffed the candles. He began to stack the abandoned plates on the table. Then he stopped. His eyes studied me. He said: 'We'll rebuild that friendship.'

I reached for my glass and took a last swallow of champagne. 'That's what I want.'

He was silent for a moment. Then he said resignedly: 'The colleague whose flat I'm using comes back the day after tomorrow. I suppose he might let me stay on temporarily.'

We loaded the dishwasher together, talking of the children. I told Richard of Danny's girlfriend, his first, a shy little redhead with big eyes and a penchant for early music, and of the bliss of hearing gentle madrigals emanating from his room in the evenings. We spoke of Oliver coming first in last term's mathematics examinations, and how often mathematical and musical abilities run together. And we agreed how pleased we were with Sara's enthusiasm for her new interests; how relieved no longer to hear the word 'boring' fall like a stone from sullen lips.

When our talking slowed and the kitchen was cleared it was late. Richard said he would go, and take Sara with him.

At the front door, our goodbyes were interrupted by Sara, outraged that Richard was not staying, that the lift he was giving her back to Fulham was only a part of his journey. She fired at each of us impartially, shocked at my desire for a break from my marriage, disgusted with what she called Richard's weak-kneed acquiescence.

'And after all the effort I've made to get you two back together!' she observed from the car, slamming the door thunderously.

Richard gave me a quick formal kiss on the steps, self-conscious under the basilisk glare of Sara's eyes.

'When do we meet again?' he asked.

'We have an engagement for the day after tomorrow.'

'We do?'

'We're invited to dinner with Alan and Hyacinth. You don't want to miss Hyacinth's cooking, do you?'

'Oh, good God, Hyacinth's cooking! How could I do without Hyacinth's food!' He chuckled. 'But next week? Could we not go to a concert, a play? Like we used to do in the old days with Oliver? I'll discover what's on. You'll come?'

'Yes,' I said.

As he drove off I turned to go indoors, away from the January cold. On the hall table was the new vase, the vase to replace Oliver's gift. I caressed it with my eyes, touched it with my fingertips. It made me feel warm just to look at it. There had been a gap that now could be filled.